Isla's Song

Love of a Child

Darren Mort

Published by:
Wilkinson Publishing Pty Ltd
ACN 006 042 173
PO Box 24135
Melbourne, Vic 3001
Ph: 03 9654 5446

enquiries@wilkinsonpublishing.com.au
www.wilkinsonpublishing.com.au

Title: Isla's Song
ISBN: 9781922810793

A catalogue record of this book is available from the National Library of Australia.

Design by Spike Creative Pty Ltd
Ph: (03) 9427 9500
spikecreative.com.au
Printed and bound in Australia by Ligare Book Printers.

Contents

Foreword

Isla's Song, based partly on fiction, partly on true events, promises
to take you on a unique adventure within a factual matrix. As you
accompany Isla on her ride, whether you are a parent, grandparent,
aunt, uncle or other child-related carer, I implore you to question
whether you believe that your child feels loved. Does he or she feel
secure and safe? How do you know? Have you truly been listening to
your child and to his or her wishes?

Communication with a child is always king and although this book
is not meant to be a guide to parenting, it is intended to give the reader
a special insight into the mind of one child battling her internal demons
whilst she matures, striving for resolution and a form of peace.
Special thanks to: my incredible book coach and editor, Gail Tagarro,
who held my hand on this journey. She was so instrumental and I am
deeply indebted to her; Dr Freeman who sparked this journey for me; and
finally to my beautiful family and their ongoing loving support.

Thanks also to Joni Mitchell, one of the most influential singer-
songwriters to emerge from the 1960's folk music circuit. Each chapter
is named after one of her songs, with her music truly inspiring my
writing journey.

Chapter 1
Overture

January 1955

Like a conductor, the chestnut metronome commanded centre stage on the antique grand Steinway, continuously moving its arm from side to side, tick-tack, tick-tack. It was surrounded by a timeless mahogany bookshelf filled with stories of composers past and present, volumes of sheet music, glass figurines, trinkets from overseas adventures, photos of happier times and a complete edition of *Encyclopaedia Britannica*. Nearby, a well-worn Chesterfield decorated with assorted plush velvet cushions occupied a California-bungalow-style bay window. Specks of dust floated in the light emanating from the rear French doors.

A beam of light appeared as a spotlight on the walnut instrument. In the spaces between the metronome's timely rhythm came the giggles of a little four-year-old girl. She was sharing a rickety piano stool with her father.

'Show me again, show me again, Daddy!'

Oliver smiled, consumed by the joy of the moment. 'Okay, okay, l'il one.' He directed Isla to the manuscript. 'You see, C, E, G, C, F sharp, G. The start of your song.'

Isla grinned with delight. Her brow furrowed as her concentration intensified. She was determined to make her father proud and carefully placed her small fine fingers on the ivory keys, ensuring her playing kept to the timely beat of the metronome.

Upon successfully completing the first two bars of music, she turned and gleamed at her father, seeking his approval.

'You have done so well, l'il one! I do believe you'll be a famous pianist one day.'

In the stillness of the drawing room a special memory was created. They glanced at each other, their strong attachment evident. Nothing needed to be said, they just knew.

'Okay, l'il one, that's all for today. You have a big day in front of you. Time to put on your favourite party dress. Our special guests will be arriving soon.'

'With presents?' Isla said cheekily.

'Only if you're a good girl. Now off you go!' Oliver smiled.

'Catch me! Bet you can't.'

Isla scurried off down the wooden hallway to her bedroom.

Oliver stood there watching her disappear into her room. Sitting on the piano stool, breathing in the room's serenity, he took out his pencil and wrote the words *Isla's Song* at the top of the music sheet. He sat back grinning, scratched his curly brown locks and smiled, whispering to himself, 'That's my girl.'

In the kitchen, Jess, Isla's mother, could hear what seemed to be laughter emanate from the drawing room and the scurrying steps of Isla down the hallway. There were no clear sounds, simply white noise.

Jess had not been well. She was absorbed by a hovering blackness from which she was unable to escape. There were no exit doors, no lifebuoy, and she stood at the kitchen sink staring out the window into a grey void, grasping onto a tea towel, alone and consumed by feckless thoughts.

Wearing a dusk-pink pleated skirt, beige silk shirt and a single string of pearls, Jess's haute couture façade was at odds with her thin frame and battle-weary appearance. Her bent figure hid her previous model stature, and her once reckless flowing blonde locks were pulled back in a severe netted bun.

Looking into the yard, she spied her previously thriving vegetable patch now crying out for attention. The flourishing tomato plants had withered on their wooden stakes, lettuces were half eaten by armies of snails and her prized lemon tree stood sadly undernourished displaying one sad piece of fruit.

Her racing thoughts consumed her. Every so often, she reminded herself that guests would be arriving soon. *I must get moving*, she thought.

The freshly baked chocolate cake sat alone on the Laminex kitchen table, awaiting icing. Any effort was a struggle. She pushed herself away from the sink, feeling ashamed of herself in her struggle to shake off her gloom, but the monkey was firmly attached to her back. Tiny things would niggle at her, people would annoy her and her patience was short.

To cheer herself up, she tried recalling happier times: the first time she met Oliver at the university cafeteria; his dreamy brown eyes; his maroon and olive-green uni sweater; the smell of his pipe tobacco; their heated philosophical arguments; and their passionate embraces. She recalled their first real kiss under the clocks at Flinders Street Railway Station during a typical stormy Melbourne downpour. Most of all, Jess recalled Oliver's cheeky smile and the way it lit up his face. She loved him so much but try as she might, she was unable to reignite the flame. More and more, a great sense of loss overwhelmed her memories of the good times and failed to appease her anxieties.

In the midst of this miasma, Jess felt her knuckles whiten as she gripped the tea towel. So afraid, she was trapped in life's pressure cooker with a lid about to burst. At times, it was hard for her to contain her anxieties and she had to call on her every strength to put on a happy face for the sake of her family. Each day became more difficult.

As she attempted to shake off her blues, Isla crept up behind her without warning, holding up her party dress. Tugging at her mother's pleated dress, she said, 'Mummy, Mummy, can I wear this dress?'

'Ah… yes, Isla, and you know what? You look as pretty as a picture.

Now let me put some red ribbons in that golden hair of yours. You are so beautiful and Mummy does love you so much. You know that, right?'

Isla threw her arms around her mother's legs and replied, 'Yes, I love you too, Mummy.'

For Jess, the comment was so simple, so honest and yet, she found it difficult to decipher in her sea of confusion.

After she placed an apron on Isla, they both iced the chocolate birthday cake that had been left cooling on the kitchen table. Isla loved decorating cakes and her favourite part was tasting the icing.

Once the cake was covered with her favourite peppermint chocolate cream and decorated with coloured chocolate smarties, Jess gave her some candles. 'How many candles should we put on this cake for you, Isla?'

'I think five candles, Mummy, 'cause I'm a big girl now!'

Jess dipped her finger in the icing and placed a small dollop on the tip of Isla's nose. 'Yes you are, you are a big girl now!'

They both laughed. For a moment, Jess felt present in the eye of the storm. She captured that flash and held it close to her heart, despite being weighed down by her debilitating emotional malaise.

She remembered when she'd first discovered she was pregnant with Isla. The birth of their daughter was a unique and joyous occasion and although she was without her London family, she had felt secure with Oliver and supported by his family members. For her, Isla was like a special gift from heaven. Despite her current state, Jess was determined to be the best mother possible.

Mixed feelings and guilt had plagued and burdened her after the birth. She had always thought that after giving birth there would be a natural attachment to her baby. However, she had struggled. Breastfeeding was a chore at first and then totally impractical and worst of all, she was crushingly tired all the time. Despite her efforts, nothing seemed to make a difference. Her doctors prescribed hormonal medications and even sleeping tablets, but her lethargy gained momentum and she struggled. No-one really listened to her or understood her predicament, not even Oliver.

She felt as if she was drowning in expectations. They needed the money and although she was only working part time as a nurse, she resented not being able to prioritise being a mother. She was like that lemon on the backyard tree, lonely and unsupported.

Jess's reflections were disturbed when Oliver burst through the kitchen door. 'There you are, covered in icing, I'm going to eat you all up… hmmm yum yum!'

Isla screamed for joy, trying to escape her father's reach. 'I'm coming to get you, li'l one… here I come!'

'Enough, you two,' Jess chided, 'the guests will be here and there's so much to do. Oh please, don't get her riled up, Oliver. Do something useful to help me, for a change.'

Oliver went to reply but thought better of it. He could see and hear in her voice that Jess was not quite herself.

'Alright then, how can I help?'

'You shouldn't have to ask, Oliver, just look around!'

Isla didn't like it when her parents spoke like this. After all, in her mind she was made up of her mum and her dad and she felt sad when they were critical of each other.

More frequently, she had become clever at managing their conflict by diverting their attention. 'Daddy, let's make the fairy bread.'

'Good idea, princess, my favourite job!'

Before long the kitchen table was laden with all sorts of wonderful treats: coloured fairy bread, sweet biscuits, a multi-tiered cupcake stand, bowls of treats including frogs in red and green jelly ponds and plates full of warm party pies, sausage rolls and frankfurters. Soon after, the joyful, happy cries of children bearing gifts for Isla engulfed the kitchen.

Whilst Oliver was at the front door greeting guests, his sister Olivia and her husband Richard rolled up in their brand-new 1955 Chevy Bel Air. It was a stunning piece of machinery with a fetching red duco, quite the addition to the streetscape on Stradbroke Avenue. Olivia alighted from the vehicle wearing a form-fitting apricot sheath dress, finished with a pearl necklace and a turtle brooch. Arriving at the front door, she peered over her turquoise horn-rimmed sunglasses, air-kissing Oliver's cheeks. 'You know that I'm here for Isla, darling, after all, I am her favourite godmother.'

Richard raised his eyebrows and smirked at Oliver, tipping his grey Akubra hat.

'Fancy set of wheels, old boy!' Oliver ribbed him.

Richard smiled, 'Well, you know we real estate agents need to look the goods and after all, I am the primary breadwinner!'

Olivia scoffed as she headed into the party, 'And the primary spender, it seems!'

'If only,' sighed Richard.

Isla immediately spotted her aunt and uncle in the hallway and dashed up to Olivia, hugging her legs. Olivia crouched down, giving her a warm embrace. 'Happy birthday, beautiful girl! You are so grown up.'

Isla smiled. 'You know, Aunt Ollie, I'm going to school this year and I'm going to learn how to read and write properly.'

Oliver butted in, 'And learn piano, li'l one!'

'Yes, yes, Daddy, I promise, I am going to be the best piano player ever.'

Jess navigated through the army of children and greeted Olivia and Richard, who had made it as far as the drawing room. Although Jess appeared warm and inviting, Olivia could tell by her strained features and puffy eyes that something was not quite right.

Oliver provided drinks for his guests and clapping his hands to gain attention, announced that a game of pin the tail on the donkey was about to commence. Isla was first to play and caused much laughter when she managed to pin the tail on the donkey's nose.

'You made me so dizzy, Daddy!' she said, removing her blindfold.

Oliver laughed, giving her a big hug. 'You are too funny, li'l one.'

The sounds of shrieking children were silenced by Jess ringing a small service bell.

'Everyone, into the kitchen, it's time for food!'

The tidal wave of children approached the kitchen, all vying for spots next to the party girl. A sea of hands clawed at the carefully designed party plates of food, amidst much laughter. Jess and Oliver dutifully assisted the children with their food and soft drinks, whilst Olivia took charge of the Kodak Brownie. Richard located a spot in the kitchen corner, sipping on his malt whisky, wishing he were at home listening to his favourite radio show, HSV-7's weekly sports program. Aunty Elsie snuck in late via the back door, sidled up to Richard and commenced chewing his ear about the coming football season and her favourite Collingwood players. Richard pretended to listen intently, whilst knocking back a few mouthfuls of scotch.

'Smile,' said Olivia to the children gathered around the table with cheesy grins and mouths full of sugary delights.

'I bet you wouldn't give up your day job for this, sis,' smirked Oliver.

Olivia retorted, 'Give me obstetrics any day, little brother. However, I am quite an accomplished photographer, if I do say so myself!'

Once the first wave of mayhem passed, the next one followed. Time for the birthday cake. The children gathered around Isla whilst Oliver carefully lit the five candles on the decorated cake. Silence momentarily captured the room. Each child watched the flickering flames, the magical lights bouncing off Isla's face. The flash of the camera added to the atmosphere, and Oliver sang happy birthday with a chorus of Isla's friends. Filling her lungs, she blew out all five candles in one hit, looking up at her parents proudly.

Oliver and Jess crouched down beside her and Jess whispered in her ear, 'Here is the fun part, Isla. Now be careful. Cut the cake but not right down to the bottom, and then make your special wish. If you touch the bottom, your wish will be broken, so be very careful.'

Isla glanced at her parents, feeling safe and secure. Everyone watched on in silence, waiting for her to cut the cake. She squeezed her bright blue eyes tightly, looked up to the heavens, took a deep breath and made her wish.

Opening her eyes, she smiled at her parents. 'You know if I tell you, it won't come true?'

Oliver kissed her on the cheek. 'We know, li'l one. We know.'

Chapter 2

Both Sides Now

February 1955

It was the witching hour at the hospital. In the nurses' station, Jess sat slumped over her patient's medical files, attempting to complete her observation entries. Her sister-in-law Olivia had just examined her last patient and newborn for the night. The ward was isolated and still. For a moment, Jess was distracted by a crying baby from the next-door delivery ward. It was a brief interlude, but it triggered her to reflect on her days at St Vincent's Hospital.

– – –

She had arrived in Australia in 1937, two years before the declaration of war. The boat trip from London had been arduous. Jess suffered from sea sickness and spent most of her time couped up in a very modest cabin. It was a huge relief to step on solid ground once the ship docked at Port Melbourne, although she had mixed emotions.

Jess was very close to her only sister, Geraldine, who was eight years her senior. She would miss her sister and her sister's close-knit family dreadfully. Geraldine, affectionately known as Gerry, had raised Jess, due to the sudden death of their mother who had died of a broken heart, never having recovered from the death of their father after World War 1. Theirs was a humble family but despite the emotional fall-out from the war and the financial burdens, they were able to make things work. Gerry toiled around the clock at a clothing factory and Jess worked part time at a local baker's, often bringing home at day's end leftover bread and sweet buns. Both sisters delighted in the odd vanilla slice topped with strawberry-pink icing.

Gerry was very weight conscious and she often said to Jess, 'I wish I knew the day I was going to die because then I'd fill my face with vanilla slices.' The thought of her sister scoffing into a tray of vanilla slices always made Jess burst into laughter.

Jess had always wanted to travel and explore the world. Australia seemed as good a place as any. Her mother, Eileen, had been a nurse, employed as part of the World War I effort. She had loved her mother, but they were never close. When she wasn't working or looking after her two girls, Eileen spent much of her time sitting in her green velvet rocking chair knitting jumpers and scarves. She was a very private person; some might even have called her cold. Jess recalled spying on her and often discovering her crying alone in the dark. She regretted that she had never been brave enough to comfort her but had always felt helpless to do so. Gerry was too busy at either school or work, so there was nothing Jess could do but watch her mother consumed with grief, a malaise that ended her life prematurely. She often thought to herself that she would never wish to live a life like hers, a life filled with regret.

When Jess's application to study nursing at St Vincent's in Melbourne was successful, it seemed like a golden ticket to escape and leave a difficult childhood behind her. *There was much to look forward to*, she thought, and having a family was high on her priority list. If she were ever fortunate enough to have a child, she would be the best mother possible. She dreamt of having a special bond with her child, one that she had never shared with her own mother. It was one of the reasons that she was drawn to the vocation of midwifery.

St Vincent's on Victoria Parade had opened some 44 years previously, having been a converted terrace house run by the Sisters of Charity.

Shortly after opening as a hospital, its clinical school was founded and it was the first school to have a formal agreement with the University of Melbourne. The new main hospital block was world standard. The nursing quarters, although basic, provided for a collegiality that Jess had never previously experienced. Strict curfews were imposed and the girls were always on their best behaviour, at least when the officious Sister Felicia was guarding the entrance door to their quarters. God forbid if ever one of the girls secreted a male companion into the rooming house. Sister Felicia stood tall and thin. She never smiled. Her face was perfectly framed by her habit, exposing a withered face, sharp nose and mean, thin lips. Her eyes were often bloodshot and the girls used to joke that it was due to her over-imbibing Father O'Flaherty's altar wine. She wore a fob watch pinned to her starched uniform bodice and often checked the time, as if she had some place better to be.

The entrance door of the nurses' home was locked promptly at 9.00 p.m. Entry was banned after that time, without question. If it were an emergency, nurses would be led back via the tunnels under the emergency department. Nevertheless, Old Kenny the caretaker, always one to rescue a student nurse in despair, would often assist latecomers.

'Oh, Nurse Baker, another emergency?' he would grin.

'Yes, Kenny, you wouldn't believe what happened. I was just...'

Kenny would interrupt by lifting his index finger to his lips.

'You need say no more, I'm just saving you another three Hail Marys at confessional tomorrow mornin', Miss.' Kenny's warm smile always gave Jess comfort and reassurance.

Another fallen angel, he would smile to himself.

In the last year of study, a handful of lectures, including pharmacology and biochemistry, was held at the university for the student nurses. Neither of these subjects were favourites of Jess. Following the lectures the next day, the nurses attended tutorials conducted by the nuns. In her study group, Jess became friendly with a country girl, Bernadette. She was a bit rough around the edges, but possessed a heart of gold. She was also very clever and assisted Jess with her studies. It was nice to have Bern around. It was like having a sister once more. Bern even reminded her of Gerry. A little overweight, often wearing pleated trousers and short-sleeved shirts. She was not very feminine and rarely wore any jewellery, save for a pendant around her neck that held a small picture of her parents. Her brown hair was curly and wild, and she was often reprimanded for smoking inside the nurses' dorm.

After the tutorial in biochem, Bern said, 'Let's go to the uni caf and do some spotting.'

'What do you mean?' said Jess, her cheeks turning rosy.

'You know what I mean, Jessie! Check out those hotties over a milkshake. I've got my eye on that bloke David. You know, the arts student. He makes me kinda randy. Those sexy brown eyes, black wavy hair, chiselled jaw and all-knowing round specs. Oh my, my heart's fluttering already.'

'Calm down,' said Jess, 'you're making me flustered too.'

Bravely, they walked into the café. It was abuzz with chatter and laughter. Some rebel students were sitting around in their flannel pyjamas, trying to be cool and out there. Others were sitting in groups, discussing the day's lesson, whilst others were gulping their meals down to make their next lecture.

Jess and Bernadette scored a table not far from the check-out counter.

'You stay there, Jess, and mind the table. My shout. Usual chocolate milkshake, Nurse Baker?'

Jess nodded, licking her lips at the thought of it. She opened her study text, accidentally bumping one of her other books off the table. Just then, someone appeared beside her, picked up her book and handed it to her. 'I believe this is yours?' he said.

'Why thank you,' Jess blushed, 'that is very kind of you.'

'It's my pleasure. Always happy to rescue a damsel… I mean nurse… in distress,' he said.

Jess looked down and remembered that she was still in uniform, fob watch and all. The only thing missing was her nurse's cap. She laughed, coyly peering up at her well-mannered knight.

'Well, I am not *exactly* in distress, sir, but I am pleased you made the effort.' *Oh my God*, she thought, *why did I say that? Was it too forward? Did I sound like an idiot?*

'My name is Oliver. Oliver Johnson. My friends call me Ollie, which is a bit confusing as my sister is Olivia and her nickname is Ollie too. It's like the Greeks calling their kids George and Georgia. You know, no inventiveness, my parents. But I suppose that's what Adelaide does to you. Anyhow, I'm babbling on, so sorry.'

Jess smiled. 'My name is Jessica, but call me Jess.' His presence was warm and comforting. He was so dreamy. 'What do you do?'

'I'm a music major, my sub-major is philosophy. How about you?'

Jess was so taken by him, she paused for a moment. Time stood awkwardly still.

'Are you alright?' enquired Oliver.

'Oh, um yes, yes… um, quite fine. I'm a final year nurse at St V's. I'm here with my…' Jess was interrupted.

'Bernadette. Bern Peters to her mates,' said Bernadette, bowling into the conversation.

'Well, very pleased to meet both of you. Hey, the lads at Newman College are having a get-together tonight. How about you two join us?'

Bernadette jumped in, 'Yes, we would love that!' She elbowed Jess inconspicuously. 'Wouldn't we, Jess?' She gave her a meaningful stare and nudged her shoulder, whilst trying to juggle two chocolate milkshakes.

'Oh, ah, yes, yes that would be most lovely,' Jess said.

'Great, well I'll see you both at 7.00 p.m., front door entrance of the college. Follow the red arrows to party central. Look forward to seeing you both.'

Jess watched Oliver disappear through the hordes of students and a thick layer of clamour. He was tall, handsome and had an aloofness about him that was most appealing. She felt her heart skip a beat or two.

'Who's in love then, nurse?' cheered Bernadette.

'Oh stop it, Bern. Stop teasing me,' said Jess.

'I know what I saw,' said Bern, 'and it looked like lurv to me, Nurse Baker,' she laughed. 'Here's your shake, drink it up, you'll need all your energy, missy. Cheers!'

As they sipped on their drinks, they grinned broadly, Jess wondering how her friend could read her mind so well.

Days at the hospital were highly structured. Mass commenced at 6.00 a.m. every day. Breakfast, including preparation and clean-up, was from 7.30 a.m. to 8.30 a.m., training and education consumed the rest of the day and dinner was at 6 p.m. sharp. They were expected to be in bed by 9.00 p.m.

A little less about structure back then, Jess was easily led by Bern. The thought of attending Newman College later that night made her flushed and breathless. They darted back to nurses' quarters and changed for the occasion. Bern simply swapped tops and carefully placed a shade of pink on her lips. Jess decided upon her red swing dress with a petticoat for fullness. She complemented the dress with her preferred black kitten heels, accessorised with her favourite string of pearls.

Upon entering Newman College, the girls were overcome by its solid commanding structure and empowering façade. They followed the arrows to the main dining room. Sounds of laughter and cheer could be heard, interspersed with the music of Buddy Holly. Reaching the epicentre, they spied a large dome decorated with paintings of the disciples above a fortress of sandstone walls, seemingly protecting the aspirations within from the profane outer world. The surrounds emanated a feeling of inclusion based on Christian teachings of companionship, love, trust and honour. Inexplicably, Jess sensed that she was safe, despite a touch of nervousness laced with anticipation.

'I'm so glad you both made it,' said Oliver.

'Why, thank you for your kind invite,' said Jess.

'Why, thank you as well,' smiled Bernadette. 'I'm off to explore, Jess. You're a big girl, I'll be back soon. Remember, lock-out is 9.00 p.m. and we don't want to have to deal with Sister Felicia!'

Before Jess could say anything, Bernadette disappeared into a fog of Players No.6 Woodbine smoke.

'Could I interest you in a dance, Jess?'

Jess smiled nervously when Oliver lightly took her sweaty hand. *Unforgettable* by Nat King Cole played and Oliver drew her in closely. All other noises in the dining room faded for a time except for the music. The dance was slow and they each sensed a kindred spirit. This moment belonged to them. As the song concluded, still in an embrace, Oliver slowly and gently released Jess's hands. They gazed at each other in silence for a moment longer, discovering each other's faces; Jess's determined jawline and Oliver's sculpted chin.

I could stare into his eyes forever, she thought.

He bent down and gave her a delicate kiss on the cheek. Jess felt all abuzz, electricity shooting through her body. Standing under the dome, their togetherness seemed to meet with the approval of the disciples gazing down from above, or so Jess thought, imagining a wink from St Peter.

'Way to go, ol' boy!' yelled one of Oliver's classmates.

Jess, embarrassed, broke the embrace, but not before giving Oliver a hug.

'I must go, Oliver. I would love to see you again, if you like. Oh gosh, a bit bold of me.'

'Hmmm, let me think about that one,' Oliver said teasingly. 'Like to? I would love to!'

Capturing one last brief kiss from him before removing her heels, she ran like Cinderella towards the main door, grabbing Bernadette on the way through and exclaiming, 'Quick, Bern, Felicia will be on the warpath!'

Sculling her Pimms and lemonade, Bern blurted, 'Methinks a good day's work was achieved, Nurse Baker. Yes indeed… a very good day's work.'

She saluted Jess and both girls laughed, trying to dodge raindrops with heels in hand, running towards the Exhibition Gardens to beat the curfew. It must be late, Jess thought, as they followed the line of street lamps that were like a runway to the hospital quarters.

– – –

Jess was startled by a tap on her shoulder from her charge nurse. It appeared she had fallen asleep. Cold tea had partially split over the medical files before her, and the file entries remained incomplete.

'Sister Baker, if you want to retain your job here at the hospital, please refrain from continually falling asleep at work. You have a job to do, a responsible one, and I expect my staff to comply with a level of professionalism. Sleep at home, if you must. Now you can stay back and complete those files for handover in time for the morning shift workers.'

'But it's my daughter's first day of school. I can't be late. Please!' begged Jess.

'*Well*, you should have thought of that before you fell asleep. No excuses, Sister. Now do your job and report to me once those files are complete.'

Jess pleaded again in vain. How was she ever going to explain this to Isla? She held her head, resigned to the fact that a special memory would be lost today – witnessing Isla's first day of school. A tear or two beaded upon her cheek. She tried very hard to maintain her composure despite her exhaustion and sleep deprivation, feeling as if she had reached the end of her tether.

– – –

It was 8.30 a.m. No sign of Jess. Oliver had tried calling the hospital, but there was some difficulty connecting his call. By then, Isla was dressed in her new school uniform. The dress was rose-pink and knee-length with small checks. It was fringed with wide white bands around its short sleeves and had a white collar and white buttons. The fashion statement was finished with white socks and black sandals. Isla felt very grown up and special. Oliver thought the same. It was a joyous moment, but one also filled with mixed emotions. A part of him felt as if he was losing his little girl – his li'l one. He was also distressed that Jess was curiously absent and hoped that it was nothing serious, guessing that work had caused her tardiness.

'Where's Mummy?'

'I don't know, li'l one, but I bet my bottom dollar she meets us at the school. Quick now, you'll miss the first bell.'

'Are we walking, Daddy?'

'Yes, I think we'll give the old girl's wheels a rest this fine day!' Oliver so loved his motorcar. When he was not playing or teaching piano, he was often washing or shining his prized 1947 black Chevrolet, which he fondly referred to as 'The Beast'.

After a brief walk down an oak-tree-lined street, the two turned a corner and found themselves at the entrance gate to Isla's school, Camberwell Primary School. The building was solid and all-knowing, ready to take on another class of eager newcomers into its rooms of discovery. Isla gripped her father's hand tightly. The main door to the school loomed large, and unfamiliar faces from the crowd suffocated her.

Oliver's gaze was darting in all directions trying to locate Jess. She was nowhere to be seen.

'Is Mummy coming, Daddy?' said Isla, snapping his attention back to her.

'I'm sure she's on her way, li'l one. Probably caught up at work with some very important patient.'

Just at that moment, they were approached by Mildred Maloney, a refined woman in her late thirties, with her daughter Linda in tow. Oliver taught Mildred and Linda piano and was often secretly bemused by their complete lack of talent. Mildred was dressed as if she was on her way to high tea at the Windsor, wearing her signature sky-blue velvet crescent hat along with pearls and gloves.

'Hello, Oliver, what a wonderful surprise to see you and darling Izzy here!'

How Oliver detested her air of pretence, even more her informal way of shortening Isla's name.

'Yes, yes it is. *Isla's* first day of school and it seems Mummy is late,' said Oliver.

'It's better late than never, I always say, Oliver. How unfortunate not to be here for your daughter's first day of school. I suppose that's what happens when mummies work. Memories are etched forever in time, darling. Let's hope Jess makes it. *It would be such a pity.* My little Linda is a big grade five girl this year. Aren't you, dear?' she said, pinching Linda's chubby cheek. 'Before you know it, she will be off to Methodist Ladies College. Lucky her daddy is a lawyer and able to afford the fees.' She laughed. 'Well, ta ta for now, see you later on. Oh, by the way, I have been putting in some work on that music piece, Oliver. You will be amazed.'

Oliver had no doubt he would be 'amazed'. He only wished he could wear earplugs.

As Mildred and Linda disappeared into the school's entrance door like a pair of salmon swimming upstream, the school bell rang. Oliver was dismayed that Jess had not made it for Isla's sake. As much as he detested Mildred, he knew that Isla *would* remember this day for many years to come. No doubt it was not Jess's fault. However, he was concerned that as the years passed, Isla's memory might be laced with a pinch of judgement.

'Off you go now, Isla. Don't want to be late.' Oliver grinned at her.

'Bye, Daddy. Yes, I don't want to get into trouble. I guess Mummy must be busy. I know she would have wanted to be here. I am glad you are anyway. I love you, Daddy.'

Oliver bent over and Isla wrapped her tiny arms around his neck, giving him an impressive hug. He kissed her on the cheek and said, 'I am so proud of you, li'l one. You know you're a big girl now. Daddy and Mummy love you so much. I will be right here to meet you at the end of the day.'

'I love you too, Daddy… and Mummy. See you soon, Daddy of mine.'

Oliver's face lit up with a proud cheesy smile, 'See you soon, li'l one of mine.'

Isla laughed and waved all at once, 'Copycat.'

Parting ways, Oliver disappeared around the corner just as Jess arrived from the tram stop. There were no parents to be seen at the school entrance and it was apparent the children were now in class.

Jess thumped the school's red letterbox with her fist, cursing her late arrival and miserably sliding down the white picket fence to sit on the ground. Putting her face in her hands, she wept uncontrollably, hardly able to catch her breath. She didn't care who might see her. As far as she was concerned, she was a failure as a parent. Nevertheless, however hard she was on herself, she did not allow Oliver the luxury of absolution. *If I didn't have to work, this would never have occurred*, she thought. Why doesn't he get a proper well-paid job and support his family like other men? Why should I be the main breadwinner?

As these bitter thoughts crossed her mind, she pulled herself up from the concrete pavement, brushing down her nurse's uniform. Wiping away her tears, she stood firm and headed home. There was a real purpose in her stride and armed with the fierceness of a mother lioness, she was hell-bent on giving Oliver a piece of her mind.

Chapter 3
Borderline

Oliver was sitting at the piano playing his favourite Schubert Symphony No. 9 in C Major. It brought a grin to his face and made his soul sing. Just as he was about to embark on the second coda, the front door slammed and Jess stormed into the drawing room.

'Who do you think you are?'

Oliver's playing ended abruptly. He looked sheepishly at Jess. 'I'm so sorry you missed Isla's first day at the school. What happened?'

Jess took a deep breath. Her hands were clenched by her sides. Her face was flushed and her bottom lip quivered. 'What happened? What happened? I got held up at work! I'm so tired, Oliver, and I'm just not coping. You don't even seem to notice me. I do everything around the house whilst you just sit on your piano stool scribbling music and teaching the odd student. Why can't you get a proper job? Why am I the one who must work so hard and earn us a decent income? I'm fed up and I can't handle it anymore. Something has to give! I can't do this!'

She collapsed onto the Chesterfield, her thin legs giving way to her tiredness. With her emotions spent, she could no longer fight back her tears.

Oliver carefully approached her, two steps forward, one step back, unsure whether his intended solace would be welcomed. Eventually, he sidled up to her on the couch to comfort her. He recalled how easy it used to be talking to Jess and how after Isla's birth, a tyranny of emotional distance had increasingly formed between them. It seemed that he could do nothing right. He had tried. He was a good dad. However despite his efforts, nothing seemed to satisfy Jess.

He tried to wrap his arm around her, but she curtly rose to her feet. Looking down on him, she said, 'I don't need your comfort. I need you to be a man and to start acting like one. Think about it!'

As quickly as she had entered the room, she left it. Oliver heard the bedroom door close. He was confused by her extreme emotions and sat there on the couch for a time collecting his thoughts. Is it something I did wrong? he thought. Is she just taking it out on me to get her feelings off her chest? He knew that she would be upset missing Isla's first day of school but he had never seen her in such a state before. He reflected on her sleepless nights and her inability to cope with the smallest annoyances. She's not coping, he thought. She's right, but I have tried.

Every time Oliver suggested that Jess consult with her doctor, he was met with her pleas of denial. Helpless, he so desperately wanted the old Jess back. But where is she? he thought. Where is that girl I first danced with at Newman College? She's vanished.

His gaze into the abyss of the dusty bookshelf was unexpectedly interrupted by the doorbell. It was his first student for the day, Barbara.

He opened the front door to a woman in her 40s. She was short, and wore a Tuscan dress displaying a pattern of green palm fronds. Her red nail polish matched the colour of her lips, and her bright red locks neatly framed her oval face.

'Good morning, Mr Johnson,' she said, 'what a beautiful morning and what a way to start the day with my piano lesson.'

'And good morning to you, Miss Jenkins. It is a wonderful day,' said Oliver, trying to cover up the morning's recent events. 'Please come in and let's get started. I believe we are working on that piece by Bach, Allegro in A. How's it coming along?'

'I'll let you be the judge, Mr Johnson,' she replied, tossing back her curls, filling the air with the sweet overpowering scent of the Myer ground-floor perfume department.

Oliver had four students that day, all women. His last lesson was at 1.30 p.m. with Mildred Maloney. He had developed quite a reputation amongst the local mothers, because of his charm and charisma. Many of his students caught up from time to time at the local coffee shop and exchanged embellished notes about their encounters with Oliver. Despite their musings, Oliver never crossed any forbidden lines and never behaved inappropriately. However, his boyish good looks and allure often sent the imagination of these women into a girlish frenzy.

Between student lessons, Oliver turned his mind to the manuscript for *Isla's Song,* at the ready on top of the piano. He picked up his finely sharpened pencil and went to work. Each motion of the composition filled his heart with joy and took him to a place where wildness was free to roam, where borders were unknown and time was no enemy. As the notes played in his mind's eye, he pictured a young girl dancing, swirling and moving fluidly from one chord to another. He could see her smile and the way she embraced her freedom. Her exhilaration fuelled such excitement that she appeared to be floating on air. Drilling down further, the image became clearer and he could see Isla, his li'l one. Her happiness made him happy. Her joy filled his very essence. Just as he was drawing the second verse to a conclusion, his rhythm was broken by a crash in the kitchen.

He rushed in to discover Jess picking up the broken pieces of a plate, cursing under her breath.

'I was just going to bring you in a cup of tea with some Anzac cookies. Trying to do too much and the damn plate slipped out of my hand. I don't know what's wrong with me. Oh well...'

'That's okay, darling. Don't worry about it.'

'So much for my attempt at a peace treaty, Ollie,' she said, continuing to pick up the broken bread plate.

'Don't worry, Jess. It's the thought that counts. And I think it was a beautiful thought!'

Oliver's eyes welled up. His emotions were already stirred by his composition work but seeing Jess bent over broken pieces of ceramic, armed with a dustpan, made him even more emotional. She was damaged, he thought. It was not a simple measure of picking up her broken pieces and gluing them back together. It was much more complicated than that, and he had no idea where to start. All he could do was be there for her and support her as much as he could do in the circumstances. However, he was scared that his good intentions were simply not enough. He'd been living with the hope that his bride would resurface from the chasm in which she found herself, yet as time progressed, his hope was withering on the vine.

Jess stood up, emptied the shattered plate into the nearby waste bin and turned around to face him. He gently wiped a tear from her face. As he did so, a tear fell from his eye. It rolled down his cheek in slow motion, tenderly caught by Jess. There was a stillness between them, a sharing of thoughts as they gazed into each other's eyes. There were no answers, just questions. Oliver then held her close and could feel her bony ribs through her cotton nightgown. He felt so helpless and all he could do was hold her and not let go. For Jess in that moment, Oliver was a lifebuoy. Although her grip was weak and she was all at sea, she knew in her heart that something had to change, if she were to survive. The problem was that she didn't know what.

Their embrace was interrupted by the chimes of the doorbell. It was Mildred Maloney. Great timing as usual.

No sooner had Oliver opened the front door than Mildred bowled in as if she owned the premises.

'I have done so much practice this week, Oliver. Often hard to find the time between my committee meetings and beauty appointments but I did, and you know why, pet?'

'I have no idea, Mildred. However, I have a feeling you are about to share it with me.'

'Well pet, it's because these lessons and the time that I spend with you each week mean the world to me. It takes me out of my little bubble and away from some of those non-creative types. I can see how you look upon me as a real protege, someone who has exquisite potential and the ability to take my piano playing further. It's like you see this inspirational flame burn within me and discern that it is your job to keep that conflagration ablaze. I can just feel it,' she said, like a young prep school girl gasping for air.

There was an awkward silence where Oliver was stuck for words. He wondered whether Mildred had shared her inner desires with the coffee club women or whether her intimate thoughts were something she privately shared with him.

'Well let's get to it, Mildred. I look forward to hearing your study piece.'

Mildred approached the piano and slowly and deliberately removed her lace gloves and hat. She positioned herself on the piano stool with the cool intention of a concert pianist about to entertain a recital audience. Oliver stood at her side as she opened her sheet music to page one, Benda Sonatina in A minor, her hands hovering over the keys. Oliver gave her a slight nod and she began playing.

He was speechless.

It was evident from the start her fingering was off-key and her timing imprecise, with her B flats incorrectly substituted for F sharps. It was like listening to nails scraping against a blackboard. Oliver hoped Jess had a good supply of Bex powder in the cupboard for his looming headache.

As Mildred finished, her fingers held the last bung notes before they lifted smoothly from the keyboard. She looked to Oliver with a proud, broad smile.

'Well, what do you think? Don't be shy, I am all too prepared for constructive criticism, however, I do believe that I performed marvellously. All that practice is clearly making a significant difference to my performance ability. And you know what, Oliver? It's all due to you and your level of devotion to me as your favourite student.'

Oliver approached the bay window, gaping, wanting to fill his mouth with words but unable to do so. Collecting his thoughts, he finally turned to his student.

'Yes, Mildred, I can see that you have been practising and indeed, you are to be congratulated.' Clearing his throat, he resumed, 'Well for a start, I don't believe you've ever been able to play that piece from start to finish without stopping. That is a real achievement, and as you are aware, this classical piece with its broken chords and short sections of scale work lends itself to a variety of touches, phrasing and dynamic treatments. All I can say is that it is definitely coming along.'

'Coming along?' said Mildred aloofly. 'I think you need to hear it again, Oliver. You obviously missed my exquisite intonation and the heartfelt joy with which I played it...'

He cut in, 'Oh no, I gathered the *heartfelt joy* bit. I do believe that you could achieve much more fluidity in your playing if we get your finger placement correct. Let's have a try.'

She moved to the right along the piano stool, leaving space for him. It was a little cosy. The strong smell of her floral perfume was overpowering, burning the inside of his nostrils. More Bex, he thought. Now, please.

He took Mildred's right hand and sensitively displayed her fingers on the treble keys, then had her read the sheet music and play accordingly.

'You see how it makes playing so much easier if your fingers remain placed correctly?'

'Oh yes, Oliver. Why yes. Let me do it again,' she implored him.

As she played, her right hand crept downwards, resting awkwardly on his knee. She looked longingly at him. Unexpectedly, the kitchen door swung open. It was Jess carrying a tray laden with Anzac and Monte Carlo biscuits along with a pot of tea and cups.

Mildred abruptly rose to her feet, straightening herself, followed by Oliver.

'Is the lesson over already?' Jess asked.

'Oh, I do believe we have achieved a lot today and I consider it would be worthwhile for Mildred to take on board what she has learnt and to practise some more before we meet next time.' Oliver was spluttering so much that Jess could hardly decipher his words.

'Oh yes, yes, I do agree Oliver. Always take the teacher's lead, I say. Always. It's been wonderful. I best go. I have a few items to collect from the greengrocers before I pick up Linda from school. Ta ta. And thanks again, Oliver. So very much.' She gave him a knowing look, making him feel that she was undressing him.

'I'll show myself out, pet. Bye, Jessica. Bikkies next time perhaps. However, us girls do have to watch the waistline. At our age, we can't afford to let ourselves go.'

'Ta ta,' said Jess, giving Oliver a contemptuous look.

After the front door closed, she asked, 'So, what was going on there, Ollie?'

'Oh nothing, nothing, usual high-maintenance client. I have a splitting headache Jess, how about a Bex powder?' He did not want to worry her unnecessarily.

Jess headed to the kitchen to retrieve Oliver's remedy. She had a bit of a chuckle to herself, being used to Oliver's students. When some of these women crossed paths with her, they looked down on her. But despite their impassioned glares, she trusted Oliver and felt secure in their marriage, always believing that he would never stray or be unfaithful to her. It was the least of her problems. She herself was growing apart from him. She thought that he had been less understanding about her needs since Isla's birth, that he was more focussed on being a dad. She so missed being away from Isla whilst at work. She was being cheated of Isla's developing years. On the one hand she knew she was being unreasonable, however, on the other, she resented Oliver's strong attachment to Isla. Her thoughts were irreconcilable.

When Jess left the room, Oliver slumped onto the piano stool feeling curiously dishonest. His heart sank and a cloud of dread loomed over him as he thought about Mildred's next lesson. I will never allow myself to be put in that position again, he promised himself.

He also thought how much he missed Jess's tenderness, her affection, and how he could well do without the continual walking on eggshells around her.

The grandfather clock chimed 3.00 o'clock.

Jess was not on night duty and Oliver suggested that they both collect Isla from school. She was thrilled at the prospect, a welcome invitation after an average start to the day. It would make up somewhat for not being there at the start of school.

Just as they were leaving, the postman delivered a parcel from Jess's sister, Gerry. Because they were running late, Jess left the parcel behind the planter on the front porch. The walk took a bit longer than usual due to the intolerable heat. When they turned the corner, they spied Mildred Maloney darting out of the school entrance in the opposite direction, lugging Linda along with her. Oliver raised his eyebrows and Jess gave him a small pinch to the side.

Upon arriving at the school gate, Isla met her parents with exquisite timing, her bright blue eyes shining with delight to see them both there to greet her.

'Oh Mummy, Daddy, I am so lucky. I have so much to tell you. I love my teacher, Mrs Wilkinson. We made Chinese lanterns and paper chains today and we read a book about playmates. I met a new friend, Anne. It's with an 'e' she told me. Also, we had lunch and played doll's houses, but not with the boys, they're not allowed.' She ran out of breath.

'Oh, *our girl* did have a big day,' Jess smiled, 'give Mummy a hug. I've missed you.'

'I've missed you too, Mummy and Daddy. I especially missed you this morning, but Daddy was here.'

'But Mummy was working,' Oliver said. 'I told you, li'l one. Your mummy is very special and works so hard for all of us. Daddy's very lucky to have your mummy too.'

'I know, Daddy. I just missed her that's all,' said Isla.

'I know Isla, but I'm here now. We're going to make you a special meal tonight, spaghetti bolognaise, and then after, if you're good, vanilla ice-cream with fairy sprinkles,' Jess said.

'Yum yum yummy! I can't wait, and I will tell you everything about today,' exclaimed Isla.

'That you will, li'l one,' said Oliver.

They all walked hand in hand down the street and around the corner, shaded by oak trees. Their steps faltered at times when they stumbled on fallen acorns.

As they opened the front door, the telephone was ringing. Jess answered it, an operator informing her it was a collect call from Gerry Baker in the United Kingdom. Jess's eyes lit up. 'It's my sister!' she exclaimed to Oliver and Isla.

'Hello, hello, is that you Gerry, can you hear me, hello?'

'I can hear you alright. How would you be, little sister?'

'I'm okay Gerry, I'm okay,' said Jess, her voice becoming subdued.

'You could be a little more convincing!' Gerry said. 'Listen, I sent you a parcel recently, did you receive it?'

'Hang on, yes, it arrived today just as we were leaving to pick up Isla!' Jess picked up the parcel and tore off its brown paper wrapping.

'Oh my God, oh my God, it's stunning! It's beautiful. But a winter coat, Gerry? Do you know how hot it is here?' Jess laughed.

'I know, you duffer, it's for you to wear over here, at the end of the year. I want you to come and spend some time with me. Just you. Just for three weeks. You need a break. Oliver wrote me about how you've been finding things a little difficult lately and a fresh break back in our old hometown might lift your spirits, lass. What say you?'

Jess wondered what he had said in that letter. Why hadn't he told her about it? Why was he being so secretive? Was he also hiding other things from her? Were her fluctuating moods so obvious?

Gerry interrupted the silence, 'Are you there, Jess? Can you hear me?'

'I can hear you well, Gerry. It's a lovely thought, but I don't think I can. There's too much… I'm not… the 12-month roster's been done. I'd lose my job, sis. Besides, I wouldn't like to leave Isla.'

'Isla will be fine with Oliver. You can call her every day if you like. I'm worried about you, Jess. I wish I were closer, but I'm not. I want you here with me. Be like old time's sake. Oh, and you can meet the two other kids I hatched after you left. And my new old man, Bob. Come on. What do you say?' pleaded Gerry.

'I say it's a lovely offer, but…'

Gerry knew a roadblock when she saw one. She interjected before Jess could complete her sentence.

'Okay then, so at least you will think about it. That's what I'm hearing. I'll call again soon. And remember, I'm here anytime you want to talk to me. I don't want you to finish like Mum. You hear me, sis? I won't let it happen. It will not happen on my watch. I love you. And know that I would do anything for you, Jess.' Gerry's voice began to break.

Isla crept up to Jess, pulling on her mother's shirt. 'Mummy, when are we cooking dinner? I'm hungry.'

'In a minute, Isla. I'm on the phone to Aunty Gerry. Soon, soon, I won't be long. Off you go please. OLIVER!'

When Isla had vanished, Jess returned her attention to Gerry on the phone. 'Listen sis, I've got my hands full at present. I did hear what you said. Means the world to me, it does. And I love you too. I will think about it. Promise. Love you so much, sis.'

'I will cherish that promise, Jess, and hold it close to me heart. Love you too. Give Isla and Oliver a hug for me. Love you.' Gerry's call disconnected.

Jess held the phone to her ear for a moment longer. The sound of her sister's voice tore her apart. She was stuck in a deep hole, punctuated from time to time by bright flashes that were all too often suppressed by a mind-numbing fog. Still holding the receiver in her hand, she imagined Gerry's hands stretched out towards her. She was unable to seize them and get the help she needed. She couldn't and she didn't know why.

She carefully placed the receiver back into its cradle, then hugged Gerry's gift tightly, warm memories flittering past her mind. She heard Isla's laughter from the kitchen and the tinkering of notes from the drawing room.

Is that what is wrong with me? Jess thought. Am I not really home?

Chapter 4
I Think I Understand

There was much to celebrate. Oliver had just received word that one of his compositions had been commissioned for an Australian film. More importantly, it was 14 February and that not only meant St Valentine's Day but his and Jess's sixth wedding anniversary.

Oliver busied himself in the kitchen making a fresh pot of tea and French toast. He had prepared a tray adorned with a small crystal vase holding a single red rose, picked from the front garden.

He heard Isla practising *Isla's Song* in the drawing room and stuck his head around the kitchen door. 'Hey li'l one, you're sounding so good. Your song is really coming along.'

Isla grinned from ear to ear, raising her eyebrows. 'Yes, Daddy, I've been practising very hard. I want to show you later. Can you…'

Oliver cut in, pre-empting her, 'Of course I can. Let's try and work out that chorus part.'

Isla gave him an approving nod before returning to her playing.

The scent of the fresh cinnamon toast and English breakfast tea was soothing as Oliver crept down the hallway into their bedroom. Jess was fast asleep. It was Monday morning. She had finished night shift on Sunday morning and was off work now until Tuesday evening. She had had a rough night, tossing and turning. Her mood swings were getting worse and unpredictable, probably due to interrupted sleep, he thought.

He meticulously placed the tray on her bedside table, careful not to displace its floral centrepiece. Then he softly nudged her. 'It's 9.30, love… wakey wakey.'

Jess grumbled indecipherably and rolled over.

Deciding upon another tactic, Oliver headed to the bedroom window. He tugged on the blind cord, accidentally releasing it and causing it to spin round and round on its roller, opening the way for a channel of bright light to hit Jess on the face.

'What the hell, Oliver!'

'Whoops, I'm so sorry love, I didn't mean it to… I mean, I was trying to wake… Oh hell! Take two!'

Jess sat up, rubbing sleep from her eyes. Oliver swiftly removed the tray and exited the bedroom, using his right foot to close the door behind him. Standing outside the room, he cleared his throat and said, 'Excuse me, madam, breakfast is served. Is madam respectably attired to receive her morning nourishment? Or shall I return at a more convenient hour?'

By this time, Isla had ceased her playing and joined in the charade. Oliver pursed his lips, 'Ssshh!' Holding her hand up to her mouth and trying not to laugh, Isla removed the small vase from the tray to take part in the processional.

Jess did not much feel up for it. She was overtired and a little nauseated, but she could see that Oliver was trying to make an effort. She thought that maybe if she met him halfway, things might start to turn about for her. She so desperately wanted to rediscover her feelings for him and experience the spark that had once ignited her love for him.

'Enter, sir,' she said in a refined voice, hearing Isla's squeaky giggles, 'and li'l madam. Entrez if you will.'

Isla ran into the room ahead of her father, 'Look what Daddy picked, look Mummy, look!'

'I can see, Isla, it's beautiful. Just like you!' said Jess.

'I know, I know, he bought it just for you, Mummy. It's beautiful like you and me. If I was a flower, I would be a rose, a red one, and we would be the same flower, Mummy. We would both be beautiful and Daddy's girls.'

Oliver noticed that Isla was pinpointed by the beam of light through the window, just as Jess was. It felt as if he was in the presence of angels. Dust particles caught the sunlight and the mirrors, small crystal statues and trinkets also sparkled in the light, filling the room with rainbows. It was magical. But above all, Oliver saw a joy in his wife that he had not seen for some time. He leant against the bedroom wall, hands in pockets, feet crossed, wearing a big grin.

'Well, I didn't buy it, but I did pick it freshly from our front garden. It reminded me of Mummy and you. My two stunning roses, perfect in every way.'

Jess took the tray from Oliver, noticing his devotion. 'Oh this is amazing, Ollie. You've gone to so much trouble.'

'Nothing is too much trouble for my bride of six years. Happy anniversary, Jess,' he said softly.

He bent over and kissed her forehead. Isla watched on, taking in every loving moment.

'Oh... yes,' said Jess, trying to cover up her forgetfulness, 'happy anniversary, Ollie.'

Observing her unconvincing salutation, Oliver reached into his pocket and pulled out a small black velvet box to mark their special milestone. Handing it to her, he kissed her again.

'Oh, I'm sorry, Ollie, I have nothing for you! I'm so sorry... I meant to... work has been...'

Sensing her guilt, Oliver reassured her, 'Aw, don't worry, I don't need anything except my girls. Now open it up, quick, your tea and toast will get cold.'

Jess opened the present. It was a delicate, iron, gold-painted, heart-shaped locket with the initials 'J & O' engraved on it. She opened it up to discover a tiny picture of her and Oliver on their wedding day. He's thought of everything, she reflected.

'Six years means a gift of iron in some parts of the world. Durable and long-lasting, so they say.' Oliver winked. 'Let me put it on you, love.'

'Oh yes, Daddy, I want to see it on Mummy! It's so beautiful,' said Isla, jumping onto the bed.

'Careful now, Isla, Mummy doesn't want tea all over her and the bed,' said Jess.

Isla positioned herself close to her mother, sitting back and crouching on her knees. She watched her mother bend her fine neck forward and Oliver fasten the locket.

'It's beautiful, Ollie.'

'It is beautiful,' said Isla.

Oliver and Jess kissed.

'Okay, let's give Mummy some peace whilst we go and make us some French toast, li'l one.' He ushered Isla from the room but almost immediately popped his head in again, reminding Jess that he was taking her out for their customary anniversary dinner.

'Now don't you worry, Mrs Peters told me after mass on Sunday that she would be happy to babysit. 6.30 sharp. I've organised the reservation. And don't worry about the cost, I scored that commission I was telling you about. Rest up, just going to take Isla for a milkshake. Enjoy the peace.' He winked at Jess and exited before she could say a word.

Jess hesitated before smiling. When the door shut, she held onto the locket for some time, pondering into the depths of her teacup. The positive moments of the morning had escaped her already. It had all happened so quickly, but she was determined to recapture them along with her other good memories.

Clapping and congratulations sounded from within as the church doors flung open to reveal Jess and Oliver in their late 20s. A hail of rice and confetti showered them both, and excited family and friends cheered them on.

Jess was the classic bride, wearing a white dress adorned with nature-inspired lace from the sweetheart V-neckline to the bottom of the full ballgown skirt. Her off-the-shoulder straps and a subtle V-back added a little cheeky drama to the gown. Oliver wore the traditional black tuxedo with a white rose pinned to his lapel, matching Jess's soft bridal bouquet. The tall skinny photographer tried his best to capture the happy couple, but the crowd formed a persistent well-wishing barrier against his efforts. Constant hugs and kisses spoilt any chance of a decent photograph.

Jess and Oliver made their way to a waiting Austin 8 Tourer and just before they reached it, the photographer said, 'Mr and Mrs Johnson. One for the keeps box!' Finally, some prize snaps of the kissing couple.

Nearby, Oliver's uncle, Big Bert, a large jocular man in his mid 50s, yelled at Oliver and Jess as they were kissing at the car. 'Crikey, Ollie boy! She's a good-lookin' sheila but don't swallow her. Don't need any awkward questions from the kids later.' They broke apart and peered at Bert, raising their eyebrows and giving awkward smiles before getting into the car to be driven to the reception party.

Later that night with the wedding garden party in full swing, the guests danced to 1940's music and helped themselves to the buffet table, abundant with fine foods and deli items, compliments of the neighbourhood church ladies. The open tent was decorated with fairy lights, a few hanging kerosene lanterns providing further atmosphere. It was a joyous heartfelt occasion, with Gerry making it all the way from England and Oliver's aunts and uncles trekking down from northern Victoria. Oliver's parents had passed away some years before.

Jess and Oliver spent the day wrapped in each other's arms, clinking champagne glasses, giving each other cheeky stares and smiling at each other in disbelief that they were finally united in marriage. Their faces were alight with passion and their hearts filled with hopes for the future. At times when they lost themselves in each other's gaze, there was a shared knowing that the road ahead would have joyous times and they would have respect for each other. As Perry Como's *I'm Gonna Love That Gal* came to an end, they kissed again.

'I'm sitting the next one out, Ollie. I need a drink of water.'

Just then, Olivia, with her boyfriend Richard in tow, joined them on the dance floor, armed with a couple of glasses of champagne. 'Brought you something,' said Olivia, shoving the glass into Jess's hand with her usual brazenness.

'Oh! I was just about to… thanks!' Jess replied.

'Congrats you two. It's so lovely to have a sister and about time my brother got his act into gear,' smiled Olivia.

There were hugs all round, with Oliver retorting, 'You'll be next, sis. You're the most eligible out of this lot.' He jerked his chin towards a group of nearby elderly church women.

'Gee thanks, little brother. Convince Richard. Married or otherwise, I might remain Dr Johnson. I've decided I'm making a career for myself now. I am the *modern woman*, as you well know!'

'Oh, I don't know about that. Liv Young does have quite a nice ring to it!'

Olivia laughed, took a sip from her bubbles and gave her brother another hug. 'Yes, perhaps it does, we will see, brother of mine. On a more pressing note, I want you to know, Ollie, that I am truly happy for you. Truly, dear!'

Oliver hugged her tightly, 'That means a lot to me, sis, you mean the world to me.'

Olivia gave him another peck on the cheek before lifting her glass and raising it to Jess. 'To happiness!' As she turned to leave, she bumped into Big Bert, spilling champagne all over his tux. 'Sorry… whoops…'

Big Bert simply laughed loudly. 'No worries, lovely Liv. Not the first time a bird has spilled on me. And it won't be the last!'

A party classic began to play, with Big Bert quick to take Jess's hand and saying, 'Fancy a spin?'

Jess glanced over to Oliver to save her.

'She's all yours, Big Bert,' said Oliver, trying hard not to show his amusement. As she was whisked away, she peered over her left shoulder at Oliver, brow furrowed. He and Olivia were having a laugh at her expense.

Later in the evening, Jess sat exhausted in a folding chair at the edge of the tent, a half-empty champagne glass in her hand. Relaxed, she glanced at the remaining wedding guests, some of whom were still dancing. Some had fallen asleep, including Big Bert. Only scraps were left on the buffet table, and every available spot was taken up by empty beer cans and wine bottles. Her gaze settled on Oliver standing in the far corner, talking to a young couple with a baby. She imagined what her own family might look like and smiled. The adventures ahead were all with Oliver. The tingles she felt gave her a real sense of good things to come.

After some brief work on *Isla's Song,* Oliver and Isla headed off to their favourite delicatessen in Camberwell, Dom's Deli. As it was a little too far to walk, Oliver decided to take the Beast for a spin.

'Daddy, I can see my face in your car,' smiled Isla.

Oliver smiled proudly.

'In you hop, miss.'

Isla climbed onto the maroon leather bench seat. In front of her was a white leather handle attached to the dashboard, which allowed her something to hang onto if she wanted to stand. She adored travelling with her dad in his car. She especially loved observing the fashion of the passers-by. Driving along the main road, she spotted some school friends with their dogs.

'I want a dog, Daddy. Can you get me one?'

'Please,' said Oliver.

'Please, Daddy, please, please.'

'Well, we have to ask Mummy first, li'l one, but can I tell you a secret? You can't tell anyone though. Promise?'

'I promise, I promise.'

'Well, I've already been thinking about it, li'l one. Daddy had a dog when he was little.'

'Where is he now, Daddy?'

'He would be quite old now,' laughed Oliver, 'but he was a bit naughty, as I recall. My dad ended up taking him away to a farm to stay, so he could run all day. I missed him. I would like to get you one. I think it's time. Just have to make sure Mummy is okay with it. Okay?'

'Okay, let's ask Mummy, but first let's make sure she's in a good mood, Daddy. I don't want her to say no.'

Oliver was affected by Isla's response. *He* knew that Jess had not been travelling well, but he was concerned that her mood fluctuations were becoming apparent to Isla. He was also frustrated, as Jess continually refused to seek professional help. He thought that it was something that he needed to address seriously with Jess, not only for her benefit, but to protect Isla. Perhaps if he used Isla as a reason, Jess might have the sense to do something about her behaviour.

They pulled up and parked right outside Dom's Deli. 'The parking angel worked her magic for us again, li'l one.' Oliver beamed.

'I love that parking angel, Daddy,' smiled Isla.

They entered the shop to the sound of a tinny bell. It heralded a world of welcome smells, sights and tastes. The mix of the continental aromas was a delight to Oliver's senses. He smelt the strong fragrance of freshly

I THINK I UNDERSTAND

ground coffee beans, the acidic cheesy odour of cured meats and the pungent scent of the many cheeses on display.

Isla's favourite section of the deli was the glass stand displaying the continental cakes. She so loved the creamy chocolate eclairs, the vanilla slices with raspberry jam and the flaky pastry matchsticks filled with fresh cream and strawberry jam. When it came to sweets, Isla's eyes were bigger than her belly.

Oliver often guided her away from these sweet delicacies and headed to the cheese area of the deli. Isla thought the cheeses smelt like Daddy's dirty socks. It was her least favourite moment at Dom's Deli, but Oliver would always stop there and taste some of the cheeses on special. His favourite was 'Stinking Bishop'. When he first tried to tell Jess about this cheese, she thought he was committing blasphemy and jokingly told him he should go to confession. He liked to think of himself as a connoisseur of fromage; the smellier the better.

'I'll take home a small wedge of that Stinking Bishop, Dom,' he said.

'Shall I wrap it in holy robes or paper today, Ollie?' Dom chuckled.

'Paper I think will do today, don't want to draw any attention to myself,' Oliver laughed.

'Fine,' said Dom, 'and what about the little signorina? The usual chocolate milkshake? And espresso for you, sir?'

'Grazie, molto bene,' Oliver said, as he removed his brown Swagger hat.

They sat at their usual table looking onto Riversdale Road. It was a quaint white table setting with white wooden high-back chairs. In the bay window were baskets full of geraniums and daisies, just like a European deli. Being a Monday morning, there were a lot of people going about their usual business. It was a sunny Melbourne day and Oliver noticed a lot of women in their summer finest, and men wearing braces with baggy business trousers, suit jackets slung over their shoulders. I wonder where all these people are headed, he thought, I wonder if they're happy, content.

'Daddy, Daddy, can I have a choc chip cookie now please?' said Isla, tugging on his shirt sleeve. He took a moment to settle his thoughts and looked at his adorable little girl. Touching her on the nose, said, 'I think your tummy has had enough chocolate for one day, missy. Time to head off. Mummy and I have a special evening ahead of us.'

It was 6 o'clock and Oliver was feeding Isla the last pieces of her egg on toast. Jess was getting ready in the front room, Oliver having already preened himself. The doorbell rang and he opened the front door to greet the babysitter, Mrs Peters. She was a warm and hearty woman in her early 60s. She often overdid her make-up with bright blue eyeshadow, thickly pencilled eyebrows and bright rouged cheeks, finished with an impenetrable ruby-red lipstick. The worst thing was she was often too familiar, in an innocent way, kissing Oliver on his lips. Despite his last-minute attempts to turn his head, it was always in vain; she had a fine-tuned radar. Every time without fail, she would hit the bullseye. Her gesture repulsed Oliver, but it had become his private joke with Jess. They often referred to her as the Catholic Drag Queen Gladys Peters. Hollywood is calling for her, they would laugh, as Oliver wiped her spittle from his lips.

Leaving Mrs Peters in control of the house, they headed to the nearby tram stop, alighted the next tram and sat comfortably, taking in the sights of Melbourne. Oliver had booked a table at their favourite restaurant, Ricco's in Spring Street opposite Parliament House. The restaurant was classic Italian, its flavours enhanced by background piano playing and Victor Ricco's roaming violin. The highlight always was the singing waiters.

Looking down Collins Street from Spring Street, they took in a vista of three-storey bluestone and sandstone office buildings and hotels dating from the boom years of the late nineteenth century. Some of them, like the Melbourne Club, had a patrician air of elegance and affluence, whilst others were more flamboyant with pediments, urns, pineapples and other exotic ornamentation. The buildings were softened by rows of feathery trees and on autumn days, when the mist clung to the air, the effect was magical. It evoked the streetscapes of Pissarro and, not surprisingly, was known affectionately as the Paris End. At street level there were cafés and coffee lounges where actors, musicians and journalists commonly met.

They entered Ricco's and were ushered to a candlelit table intimately set for two, tucked into a secluded corner. The wooden panels were decorated with colourful artifacts, including plates from the Italian mainland. The lights were dim and the music lulled one into a sense of belonging. Oliver and Jess clinked their champagne glasses filled with sweet sparkling.

After some bruschetta, they enjoyed their favourite pasta. Oliver soaked up the last bit of marinara sauce with freshly baked panne. He then gently took Jess's hand and waiting for the right moment, looked directly at her and said, 'How are you travelling, Jess? I'm worried about you.'

'I'm okay, Ollie. I'm a bit tired and I'm not sleeping… I don't know, Ollie.'

He stared into her sunken blue eyes. 'Well, I still think you should see a doctor, Jess. It's not right, you're not right.' A moment passed before he shyly asked, 'Is it me, Jess? Is that what it is?'

Jess pulled her hand out of Oliver's and placed them at her side, gripping the edges of the seat, not wanting to let go. She peered down at her half-eaten carbonara, her locket dangling loosely around her neck. She went to respond but then held her breath. She wanted to cry, but couldn't, even though she didn't care that she was in a public place. All she wanted to do was cry, but she was numb, frozen, empty. She had fought hard to remain in control up to this point, but she was losing the battle.

'What's wrong, love, are you okay? Jess, are you okay? Do you need help?' Oliver's voice rose.

Jess broke her silence. 'I have thought about it, Oliver. I'm going to stay with Gerry for a short time. I need some space, a change of scenery. I think it will be good for me... for us. I don't know what else to do.'

'For us? What do you mean 'us', what do you mean by you need space?'

'I mean I think I need some time apart to get my head straight, Oliver. I'm not right. I don't know what's wrong with me. I'm sick of myself. Maybe it's me, maybe it's you... us, I don't know. Perhaps some time away will give me the perspective I need to work things out. I'm thinking about taking Isla with me. It would only be for a short time anyway, so she wouldn't miss too much school.'

The mention of removing Isla increased Oliver's tension. 'No, you go yourself. Sort yourself out. I'm here for you, Jess. I'll wait. But you are not taking Isla. You hear me? Do you hear me? She stays here!' Oliver hit the table with his fist and then quickly looked about to see if anyone was watching. 'It's not fair on her. She's just started school, she's meeting new friends and it will destabilise her. No way, Jess.'

Jess did not say a word. She just sat opposite him staring blindly into the candle flame. She had said more than she anticipated. Saying the words out loud terrified her.

Oliver rose to his feet, nearly falling over, his legs giving in to the tension. He headed to the bathroom, brushing past one of the waiters, who enquired after his well-being. Reaching the men's, he turned on the cold-water tap, filled his cupped hands and splashed his face. He wiped his face and stared into the oval gold-framed mirror. Thoughts rushed through his mind, happy times, sad times, joyous celebrations and the birth of his li'l one. At each turning point, he tried to flag his own culpability, but as he did so, he began to understand that perhaps the reason for the relationship demise was not as complex as he had once thought. Perhaps it was as simple as Jess had fallen out of love with him.

With that thought, Oliver's knees collapsed from beneath him and he hugged the porcelain basin like some baptismal font.

Chapter 5
Born to be Wild
30 January 1950

The kitchen clock ticked over to 11.00 a.m. Jess stood bent over the kitchen sink, holding her aching bump. Suddenly, a stream of warm fluid cascaded from her, spraying her thighs and spilling onto the kitchen floor. The shock caused her to catch her breath before she yelled to Oliver for help.

Oliver was between clients in the drawing room, working on his composition piece. He heard Jess's cry. The pencil dropped from his mouth, he pushed the piano stool out of the way and sprinted to her aid.

In the kitchen he immediately saw the small pool at Jess's feet. 'Oh my lord, Jesus, it's happening, it's happening, Jesus! Hell! Have you packed? Where's your overnight bag? Where's my keys? Shit, what did I do with my keys?' As Oliver opened one kitchen drawer after another looking for his car keys, Jess picked them up from the window shelf and dangled them in the air.

'Looking for these, Ollie? Now breathe, Ollie… in one, two, three… hold… out… one, two, three,' she said ironically.

Although Jess appeared to be taking matters in her stride, inwardly, she was more than a little anxious. However, watching Oliver rush about the house, seemingly possessed by a tornadic force, she grinned. *It was a memory worth collecting*, she thought. A striking cramp-like pain then engulfed her, erasing the smile from her face. She gripped the kitchen sink tightly. 'Ollie, okay, enough with the birth dance, just get the car, it's happening… Ollie… it's really happening!'

Oliver grabbed the keys from her, collected her overnight bag that was conspicuously sitting at the front door and ushered his expectant wife to the car.

He helped her into the car, darted back into the house to collect her toothbrush and paste, rushed outside and then ran back indoors, remembering in his haste that he had placed a hot towel in the bathroom sink as a precautionary measure. After stowing the items on the back seat, he stood outside the car, shuffling through his pockets. 'Hell, what did I do with my keys?'

In between cramping pains, Jess pointed to the keys in the ignition.

'Oh yes, thanks, yes… okay, okay… I know,' he said, letting out a big sigh. He grabbed them, returned to the house to lock the front door, sat in the driver's seat, switched on the motor and sped off, leaving a trail of exhaust smoke behind them.

'Slow down, slow down, we want to get there in one piece, Oliver! Oh, and by the way, I had packed a toiletry bag already. Just an FYI, Ollie,' she quipped.

'I know, I know, always better to have a back-up plan, in case. I mean, you might run out of toothpaste or something,' he said, attempting to underscore his usefulness.

'Yes, I can see that your plan is working so well for you,' said Jess, cheekily raising her eyebrows.

Without warning, she was hit with a strong contraction. She grabbed her bump, groaning in pain, sweating and overcome with fear that they would not reach the hospital in time. She rubbed her stomach round and round, taking shallow breaths, curling her toes tightly each time a contraction peaked. Any attempt by Oliver to calm her was met with a severe tongue-lashing and a spray of profanities.

'Oh my God, Oliver, will you just drive! Drive, I don't want a Chevy birth delivery. Besides, *imagine* the mess, Ollie,' she exclaimed, knowing how Oliver loved his precious vehicle.

Over her groans, Oliver looked at her despairingly. 'You wouldn't. You couldn't. No... '

Jess cut him off, 'Well, I will if you don't bloody well get a move on.'

About 10 minutes from St Vincent's Hospital, Oliver looked down and noticed the petrol gauge was near empty. It was one of Jess's common complaints that he always failed to fill his car with petrol. Time and time again she had warned him that a day would come when his failure to pay attention to such matters would cause much despair. Well, as far as Oliver was concerned, the day had finally arrived, her prediction had proved true and he braced himself for a loud, 'I told you so!'

Passing a nearby petrol station, he swiftly executed a sharp right, narrowly missing an oncoming vehicle and mounting the kerb. Screeching his brakes, he pulled up outside a petrol bowser. The abrupt stop caused Jess to fall forward, lightly bumping her head on the dashboard.

'Oh shit, Oliver, what the heck are you doing?' she screamed.

'I'm sorry, love, I'm so sorry. Are you alright? Would you like a hot towel? I brought some with me. Here.' Oliver passed her a lukewarm towel from the rear seat.

'Oh hell, Oliver, I don't want a towel!' she said, throwing it back at him. Noting the car was positioned at a petrol pump, Jess furiously turned to her driver. 'Tell me you didn't, you couldn't, please tell me you didn't, Ollie.'

'Um I did... I'm so sorry, love... I won't be long!' he cried, jumping out of the car and returning the towel to her. 'I've seen in the movies what they say about using a hot towel when women are giving birth.'

Jess could not believe what she was hearing.

A nearby bowser attendant approached Oliver, 'What will it be, sir?'

'Just fill it up with super please. And please hurry,' said Oliver, 'my wife is... ' Before Oliver could complete his sentence, Jess unexpectedly jumped out of the car, stood beside it, held her stomach, looked to the heavens and yelled like a banshee, 'SHHHIIIIIITTTTTTTT!'

Oliver looked to the attendant, 'As I said, my wife is having a baby. If I were you, I'd hurry, you wouldn't want to mess with her!'

With his eyes popping from his head, the attendant nervously filled the tank and before long, they were on their way again.

On arrival at St Vincent's, Jess was eventually settled in a birthing suite. Oliver waited in a nearby room along with a number of other expectant fathers, all pacing up and down. He observed their looks of nervous anticipation, pacing with brows swimming in beads of sweat.

No-one spoke and the air was thick with unanswered concerns. Oliver poured himself a glass of water before being interrupted by a midwife , 'Is there a Mr Johnson here?'

'Yes, yes, that's me, Oliver Johnson,' he said.

'May I have a private word please, outside?' she replied.

Oliver did not like the way she sounded. There was no smile on her face. There was nothing warm about her enquiry. His breathing became more rapid, his heart beating in his throat. 'Is there anything wrong, Sister?'

The nurse motioned him to take a nearby seat and sat next to him. 'No, not at all. My name is Sister Meale. I'll be assisting Dr Brown with the delivery of your bonnie baby. Just letting ya know, there be a little complication, but there is nothing to worry yourself about. I assure you.'

Although her voice was calming to a degree, Oliver was still anxious. He gripped his kneecaps, momentarily lost for words, then looked at the nurse directly and pleaded for a straight answer. 'Is there anything I should be worrying about? Please. I need you to be honest with me. I love Jess, and if anything ever happened to her, I...'

Before Oliver could finish, Sister Meale interjected, 'No, Mr Johnson, there be absolutely nothin' to cause ya worry, it's just that it may be a wee bit longer than anticipated due to the wee bonnie's breach position.'

The lilt of her empathic, fluid, Irish accent calmed Oliver down a little. 'So what does that mean, Sister?'

'It's just that instead of the head of the bonnie pointing down for delivery, the feet are in that position. Bit of a gymnast, that baby of yours. Dr Brown will try to turn the baby around in utero to make for a normal birthing position, however, we can still deliver you a healthy baby in the breach position, without there bein' any harm caused to the mum. Are you understandin' me, Mr Johnson?'

Oliver briefly pondered, taking in the advice but wanting to be by Jess's side supporting her. He wanted to reassure and comfort her so she didn't feel alone. Sitting there helpless for a moment, he stood up and then paced for a short distance. Upon returning to his seat, he expelled a huge sigh. He knew that he had no choice with the predicament at hand. 'Yes, I get it. Well, I'll just wait and try to be patient.' Tipping his head, he continued, 'Please let me know if there is anything I can do and let me know how she's doing.'

Sister Meale softly tapped him on the knee. She smiled compassionately at him, 'Aye, you can count on that, Mr Johnson.' With that, she stood up and disappeared behind the nearby ward doors. Oliver sat there, his elbows on his knees holding the weight of his head, staring into the distance trying to be confident and positive, yet unsure how the night might unfold.

Some 12 hours passed, with Oliver receiving only intermittent reports of Jess's progress. Finally, Sister Meale scurried into the waiting room and spotting Oliver, called, 'Mr Johnson, Mr Johnson, oh there you be! Please may I have another private word?'

She quickly ushered him outside, once again asking him to sit down. Oliver was on high alert, his breathing shallow, his left foot rapidly tapping the floor. 'What is it, what is it? Please, is she alright, tell me, is she alright?'

Oliver was in quite a state but Sister Meale was accustomed to agitated expectant fathers. She took in a deep breath and looked at him with the most comforting smile she could conjure. 'Yes, yes, she be doin' fine, Mr Johnson. Due to the position of the wee bonnie, Dr Brown has been struggling to turn that li'l one about. Well the baby, he's a stubborn one and seems not to be wanting to venture into this world head first. Your wife also keeps rejectin' the pain meds. She's made of iron, that one. If it were me, Mr Johnson, I'd be chewin' the whole packet of meds and askin' for refills.'

The thought of Jess's dogged nature and how her determination might be affecting the unsuspecting nurses made Oliver chortle.

'Now there you go, Mr Johnson, better out than in… Now where was I, oh yes, Dr Brown wants to continue the trial of labour, it's only been 12 hours. If nothin' turns around soon… whoops, excuse the pun… well Dr Brown says the only option be a caesarean section. But patience is a virtue, Mr Johnson, and rest assured we'll get there. Now you have a cat nap and I'll give you a bit of a shake when the time comes. You okay?'

Oliver's leg ceased shaking and he looked at Sister Meale, nodding to signal his trust in her and thanking her. With that, she disappeared again before he could ask her how she knew he was having a boy. In any event, Oliver was not so much concerned about the gender of the child as he was focussed upon Jess and her welfare.

He did not sleep well that night. There were three other men in the waiting room snoring at various pitches and intervals. Their semi-musical discord pierced the air without any sense of rhythm and interfered with Oliver's desire for a more serene frequency. He thought that a suburban fence full of squealing midnight alley cats would proffer a more alluring tune.

Monday 31 January 1950 arrived. It was 10.52 a.m. and the age of Aquarius was upon them. As he dragged his feet to a nearby coffee jug,

Sister Meale busted through the waiting room door exclaiming, 'It's happening, your wee bonnie is on his way! Dr Brown wants to try for a natural delivery, well, feet first at least. On all accounts, we be ripe to go. Got to fly, Mr Johnson, I hope I'll be back soon with the good news.'

As quickly as she had arrived, she disappeared. Oliver sculled his coffee and poured himself another one, praying for something a little stronger.

As a further hour ticked by, then two, three and four, Oliver's pacing was beginning to wear a channel through the timber floors. He had smoked a packet of cigarettes, continuing to tap the celebratory Cuban cigar sitting in his top pocket as a form of a good omen. After a brief spell of fresh air, he was walking up the hallowed wooden staircase when he heard his name echoing from above, with an Irish intonation. His step gathered momentum and Sister Meale spied him climbing the staircase. 'Get yourself up here, Mr Johnson, quick! I'm pleased to say you be a father,' she exclaimed. Oliver trekked the five flights of stairs in record time to greet Sister Meale.

'Where have you been, mister? I be lookin' for 10 minutes,' she said. 'Well, as I said, the good news I promised you is you are the father of a bonnie wee lass and she is the most beautiful baby I have seen in a long time... and I've seen some ugly ones, I might add,' she laughed.

'Oh my, oh my God!' Oliver shouted, picking up the nurse, giving her a huge kiss on the cheek and swinging her about. He felt as if he were floating on air.

'You best put me down now, Mr Johnson, I don't wish to find us both at the bottom of that holy staircase,' she said, 'now let's go and see your li'l one.'

'How's Jess, is she okay?

'She be fine, Mr Johnson, a bit fatigued but with a wee bit of love and attention, I am sure she will be up and about in no time. Now follow me.'

Finally, Oliver made it past those flapping ward doors, following Sister

Meale. Passing by several ward beds, he was taken to a glass window framing a number of baby capsules, each with the family surname attached to a pink or a blue flag. Oliver's eyes darted from one baby to another, finally arriving at his newborn daughter, 'There she is, Sister Meale. The pink flag, Johnson. Oh my… she's beautiful.' He proudly gazed upon her perfect cupid lips, her rosy cheeks, tiny fingers and cap of dark brown hair. He noticed the baby grinning at him.

'Look, Sister Meale, she's already grinning at me!'

Sister Meale chuckled a little. 'Oh she will in time no doubt, Mr Johnson, but before the lass gets to know ya, I'm guessing her smile might be a wee bit of gas.'

Oliver chose to ignore the comment, preferring his explanation.

'Well, Mrs Johnson be in room six on this floor. You might want to go visit her, before her feeding chores begin. I'll show ya to her room. We need to get her cleaned up a bit, it's been a journey and a half getting that li'l tiger out, but as I said, she'll be as right as rain and up and about before you know it. Dr Brown give her a few stitches down below. Not uncommon when ya baby arrives feet first. She'll be okay, Mr Johnson. Don't you be worrying about that one.'

Sister Meale's direct explanation instilled Oliver with confidence.

When he arrived at Jess's room, he could see that she was indeed spent. She was lying in her bed, arms limp hanging from her bedside, her blonde locks dank, her pale face angled at the ceiling, wearing a hospital gown covered in fresh patches of bright red blood.

'How are you, Jess?' Oliver approached her cautiously but caringly, holding her hand. 'I'm so, so proud of you, love. You did amazingly. You have given us a beautiful little girl. She is perfect in every way, Jess.' He leant forward and kissed her on the forehead.

Jess didn't say anything at first. She was totally exhausted. In a faint whisper, she turned to him. 'I know, Ollie. She is beautiful, but like her star sign would dictate, very stubborn. I thought she would never come out and when she did, it was like I was being ripped apart with long sharp fiery nails. When I screamed out for Dr Brown to stop using his birthing device on me, he said he was not even touching me! I never imagined it would be so painful, Ollie.'

'That's okay, love. It's done now. You survived and you've given us the most wonderful gift.' Oliver kissed her hand gently. 'I will never forget what you went through for us. What we have created is so special and now we're a true family. I love you so much.'

Jess smiled at him, sensing his concern over her. 'I love you too, Ollie.'

At that moment, Sister Meale wheeled in a trolley holding the crib with their little girl. 'Now, it's time to feed the wee lass. She'll be hungry given the length of the journey. It's just the pre-milk, colostrum, before the real stuff starts to flow in a couple of days' time. The wonders of nature, Mrs Johnson. I know you be tired, but let's see what you can muster. Us women, we're machines. Wouldn't you agree, Mr Johnson?'

'Oh yes,' smiled Oliver, 'I dare not disagree, particularly with you, Sister Meale.'

'A very wise man you've chosen there, Mrs Johnson,' she laughed.

Sister Meale gently lifted the tightly wrapped baby from her crib. She was wide-awake and with her sparkling blue eyes, seemed to be getting a sense of her surroundings. From a short distance, she could smell her mother, which ignited her appetite and her vocal chords.

'Oh my, she does have a good set of lungs,' said Oliver.

Sister Meale gently rested the baby on Jess, in a position to accommodate her feeding. It took some time before the baby finally attached to Jess's nipple.

Each time it seemed that there was success, the baby would detach again and start squealing. Her raw screams made Jess wonder what she was doing wrong. *I am a nurse*, she thought, *why isn't this happening?*

Despite her efforts, she could do nothing to calm the babe or appease her cries. *What the hell*, she thought. *These other nurses must think I'm useless. I'm so tired, but I mustn't let Ollie notice. I need to be stronger than this, stronger for us.* She shuffled in the bed, moving the baby to her other breast, thinking that might make a difference. It didn't. The baby continued screaming, her piercing cries sending shockwaves through Jess's nerve endings. *What sort of mother am I?* she thought. *Why am I so annoyed with my child already? Is that normal? This is not what I was taught about attachment theory.* Trying not to alert the room to her dismay, she smiled intermittently to fob off any alarm bells that she might not be coping.

It's my mother, Jess thought. It's her fault. Why didn't she teach me better? Where's Gerry when I need her? One inward scream after another tormented her. Her passing smiles were overtaken by signs of frustration with the child. What the hell is wrong with me!

Sister Meale detected Jess's exasperation and carefully helped her cradle the baby, adjusting her position to assist with nipple attachment. Jess was trying to hold back tears, her feelings of despair terrifying her. She had never experienced such black empty moments, gasping for air, beating off repeated internal messages that she lacked the intuition to be a natural mother.

Oliver noticed that the baby's unsettled behaviour was unhinging Jess. 'Let's try some more in a little time, Jess. Here, give her to me. Rest a little, love. You've earned it. It's okay. Give it time, babe.'

He took the small bundle into his arms. It was the first time he had held his daughter. For him, the attachment seemed spontaneous. As the baby looked at him, she immediately ceased crying, checking out his every feature. Jess looked at Oliver holding their baby, wondering why she had not been able to soothe the child, why she was so calm in his arms. *Why is she not like that with me?* she thought. *After what I have been through, how can Oliver just walk in here and take over like that?* Her thoughts rolled by one after the other, causing her to dwell on and resent the child's attachment to her father. She knew it wasn't rational to think like this, but her emotions were spinning wildly out of control.

Oliver walked the baby over to the nearby window, gooing and gaaing at his daughter, examining her tiny fingernails and digits, her cute button nose, her rosebud lips and her perfect little ears. He bent his head to smell the crown of her head with that infatuating newborn odour that was fresh, warm and unique. With their eyes fixed upon each other, Jess saw there was a bond of peace, comfort and love between them that she did not share. Oliver smiled broadly at his daughter and looked over at Jess. Not knowing whether it was the right time, he was so overcome with emotion he said, 'Well, I think it's time we named our li'l girl. I know we've discussed a few options, but Jess, I still think now she's here, she looks like an 'Isla' to me. What do you think?'

Jess had always loved the name. It had a force about it. She loved its Scottish origin of 'island' and its meaning emanating from a desire to connect with others, a nature that was not only curious, but impulsive and free-spirited. There was something wild and liberating about the name 'Isla' with its potential to speak from the heart and touch the hearts of others. For Jess, the name possessed a potential sense of power ready to be tapped.

'Yes, yes, Ollie. I agree. It's perfect. Isla Elizabeth Johnson.'

Oliver nodded, grinning from ear to ear. He looked at his darling daughter, holding her out a little so that the sun washed over her skin for the first time. In an uplifting but soothing tone, he said, 'Welcome to the world, Isla Elizabeth Johnson… my li'l one.' He cradled her closely and as he did so, a tear of joy rolled down his cheek. Curiously, it landed on Isla's forehead, like a blessing, marking her official graduation into a world of opportunity.

Chapter 6

Dog Day Afternoon

Mid-September 1955

Winter in Melbourne was being chased away by a flurry of fine spring mornings, but Oliver and Jess's ill-fated anniversary dinner continued to haunt them. There was an absence of laughter in the home, Oliver's carefree displays were less frequent and Jess spent increasing time on the phone to her sister.

They were never able to speak again about that night at Rocco's. Just the thought of it called into question their unlikely future together.

Exhausted, Jess's shifts at the hospital weighed her down and depleted her energy. She had kept a smile painted on her face for too long and could no longer wear the mask. There was a deep feeling within her that she was falling out of love with Oliver. She searched within herself, trying to find that spark again, that feeling of longing and lust, but it was nowhere to be found. There was just emptiness. She was afraid that her feelings were becoming obvious to Oliver, even to Isla. Her failed attempts to maintain a façade kept slipping and she became increasingly riddled with guilt. Her change of heart fell upon her slowly, like an evening mist, leaving her lost and directionless and unable to reconcile her feelings.

The past cause of her malaise mattered no longer, as its current form continued to rob her of life. She was suspended over a great chasm, experiencing a crisis which seemed impossible to conquer. With no apparent solution, the threat of annihilation loomed large. She pondered a life without Oliver, a life without Isla and an existence free of shadowy encumbrances. She had been anchored for too long; now was the time to form and execute an escape plan.

Gerry was the only person with whom Jess felt she could share her feelings of despair. She understood her and despite the tyranny of distance, Gerry was always able to give her emotional support, which she felt was missing with Oliver. She thought that perhaps her own fears about expressing herself and hurting his feelings inhibited her from sharing them with him.

She often resented how critical Oliver was of her parenting. It was random little things like mentioning her being late for mealtimes due to work, being late for Isla's pick-ups at school and never having enough time to help with Isla's reading and writing. Although he never expressed his frustrations, Jess intuitively sensed his disappointment. In the past she had raised his judgements with him, however, these days she simply did not have the energy to do so. *Is it because I don't care anymore*, she thought, *or is it that I'm just over the conflict?*

For his part, Oliver was steering a rudderless boat, attempting to navigate a storm. He often pictured himself standing at a ship's helm, being battered by waves of discontent and winds of emotional turmoil. Yet he remained determined; he was not prepared to give up on Jess just yet. Over and over in his mind he thought of ways to inject some excitement and happiness back into their union. I

know just the medicine, he thought. It's about time we had an addition to our family unit. He grinned. Perfect. A puppy.

After concluding his lesson with Mildred Maloney and successfully avoiding her wandering left hand, Oliver escaped the home in search of the perfect pooch. Isla was at school and Jess had taken an additional day shift and would pick her up, so his secret was safe.

With a spring in his step, he took himself off to the local pet shop, hoping to spy their new family member. He approached the shop window to discover a cage filled with furry four-legged treats, all different sizes, colours and levels of cuteness, rolling about, wrestling and cavorting with one another.

As he entered Harry's Pet Emporium, one puppy's glance followed him all the way into the shop. A mischievous little specimen with a drooling pink tongue, black coat and chubby rear attached to a wagging tail.

'G'day, how much for the cheeky looking one?' Oliver pointed to the pup with the wide smile.

'That one is two quid. He's quite a cheeky one that li'l labrador. Always muckin' around with the others, causing a stew. I could watch all day what he gets up to.' The man laughed.

'Good then, I'll grab him before someone else steals him away.' Oliver reached for his wallet.

Before he knew it, he was outside the store grasping the crate with howling puppy on board. 'Oh my God,' he whispered to himself, 'what have I done? I just hope this little bundle is the catalyst for a new beginning. You better behave yourself mister, or else I'll be marching you back here.'

Back home, he opened the front door slowly and crept inside, finger poised on his lips as if this would silence his mischievous cargo. From the kitchen window, he could see Jess at the makeshift clothesline pegging out the washing. Behind the line was Isla playing on her swing set. As he approached, Jess was conveniently masked by a couple of rows of white sheets.

'Boo!' he said, sticking his head around a sheet and hiding the puppy behind his back.

'Oh Oliver, stop it, you frightened me,' she said.

'Daddy, Daddy! It's you!' Isla ran towards him.

'Now, now, wait li'l one. Before you pass this row of sheets, I have a surprise!'

'What is it, what is it Daddy?'

'Yes, what has Daddy done this time?' Jess paused in hanging out the sheets and frowned at him.

Oliver pinned the corner of the sheet to his midriff and circled about, enclosing himself and the crate in a cotton cocoon.

Isla's curiosity peaked. 'Daddy, Daddy, what is it? What's the surprise? Let me see!'

'Okay, time for the butterfly to reveal himself to the world.'

Isla laughed. Such joy was a welcome visitor for Oliver.

Isla started unravelling her father, giggling the whole time, until she finally arrived at her surprise. She peered in and let out a huge cry of delight, 'Mummy, Mummy, it's a puppy, it's a black puppy! Oh Daddy!'

She wasted no time in opening the crate door and embraced the ball of fluff. 'Is he mine, Daddy? Is he all mine to keep?'

'What do you think, Mummy?' said Oliver.

'Oh… well… we may need to think about that. I mean dogs are a huge responsibility… and I mean Mummy and Daddy *need to talk about these things* before we make such *big decisions*, don't we Daddy?' She glared at Oliver, unimpressed.

'But we did, we did at Dom's Deli before, didn't we Daddy, didn't we? Oh, I want to keep him, I do. I will look after him Mummy, I promise. I'll walk him and feed him and love him forever.'

'Forever is a long time, Isla, and Mummy and Daddy will need to talk about it first, won't we Daddy?' Jess sighed.

'I think having a dog will be good for this family. I mean, I had a dog growing up, Jess, and it gave me a real sense of responsibility. It teaches children to care. The puppy will warm up the house and I think it'll be good for our li'l girl.'

'It would be *nice* for Daddy to have these conversations in the absence of little ears,' said Jess.

Oliver knew that he should have had this conversation with Jess before buying the puppy, but he hadn't wanted her undermining his strategic rescue remedy and destroying his plan to make things right. He believed that a puppy would be just the medicine, even if Jess didn't realise it yet.

'So what do you say, Mummy? No puppy for li'l miss or the puppy stays?' He winked at Jess.

Isla looked at her mother, bottom lip protruding. Her face had dropped and her pixie nose was slightly scrunched. 'Please Mummy, I'll be the best girl... *pleeeeeeze!*'

Jess was blindsided. Raising her eyebrows and taking a deep breath, her hands firmly on her hips, she said, 'Oh alright then, I give up. But you and your father are responsible for him, not me. You understand?'

'Yes, yes!' said Isla gleefully, holding up the puppy to her face and gently kissing the back of his head.

Jess snuck a scowl in Oliver's direction, 'And I'm not picking up any of his business, that's your job, Oliver.'

'The least I could do!' said Oliver, secretly smiling within.

'Okay, so what do we call him li'l one? He's a labrador.'

'I think *Larry*, Daddy, *Larry the labrador*,' smiled Isla.

'Perfect!' said Oliver.

'Yes, perfect!' sighed Jess.

Chapter 7

Don't Interrupt the Sorrow

By the end of October, Larry had sparked some glee in the Johnson household. Isla doted over her puppy and the two were inseparable. She fed and groomed him, stealing him into her bed at night for cuddles. They played games like fetch together. Larry was skilful with balls and sticks and with digging unwanted holes and delivering the occasional dead bird to the back doorstep. Oliver loved watching Isla bond with her new responsibility and revelled in the joy Larry gave her.

Despite the new arrival, Jess's mental anguish persisted. She was not sleeping and often visited the kitchen sink at night, staring at the backyard lemon tree, which was still devoid of fruit. Occasionally, when Isla was sneaking Larry into her room, she would spy her mother standing there, alone and seemingly upset. She wanted so much to give her mother a hug but was scared for fear of being reprimanded. She was confused by her mother's behaviour. Unable to understand it, all she knew was that Jess was not right and that, unlike her father, she didn't smile much. Her mother was sad and she wished that she could fix it somehow.

It was early morning, Melbourne Cup Day. Jess put the phone down and ran into the drawing room. Oliver was there in his blue checked dressing-gown playing with Isla and Larry, all of them spread-eagled on the Persian rug. Larry was grasping the end of a piece of rope with his teeth, whilst Oliver and Isla were hanging on to the other end in a game of tug o' war. It was hard for Jess to make herself heard over the exuberant screams of laughter.

'At least he's given up chewing on your pink and white socks, li'l one,' laughed Oliver.

Jess tried to interrupt, 'I've just got off the phone from Gerry and I'm going, I've decided, just for a short time.'

Oliver and Isla continued to battle joyfully with Larry, without apparently hearing Jess's announcement.

'Did you hear me you two? Hello… hello!'

'Oh, I'm sorry love,' laughed Oliver, 'but this little tiger is giving Isla and me a real struggle. I'm so sorry, what did you say?' He dropped the end of the rope and left Isla to wrangle with the puppy.

'I said, I've spoken to Gerry and decided to take her up on her offer to spend some time in London. I plan to go at the end of next week… 15 November. I'll be back for Christmas. What do you think?' She hoped Oliver would agree with her travel plans.

By this stage, Isla was also listening. The magic word 'Christmas' hit her between the eyes, with thoughts of Santa, fairy lights, colourful Christmas ball bells and brightly wrapped gifts.

'You will be home for Christmas. Are you sure Jess?' said Oliver.

'Yes, I will Ollie. Promise. Can I go? Are you okay with it?'

Oliver held his breath. His thoughts returned to their anniversary dinner and Jess's conversation with him. Is she leaving me for good? he thought. Is this an escape plan hatched between Gerry and Jess? Isla is not going anywhere, that's for sure. With a million thoughts running through his head, her voice became muffled.

'Ollie, Oliver, are you okay, are you okay with me going?' Jess persisted.

Oliver shook his head to clear his thoughts. 'Yes… I guess so. If you really want to, a change of scene might do you good, do us good, and besides, you haven't seen Gerry in such a long time. I remember how upset you were when we were supposed to travel with Isla two years ago and ended up not going. So perhaps this is a good thing. You can use the money we saved up for that trip.'

'No, it's all good Ollie. Gerry said she would shout. She's actually using some of my inheritance money that Mum put aside for me. What better use! How lucky am I?'

'Yes, lucky. Okay… well it's all planned then. You and Gerry have worked it all out, I guess. And what about Isla? She's not going. She's just started school.' He sighed.

'Um, no, no, that's okay,' Jess said, peering over at Larry. 'Isla can stay with you and go to school.'

Oliver was relieved, although Jess's response did not entirely convince him. He was unable to put his finger on it but an uneasiness remained with him. 'Well, alright, 15 November, not long. You better start packing, I guess.' He tried to make light of things.

'Mummy, you won't be gone long, will you? And Santa. You will be home for Christmas time? I'll miss you,' said Isla.

Jess wondered why Isla did not ask to travel with her. Perhaps it was because she did not want to leave Larry but still, it hurt her, although she was determined not to let it show. She didn't want Oliver to notice anything out of the ordinary about her half-truths. She was now in survival mode and everything else took a back seat to her priorities.

The next day, Jess took the tram into Melbourne city and headed to the travel agency where Gerry had wired funds for her air ticket. She told Gerry that she could purchase a return ticket after she arrived, as she was still uncertain about the dates. However, she knew exactly what she was planning. She entered the agency and after being greeted by the travel agent peering at her over large tortoise-shell glasses, took a seat. The agent, Eileen, wore a woollen emerald jacket, a green and rouge floral scarf and a red pencil skirt, with lipstick to match. Her brunette hair was pulled back into a tight bun, exposing her angular yet youthful features. 'Yes madam, how may I assist you?'

Jess gave her the booking details and handed her an envelope containing a wad of cash.

'I'm sorry madam, what's that?' Eileen asked.

'It's money for a ticket.'

Eileen rechecked the details. 'Looking at your booking, Mrs Johnson, it appears your ticket has been paid for by a Mrs Gerry Baker. We are holding your ticket order here. Just need to formally issue it.'

'Yes, she's my sister. This money is for an additional ticket, for my daughter, Isla Elizabeth Johnson, to travel with me. I have her passport here.'

Jess reached into her black velvet clutch bag, retrieving her passport and Isla's, and handed them to the agent.

'Oh I see, no problem Mrs Johnson. I'm just going to make a call and ensure there are no problems with getting the little one onto that flight. Always busy this time of year, you know, all these Collins Street bankers flying their families to Europe for a white Christmas. Oh, how I would love a white Christmas one day! So romantic. Bing Crosby, I love him! Do you? One day soon, one of those bankers will jump my desk, go on bent knee, propose to me, place a four-carat diamond on my finger and whisk me away to gay Paree and then...'

Jess cleared her throat, politely prompting Eileen to float back to earth. 'I don't mean to be rude, but I am in a little bit of a hurry, so if you don't mind...'

'Yes, of course Mrs Johnson, of course, I'm sorry, forgive me. That's why I love my job. I get to travel vicariously, Mrs Johnson. I get to dream, to travel in my imagination, to venture to areas others can only dream of, to explore the nether regions of the world, to...' Loosening her scarf, she added, 'My, it's getting warm in here. Where was I, oh I know, I was saying... to...'

Jess cleared her throat again, raising her eyebrows.

'Going, Mrs Johnson, I'm onto it. I know you're in a hurry. Sorry, I do get caried away a little but you can count on me!' Eileen fanned herself.

Some two hours later, Eileen reappeared waving two tickets in the air. 'I did it, I did it Mrs Johnson! I have arranged your two tickets for 14 November, as requested. You will arrive in London on 16 November. Stopovers in Brisbane, Singapore and Cairo. What a journey, what an experience. Camels, pyramids, peanuts at Raffles and don't forget the Singapore slings. Just you, not the little one of course! And... oh, the shopping, oh my, can you imagine Mrs Johnson...'

Jess had given up on further prompts. She simply grabbed the tickets with the itineraries attached that Eileen was waving at her. 'Goodbye and thank you. I will send you a postcard, I promise,' she said briskly, fleeing out the door. Before the agent could offer her a travel pouch, she was gone.

Jess's luggage had been sitting at the front door for a few days and over this time, Oliver had noticed her mood become more stable. She smiled from time to time and her sleep was less interrupted. Isla had even been able to get Jess to show a little interest in Larry.

On 14 November, Oliver came home from Isla's morning recital at school. Jess was at work, finishing off her fortnightly cycle of night duty. He so wished she could have been with him to hear Isla. He was so proud of his li'l one. She had played *Isla's Song*. It was only the bare bones and it needed further attention, but the piece had so much potential.

Oliver sat there listening as Isla's fingers delicately tickled the ivory keys. He leant back and shut his eyes, mesmerised by the melody and the spirited tune, the way it happily bounced bridges, hit its crescendo and melted into a sea of longing and love. He reflected on its heartfelt warmth and maturity, extending beyond Isla's years. It was something that she would grow into, he thought, a song which one day would attract lyrics penned from her own soul. Her tiny frame sitting on stage was engulfed by the piano. When she played her last note, her fingers lifting ever so delicately off the keys, there was a stillness, a silence, that was hypnotic. A round of applause broke the atmosphere, with cheers of adoration from her classmates and audience members. Before taking a bow, Isla clutched her music sheets and blew a kiss to Oliver. His whole body trembled with pride and his eyes welled up with joy. He loved his li'l one. *Isla's Song* was their piece, representing a small measure of each of their hearts, their hopes and their attachment to each other. It was a work sealed with the love of a unique father–daughter bond.

Oliver approached the stage and knelt at Isla's tiny feet. He moved in close, whispering into her right ear, 'Daddy is so proud of you li'l one. I love you so much… to the moon and back. I love our song, but I love you more.' He gently kissed her on the cheek and waved her farewell. Before he exited the auditorium, he turned to catch Isla standing centre stage, waving at him. There was his little girl displaying a sunny smile, as cute as could be.

Jess arrived home from work, having difficulty inserting the key in the front door and dropping her keys between attempts. She was greeted by Larry jumping up on her legs. She pushed him aside, dashed to Isla's room, grabbed a bundle of clothes from her drawers and stuffed them into one of the cases at the front door. As she was zipping up the case, the front door opened. It was Oliver.

'What are you doing Jess?'

'Oh nothing, I just forgot to pack my pink cardigan, you know, my favourite one. Thought I better throw it now in case I forget tomorrow… you know me!' Jess babbled.

'Are you okay Jess? You seem a little flustered.'

'I'm fine, in fact I feel really good Ollie, even though night shift was a little taxing.' She was trying to distract him. 'Now let's get us a cup of tea. I want to hear all about Isla's performance. Plus, I'm gathering you'll need a recharge before starting the day's lessons with your female fan club!' She laughed.

'That's true, love… maybe two cups!' Impulsively, he grabbed her around the waist, leant into her and kissed her passionately. He was overcome by the emotions from Isla's morning recital and his love for Jess.

'Wow, where did that come from, Oliver?' For a moment, Jess felt the pain of guilt and confusion around her escape plans with Isla to London. Am I really making the right decision? Will this make me feel better? Will I regret my choice later? Is Oliver the real problem or is it me? Am I going crazy? How will I parent alone? Her conscience prevented her from addressing any possible effects on Isla.

As they sat drinking their tea, Oliver told her about Isla's performance, pride sweeping across his face. Jess noticed how any mention of his 'li'l one' lit up his face and raised a grin. His joy further tarnished her sense of shame and guilt. I mustn't look back, *I needed to make this decision, it's my only way out of this hole*, she thought. The silence between them lingered, the air feeling dense, like a solid wall that prevented them from speaking openly. In the past, these still moments had been comfortable. These days, their communication was undermined by a lack of trust and mixed messaging. Although he knew nothing of her plans about moving forward at any cost, Oliver felt abandoned in no-man's land, too scared to talk, wondering why their relationship had disintegrated.

Although Larry had been a welcome addition to the family, even his cuteness and welcoming grin could not abate their troubled dynamic. The ring of the doorbell fortuitously broke the silence. Oliver opened the door to his first student for the day, greeting her with his customary charm, leaving his troubles behind him – at least temporarily.

It was 2.45 p.m. and Oliver was still occupied in the drawing room with his penultimate student for the day.

Jess had pre-booked a taxi to collect her from Camberwell Primary School at 3.10 p.m. Despite the warm, breezy, spring day, she put on her black trench coat over her plain grey dress. Her blonde hair was tightly pinned back and her faced disguised with black horn-rimmed sunglasses. She wore no make-up. Creeping past the closed doors of the drawing room, she collected her two cases at the front door. She then checked her purse for the tickets and passports and exited the home, quietly closing the front door behind her whilst trying to prevent Larry from escaping with her. Her heart was beating rapidly and she felt heady due to her shallow breathing. She briskly walked past their white picket fence without a backward glance and headed down the acorn-strewn path towards Isla's school.

Leaving her travel cases just outside the school office, Jess proceeded to the bursar's office and asked to have Isla released from class early. The Principal, Mrs Headsworth, stuck her head out of her office. 'Is everything alright, Mrs Johnson?' She couldn't help noticing that Jess appeared dressed like Mata Hari in one of those WW1 spy movies.

'Oh yes,' replied Jess, peering over her sunglasses, 'fine, just fine, I have a dentist appointment for Isla and need to collect her now, that's all.'

Within a short time, Isla appeared, holding her school case. 'Mummy, what are you doing here? The school bell hasn't rung yet.'

'Don't worry Isla, we have to go, Mummy's in a hurry.' Jess bid farewell to the bursar and the principal and hurriedly left the office, collecting her luggage on the way.

Before she got far, she heard the principal calling out to her. She turned around very slowly, trying not to let her escape plans unravel.

'Mrs Johnson, you forgot your purse,' said Mrs Headsworth. The woman saw Jess's two cases.

Jess saw that the woman was sizing her up. Not daring to give her a moment for any inquiry, she said, 'Oh thank you, thank you so much. I'd better run. Quick Isla. Thanks again Mrs Headsworth.'

They exited the school gate, just in time to meet the awaiting taxi. Jess had Isla enter the car whilst the driver stored their luggage.

'Essendon Airport, please driver. And hurry please, we can't be late.' She said this in a strained whisper. From her intonation it was clear that she had no time for chit-chat, whilst her eyes darted backwards and forwards out the car window, spying Mrs Headsworth, arms folded, at the school gate.

'Very well madam,' he said, capturing Jess's tortured frown in the rear-vision mirror.

'Where are we going Mummy? And where is Daddy? Is he bringing Larry? I forgot my lunchbox Mummy!'

'Not to worry, Mummy will buy you another one. And yes darling, Daddy is coming later with Larry, of course. Now just sit still. Everything is going to be fine. Mummy loves you.' Jess closed her eyes and sat back, her heart beating in her throat, her head pounding.

Isla was confused. She did not recall any prior talk of a holiday with her mum and dad. If they were going away, she wondered why her father was not travelling with them. *All the other holidays we went away together,* she thought. She was also concerned for Larry, who was too little to be left alone. She only hoped that her father would remember him. We must be going on a plane, Mummy said airport. I've never been on a plane before, neither has Larry. I hope Daddy isn't late.

Looking across to her mother, she noticed she had her head titled back and her eyes shut. She also caught the taxi driver's beady eyes in the rear-vision mirror staring back at her. He made her feel uneasy, causing her to shift in her seat and look away.

Placing her small school case on her lap, she opened it. There were some drawings of Larry, some pieces of chalk and her sheet music from the morning's performance of *Isla's Song*. She thought about her performance and her father's parting words. A little corner of her heart burst with joy and the corners of her mouth lifted in a smile. Just then, the taxi came to a halt. 'Airport madam. Overseas or domestic?'

Jess was abruptly awoken by the sudden braking. 'Oh, yes, international, driver.'

'Very well.'

The driver placed the luggage on the terminal footpath and tipped his hat to them before leaving.

'Where's Daddy, Mummy? Where's Larry?' exclaimed Isla.

'Quick Isla, I do not have time for this. Hurry!'

As they approached the check-in area, Isla planted her feet and started crying. She was inconsolable. So much had confused her in such a short time and she was upset and fed up. Her tantrum escalated, with passing travellers giving Jess judgemental, unnerving stares. *I feel bad enough, they can bugger off,* she thought.

In a soft tone, Jess crouched down to Isla's level. 'Look Isla, Mummy knows you're upset, but Daddy said if he's late to the airport for us to go and he will catch up. I know this is all a bit rushed darling, but Aunty Gerry only called Mummy late last night, and guess what? We are all going to spend Christmas this year in London! Now isn't that exciting? Father Christmas, candy canes, presents. So don't cry. It's all going to be okay. The best Christmas ever!'

Isla settled down after her mother's soothing words. 'Okay Mummy, it sounds fun. But what about Larry? What if Daddy doesn't bring him? He might not even be allowed on a plane. He is a dog, Mummy.'

'Yes, well, we will have to see about that. I know Daddy was calling the airport man today and if Larry can't fly to London, Mrs Peters will take care of him.' Jess feared that this moment would haunt her forever. She had never lied to Isla and despite her state of desperation, it did not sit well with her.

'Okay Mummy. Mrs Peters loves Larry. She will be kind to him. When are we coming home though?'

'We haven't got there yet Isla!' laughed Jess, trying to cheer her up and allay her fears. 'Just over Christmas, that's all. Now we best get a move on or we will miss that plane. If Daddy is late, we will see him in London. Okay?'

Isla squeezed her mother's hand and came to a halt.

'What is it now Isla?'

'How come Daddy didn't tell me about the holiday today or about Larry coming on a plane with us?'

There was no effective response, just another lie, and Jess was saved this by the timely announcement of their flight boarding.

'Quick, better hurry, let's go!' she said.

Isla, her face stained with dried tears, looked up at her mother, unconvinced. People were rushing past, back and forth, loud announcements boomed out over the airport speakers and there was luggage everywhere.

Meanwhile, Oliver had concluded his last lesson for the day. It was 5.15 p.m. and there was no sign of Jess or Isla. As he wandered from the kitchen to the hallway, he noticed that Jess's luggage had gone. He peered into their bedroom to see if they had been shifted. They were nowhere to be seen. Panicked, he rushed into Isla's room only to discover open drawers with clothes removed. He ran to the back yard thinking that perhaps Isla might be there playing with Larry, but the puppy was alone chewing again on Isla's favourite socks.

Oliver immediately telephoned the school, hoping his call would be answered despite the late hour. By chance, Mrs Headsworth was working back and answered his call. She informed him that Jess had removed Isla from school early, carrying travel luggage, and she had seen them boarding a taxi.

Oliver was in a complete spin, thinking the worst. Beads of sweat began dripping from his brow, his heart beating so fast he felt dizzy. It was too late to report the matter to the police, he thought. The airport… the airport! That's why she's been on the phone to Gerry so often. 'The bitch, the fucking bitch!' he screamed. 'She's taken Isla. She lied to me. Fuck! Fuck!'

In an emotional whirlwind, Oliver grabbed his car keys and floored it to the airport. He didn't care if the police pulled him over for speeding, there were much greater things at stake. All he could focus on was Isla and the fact that he might never see her again. He felt he was suffocating, gasping over a great emptiness, unable to grab enough air, and he had tears flooding down his cheeks.

Isla and Jess were in the boarding lounge, Isla still clutching onto her school case. Before long, the boarding announcement came. 'All passengers travelling to London via Brisbane, Singapore and Cairo are now requested to board Qantas flight QF231 at Gate Lounge 3. Final call for all passengers. Please proceed to the boarding gate.'

Isla stopped in her tracks and demanded, 'When's Daddy coming?'

'Later,' said Jess.

'Will the plane wait for him if he's late?' cried Isla.

'Looks like he's late, love. He'll join us there, as I said. You know Daddy's always late.'

'But you said Daddy was coming.'

'He is. Just not today it seems. He'll meet us there. Look, not many little girls are lucky enough to go on a big airplane.'

'Why can't I go with him? I miss Larry.'

Jess observed two security officers looking in her direction, so she quickly pulled Isla closer to her. 'Stay close to me. And no more questions. It's quite inappropriate, miss. Daddy is joining us in London. That's just the way it is.'

'It's not fair!' protested Isla.

'Stop misbehaving. People are looking.'

Jess dragged Isla to have their tickets checked and after climbing the stairs to board the plane, she smiled awkwardly at the stewardess as Isla kept trying to pull herself from her mother's grasp.

'Let me go, let me go!' she cried.

'Ssshh!' said Jess. 'Stop being so naughty!'

'I'm not naughty, you are. You're telling lies, Daddy and Larry are not coming. Let me go!'

'Be quiet! They are! Now stop it Isla or there'll be no Christmas, no Aunty Gerry and no holiday.'

The stewardess gave Jess a concerned look. 'Is everything alright madam?'

'Oh yes, yes, first time on a plane and she's just a little scared, that's all. She'll be fine!'

'No I won't, I won't, let me go!' yelled Isla.

Jess tugged hard on Isla's hand to pull her to their seats, but Isla squirmed and turned to look back out of the aircraft. 'Not fair! Daddy! Larry!' she screamed. Jess gave her hand another tug and the cabin door finally closed as the plane prepared for take-off.

Meanwhile, outside the terminal, Oliver's Chevy came screeching to a halt. He doubled-parked without thinking twice and sprinted into the airport, ignoring the abuse levelled at him by a nearby airport parking attendant. He scanned the fight schedule board, noting the London flight was boarding. With no time to lose, he sprinted past customs and without explanation, jumped the turnstiles. Whistles blew from officials, who then chased him down the terminal corridor to the gate lounge.

'Stop the plane! Stop the plane!' he yelled at the gate.

Out of breath, he expelled his last bit of air with, 'Stop the bloody plane! Stop it please, my li'l girl is on board! Stop it!'

Only the remaining ticket staff were present. The gate was closed. Customs caught up with him and grabbed him by the shoulder.

'Fuck off! My li'l girl is on that plane that's about to leave. You have to stop it!' Oliver shrugged off their grip, collapsing against the nearby customer service desk.

'I'm sorry sir, that flight has just taken off,' said the officer, pointing out the terminal window.

Oliver rushed over to the window, only to observe the Qantas flight soaring into the sky, piercing the clouds and increasing its distance between Isla and him.

Trance-like, he pressed his face and hands against the viewing window. As the plane eventually disappeared into the distance, he collapsed on the floor, allowing his emotions to free-fall. People stood around him, shuffling about, attempting to comfort him, but he did not acknowledge their presence. He was alone in his sorrow and despair, tolerating no interruption and shrugging off any attempt at consolation. The world could go to hell. How could she do this? How could she lie to me and take our precious li'l girl!

He took in a deep breath, held onto it and then exhaled with a sense of purpose. The image of Isla flashed into his mind, filling his heart with a newfound sense of power. As he climbed out of his black hole, he wiped the tears from his eyes. Using the window frame to support him, he turned to the customs officer.

'Well, she might have won this battle, but lads, the war has just begun.'

Chapter 8
Go Tell the Drummer Man

Oliver hardly slept at all that night. He tossed and turned, his pillow drenched with tears. He went over and over things in his mind, with no answers forthcoming. He was unable to comprehend why Jess would do this to him and hurt him so badly. It was true that she had been battling her demons for some time, and he had done his best to navigate her extreme mood changes, but what she had done was unforgiveable.

Their finances were tight, he knew, but nonetheless they made ends meet. He understood that Jess hated working night duty, but marriage was a partnership and they both contributed in different ways for the sake of their family. His relationship with Jess had drifted since Isla's birth, he acknowledged, but he had tried, really tried.

He was so frustrated that Jess had never sought professional help. Time and time again, he had attempted to broach with her the sensitive topic of her mental health, but she simply shrugged off any advice he proffered. He often thought that being a nurse, she would have some insight. Perhaps it was simply due to her stubborn nature, or to feelings of shame, inadequacy or fear.

Apart from Gerry, Jess had never discussed her family with Oliver. He knew little of her father, apart from being an army officer serving England in WW1 and then dying some short time after returning home from duty. He did not know much about Jess's mother either. Every time her name was raised, Jess subtly diverted the conversation and avoided discussing her. Her guardedness often left him perplexed.

Even at their wedding, Oliver had felt that Gerry was dodging his probing questions. This only further fuelled his curiosity.

On the flipside, Oliver had experienced a wonderful family. Although both his parents had died relatively young, his memory brimmed with fond memories of growing up, like happy holidays, family dinners and birthdays. He loved his parents very much and missed them every day. However, he often thought how fortunate he was to have his sister, Olivia. Although she was a bit tough and matter-of-fact at times, he cherished her and knew that she would do anything for him. For now, Oliver needed her more than ever.

He turned in bed, facing Jess's side. The gold coach clock on her bedside table read 6.55 a.m. What the fuck was she thinking? he cursed, crying and putting Jess's pillow over his face to inhale her scent.

Soon, his muffled cries were interrupted by a loud knock at the door. He discarded the pillow and swiped at his eyes, put on his dressing-gown and opened the front door to two police officers. Behind them, Olivia and Richard had just pulled up in their car and were making their way to the house.

'Good morning, Mr. Johnson? Apologies for the hour of the morning, but may we come in?'

'Yes, that's me. Come in,' said Oliver in a broken voice.

Olivia barged between them, 'And I'm his sister, Officer, Dr Olivia Johnson... oh, and my husband, Richard. And you are?'

'Constable Baker and I'm Senior Constable Riley.'

Olivia firmly shook hands with them both.

'Pleased to meet you. I know 7.00 a.m. is early, but the station received a message early this morning from the airport officials with some information that we needed to follow up with you,' said Senior Constable Riley.

'Yes well, *we* got our message at 6.00 this morning, *didn't we Ollie*? You could've called us last night, little brother! Might have been, hmmmm... let's say, thoughtful even!' Olivia wagged her finger at Oliver.

'I'm sorry sis, I got home so late. I was at the airport talking to the police. I was so distraught, the room was spinning, I was crippled. I just needed time to process. I'm sorry. At least you got the message. I did tell the airport officers to call you as soon as possible. I'm sorry…'

Olivia interrupted her brother, holding him tightly. 'I know love, it will be okay, it will. Richard and I are here for you, that's the main thing.'

Olivia turned back to the police officers. 'So how do we get her back, Officers?'

'Alright, first things first. Can we come inside and sit down?' asked the senior officer.

Once inside, they all sat in the drawing room. Oliver slumped over, sitting on the chesterfield, his hands covering his face. His sobs were muffled and Olivia sat close by, her arm wrapped around his shoulder, comforting him in his distress. Catching his breath, Oliver wiped away his tears and peered over to the piano. There she was again, his li'l one, pretty as a picture, squinting at her sheet music and looking down at her finger positioning, enjoying every focussed moment. The picture was clear, heart-warming, yet painful. Would he ever see Isla again?

'Mr Johnson. Mr Johnson, are you alright?' said Senior Constable Riley.

'Oh… yes.' Oliver came out of his trance-like state. 'I'll be… okay, I guess. I'm just so worried about Isla.'

'Now, we know your wife and daughter were booked on a Southern Route flight to London arriving at Heathrow on 16 November. The tickets were issued by a travel agency in Melbourne. I understand that there are no custody orders in place and the child travelled with her mother on her own passport. By law, your wife's done nothing wrong.'

Oliver jumped to his feet.

'*Nothing wrong? Nothing wrong!* That bloody bitch! How could she do this? How can you say that? We were supposed to travel to the UK a couple of years ago but we had to pull the pin. We got Isla's passport then. Jess uses her UK passport. She was born there. Her sister, Gerry, lives there in Chelsea, I think. Actually, she's been speaking with Jess quite often lately. What the fuck! I thought Gerry liked me. Why would her sister help her steal Isla away from me? Fuck!' Oliver paced back and forth. 'I have to get to the airport!'

'Ollie, sit down, you'll wear out the rug. Come, sit here!' Olivia motioned to her brother to resume his seat next to her. 'Deep breaths love!'

Oliver refused to listen and continued with his determined stride.

'There'll be no more flights till tomorrow night I believe, sir. I suggest you pack your bags and head off on that flight. It's a commercial flight. You can contact the police in London once you arrive. We will notify the authorities in Britain, so at least they'll have a file upon your arrival. We will need recent pictures if you have them. I suppose it's likely she'll head to her sister's… ' Riley paused before continuing. 'Try and get a good night's sleep tonight, Mr Johnson.'

'No. We have to go right now! There's no time… ' said Oliver.

He was interrupted by Olivia, 'Yes, Officer, that's very sensible advice. Thank you.'

Oliver butted in loudly, 'We're just losing time. She kidnapped my daughter. Don't you see that? Does anyone get that?'

'Sir, please refrain from raising your voice,' said Constable Baker, awkwardly trying to assert himself.

Riley looked at Oliver, raising his eyebrows. 'Yes, no need for that Mr Johnson, we *are* trying to help.'

'Well you're not fucking helping, you're fucking doing nothing. This feels like a bloody funeral.'

He dragged out the piano stool and collapsed onto it. His elbows landed on the keyboard, causing a clambering of random notes. His head fell into his trembling hands and tears streamed down his face. Everyone in the room was uncomfortable watching him break down before their eyes. After a moment, Olivia could bear it no more.

'Alright, thank you gentlemen for all your help. We will do what we need to do, rest assured. I'll see you both out.'

Richard poured Oliver a whisky. 'I know it's a bit early old chum, but it can't hurt.'

Oliver took his medicine with one swallow, holding out the tumbler for a refill, which Richard willingly obliged. After he caught his breath, he looked up at his sister. 'Will you come with me?'

'Of course Ollie, there was never any question,' she said.

'What will I do with Larry?' Oliver looked at Richard.

'There was never any question,' smiled Richard, 'I'll take that sock he's chewing on too, if you don't mind!'

'It's Isla's. He won't sleep without it,' said Oliver, trying to stand up, but looking as if he had been kicked in the stomach. 'Am I a bad husband? Is that why she left me?'

Olivia took a deep breath and moving to her brother, placed a hand on his shoulders. She looked at him directly in the eyes, determined to speak to his heart. 'No darling Ollie, of course you're not a bad husband. It's not your fault.' She hugged him. 'We'll find them, I promise.'

That night, Oliver found himself in the drawing room seated at the piano, Isla at the forefront of his mind. He started sifting through the sheet music spread over the top of the piano. 'Where is it?' he asked himself, flicking through the pages. 'Where is her song, where is *Isla's Song*? It's gone! She's gone!' Impulsively, he gathered all the sheet music and threw it about the room, kicked the piano stool aside and pulled music books from the nearby shelving, tossing them about the room and uttering guttural cries. Then he collapsed on the floor, lying in a sea of music scores dampened by sweat and tears.

He could not sleep again that night. By 2.00 p.m. his bag was packed, Larry had been collected by Mrs Peters, the home blinds had been pulled and the doors locked whilst he anxiously awaited his sister's arrival. In her usual timely fashion, her arrival was announced by Richard's car horn tooting and he rushed out the front door, threw his luggage into the boot and got in the car. He did not dare look back.

Upon arriving at Essendon Airport with passports and tickets in hand, they bid Richard farewell and headed to the boarding lounge, their actions fuelling a sense of hope.

Three days later, Jess and Isla exited customs at London Airport. Isla was exhausted after the long, disjointed trip and remained a few steps behind her mother. Jess scanned the public area and finally spotted Gerry with her husband Bob and two younger children, Billy and Gertie.

Jess grabbed Isla's hand and ran towards her sister, hugging Gerry, holding onto her for support. She so needed the touch of a loved one. Her tears fell and she laughed awkwardly, hiding her pain. Pulling away from her sister, she then embraced Bob and the children. 'It's so nice to be here, to see you all. It has been such a journey. This is Isla. Isla, meet your Aunty Gerry, Uncle Bob and oh, this must be Billy and Gertrude.'

'It's Gertie, not Gertrude, and I'm eight years old anyway. Who are you?'

'Gertie, please! This is your Aunty Jess, Mummy's sister,' said Gerry. 'You know, I've told you she would be visiting?'

'I thought you said she was younger than you Mummy. She doesn't... '

Gerry quickly intercepted the verbal missile, 'Well little madam, if you don't act like a lady and keep your bad manners to y'self, you'll be havin' no dinner tonight!'

Jess smiled awkwardly, 'It's okay, I must look like a complete wreck!'

Gerry bent down and hugged Isla, kissing her forehead. 'Well, I wasn't expecting this little one as well. Jess?'

Jess quickly winked at Gerry, pursing her lips and shaking her head. 'We'll talk about the trip and all that when we get home. I'm exhausted and longing for a cup of English tea.'

'I think we can manage that Bob, can't we?' smiled Gerry.

'Ah yes,' said Bob, collecting the luggage and leading them all to his car parked just outside the main doors. 'Nothing a good cuppa tea can't cure!'

Isla continued dragging her feet behind Jess. She was pale, her hair was unkempt and her clothes hung off her. Observing her struggles, Billy walked up to her and said, 'You are so lucky. I've never been on a plane. I want to fly a plane when I get big. I'm six, that's pretty big, but I need to get bigger like Dad. When we get home I'll show you my room and my planes me and Dad made. I glued them and all.'

Isla did not properly take in what he was saying. There were all sorts of people coming and going, some speaking English but in a different way to what she was used to, loudspeakers with announcements every so often and so many different smells. Her senses were on high alert. 'Who are all these people? Where am I? I want to go home. I want my daddy. I want Larry.' She froze, suddenly frightened, overcome by all sorts of feelings. Her tummy was abuzz with butterflies and she was lightheaded. She wanted to cry but couldn't and it scared her. Billy grabbed her shoulders and shook her, 'Isla, Isla, what's wrong? Mummy, Mummy!' he yelled.

Jess saw what was happening and ran back to her daughter, who appeared dazed. She knelt down in front of her. 'Isla, Isla, can you hear me? Isla, can you hear me, are you alright?'

The child fell into her mother's arms, clasping her like a piece of driftwood in a sea of doubt, hanging onto her for her life.

'I'm here Isla, Mummy's here, Mummy's here.' Jess kissed her several times then held her tightly. 'Mummy's here.'

Isla didn't feel that kiss. She felt nothing. She was numb.

'When are we going home, Mummy? I want to go home,' she sobbed.

By then, Gerry and Gertrude had joined the closed circle.

'First, we will go with Aunty Gerry. Daddy should be here soon,' said Jess, trying to comfort her.

'And Larry?' said Isla feebly.

'We'll see, Isla. Now let's go and get some nice hot chocolate into that belly and who knows, maybe Aunty Gerry has some sweeties for you.' She smiled.

Gerry looked at Jess wondering what was going on. Isla's arrival was totally unexpected and she wanted to hear the full story.

Bob's Rover was jam-packed, the kids packed in amongst the luggage like sardines. As the car rolled into the council estate, Jess had fleeting memories of a past long gone. Entering the house, she could hear the shrills of children's voices from upstairs.

'We're home loves, come down!' shouted Gerry. 'Stoke the fire Bob, it's bloody freezing, must be those council pipes again. The buggers always freeze up this time of year,' she grinned.

Bob disappeared into the rear room and Margaret and Phillip bolted down the rickety staircase.

'He did it again Mum. Tell him to give it back. He's got my diary!' said Margaret. Phillip stood there performing a native American war dance, waving about Margaret's diary in the air, provoking her.

'Oh you two! *Will you give up*! Fight, fight, fight. We have guests. *Please*!' said Gerry, turning to Jess and Isla. 'Now, this is your Aunty Jess and your cousin Isla. Please behave yourselves. Margaret, you will be moving into Phillip's room whilst our guests are here.'

'What the hell. I'm not moving in with that idiot, Mum. He smells, and a girl needs her privacy.'

'It's not forever, so do as you're told!' said Gerry.

'Nice to meet you, Aunty Jess and Isla,' said Phillip and Margaret in unison, before running down the narrow hallway, with Margaret still trying to snatch her diary from Phillip's tormenting hands.

Billy took Isla's hand and led her upstairs to his bedroom with Gertie to explore his plane collection.

'Billy, I hope you haven't made a mess of your room. Be nice, both of you, Isla's our very special guest,' exclaimed Gerry, watching them disappear from sight.

'Gosh, Gerry, when you said you live in London, I thought you meant in the city. This is like another town,' said Jess, collapsing onto the nearby couch.

'Can't afford anything in London. This is the best we can do for now,' said Gerry, interrupting herself by yelling at Margaret and Phillip again. 'Brian left me with little, the gambling prick, so Bob and I make do. Not easy, but you know me, always up for a challenge, sis.'

Gerry sat down next to Jess. There was a quiet moment before she gently placed her hand on her knee. 'Now, let me take a good look at you. It's been a while.' She reached out to her sister, put her arms around her and gave her a tight hug. 'I've really missed you, ya know.' They looked at each other in silence. Gerry tracked Jess's sunken cheeks, blackened violet rings under her once sparkling blue eyes, her creased brow and rigid jaw. This was not how she remembered her little sister. A lump formed in her throat. In an attempt to dislodge her angst, Gerry sparked up, tapping Jess's knee. 'Alright, as promised, I'll get you that cuppa… and for memory's sake, a vanilla slice, just as you like them. Won't be long. Then a spot of dinner, and off to bed for you and Isla. You need your rest. We will talk in the morning.'

Jess awoke early the next morning. She had forgotten how cold it could be in London. She quietly snuck out of bed, leaving Isla curled up under the coloured crochet woollen blankets.

Each step down the aged staircase let out its own individual creak, and Jess was careful not to wake the household.

Upon arriving at the end of the hallway, she discovered Gerry sitting in the kitchen, reading the newspaper. She was wearing her fluffy pink dressing-gown, and her brown locks were wrapped in a variety of coloured rollers. Her make-up was faded but still obvious from the day before, with a cigarette hanging from her wrinkled mouth. Wafts of smoke engulfed the kitchen table area.

'Morning, sleep well?' she asked her sister, peering up from the newspaper.

'Yes, I did, thank you.'

Jess grabbed herself a cup of water and joined Gerry at the table. Slowly, Gerry folded the paper, taking a long drag on her cigarette and gazing at Jess, patiently awaiting an explanation.

'He *will* come looking for me. Also, his brother-in-law has money, so I'm sure he'll contribute. Oliver will stop at nothing to find me and Isla.'

'I thought as much. Why Jess, why?' said Gerry. 'What about Isla?'

'I… uhm… I don't know. I mean… ' Jess pondered what she had rehearsed over and over on the plane. 'I've been sick for ages. Not feeling well. I don't know what's wrong with me, Gerry. I haven't been able to sleep, my appetite's gone. I feel that I haven't been there for Isla. It's a mess.' She broke down in tears. Eventually, she caught her breath. ' I think it's him. Our relationship. It's not right. I don't love him. I told him. It's my health Gerry, I just can't take it anymore. It got to a stage where I thought about it… I thought, I don't want to live anymore, not like this. I got scared, thus the SOS to you. I'm not finishing like Mum, I'm not Gerry, I'm not!'

'But what about Isla, sis? Did Oliver know you were bringing her?'

'No! I didn't tell him. He thought I was leaving a day later. I emptied our account, bought her a ticket and escaped.'

Gerry looked at her in disbelief. This was not her Jess, a girl full of life, smiles and compassion for others. Gerry had always loved Oliver. As far as she was concerned, he was a loving husband and father and she had always thought their match was one made in heaven, and Isla their God-sent little angel. She held a spot in her heart for Oliver, and felt very torn. However, she also felt obligated to her sister. They had a history that bound them closely and she refused to give up on her now. *Blood is thicker*, she thought.

'Jess, Isla has a father. Have you thought about Isla? The impact on her? On Oliver? Have you thought this through, love? I mean Bob and I are here for you, but travelling to the other side of the world, without a hint… well Jess, it doesn't seem right.' Gerry knew well that she was walking on eggshells.

'Right! Right!' Jess shouted. 'You have no idea what I've been feeling. I've felt I'm losing my mind, Gerry. I can't control my racing thoughts and every night after midnight, when I was standing at the fucking kitchen sink, I wondered when it would end… this life … my life! I just can't do it anymore Gerry, I won't. You *have to* help me!'

'Okay, okay,' said Gerry, grabbing Jess's hand. 'So how long are you staying?'

'I don't know. I don't think I can go back, Gerry.'

Gerry picked up her cigarette from a butt-filled ashtray and took a long drawback. 'Okay. Well, he *will* come looking for you. He only has my old address with Brian in Chelsea, but he'll find you here eventually, and God help us all.' She stood up, picked up the teapot, emptied it, replenished it with some fresh tea and resumed her seat. She replaced the teapot's pink crocheted cover and turned the pot for the leaves to draw. Following a few rotations, her eyes again fixed upon Jess.

'Okay. You'll stay here a couple of nights and then, the day after that, plan to head to Glasgow by train. There's an inn there, Crowcaddies. I'll give you the address. Ask for Gwendolyn; she's an old friend mine. She'll put you up for the night in a room above the pub. It's nothing fancy but you'll have a roof over your heads and a bed to sleep in. She'll give you something to eat too. After that, we'll talk. I'll make some further enquiries. I have some thoughts, nothin' concrete, but we'll work it out, Jess. You and Isla will be fine. But I don't want you here if Oliver turns up on my doorstep. Do y'hear? It's for the best, sis.'

Dazed and speechless, Jess was well aware of the difficult position in which she was placing her sister.

Taking one last draw on her cigarette before extinguishing it, Gerry exhaled and thoughtfully blew away the specks of dust captured by the morning's rays filtering through the kitchen window.

She said to Jess, 'Have you heard of the drummer boy? Part of the battlefield music for centuries. There, those young ones, with a bass drum strapped to their tiny shoulders, would signal commands from officers to troops. Well I fear, sis, that Oliver may have already heard the beat of his drum. War is on the horizon and the battlefield is a dangerous place to be, little sis.' Pouring a fresh brew into Jess's cup, she said, 'Drink up sis, calm yourself, catch your breath, you'll be needing nerves of steel. Let's get a move on before it's too late. I'll make sure the rest of your arrangements are in place once you arrive at Crowcaddies. I've a few calls to make but don't you worry, that's what sisters are for.'

Chapter 9
Let the Wind Carry Me

It was their last night in London. Gerry and Bob's home filled Jess with mixed emotions. Memories of the past haunted her. She felt clammy and her stomach was upset. Each hour upon the hour, the old grandfather clock that had once belonging to her mother resonated throughout the household. As midnight struck, Jess looked outside her frosted windowpane. The night was bleak, with howling winds and snowflakes peppering the pavements. A single ornate street lamp stood firm, its light pulsating into the night mist. The atmosphere was ominous and haunting, as if enticing spirits from another realm. 'I hope the invitation doesn't extend to my mother, God bless her. The last thing I need is her jumping out of that blasted clock,' Jess said to herself, holding her blankets up to her chin.

The morning sun warmed the layered frost. Jess hoped a fresh new day was a good omen for her adventure ahead with Isla. 'It's for the best,' she whispered and with that, her thought was punctuated by another gong of the clock. 'Okay, okay, I hear you Mum!'

Oliver and Liv finally touched down at London airport. The journey had been marred by mechanical issues, lost baggage in Singapore and a case of mistaken identity by customs in Egypt, resulting in further delays. Despite those certain frustrations, Olivia had lapped up the attention of being confused with Grace Kelly.

In addition to the long, arduous flight, Isla's absence added to Oliver's anxieties. As he stepped from the plane, his once-pristine brown-striped suit was rumpled and dull. His brown Stanton hat hid his messed-up hair and overshadowed his tired features. Clearly on a mission, he moved quickly to the airport exit. Olivia dutifully kept up with her brother's pace, managing an awkward jog in her high heels.

As soon as they were both processed through customs, Oliver collected their baggage, headed out of the airport and waved down a taxi.

'May I ask where we're going? The police station?' said Olivia, gasping for breath.

'No, Liv, I've got a strong hunch. After a short stay at Gerry's, she'll head north.'

'North? Why north?'

'Because that was our idea last time we planned to visit here, and I reckon that's what she'll do. Can't explain it. Got a gut feel. Don't ask why, I just do!' Oliver was trying to hold his anger at bay.

'Oh, I wouldn't dare,' said Liv, 'God knows you might start telling fortunes soon!'

'Funny, sis. Very funny. I know what I'm doing, alright? Don't give me a hard time. Just bear with me.' A black cab pulled up. He threw the pair's luggage into the boot. 'Victoria Station driver, please.'

The mornings at Gerry's home were mayhem. Margaret and Phillip were arguing over whose turn it was to wash the dishes, Billy refused to get dressed for school as he hadn't finished gluing his fighter jet, Gertie was constipated from consuming a large portion of green bananas and caramel sauce the night before and Bob was Bob, grumpy as ever.

'Would you hurry up Bob!' bellowed Gerry. 'We'll be late for the train at this rate. Billy, BILLY! Hurry up love, you'll be late for school. Gertie, what did I tell you! Margaret, stop throwing the tea towel at your brother. Jesus, Mary and St Joseph. Good lord, why me!'

Although Jess loved her sister, she was not used to such pandemonium. Her life in Melbourne was more measured and predictable. She was very much looking forward to peace once more. It will be different, but it will be good medicine, she reassured herself.

The trip to the train station was as eventful as the morning's household antics. Bob's car continually fogged up, with Gerry spitting on her handkerchief and wiping it.

'Will everyone hold their breath please, or breathe lightly, this bloody window keeps fogging up. Bob can't see at the best of times and we want to get to the train station in one piece!' As Bob drove along, the car slid across the road because of the black ice. On one occasion it slid through the intersection against a red light, narrowly missing an elderly woman walking her three basset hounds, and everyone in the car held their heads and screamed.

Finally, they arrived at their destination, London station, a prime example of the city's proud Victorian architecture with striking sculptures encircled by ornate arches.

Bob pulled up at the drop-off spot just in front of the train station. It was cold, glum and windy. Isla wanted to stay inside the car and continue to soak up the warmth. Bob grabbed their luggage, whilst Gerry smothered her sister and niece with warm embraces.

'Now you look after your mum, you hear Isla? You're a big girl now. We will see you soon. Take care, li'l one.'

'My dad calls me that,' said Isla.

'What, dear?'

'Li'l one, Aunty Gerry,' exclaimed Isla proudly, 'when is Daddy coming Mummy?'

'Oh, look at all those pretty coloured balloons over there, Isla,' Jess said to divert Isla's attention, pointing to a vendor's brightly covered stand. 'Aren't they beautiful? Look, the red ones match the colour of your coat. If you're good, Mummy will buy you one later.'

Jess reached out to embrace her sister again, whispering softly into her ear, 'Thank you sis. You have been more than amazing. I know you don't understand me, I do, but one day maybe… '

Gerry gently kissed her on the cheek. 'I love you sis. I don't have to understand for now. Maybe one day. Maybe. In the meantime you take care of the both of you. Be safe. Be well. And ring me sis. Ring me when you get there. I'll make sure you have the extra information by then. Travel safe!'

'I will. I will never forget your help,' said Jess.

With that, she picked up their luggage, motioning to Isla to follow her. She didn't look back and as they entered the train station, she spotted a large ornate clock and said under her breath, 'No looking back now!'

Minutes after Bob's car headed west from the station, Oliver and Liv's cab made an abrupt stop outside the station, skidding on the asphalt.

'Two quid, gov,' said the driver.

He had hardly finished his sentence before Oliver alighted from the vehicle and removed their luggage. He handed the money to the driver and bid him farewell, tipping his hat.

'Right, we must check every train and bus station. Every damn taxi stand. Everything that moves. If we wait too long, we may never find her.'

'Ollie, she might not even be here. What about the police? This place is massive, you have to be… '

Before she could finish, Oliver butted in, 'Liv, we haven't time to argue. No police for now. Dump the luggage at that counter over there and let's spread out. Time is our enemy, sis. You start checking the rental car dealers. See if she's hired a car. I'll check the station platforms. Meet you at that sandwich bar over there.' He pointed to Sam's Café.

Although the peak hour rush had passed, many travellers remained in the vast building.

Throughout the plane journey, Oliver had thought very carefully about his strategy. He thought that he knew Jess better than most and believed he had a handle on her and her anticipated travel plans. He had no idea what he would do once he found them as for now, his energy and focus were totally concentrated on locating Isla.

He explored each train platform, waving a photograph of Jess and Isla under the noses of random unsuspecting commuters, praying that someone would recognise them.

As he was standing on platform eight, he noticed across the way on platform seven a woman and a child who reminded him of Jess and Isla. He could only see their backs, but their features sparked his hopes. The blonde woman was wearing a black winter coat and a grey woollen pillbox hat. The young girl was dressed in a pretty blue dress and cream jacket. Her curly brown locks masked her features at times, due to the blustery wind conditions.

Oliver immediately took flight, up the platform eight ramp and then down the adjacent ramp onto platform seven. As he approached, the woman and child were heading to the end of the platform to seek refuge in a nearby seating area. Oliver's heart began to pound as he closed in on them. Moments away, he experienced a sense of knowing. He grabbed the small child by the hand, 'Isla! Isla!' he shouted.

As the child turned, it was apparent that his intuition had been misguided. The little girl looked at him horrified, screaming.

'What do you think you're doing, sir?' shrieked the child's mother. 'Get your hands off her, or I'll call the police. Get away. Leave her alone!'

Oliver immediately released the child's hand. 'I'm so sorry, I didn't mean to… Please forgive me. It's just that I'm… ' Oliver reached into his coat pocket, 'I'm looking for this woman and child, my daughter. Have you seen them?'

The woman looked at him and sized him up as someone in need of therapy. 'No, I have not! Go away!' Turning about on the spot, she took her daughter by the hand and marched off in the opposite direction.

Jess made her way inconspicuously to the ticket box to collect her travel tickets. Isla stood behind her, constantly reminding her mother of her hunger pains.

'In a minute Isla, *in a minute*. Just give me a minute!' she said, shaking her off from tugging at her winter coat.

With tickets and suitcase in one hand and Isla in the other, Jess raced off to platform five. They descended the old iron staircase from the ticket booth, which was opposite the ramp down to platform seven. As they reached the bottom steps, Oliver was just exiting the top of the ramp, turning left to Sam's Café. Neither one spotted the other.

Jess's eyes were on high alert. She well anticipated that Oliver could have the police on her trail. *Who knows*, she thought, *he might be in London, trying to track down Gerry. I don't think he has Brian's number or he would know where to find him. He certainly doesn't know Bob or Gerry's new address.* This she assumed, attempting to appease her escalating anxieties.

To the right of the staircase, Jess spotted the sign to platform five in the distance. Nearly there, Jess, nearly there. You can do it, she affirmed to herself. A short distance in the other direction was Sam's Café, where Liv was anxiously waiting for Oliver.

Isla lagged behind. She was tired, hungry and failing.

'Will you hurry up, Isla, *hurry up*,' said Jess, tightening her grip on Isla's hand.

'You're hurting me! Stop it! *Stop, Mummy*!' she screamed. People were beginning to stare at them.

Jess paid her little heed, save for hushing her now and then. She had no time. On platform six, she saw two police officers standing, having a smoke and a laugh. Jess settled her pace, holding Isla close by, looking ahead and trying not to draw any attention to them.

As if on cue, the grand London station clock chimed, marking Oliver's arrival at Sam's Café, his back facing the platform five sign now positioned directly above Jess and Isla.

A train whistle from platform five pierced the busy station, the train releasing a large plume of smoke into the air. A rumbling sound signalled that the train was beginning to move.

'No sign of them, Liv?' queried Oliver.

'No, no sign. Car rentals have no records of Jess.'

Oliver hung his head, put his hands in his pockets and stared at his brogues, appearing lost for words.

Over Oliver's left shoulder, Liv spotted a flash of red. As she focussed, she could see it was a small girl in a red coat holding a familiar little overnight case, hand in hand with a young blonde woman. It was only a glimpse, but it was enough for Liv to race to a conclusion as she spied the pair disappearing down the ramp to the train platform.

'Quick, Ollie, quick I think it's them! It's them, run!' she shouted, removing her fine mint-coloured stilettos to pursue them in true athletic style.

Oliver's head jerked up, Olivia's words hitting him like a frying pan on the back of his head.

'What the hell! Jesus,' he said, sprinting and overtaking his sister. 'Stop them, *stop them*!' he roared, the two smoking police officers joining the chase, blowing their whistles.

As Oliver reached the top of the ramp, his pace was fuelled by the desire to hold Isla once more. Dashing to the platform, he bowled and hurdled over morning travellers heading upstream. Arriving at the platform, he spotted Jess and Isla boarding the last train carriage, which was already two thirds up the platform. His guttural cries pierced the air, as he saw Jess pushing Isla onto the slowly moving train. Hearing the scream, Jess turned her head, catching a glimpse of Oliver running towards her. His eyes were tightly focussed on her, his stare one of pure rage, his pace increasing. She could not believe her eyes, with little time to register what seemed like a raging bull narrowing the distance between them. Flight kicked in. She leapt onto the train, grasping the long door handle inside and then hanging out of the train to watch Oliver trying to run to Isla's rescue.

'*Stop! Stop that woman!*' he screamed, '*Stop her, she's got my child!*'

The final carriage bid farewell to platform five as Oliver reached its terminal. Totally spent, he collapsed on the ground in a crucifixion pose.

He was too late.

Jess watched him, trying to make sense of the moment, but she was just relieved to have made her escape. Closing the train door, she felt a hardness overcome her, a bitterness that she had never quite experienced before. A flood of emotions overcame her, paralysing her momentarily. She became angry and sad, then empty and lost. Reaching her seat next to Isla, she collapsed under the pressure of what had just occurred, pressing her face against the carriage window. Buildings, houses, people and children flitted past, making her dizzy. A wave of nausea overcame her and she bent over, holding her stomach and dry-retching, with nothing to expel but emptiness.

Shortly after, Liv and the two police officers reached Oliver, who was still lying on the platform, trying to catch his breath.

'I nearly had her, I fucking nearly had her Liv! All I needed was the wind to carry me and I would've fucken had her. And I saw her look at me with steely blue eyes. She was so full of hate. It wasn't her Liv, it was like, I didn't know that woman. Who was she? Who was that woman who took my child?'

Oliver sat up and Liv passed him his Stanton that had blown off his head in the chase. Snow drifted around them, carried on the winter breeze. Before long, Oliver was enveloped in a thin white pelt, which he shook off when he stood up. There were no tears. There was no carry-on. Liv looked at her brother and for the first time in a long time, she saw in him a sense of real determination. *This man means business*, she thought. Smiling inwardly, she could see that this episode had changed her little brother. He had manned up. No more aloofness, no more being walked over. *This is a man on a mission*, she thought proudly, and *God help anyone who gets in his way!*

'You right, gov?' said one of the police officers.

'I'll be fine when I get my daughter back, officer. Do you reckon you might be able to help me do that?'

Chapter 10
Big Yellow Taxi
Jess's Family Home, North London, 1927

Gerry and Jess were busily peeling potatoes for their mother, Dorothy. It was nearly 6.00 pm and the local pub was about to serve its last round of beers.

'Would you two get a hurry on? Your father'll be home soon and you know how he likes his dinner on the table on time,' said Dorothy.

'I'm hungry!' Jess complained.

'Well, you can go hungry if there's any more of this nonsense, young lady.'

'I'm tired of this. Anyhow, I want to go play now. I've already done the beans.' Jess sighed.

Gerry slyly kicked Jess under the table. She could see that her little sister was pushing their mother's buttons again. There's not room enough for two bulls in this paddock, she sighed to herself.

'You listen here missy, when I was your age I worked in my mother's bakehouse all day long. Dawn till dusk. Without a complaint. So stop your whingin' or the wrong end of the wooden spoon will meet your backside again!' Dorothy's patience was wearing thin.

Jess frowned. There was a brief interlude and just as she was about to get herself into more trouble, Gerry abruptly butted in, 'Yes, yes, there's time to play later sis, I promise. Now let's get this done for Mumma.'

'Now that's what I like to hear! A bit of co-operation goes a long way in my eyes. Now hurry, girls. Ten minutes and your father'll be landing at that door, in God only knows what state.'

A few moments later, the chime of the grandfather clock reminded them all it was time. Dorothy tore off her apron and sculled her third vintage port for the afternoon.

'Off you both go now. Wash your hands and face!'

Before Jess retreated, her mother clasped her chin with her hand, 'And just look at you Jess. You're a mess. Hurry and clean up. And for God's sake put on some fresh clothes. HURRY!' she exclaimed, releasing her grip.

Jess slinked to her bedroom, rubbing her chin. She used a jug of water and a bowl in her room to wash her face and hands. After changing her clothes, she was startled by the opening and slamming shut of the front door. She was always on edge at this time, as her father would often return from the pub overly cheery before he raised his voice against Mother, and made aggressive physical threats. She put her ear to the gap in her partially closed bedroom door and listened to the rhythmic beat of her father's limp leg, his only badge of honour from World War 1.

'I hope dinner's ready, Dot!' he bellowed.

'Coming, Frank!' Dorothy answered immediately.

As he passed her door, Jess caught a waft of stale cigar smoke mixed with the sweet scent of alcohol. He always adjusted the framed pictures lining the narrow hallway walls as he staggered to the dining room. 'Where the hell is my dinner, woman?'

'It's coming, it's coming! Girls! Where are you girls? Come help me in the kitchen,' Dorothy shouted from the kitchen.

One by one the three of them placed the plates of food on the dining table in front of Frank, who was seated at the head of the table. A finely baked roast chicken was accompanied by bowls of peas, beans and steamed potatoes sprinkled with parsley and drizzled with butter.

'Well, that's more like it!' said Frank, chuckling to himself. 'Get me a red, dear, whilst you're up.'

Once they were all seated, Jess impulsively reached for one of the hot potatoes in the nearby bowl. It was so hot it burnt her fingers, causing her to throw it up in the air. Simultaneously, Dorothy jumped from her chair as the potato flew across the table and landed on her husband's lap.

'JESS! JESS! What the hell are you doing, child?' her mother yelled.

Frank also jumped to his feet and flicked the hot spud from his lap.

Dorothy reached across the table and forcefully smacked Jess on the hand. 'Get to your room, miss!'

Despite her unfortunate misdeed, Frank said, 'Oh, leave her be Dot. She's just a wee child. And if there's any hitting about this house, it'll be my doing. Now just behave yourself, woman! You too, Jess. Sit down and let's give thanks to the Lord.'

Jess looked up at her father sheepishly. The corners of her mouth relaxed upwards as she caught a quick wink from him.

Hanging on the wall behind her father was a scene of the crucifix. She observed the look of anguish on Jesus's face, empathising with his silent cries of pain, wishing someone would address her grief by actually showing her some love. Apart from Gerry, she felt alone, fearful and scared in that house at times.

Jess often spied on her father sitting in his club chair, smoking his pipe and downing glass tumblers of whisky. She so wished that one day she could sit on his lap and have him read to her, like other kids' fathers. She knew something was not right, as she was often awoken by her father's night terrors. Her mother would hush him back to sleep, her distress evident in her soft whispers. Dorothy ruled the roost at home during the day with an iron fist, but when it came to her husband, she remained unquestioning and subservient to his needs. She knew her place, unlike Jess, who continually tested boundaries.

'Alright, let's start that again,' said Frank. 'In the name of the Father, the Son and the Holy Ghost... '

As her father prayed, Jess looked at Jesus, wondering whether he felt butterflies in his stomach too.

Isla peered out of the train window and stared at the snow-laden fields dotted with livestock, and the cupcake hay mounds as if sprinkled with icing. Although the winter wind swept across the land, the afternoon sunlight gently illuminated the frosty fields, making the surface glisten and twinkle like the night sky.

'Pretty, isn't it?' said Jess. Isla nestled into her mother, who placed her woollen cardigan over her to make sure she was warm enough. It was getting dark as the train approached another town.

The police officer was only too glad to assist Oliver and Liv. Once they returned to the London police station, after some helpful guidance, the two of them chartered a plane to Carlisle, just outside the Scottish border. Oliver had previously researched the train route and was fully aware that not only did Carlisle have an airstrip, but the train would be making its stop there before heading north to Glasgow.

'Liv, what would I do without you and Richard! This is costing a fortune, but I will repay you sis, I will. I promise,' he said, grabbing both her hands.

'I know, I know dear, but first things first. Let's get to Isla and worry about money later,' Liv reassured him.

They boarded the small plane with the two assigned police officers and headed for Carlisle. It was a little compact but Oliver, staring out the window, didn't mind, thinking only of his daughter and their anticipated reunion. It felt like the plane had barely taken off before it began making its descent. Olivia gripped Oliver's hand on touch-down when the plane made a solid landing on the snow-covered airstrip. They disembarked and headed to an awaiting police car. There was no time to lose.

Isla was still sound asleep when Jess spotted a police car speeding along the street running parallel to the railway line. She released her hold of Isla, interrupting the child's slumber.

'Mummy, Mummy, where are we?'

'Sshh! Go back to sleep love. It's alright.'

Getting out a train map from her handbag, she anxiously located the town ahead. The train slowed down to approach the station and Jess' eyes darted about. Beads of sweat formed on the cool skin of her brow. When she looked out the window again, she observed the sign on the station platform: 'Carlisle'.

The train came to a stop.

Some passengers entered the train, whilst others left with suitcases in hand. She apprehensively watched every movement. Time seemed to move so slowly. As Isla went back to sleep, Jess got to her feet. She hesitated and then put her face close to the train window, wiping away the condensation. Seconds ticked by before she heard the ring of the conductor's whistle and the signal, 'ALL ABOARD!'

The train commenced its forward motion just as Jess spied two police officers together with Oliver and Liv standing on the station. She caught her breath and watched them until they vanished from her view.

Oliver stood there devastated as the train disappeared from sight.

'We have to go. We can catch them at the next station. Let's go!' he said, pulling on the policer officer's coat.

'We can't do that, sir. Carlisle is the last station before crossing the border into Scotland.'

'I don't understand what you're saying.'

'I'm sorry sir, but we have no jurisdiction across the border. From here, we must hand you over to Scotland Yard.'

Oliver walked away from the officer, turned on his heel and paced up and down, giving a cry of frustration. Finding it unbearable, Liv walked away.

'I *am* sorry, sir. I'll phone ahead. They'll wait for them at Glasgow station. That's the final stop. We can then drive you to Scotland Yard. The file's been sent there in any event, as a precautionary measure.'

The train moved through the darkening Scottish landscape and Jess's heart sank. She had been surprised to see Oliver at London station, and staggered that he had caught up with them at Carlisle. She feared that he just might catch up with them next time. *Third time unlucky*, she thought, *I can't bear the consequences. I must focus and stay calm. It's for the best.*

Isla awoke again, disorientated and hungry. 'Mummy, where are we? I'm hungry. How much longer?'

'Not long now sweetheart. You go back to sleep and Mummy will wake you once we are there. We'll get some hot chips when we get there, but only if you're a good girl.'

Isla watched her mother intently. Something did not seem right. Jess kept giving her nervous stares, patting her arm, whilst looking out the window and about the carriage, as if she were expecting someone to burst in at any moment. Occasionally, she glared at her when she caught Isla staring at her. She was not used to seeing her mother in this state and it frightened her. At home, she had been quiet at times, staring into space. At other times, she would yell at Isla for no reason. However, since leaving Melbourne, she had noticed differences in her mother's behaviour, such as her sharp speech, the way she constantly reprimanded her by hitting her on the hand and how her eyes often darted about in a disturbing fashion. *Perhaps she was nervous travelling alone without Daddy,* she thought. Thinking about her father made her realise how much she missed him and Larry. She longed to be picked up by her father, swung about and tickled all over. *I'm a big girl now, he told me that,* she thought, *I'll look after Mummy till he gets here. He'll know what to do.*

As the conductor passed them in the aisle, Jess told Isla to stay in her seat. Isla's eyes remained fixed on her mother when she approached the conductor and spoke with him briefly. Not long after, Jess returned to her seat. Isla waited for her mother to say something, but she remained quiet. She watched her mother nervously surveying the darkened outlines of the passing countryside, and her fixed look made her stir in her seat.

After a speedy car journey from the station, Oliver and Liv were able to make it to Scotland Yard in Westminster without time to spare. The report from London including photos of Jess and Isla had already arrived and police officers appointed to the case. A police car was awaiting them. After a short debrief, they all jumped in the vehicle and sped off for Glasgow.

Oliver's heart was thumping. Finally, he thought that he would catch up with Jess and hold his little girl once more. He had not thought about what might happen afterwards, his thoughts focussed only on his mission. As the car came to a halt, Olivia grabbed his hand, giving it a little squeeze. 'Thank God we're here Ollie. We made it.'

They ran after the police officers, who raced ahead to the train station. As they stepped foot on the platform, the train was slowing down. Oliver's head swivelled back and forth and he peered into the train windows, desperately trying to catch a glimpse of Isla.

The train came to a stop, steam filling the platform, capturing the frosty air and engulfing the station.

The carriage doors opened and Oliver, Liv and the officers spread out on the platform, waiting to pounce.

Passengers alighted from the train, Oliver scanning each one. People greeted family and friends and the platform quickly became a horde of travellers and welcoming parties. The silence of the night was invaded by the cheers and embraces of the crowd, their noise muffling any attempts by the police, Oliver or Liv to communicate effectively. The swarm of people also cut off Oliver's view of Liv and the police.

With the crowd dispersing, Oliver could wait no longer and ran onto the train.

The police officers and Liv saw him, yelling out his name. As Oliver entered the rear, they jumped on the train as well, joining in the search. After a time, with no sign of Jess or Isla, they disembarked.

'Where are they?' said Oliver, desperately searching the platform. 'Isla, *ISLA*!' he screamed, as the officers grabbed his arms.

'Please sir, calm down. Do you understand? DO YOU UNDERSTAND?' said one of the officers, attempting to contain a kicking and screaming Oliver.

'Sir, if you don't desist, we will have to arrest you. Do you understand? You're frightening people. Answer me!'

'How can they not be on the train? Where are they? There was no-one at Carlisle, the train's first stop. So where the FUCK are they? Did we miss them? How could we miss them?'

He wrestled his arm from the officers' grips. His jaw was clenched, his hair flopping loosely over his face and his tie and shirt rumpled in the struggle.

'Where's my li'l girl?' he sobbed. 'Where is she?' He slumped into the hands of the officers, each one supporting him.

'Oliver, stop this right now,' said Liv. 'You getting into trouble won't do us any good. Pull yourself together. How would Isla be if she saw her father like this? Now come on. It's not over yet. We'll get that bitch! Officer, could they have alighted elsewhere?'

'The nearest station is Carluke. About an hour southeast of Glasgow,' said the officer.

Oliver straightened up and stood, using his fingers to comb back his ruffled hair. He was taken aback by Liv's comments, as he had never heard her speak about Jess in such a way. There was a real courage and determination to her voice, he thought. It refuelled his strength of purpose.

Remaining quiet for a moment, he stood there with his eyes closed breathing in the cool Scottish air as the sounds faded around him.

Some miles away, a big yellow bus was departing Carluke Bus Depot bound for Glasgow. In the rear sat Jess, her arm wrapped around Isla. This time she stared out the window and actually noticed the contours of the outside world a little more intently. With the bus heading north, venturing deeper into the land of the Scots, the fading country lights of Carluke eventually disappeared into obscurity. Jess's racing thoughts calmed and she dreamt of Scotland's rugged landscapes, the remote wilderness and its potential to veil Isla and her from discovery. *No-one will find us*, she thought. *At last we will be safe*. She pulled Isla closer to herself, stroking her curls. 'Mummy will make it better, I will be better,' she muttered to herself. Slowly, her eyes slid closed too. As she drifted off to sleep, her restless limbs betrayed her unspoken thoughts that whilst she might be able to escape Oliver, she might never be able to escape herself.

Chapter 11
Chelsea Morning

Heading back to the police station, Oliver and Liv were silent. From the car window, Oliver looked out at the lonely, cobbled streets peppered with glowing street lanterns and lined with trees swaying in the breeze. At Tolbooth, the large central clocktower chimed 12, reminding him another day had been lost with Isla escaping his grasp again.

Upon arrival at headquarters, Oliver and Liv waited near the long wooden bench separating the public from the law enforcers. Oliver noticed some etchings scratched into its surface, 'Pigs suck', 'Go to Hell Fuckers' and 'Bend over pricks'.

The inner station doors were flung open and the police sergeant bowled through, file in hand. Oliver was still gazing down, gutted.

'Interesting artwork, Sergeant?' he mumbled under his breath, indicating the graffiti.

Liv placed her arm around him, giving him a small nudge. It brought him back to the moment and he shook his head. Slowly, he looked up, catching the eye of the police sergeant. 'Is there anything more you need from us, Sergeant?'

'No, but just one thing,' said the sergeant, forearms splayed on the desk as he peered at them over the night lamp. 'Before you go, Mr Johnson, do you have any concerns for the safety of Isla?'

'Absolutely not. Jess would never harm Isla. Never!' said Oliver.

'*Uh-huh*,' he said, shoring up his thoughts.

'What do you mean, uh-huh?' said Oliver, shuffling his feet. 'Oh, I see where this is going…'

Without hesitation, the sergeant butted in, 'Look, I apologise, Mr

Johnson. But I am stating the facts as I see them before me. If there is no reasonable cause for concern, there is not much we can do until such time as it becomes blatantly clear that your wife has no intention of returning to you and that she has in fact abducted Isla. So, in the meantime, we will put out the word, and if or when your wife is found, she will be brought in for questioning as to her conduct and intentions.'

'She could be anywhere by then,' said Oliver.

'Well, all I have at this stage is your account of the events, yours and your sister's. Forgive me for saying this, but there's always two sides to a story.'

Olivia peered at him and had to bite her tongue. She tightened her grip on Oliver.

'We will be in touch if anything crops up in the meantime. We've arranged lodgings for you across the road at the local inn with the owner, Will. He's a retired member of the force. Sleep well. You both need your rest.'

Checking into their room, they fell into their beds, feet aching, bodies numb from the cold and heads pounding as a result of the day's tiring escapades.

At the other end of town, Jess and Isla were standing outside an old timber building. A sign with a three-dimensional gold crown emblem announced in Roman script 'Crowcaddies Inn.'

Jess took a moment to catch her breath. The warmth of her breath shaped a frosty plume in the night air. She rubbed one of the windows and gazed into the inn. The noise unsteadied her. There was the smell of stale beer in the air along with wafts of cigarette smoke and the stench of stale urine.

Isla looked up at her mother, shaking with cold. Her skin was paler than the snowflakes that formed epaulets on her tiny shoulders.

'C'mon Isla, let's get you warm,' Jess said, taking her by the hand.

Entering the main bar area, they observed what seemed to be a private party taking place. The room was filled with boozy men, smoking and chatting. Just then, the barman, a stocky man in his 50s with a short neck, spotted them. He threw down his bar towel, screwed up his crooked nose and with wide bloodshot eyes, lunged over the bar at them. They screamed.

'Oi! You shouldn't be in here, lassies!' he growled in a thick Scottish accent. 'Git lost!'

Jess and Isla stood rigidly, too scared to move.

'I said, you shouldn't be here. Git! Out!'

Jess stepped forward an inch, placing Isla behind her. 'I'm looking for Gwendolyn,' she said, clearing her throat.

The barman paused, looking Jess up and down. By now, the surrounding noise had subdued a little and all eyes were focussed on the two tourists.

'Back entrance!' he roared. 'Are you deaf, woman, or what? Use the back entrance and up the stairs! And for the third time, git out!'

They picked up their cases and scurried to the rear of the inn, driven out by the rollicking laughter of beer-swilling patrons.

They reached the bottom of the wooden staircase and Jess looked in her handbag, gazing sadly at the leftover money in her envelope. How are we going to make ends meet? she worried. Room two was at the top of the staircase. There was a piece of paper pinned to the door with 'Jess' scribbled on it and a brief note on the other side:

Jess, all good luv, door open. Went to bed early. Make yourself at home. Any friend of Gerry's is a friend of mine. There's a note on the bed from Gerry. See you in the morn. Gwendolyn x P.S milk's in the fridge down the end of the corridor if you fancy a tea or warm drink.

They entered the room, shutting out the thumping music from downstairs. Isla collapsed on a well-worn leather chair. She sat there staring at her odd socks. One foot was wearing solid pink and the other pink-and-white stripes. She ran her finger along the line of the stripes, as she wondered if Larry might still be chewing the other one.

'Mummy. It smells bad in here,' she said, peering up at her mother.

'I know, sweetheart. It's just for one night.'

'Are we in Glasgow?'

'Yes, we are,' sighed Jess.

'Good. I'm glad,' exclaimed Isla.

'Why's that?'

'Because Daddy will be here tomorrow. I just know it,' she said, still inspecting her odd socks.

Jess flinched, fighting back tears. In this small stench-ridden room in the middle of Glasgow, it occurred to her that, at last, she could catch her breath for a time. She was exhausted. Her numbness was not due to the cold but rather to an emotional void. She realised, despite her actions of the last few days, that she still felt nothing. It frightened her more than anything. The bedside lamp caught her reflection in the icy window. Slowly, she studied the image from top to tail, failing to recognise herself. *Who is that person? Is it me, is it really me?* she thought. Her eerie calmness unsettled Isla, who noticed tears trickling down her mother's still face.

'Why are you crying Mummy?'

'Uhm… I'm not… I… I just miss… your Daddy,' she lied.

Isla watched her for a little longer. She remained motionless. Nailed to the floor. Despite Isla's exhaustion, she rushed to her mother's side, wrapping her small arms around her waist. 'It'll be alright Mummy, it will.'

As they caught each other's eyes, Jess saw her reflection shatter and she sobbed uncontrollably.

Later, Jess tucked Isla into bed and kissed her forehead.

On her own bed, partially covered by a pillow, was the promised envelope. Inside, the handwritten note read:

Dear Jessica, I took down this note from your sister. Hope you can read my terrible writing. Trust the room is fine for you and your little one. See you in the morn. Gwendolyn.

Dear sis, hope the trip was fine. Here's the plan. Early next morning you will take the bus to the far north of Scotland. It's so wild yet beautiful and raw. They now have these window-roof buses. When you get to Longhope, take the post boat to the Orkney Islands, to a port named Stromness. There's a map at Longhope, you'll see. I've arranged for you to stay in a house there. The name of the landlady is Morag. Previous tenants left in the hurricane of '53. They'd had enough. Take care and God bless the both of you. I'll be in contact. Much love.

Three days later, Liv and Oliver found themselves back in London on the underground and exiting Sloane Square Station, Chelsea. Time spent in Glasgow had been usefully spent clearing their heads a little. It was mid-morning and Olivia was intent on changing the mood with a little levity. *Good medicine for Ollie*, she thought.

The flower merchants stood behind multi-coloured carts, some singing, others simply smiling, high on the array of floral perfumes.

'Oh, this is just like *Pygmalion*, Ollie! I wonder will we catch a glimpse of Eliza Doolittle or Professor Higgins?' she laughed.

'Oh stop it, you old drama queen. I have more important things on the agenda, like finding Gerry's place!' said Oliver.

'How about buying your sis a bunch of yellow roses?' she said.

'How about this? No. However, I will shout you a hot chocolate. It's bloody freezing.'

They ventured down a small side street lined with a palette of multi-coloured cottages, bejewelled with baskets of red geraniums hanging on wrought-iron fences.

'How about this one, Ollie? 'Bean and Gone'! It has an irony about it, love,' said Liv, mischievously attempting to raise Oliver's mood.

'As good as any, I guess. Besides, I'm freezing off my you-know-whats, sis.'

'Way too much information, brother dear!' she smiled.

The café had an air of familiarity about it, reminding Oliver of Dom's Deli back home. The same tables and chairs and flower baskets. The flashback triggered him. He stared motionless for a time, remembering the laughs he had shared with his little girl sitting in the front window, watching the world pass by. As a waiter walked past, Liv tugged on his apron.

'Sorry, I know, a bit forward, but I'm desperate!' The waiter gave Liv a contemptuous gaze. 'Well, don't look at me like that, all judgemental like. I meant it in a good way. I'm frozen to the bone. I'll have a double hot chocolate, *if you do those*, and he'll have… what will you have, Oliver? Hello? Hello Oliver, anyone home?' Liv waved her hand in front of his eyes.

'Oh, yes. Good! Yes,' said Oliver, from a faraway place.

'No, you duffer, what do you want to drink? Hot chocolate?'

'Yes, one of those too, thank you. With marshmallows, don't forget the marshmallows!'

'Good. Settled sir.'

Liv grinned. 'Two hot chocolates, marshmallows all round and one of those homemade cookies too… make it two.'

With raised eyebrows, the waiter made a quick exit.

'Oh my God, you are such a flirt, Olivia Johnson!'

'No touching, just looking, little brother. Well, a little touching, I did tug on his apron,' she laughed.

For a moment, Oliver was transported back to their childhood, sitting at the kitchen bench drinking chocolate milkshakes made by their mother, Nora.

'Mine's got two scoops of ice-cream. Yours only has one,' Liv teased.

'Mummy, I've only got one. She's got two!' exclaimed Oliver.

'Alright, alright, wouldn't want my little hero missing out on anything,' said his mother. 'And remember Ollie, saying *please* goes a long way!'

'Pleeeezzzze, Mummy!' said Oliver, laughing with his sister. 'Pleeeze!'

'Okay, I heard you! That's my boy.' She spooned some vanilla ice-cream into Oliver's shake.

Nora wiped her hands on her red checked apron. She bent over the kitchen bench, her face level with Oliver's.

'You know Ollie, Mummy loves you very much. And your sister. But one day you are going to grow up into a man. You might have kids of your own even. And I just know that whatever you want in life will be yours, God willing. You're a special little man, Oliver Johnson, and with the power of the holy spirit in you, you *will* be able to do anything, be anyone. You will achieve greatness, my boy. I can feel it in my bones. You will make Dad and me proud. You too, Liv!'

'Yeah Ollie, you *can* do anything… except beat me in a race,' laughed Liv.

———

At Crowcaddies, Isla was still fast asleep. It was early morning. Jess quietly put on her coat and got the two suitcases ready, looking around to make sure that she did not leave anything behind. A while later, she gently shook Isla to wake her up.

'C'mon Isla. Rise and shine. Mummy has got your woollies out, it's cold outside. We have to get a move on to catch that bus.'

Isla rubbed her eyes, still snug curled up under the warm blankets.

'Where are we going, Mummy?'

'I'll tell you all about it on the bus. Let's just say it's another adventure, love.'

Isla immediately thought of her father. After all, he was meeting them here today, wasn't he? *Why are we getting a bus?* she thought. *How will Daddy know where we are?*

'Mummy?'

'Yes.'

'Isn't Daddy coming today? If we go on a bus you had better leave him a note.'

Jess wondered whether this was the time to sit down with Isla and explain things. She was torn and didn't know where to start. From outside, the town clock chimed 10.00 a.m. *No time now,* she thought. *I need the right moment. Later. Yes, later.*

'Quick, grab your case, we will be late for the 10.20 bus. I've left a note for Daddy. He'll catch up soon,' she said, trying not to alarm Isla.

Soon they arrived at the shelter and boarded the glass-roofed bus headed for Thurso via Inverness.

'I am buzzing, Ollie, that hot choccie really hit the spot!' said Liv.

'Yes, well onwards we go,' said Oliver, reaching into his jacket pocket and pulling out a note.

'Here it is, 48 Ansdell Street, Royal Borough of Kensington and Chelsea. Lucky I keep a good record.'

'And what has Ansdell Street got to do with anything, dear?'

'That would be my dear sister-in-law's address,' said Oliver sarcastically.

'Of course… but I thought you liked Gerry?'

'I do… or at least I did, until she got involved with child abduction!'

They walked briskly along the tree-lined streets, passing one Regency home after another. The morning air was accompanied by a howling icy breeze which unhappily penetrated their woollen coats and mittens.

'Oh God, the things I do for you, little brother.' Liv's words were muffled by her scarf blowing up and covering her mouth.

'Now that's an improvement, sis. Keep it there… it works wonders for you!'

'Very funny Ollie! You are so amusing! Who writes your scripts. Oh no-one, that's right, you're a musician!' She laughed.

As they turned the corner, evading the windy narrow corridor of King Street, they entered Gerry's street and arrived at number 48. Oliver had never been to her home before. He had heard a lot about it, including its history and famous occupants. There was a part of him that did not want to knock on the door for fear that he would be disappointed again. I can't be like that, I must man up and be positive, he thought. I've come too far to be a wimp. My Isla is going to be behind that door and that's all that really matters.

He trudged up the front stairs, leaving Liv behind him rubbing her hands together, partly in anticipation and partly because she was freezing cold.

He knocked on the front door. And then again. He soon heard footsteps approach the entrance and then the door creaked open.

'Yes?' croaked an elderly gentleman. 'Who are you? What do you want?'

'Is Gerry or Brian McIntosh home, sir?'

'Gerry or Brian McIntosh? Oh… they be gone long ago. Mortgagee sale, my friend. Loved a card game, that Brian, or so I heard. My wife and me got the home for a steal. Poor woman, that Gerry, how he left her with those two screamin' kids. Nothing, she had. Nothing, but the clothes on her back. And he didn't care, that bastard. Not on your oath!' he said, shaking his head.

Olivia piped up, 'Well that's all very fascinating, sir, but I'm freezing my derriere out here and…'

'And,' said Oliver, cutting his sister short, 'we would just like to know if you might have a forwarding address for them. I'm her brother-in-law, Oliver, Oliver Johnson.'

'I'm a bit of a hoarder, son, and I think I might have pinned her address years ago to the corkboard in my front den. I remember her telling me that she got some place through the Salvos. I'm sure she gave me her forwarding address for mail. That was… Jesus… must be eight year ago. A lot of stuff pinned to the board, y'know. Never throw away nothing. You never know, my dad used to say. Keep things for a rainy day. Useful them corkboards in times when you don't know where to stick a piece of paper…'

'I know where you can stick a piece of paper,' said Liv impatiently.

'Yes, yes, Liv does… she does, um, papier-mâché at home. She makes candle covers, wine bottle holders …' Oliver grinned sheepishly.

Liv interrupted her brother, 'I do not. I detest …'

Oliver turned around to face her, mouthing Shut up! then pivoted back to the gentleman. 'That would be wonderful. If you have her address, it would be a huge help, as she must have given us the wrong address in error. She's a bit absent-minded that one at times.' He laughed, whilst Liv stood behind him mimicking his chuckles and his posture, hands on hips and bending backwards.

For his part, Oliver mimicked giving Liv an elbow to the ribs. Clenching his jaw as the front door closed, he sighed, 'Jesus, see what you've done?'

Before Liv could answer, the door reopened and the man was holding a piece of paper in his hand.

'You see, every room has a corkboard. The first room has corkboards with the letter 'A', so I pin addresses on those boards. And 'G' for Gerry, ladies come first, as you know. That is on the seventh board in alphabetical order. It's a tried-and-true process and it's organised,' he said, handing the paper to Oliver.

'It certainly is a process,' snarled Liv.

'Well thank you sir. I do appreciate it,' said Oliver.

He thanked him, the man closed the door and Oliver looked down at a piece of torn paper in his gloves and read, 'Mrs Gerry McIntosh, 26 Cable Street, Whitechapel.'

Heading down the stairs and waving the address in his hand, he smiled cheekily at his sister.

'Papier-mâché, bah humbug!' she exclaimed.

The bus wound along the one-way road and Jess passed Isla a piece of apple. They hadn't eaten since leaving Glasgow and Isla's tummy was rumbling. Jess peered out the window where Isla was seated and observed a breathtaking emptiness, desolate moorlands, a wild yet fragile countryside confined by rugged, brooding mountains spilling onto forgotten beaches. Flashes of white seabirds circled the grey murkiness and pierced the breeze with shrill cries. Munching on her last slice of apple, Isla thought they looked hungry .

When the bus arrived at Thurso's small port, the gateway to the Orkney Islands, it was getting dark, the winter sun hidden behind a leaden sky.

They collected their luggage and waited in a tiny shelter next to the pier. Gusts of wind hurled along the pier, sneaking through the wooden crevices of their refuge. Mother and daughter huddled together, savouring the warmth.

'What are we waiting here for Mummy?' Isla murmured.

'The ferry, Isla. It will be here soon. Aunty Gerry arranged it for Mummy. It's taking us to those islands over there.' Jess pointed at the horizon.

Isla stared for some time, squinting, the oncoming breeze making it difficult for her to discern. Slowly lifting her head, she gazed at her mother, 'But how will Daddy find us, Mummy?'

Isla's words sat profoundly with Jess. Her thoughts raced by one after another, backing her into a corner. What am I doing, Jess thought, a tinge of guilt shadowing her escape plan. She shook her head to rid herself of the feelings of culpability and caught her breath. It was time.

'What's wrong, Mummy? Why do you look so sad? Why are you crying?' Isla held onto her mother tightly, nuzzling into her and peering up at her.

Jess was silent. She was about to say something from which there was no turning back. She knew it was wrong, but her options were limited. *I must do what's best*, she thought. *It will be better in the long run. If I were not doing this, Isla would not have a mother, she would be dead, she thought over and over, trying to justify her actions. Better she has me.*

Gathering her courage and mustering every bit of strength from within, Jess looked closely at her little girl. 'Mummy's upset, Isla... You see, when Mummy went to leave a note for Daddy in Glasgow, the hotel lady, Gwendolyn, gave Mummy a note instead.'

Jess took another deep breath, trying to recall exactly how she had played out this moment in her head so many times already.

'And what did it say, Mummy?' Isla hesitated, looking to her mother and hoping for some good news.

Jess locked eyes with her, softly rubbing her back, gathering her closely. She gently kissed her on the forehead. Crouching down, she whispered softly in Isla's ear, the sound landing on a passing breeze, causing it to resonate eerily, 'He's dead, Isla… your father's dead.'

Chapter 12
Night in the City

The five-hour ferry trip to Stromness was a silent voyage, Isla in shock after discovering her father's demise. Big blue-grey waves crashed against the boat, making it rock back and forth. Huddled into her mother, she gazed starboard whilst Jess stared in the opposite direction, still trying to convince herself that she had acted in Isla's best interests.

The boat's stewardess swayed down the aisle, offering snacks and refreshments. Isla looked at her cherry-striped apron and orange sailor's hat, the colours melting into their surrounding grey. Her hunger subsided and despite her efforts to claim some warmth from her mother, coldness seeped into her bones.

How is he dead? she thought. *Where was he when he died? Why didn't he call Mummy or me? I will never see him again, ever!* Colourful moving images of her father rolled on in her mind, as if she were watching a film. His cheesy grin, the way he picked her up and swung her about, the games they played with Larry, the tea-parties and the wonderful times sitting on that rickety piano stool, watching her dad compose music and listening to him play. She used to close her eyes, listen to the music and feel like she was floating away, dancing with quavers, swinging from treble clefs and skipping along minims. A gentle tap on her knee by her dad would calm her and he would place her tiny hands on the preferred chord and encourage her to play. The memory evoked a smile, but only momentarily, as the realisation that she would not see her father again started to sink in.

She looked at her mother, thinking that she was not paying much attention to her. *Perhaps she is hurting too*, she thought. *Perhaps she just doesn't know what to say to me.*

Jess felt like she was free-falling. She only hoped for a soft landing, but there were no guarantees.

Escaping the boisterous sea and all its wild fury, the ferry turned into the safe harbour of Stromness. Isla peered out the window and could hardly see the outlines of the town.

'Here we are Isla. Stromness.'

'It's hard to see.'

'In the morning we'll explore it. I'm told there's a large Viking longboat on display in the harbour and a museum with warrior statues.'

Isla's eyes lit up. I hope those statues don't wake up Mummy!'

Just then, the boat came to an abrupt stop at an ancient stone pier, bouncing off rubber buoys, the water lapping at its sides. The air was cold, although the cove was protected from the wind. A voice boomed over the speaker system, 'Stromness, all passengers please disembark and check ye have all y'ur belongin's with ye.'

Startled by the announcement, Jess sat up sharply. In turn, Isla was alarmed by her mother's reaction. 'It's okay Mummy. We're here.'

'Oh, good, good, Isla. Mummy is so tired. You must be too. We can talk more tomorrow, but I just want to find our lodgings and go to bed. It's been a big day for both of us.'

She almost forgot that she had lied to Isla about her father's death, neglecting to take into account the impact the dishonest news would have upon her. She had broached the subject of Oliver's 'death' in such a matter-of-fact way. Pausing for a moment, she grabbed hold of Isla's small icy hand and checked in on her little girl. Her eyes were puffy and her face pallid. Dried tear tracks marked her pale skin, and her bottom lip was swollen. She was cloaked in a deep sadness and Jess was stuck for words.

'Isla, listen darling, Mummy's here. I'm not going anywhere. Alright? Alright?'

Isla gazed up at her mother and without managing a smile, softly replied, 'Alright.'

Carrying their luggage, they navigated the gangplank to reach land. To the left of a stone shelter under a dull street lamp, a short distance away, stood a figure staring at them. Isla could barely make it out, but she thought it was a woman.

She was tall and slightly built, although her true stature was masked by an impressive black shagpile coat. Her head was covered by a large dark hat with jutting edges, casting an impressive shadow over her long face. The woman's chin appeared to touch her chest, giving the appearance of a vanishing neck. Every so often, Isla observed a small burning orange light moving towards the woman's lips, followed by a puff of smoke that engulfed her. As she approached, Isla dropped her case and grabbed her mother around the waist, holding onto her tightly.

'Jessica Johnson. That be you?' the woman said, butting out her cigarette.

Jess looked at her for a second, trying to hold back the temptation to pick up Isla and run.

'Ah yes, that's right. That's me. Jessica, Jess. Yes.'

'I see, well I'm in the right spot then. Gerry told me you'd be in this boat. Lucky to make it in weather like this. Many have perished before in lesser storms, lass. Name is Morag. I'll be taking you to your lodgings.'

'Oh good. That's so good,' said Jess, 'And this is Isla.'

'I know, Jessica. Let's step to it. Bloody cold out here. Oh, and by the way, I'm your landlady.'

'Whitechapel! This is certainly not the Toorak I'm used to. The unblessed places you drag me to, darling. If I break one of my heels here, you'll have to carry me home. I'm not walking barefoot on unsanctified ground!'

'Oh for God's sake Liv, will you just zip that precious gob of yours for once. Have you forgotten why we're here? Your niece, my daughter. Let's not forget that!'

She gazed silently at her brother. His anxieties had escaped her temporarily. She felt a pang at allowing her own feelings of discomfort overshadow his much bigger worries.

Linking her arm with his, she began to match his pace. 'Yes, you are right little brother and I do love you, even if Whitechapel is not the fashion capital of London.'

Oliver greeted her apology with a grin, shaking his head, 'You are impossible, you know!' he laughed. 'But I do love you!'

Arriving at Cable Street, they saw a bleak streetscape bereft of foliage and lined with commission cottages. Regardless of the cold, there were some children kicking an old leather soccer ball on the street. Most wore threadbare clothing, some sporting old scarves, their hands partially covered with fingerless woollen mittens. It appeared that their shoes had seen better days as well. They were cheery though, laughing and calling out to one another for the ball with obvious comradery. Their sense of unity, kinship and playfulness warmed Oliver's soul and he revelled in the moment, remembering what it was like to feel.

They were soon facing number 26 on a worn, grainy, timber, commission flat door. The '6' was hanging upside down on its nail, making it look like a '9'. Before Oliver could knock on the door, it suddenly opened, and Bob fell backwards in surprise.

Composing himself, he said, 'Oh, I'm sorry, I didn't quite expect anyone there! Can I help you? You're not Child Services or anything, are you? These bloody neighbours always reporting us for no reason. Kids are a bit noisy, granted, and rough, but kids are kids. Anyhow, if you are Child Services you should know that...'

Oliver interrupted him politely, 'No sir. You have nothing to worry about on that front. We're looking for a Gerry McIntosh. Is she here?'

'Not a McIntosh anymore. Wears her maiden name. We're not legal yet. No time. No money.'

At that moment, two hobbit-like children appeared at the door with brooding eyes, one entering from under Bob's legs, the other pushing in from the side.

'I'm Gertie, and this is Billy, who are you?'

'Now children, back inside, back inside, please!' said Bob, tangling himself up in Billy's and Gertie's arms and legs. 'Will you git! Git, I said.' Bob gave Billy a soft kick in the rear.

'Damn kids, always nosey. They mean no harm.'

Oliver smiled, sensing Bob's embarrassment.

'Now, sorry, what did you want? What are you callin' for?'

'I'm wanting to see Gerry McIntosh please, I mean Gerry, if she lives here.'

At that moment, someone yelled from the end of the corridor, 'Who's at the door love?'

'Some people to see you, Gerry. Dressed all proper and like.' Bob winked at the visitors. 'Come here love, they can't wait all day!'

Oliver could not make out Gerry with Bob standing in the door frame until he stepped back and Gerry moved in front of him. She looked up and saw Oliver staring her in the face.

'Oh my Lord, it's Oliver! Oh, and Olivia!' she cried.

'Who?' said Bob.

'Oliver and Olivia. Oh, never mind Bob. Get back inside and tend to those kids. I don't need another dose of the authorities.'

Bob gave Oliver and Liv a wave before vanishing behind a wall of muffled noise.

'That be my husband, second one, Bob.'

'I gathered,' said Oliver, 'nice to see you Gerry.'

'Yes, *lovely*,' quipped Liv.

'I suppose you're wondering what Liv and I are doing here?' said Oliver, suspecting she knew all along.

'Yes, well it did cross my mind… apart from the fact it's lovely and all to see you. Where's Jess, and Isla?'

'I didn't mention them. Don't you know?' Oliver asked.

Gerry felt uneasy, her thoughts rushing, 'No, why would I? Last I heard of her was over a week ago on the phone from Australia.'

'Oh, I see. So you don't know that she flew here last week with Isla,' said Oliver.

'No, no… why would I? I mean, I'm in shock Oliver. Why wouldn't she call me? Has she lost her senses? Who have you told? Have you been to the police?'

'Yes. It's a long story, but we ended up chasing her to Glasgow.'

'Oh, I see. Well as I said… I'm shocked. I just don't understand, Oliver. She *seemed* okay last time we spoke. She said she's been a bit on edge, with work and all. But flying here and taking Isla. Are you sure? I mean are you *really* sure?'

'I'm positive! And she's drained what little we had in our bank account too.'

He looked Gerry in the eye. Each time he locked gazes with her, he noticed that she shied away, as if she couldn't bear his pain.

'Well Oliver, I don't know what to say… I need to digest it and all. Do you know if she's still in Scotland?' Gerry leant against the door frame as if she needed the support.

'No I don't, but Scotland Yard is onto it now. Liv and I have given statements and they have a photo of her and Isla. Probably be on the news. We can only pray. You might like to pray too, Gerry,' he said unconvincingly.

'Well, if I hear anything, anything at all, I'll contact you… oh, how do I do that?'

'Here, we're staying at this hotel.' Oliver passed her a card. 'I'll keep in touch. What's your number?'

Whilst Oliver searched his coat for a pen, Liv unclipped her leopard handbag and rescued a pen and small card from within. 'Now what is your number, *darling* Gerry?' she asked.

'Give it to me Olivia, I always mess it up givin' out numbers. Need to see 'em written down and like,' said Gerry.

In writing the number down, Gerry intentionally left off the last numeral. 'There you go. Now please let me know if you hear word from her. Same goes for me. I can't believe it, Oliver. I'm so sorry. Best get back to those screamin' kids. Now you take care. The both of you.'

Oliver put his foot in the door to prevent her from closing it. 'By the way, I'll be giving the police your address so they can follow up their enquiries. I know you'd be only too happy to help... that right isn't it, Gerry?'

'Yes... of course.'

Oliver smiled, removing his foot and tipping his hat to her before the door slammed shut.

On the other side Gerry stood, holding both hands to her heart, scared to take a breath. *What have I done*, she thought, *what have I done!* Gertie ran up to her and wrapped herself around her mother's legs. 'Who was that man and lady, Mummy?'

'Oh no-one sweet. They lost something and they're trying to find it.'

'Will they find it Mummy do you think?'

'Sometimes, things need to stay lost love.'

Gerry bent down and held Gertie tightly. Her mind was cursed with guilt and by the choices she had made out of a sense of duty to her sister. This self-imposed secret was already wearing her down. She slid down the door and Gertie moved in closer to her mother, gently grabbing her face in her hands in an almost maternal way, 'Now Mummy, you can tell me, don't be scared,' she said, parroting familiar words.

'Mummy will be alright, Gertie. And as long as you never get lost on me, Mummy will be just fine, love.'

She hugged Gertie a little tighter.

———

That evening, Oliver and Liv fell into a local pub in London Central, the Forget-Me-Not Inn. It was a welcome diversion and somewhere to escape the chilly outdoor breeze. As they entered, their feet almost stuck to the red carpet with its remnants of split beer and raspberry lemonades. They made their way to a wooden side booth through a haze of tobacco smoke and took a seat. Raucous laughter and talking filled the space. Steins of stout lager sat one after the other on the bar, with counter meals of bangers and mash breaking the line-up. Although still low in spirits, the atmosphere thawed Oliver's weary bones and he managed to put on a brave face for his sister.

'It's Friday, sis. How about the usual Catholic fare, fish 'n chips with a pint of ale?'

'Exactly what I feel like Ollie. And then maybe another pint after that one! God knows I need it after this day!' She smiled.

'Your wish is my command,' said Oliver.

'Since when?' retorted Liv, giving her brother a firm wink.

Oliver disappeared into the misty enclave, parting a wave of drunken patrons to the service counter to order their meal and secure two pints of well-earned ale.

By the time their meal arrived, they were already halfway through their second pint.

'I love fish 'n chip Fridays, Liv. It brings back so many happy memories, sitting around the family table Friday nights with Mum and Dad. I've been doing a lot of thinking lately, about how lucky we were growing up. But I do regret how time stole our youth so quickly and how I failed to come to terms with bits 'n pieces.'

'Whatever do you mean, little brother? You, the successful musician and composer, father and husband… oops, well you know what I mean anyway.' Olivia delicately placed a fried chip into her mouth.

'Mmmm, yes, husband. That one worked out well!' said Oliver. 'Sometimes I wonder if I'd dealt with past hang-ups better, whether I would have been a better husband to Jess.'

'Oh what a load of bollocks! You were a caring, loving, devoted partner Oliver, and don't you forget that! That woman will rue the day she up and left you, taking your child. She's clearly not right in the head.'

Oliver nodded his head approvingly.

'You remember how I used to take Dad to the orchestral concerts at Melbourne Town Hall each month? I didn't much care for it, but I wanted him to like me more, sis. I always felt he didn't like me much… or maybe *like* is a bit harsh. Approve, is a better word. I mean, sure, Mum was always blowing my trumpet, but… '

'Well you were a mummy's boy! smiled Olivia, pointing her fork at her brother.

'Yes, I suppose, but I never thought I was good enough for Dad.'

'Oh come on Ollie. Dad loved you. He always told Mummy and me about your piano playing, he would brag about your grades, you being captain of the school orchestra, oh and when you got into Newman College. He was so proud, love. I could see it, Ollie, it was obvious to all that his heart was ablaze with pride.'

'But why didn't he ever tell me, Liv, why? He was a bag full of mixed emotions and I never felt comfortable talking to him about things that truly mattered to me. I never even told him I loved him. I felt I never had permission to do so.'

'Oh come on, stop getting so maudlin little brother. Eat your chips before they get cold.' She forked one of Oliver's chips from his plate.

'I'm not, and eat your own chips,' he said, trying to raise a grin. 'It's just that when Mum rang me that day to tell me Dad was dying, I couldn't bear it. I couldn't speak to him about it. I *couldn't* speak, full stop. I remember visiting him at home before he was placed in palliative care. I specifically asked Mum that morning to leave us alone so I could spill the beans, you know, tell him what I was thinking, get his approval, tell him how much I loved him, how much I'd miss him.'

'I never knew Ollie. Mummy never told me. *You* never told me,' said Olivia, leaning in and gently squeezing his hand.

'And you know sis, there we were, Dad on his old brown leather captain's chair, his legs covered by Mum's crochet rug, his face looking gaunt and pale with wax-like skin. I could tell he was having difficulty breathing. His chest was moving rapidly up and down and every so often, he'd gasp for a pocket of air. I looked at him for what seemed like an eternity and suddenly this huge lump in my throat formed and started to pound. Despite my head exploding sis, I couldn't cry. I wouldn't let him see me cry. I wouldn't, I couldn't. And then he slowly turned to me. He didn't move, only his eyes, and they peered into my soul. "What do you want to say, my son?" he murmured. I kept staring at him and his words continued to ring in my head: *What do you want to say, my son, what do you want to say.* And then I scanned his feeble body and arrived at his tortured face. There was a man who had fought in the war, raised a family, did what he could to the best of his ability. He wasn't bad. He was a good man. Perhaps unable to express his emotions, but a good decent man nonetheless. And despite my desire to tell him how I felt, I said nothing. And you know why sis? Because he knew. He knew! He knew I loved him. And he loved me. I didn't need to say a word.'

Oliver held his head, weeping uncontrollably, and Olivia moved around the booth to sit beside her brother and comfort him.

He caught his breath and looked at her. 'And what I fear most sis is that Isla will never have that opportunity of feeling loved by her father, of knowing what it's like growing up with a dad. My greatest fear is that I will never be like Dad… experiencing the love of a child.'

He rested his head on Olivia's shoulder. She softly rubbed his shoulder and wiped away his tears. 'Never fear little brother, hope springs eternal and in that hope lives the karma bus, always just around the corner and always looking for passengers, just like Aunty Elsie always says. We *will* find Isla, rest assured, brother of mine.'

Chapter 13
I Won't Cry

Isla was awoken the next morning by the horn of a cargo boat docking in the nearby harbour. Her feet touched the cold, well-worn boards of her bedroom floor and she approached the small wooden window, standing on tippy-toes to view the outside world. *This was not like home,* she thought. There were no trees or clear roadways. Here, there were stone houses spilling down to the water, like pebbles one on top of the other. Occasionally, the sounds of barking dogs broke the noise coming from the business of the pier. On the lefthand side, she saw a grand, grey steeple attached to a timber church. It was painted white with grey window frames. Some of the windows displayed intricate coloured lead lights that sparkled in the monochromatic landscape. She could not see all that many people about the street, however, there was a small crowd gathering at the marketplace on the waterfront, which appeared abundant with fresh produce.

I wonder where all the kids are, she thought. *Where is the school? I don't want to go! What if I don't like it? I wonder when we'll go home.* As she thought about her home, images of her father and Larry flooded her mind. Thinking about it gave her butterflies in her stomach.

She grabbed a woollen jumper, deciding to venture out of her room. There was a small bathroom at the end of a narrow hallway. Off the bathroom, a little wooden door went to the outhouse toilet. Her mother's room was at the other end of the hallway, opposite a modest kitchen and dining area. The kitchen cupboards were painted pale blue and under the dining bar stood three white wooden stools. Off to the side was a compact lounge area with a worn maroon two-seater lounge, a frayed club seat, a teak coffee table and a quaint fireplace with a wooden mantle. On the walls hung framed cross-stitching, the centrepiece above the fireplace being *The Last Supper*. To the side of the lounge suite proudly sat an upright piano. Seeing it made Isla beam. She carefully opened its lid and could not resist climbing up onto the piano stool. Purposefully, she placed her hands on the keys and started playing *Mary had a Little Lamb*, singing along to the tune.

Just then, Jess entered the room, tying her bathrobe.

'Trust you to find the piano, miss! Aunt Gerry organised it with Morag before we got here. I hope you like it, love?'

'Oh yes, Mummy, I love it. And guess what, guess what?' said Isla.

'What, love?' said Jess.

'Wait, wait here.' Isla rushed down the hallway. She grabbed her small school case and ran back to the lounge area.

'Look Mummy, look!'

She placed the case on the piano stool, opened it and retrieved a few pages of sheet music.

'I had this with me at school on that last day, you know when Daddy was there. I played it for him.' Isla handed the music to her mother.

'Oh I see,' said Jess, reading the music headed *Isla's Song*. 'That's amazing.'

'Yes Mummy, yes. I can finish writing it for Daddy and when I finish it I can play it to him in the stars,' she said, her expression becoming sad.

'That you can,' said Jess, returning the music to her, overcome with emotion. 'Well, let's get some brekky. Morag has left some food for us. Lots to organise today: school, Mummy's work. Lots to do!'

Momentarily distracted by her father's writing on the sheet music, Isla said, 'Oh yes Mummy, I'm not that hungry, but I'll try.'

Following breakfast, there was a loud knock on the door. Morag invited herself in. 'Anyone home? Hello, hello!'

Jess entered the hallway to discover Morag sliding her finger along the windowpane, checking for dust. 'They never do a good job, those cleaners. I have told the owners that many times. What would I know? I have no patience for people who fail to listen to you. Mrs Johnson? Are you getting my drift?'

Jess nodded, overcome by Morag's air of authority.

'You can stop nodding now, Mrs Johnson. Where's that wee bairn of yours? Hiding?' Morag brushed past Jess, calling out, 'Isla, Isla, where are you lassie?'

'Here I am, who is it?'

Morag entered the lounge, striking a commanding figure, the crown of her head not too far from the ceiling above. The first thing she spotted was Isla sitting upright at the piano, shuffling her sheet music.

'Oh, I see you found the home treasure. Now be careful of that one. It's my grand-aunt's and it's on special loan to you. Only because your Aunt Gerry asked so nicely,' said Morag.

Jess entered the room to find Morag seated next to Isla on the piano stool.

'I hope you like it, Mrs Johnson. It's a fine piece of furniture and a better learnin' tool. A wee birdie told me this little one has a bit of flair for music. And that her father is a fine musician.'

'Daddy died, miss,' said Isla, looking up Morag's nostrils, 'he's in the stars now.'

Morag raised her eyes at Jess and moved from the piano stool to approach her, making the sign of the cross. 'Well I'm very sorry to hear that miss. I'll say a prayer for him, a few Hail Marys. Your Aunt Gerry made no mention of it to me.'

'Yes, he was a musician. A very good one. He… ' Jess interrupted herself. 'It was a tragedy,' she said, motioning Morag to the kitchen with her eyes.

'Stay there Isla and practise, dear. Practice makes perfect! Practice, practice. I'll be back.'

Jess was waiting for Morag in the kitchen, wiping non-existent crumbs from the kitchen bench pretending to clear the bench.

'I'm sorry, but I don't want to talk about her father in front of her. She's been through enough. Do you understand?' Jess was attempting to give Morag the impression of a brave front.

Morag gained height on the other side of the counter, towering over Jess. She placed her large hands on the bench, spreading her fingers and leaning forward, piercing Jess with a glacial stare.

'Aye, *I do understand* Mrs Johnson. But you understand this. I will not be patronised by anyone. I know children. I know them and I teach them at the school. They're *my* children and I care deeply for the wee bairns. Most of them don't ask for the dishes served up to them. So it's my job to help them tolerate things, scrape their plates and prepare themselves for the next rubbish meal served up. Many have had their childhoods stolen from them, but I'm here always to remind them it's okay, that Morag is here to protect them and as you will discover for yourself, Mrs Johnson, Morag doesn't cop how do y'say… bullshit! So yes, Mrs Johnson, I had no idea about Mr Johnson. I'm sorry for your loss. Your little one must be enduring a hell no-one could imagine… being so far away from home, without her father, without family, loved ones and friends. I can *well understand* Mrs Johnson, that she's been through enough, and that she might be needing a friend, Mrs Johnson. You might like to think about that one. And whilst I think of it, as well as teaching at the local school, I teach some of the wee bairns piano outside of hours, some of them during class. I know you must be struggling a little for a penny, so until you get yourself some work, I'm happy to teach Isla for free. You can fix me up later if you like. Also, rent is due last Friday of the month, otherwise the owner will have my skin for garters. The church is down the road. Father

Patrick runs a good Sunday Mass and says prayers for those in need. God knows he's never short of a prayer! Call me anytime. I stuck my number to the fridge. Anything else, Mrs Johnson, as I best be going? Lots to do!'

Jess stood there, mouth gaping, wondering what had hit her. *There goes a force to be reckoned with*, she thought, watching Morag wave goodbye to Isla and leave their new abode.

Isla rushed to the lounge window, watching Morag depart. She saw her long, thin legs masterly descend the cobbled staircase. Her black faux fur coat brushed the stairs with each step. Her posture was upright and her crooked nose extended from her face like some atmospheric rudder. Isla thought she wasn't as scary as she'd thought at first. In fact, seated on the piano stool with her, she'd felt as if a giant eagle had placed its wing around her. Morag was a bit creepy to look at, but she sensed she was full of marshmallows inside.

As Morag reached the letterbox at the bottom of the staircase, she turned and looked up at the house. Isla waved at her. Morag raised her hand, giving Isla a brisk wave and a wry smile before marching stridently to the main street.

Jess came up behind her and gently rested her hands on her shoulders, and Isla turned to gaze up at her, saying, 'I think I like that lady, Mummy!'

Jess raised her eyebrows and nodded gently without saying a word.

Isla skipped from the window to go to her room, leaving Jess gazing out at the sheer cliffs on the other side of the inlet. She wondered what was ahead of them both, never imagining she would find herself in a place like this. In spite of her efforts to embrace little moments of joy, she still found it difficult to smile. Her low mood continued to plague her, with the voice in her head increasingly reminding her of the lie she had told Isla about Oliver, fuelling her with doubts as to her motives for leaving Melbourne. Time is my friend, she murmured to herself. I've only just arrived. I need to give it a chance. I can't go back in any event.

How could I ever tell Isla the truth about her father now? Chin up and get on with it, she urged herself, sitting down on the club chair facing the fireplace.

The wind howled outside, stirring up her emotions, and then her mother's haunting words rang in her head. *'You've made your bed, now lie in it.'* As she kept staring into the dead coals littering the fireplace, she whispered under her breath, 'Yes Mother, that I have.'

London Airport was overflowing with travellers when Oliver and Liv made their way to the international departure lounge. Oliver had made his final calls to Scotland Yard and London Police Headquarters for updates, telling them he was heading back to Melbourne and exchanging contact details. He could do no more. Despite police efforts, there was still no sign of Isla and Jess and all he could do now was to wait in hope. There was no use him remaining in England as the police had no leads because of their limited information. They still had to speak with Gerry, but they'd given him no specific time frame.

The journey home was long and tiring, made more tedious by Oliver's bouts of airsickness. The two of them limped to a nearby taxi at Essendon Airport, with Oliver being dropped off at home first. Before alighting from the vehicle, Liv gave him a tight hug, whispering into his ear, 'We will find Isla, try not to worry, I'm sure the police will be in contact soon. Hang onto that courage of yours, little brother.' She kissed him goodbye.

Oliver collected his luggage, closed the taxi door and stood there watching Liv disappear down the tree-lined street.

As he entered the home, he was struck by the eerie silence, save for the regular tick of the grandfather clock. He dropped his bags and instinctively walked into Isla's bedroom, gazing at the drawings stuck to the walls, her golden teddy and golliwog slouching on the pillows and her pink tea party set scattered around her small white desk. These bits and pieces of Isla reminded Oliver of happy times and shared moments. He could hear her giggles, see her cheeky smile and sense her presence. However, as he caught a glimpse of himself in Isla's gilded mirror, her absence struck him. For the first time, he was alone.

He reached under her pillow and removed her spotted pink pyjama top, slowly raising it to his nose, picking up Isla's sweet scent. Images of her flitted through his mind and his eyes welled up. He carried her top down to the drawing room, hugging it against his face. Reaching the piano, he discarded the garment, where it ended up splayed across the piano lid. In the hush of the moment, Oliver stood there consumed by the stillness. The silence possessed him. He could take it no longer. He let out an almighty primeval scream, breaking the unwanted calm. Impulsively, he swiped the candelabra on the piano lid to the floor, randomly pulled books from the shelves, threw cushions about the room and smashed his and Jess's wedding photo. When his energy was spent, he collapsed in a pool of dense misery, pining for his previous family life, yearning to have his li'l one back in his arms. His heart was aching and he was drowning. 'Save me, save me,' he muttered, before curling into a foetal pose on the threadbare rug, clutching onto Isla's top again and crying himself to sleep.

It felt as if he had only been asleep for a short time before he was awoken by a tapping on the bay window and old familiar sound.

'Oliver, Oliver, are you in there dear?' screeched an elderly woman, hand over her forehead, nose pressed against the glass, peering into the drawing room.

Oliver used the piano to climb to his feet and went to open the front door.

'Aunty Elsie, what a surprise!' he exclaimed, wiping the remnants of sleep from his eyes.

'Well dear, Liv said I might find you at home mulling about. Little did I know you would be still sleeping and in your clothes. It's 12 noon dear. Sunday Mass done and dusted. I got up early, baked a fresh batch of scones… your favourite love, and here I am, with the sun on my back and a smile on my dial.'

Elsie thrust the basket of goodies into Oliver's unsuspecting hands. 'Oh love, you'll find the cream and jam in there too, don't mind the small flask, that's for Aunty Elsie,' she said, winking at him. 'Now follow me to the kitchen, I'll find us some plates and cutlery and us two will have a good natter.'

Oliver dragged his feet behind her, scratching his head. Elsie buzzed about the kitchen and before long, the table was adorned with scones, accompanying condiments, a fresh pot of tea and a vase brimming with freshly picked red geraniums from her garden.

'Just what I needed Aunty,' said Oliver, raising his eyebrows.

'Well, Liv told me all about it, so best not go back down a well-worn track,' she said, gently rubbing his hand. 'I don't know how you feel exactly, but I do sort of, if you get my drift. I mean, you know how Uncle Charlie left me for the cheap barmaid sheila years ago? I was made destitute because of that harlot. But I said to myself, I said Elsie, chin up, be proud, walk like there's a rod in ya back, stand tall Elsie, stand tall. Don't let the gossipers get to you, because the good Lord always has the karma bus parked around the corner ready for those who do bad things and that bus, love, it's *always* looking for passengers. My Charlie got a seat on that bus, two years after he left me. Yes, prostate cancer, couldn't get it up after the operation. The slut left him and then he died. Nasty way to end up. I'd say Charlie got a first-class ticket on that bus love.' Elsie took a swig from her hip flask and then poured some brandy into her teacup.

'So don't let it get you down, my boy. Stand tall and be patient. The good Lord will take care of you, Oliver Johnson, like He does all of us Johnsons.'

Elsie leant in to Oliver. He could smell the alcohol on her breath. As she continued to rub his hand, she gazed over her tortoiseshell-rimmed glasses, 'We Johnsons have the gift, love. I'm telling you love, Jess will soon have a seat on that bus, just like Charlie, so you needn't worry no more. Now eat your scones up, you need some fattening up. I'll have to drop around more often at this rate.' Elsie stuffed a jam and cream scone into her mouth.

Oliver smiled at his aunt, wondering whether her early morning arrival and sage advice was his karma.

After Elsie tottered off, Oliver penned a letter to Gerry, hoping to appeal to her good conscience. Upon completing the task, he sealed the envelope, addressed it to her and marked the sender 'O. Johnson'.

The next morning, Jess stirred Isla from her slumber.

'Quick, Isla, brekky, then Mummy is taking you down to school. There's papers to fill out and then you'll be off to class.'

Isla was not at all thrilled by the idea. She had only just arrived and things were moving too fast for her. Her world had been turned upside down. Her father was dead. She had lost Larry, her school friends and family. She felt dizzy, had no appetite and her tummy was sore.

'Are you alright, Isla? You don't look good. Should Mummy take you to the doctor's? Here, have some of this vitamin medicine, it'll make you feel better. Starting a new school is always a bit scary, love. You'll be okay, you'll see. Morag will keep an eye out for you.'

'I'll be okay Mummy. The medicine will help.'

They entered Stromness Primary School hand in hand. It was a stone building with a hard, cold exterior. There was a stone arch at the front with an iron sign hanging from a chain depicting the name. As they passed under the arch, Isla stood motionless looking up at the school's insignia. She tried to make out the features of the emblem.

Jess pulled on her little hand, 'C'mon Isla, we best not be late on the first day.'

Isla remembered that these were the very words mouthed so recently by her father when she had started school at Camberwell Primary School.

A gust of icy wind blew her red beret off her head. Jess leant down and scooped it up, repositioning it for her. She touched her nose, kissed her cheek then held her tight.

As she released her, she said, 'You know Mummy loves you the whole world, Isla!'

'I know Mummy, I know. And you know what else? You don't need to worry about me going to this new school. I promise I won't cry.'

Chapter 14
Just Like This Train
Monday 5 November 1961

Jess arrived home from the local medical centre, tired after a hard day's work. There were two nurses and three part-time nurse aides on the payroll, but their work schedules kept them all run off their feet. It was a local medical hot-spot for the Stromness inhabitants as well as for nearby island neighbours. The island had a small population and the centre catered to everything from cuts and bruises to orthopaedic interventions and minor surgeries. Serious cases were transferred to Glasgow.

Dr Lewis was the chief medical officer, assisted every so often by travelling doctors from the mainland. Jess worked a six-day week and had done since arriving at Stromness some years before.

She had kept her history very private. Always polite to patients and staff and greeting patients with a warm smile, she wore a veneer to hide her grief. However, the weight of her lie to Isla about her father was beginning to wear her down and her need to self-medicate with alcohol was posing problems for her. To guard against exposure, she kept concealed in her uniform pocket the requisite packet of mints to camouflage the scent of spirit.

Over time, Dr Lewis noticed a change in Jess's behaviour, her late arrivals to work becoming more common. She used lame excuses that rarely impressed her employer. Jess thought one day she might be fired and despite promises to herself to reduce her alcohol intake, she usually failed miserably, waking up the next morning in the club chair in front of extinguished embers, feeling worse for wear.

Kicking off her shoes and rubbing her feet, she went to the kitchen and reached for a tumbler in the drying tray overladen with dishes. Two ice blocks, a generous pouring of whisky and so her cycle continued. Cocooned in the club chair, she savoured her first warm sip, soon to be distracted by the bang on the front door.

'Is that you, Isla?' she shouted.

'Yes Mother. It's me.' Isla rushed to her room.

'Come here! Did you hear me? Come here, miss!'

There was silence. Jess got up and walked to Isla's room. She could hear the sounds of things being frantically shuffled about.

'What are you up to in there, Isla? Nearly a teenager but not an adult yet, miss!'

'Nothing, nothing. I'll be out shortly.'

Jess let out a huge sigh, sculled the remains of her whisky and headed back to the kitchen to replenish her glass.

Isla dreaded fronting her mother these days. She couldn't bear her drinking, knowing only too well how the night usually ended, with harshly spoken words and her own inevitable retreat to her bedroom. Although her home life had become increasingly less fulfilling, her days outside of home overflowed with joy. Her best friends, Lucy Rose and Betty, were her soul mates. They laughed, played and got into their fair share of mischief, and she found emotional refuge in their friendship.

Isla had also fully embraced her piano playing under Morag's watchful tutelage. She skipped music grades one after the other and soon became Morag's top student. Not only did she possess the gift of playing music, she also began writing music as well. Each week, she and Morag worked on a piece together, with three manuscripts in progress at any one time. Isla's favourite was *Isla's Song*. It became a dedication to her father, whom she still missed dreadfully. She was so scared that she would forget his image, the sound of his voice, the smell of his pipe. It was this song, *their song*, that kept his memory alive. Each week, *Isla's Song* became more layered, more intricate and even more special. Every time she played it, it was like opening up a communication line with her father in heaven. The music was her vehicle to express how much she loved and missed him. Each note played filled her heart with love and her soul soared. She felt sure that he could hear her; she didn't know how, but she just knew. Besides, Morag had told her that her father would hear her – and no-one dared to question Morag, *ever*.

Before arriving home, Isla, Lucy Rose and Betty had been to the local square to watch the Guy Fawkes celebrations. There was a huge effigy of Guy Fawkes surrounded by kindling with firecrackers. The days were longer this time of year, with the sun resisting the urge to set until late into the night. Notwithstanding the sun's presence, there was little warmth in the air, the wind from the sea as chilly as ever.

The locals gathered in droves to enjoy the annual celebrations, made all the merrier by Scottish fare comprising haggis, neeps, black pudding, fat hot chips and Scotch whisky. On this day commemorating a failed gunpowder plot, the girls had their own plans to add their own special memorial touch.

'Now listen you two, I appoint myself the captain of this scheme,' said Lucy Rose.

'Now hang on *captain*, I thought of it first,' said Betty.

'You're both got fools for brains, it was my idea!' exclaimed Isla. 'Anyhow, I think we can all be captains! What do you say?'

A moment's silence, a look to each other and then, 'Deal!' said Lucy Rose and Betty together, the three girls piling their hands on top of each other's to signal their pact.

'Okay, gather round,' said Isla. 'Now you see that table over there with the boxes marked *Danger*? They're the firecrackers. Lucy Rose and Betty, your job is to distract that bearded Scotsman whilst I fill this hessian bag with them crackers.'

Betty and Lucy Rose stood with eyes wide open and mouths agape.

'Are you going to be noddin' your heads, you fool lassies? What is this, some contest for the dumbest or somethin'?'

They immediately shook their heads on command.

'Thought so,' Isla laughed. 'Right, I have a plan for this wee deception, gals. Come closer,' she whispered, and the girls huddled together.

Soon, Isla was circling behind the stout, kilt-wearing Scotsman, who was carefully guarding the boxes of fireworks. Lucy Rose and Betty moved forward to greet him at his trestle table.

'What you be sellin', mister,' said Lucy Rose, 'fairy floss?'

'Yeah, what you sellin'?' Betty repeated.

'I not be sellin' any of dat sugar on a stick, lassies. What I be guarding be none of your wee lassies' nose-pokin' business. Now git you both out of 'ere!'

Lucy Rose and Betty spied Isla making her way to the rear of the Scotsman. 'Oh please, kind sir, just give us a wee peek at what's in the boxes and you'll be rid of us both. We won't bother you no more. Cross my heart. Ain't that right, Betty?' said Lucy Rose.

'Yes, that be right mister. I kin assure ye of it!' said Betty, nodding her head intently.

The Scotsman looked at them both for a moment and let out a small laugh, taken in by this devilish pair.

'Oh alright, one peek and ye be gone. But don't ye be telling any folks, or I'll git into trouble. Deal?'

'Okay, deal,' said the girls, both making the sign of the cross.

As he slowly opened the lid of the cardboard box, the girls peered in and saw layers of bright red firecrackers. At that moment, Isla let out a blood-curdling scream from just behind him, startling him and making him jump two feet in the air. 'What the blazes?' he cried.

Whilst his attention was on Isla, Lucy Rose and Betty grabbed a handful of crackers each and took off like lightning bolts. With that, the Scotsman realised what the girls had done and took chase, yelling, 'Come back y' scoundrels, your lives won't be worth livin' when I grab ye and bang y' heads together!' Jumping over trestle tables and chairs, barrelling through people like bowling pins, he raced after the bandits.

With the table left unattended, Isla surreptitiously commenced filling her hessian bag with more firecrackers. Upon completing the task and making a hurried escape, she signalled to her partners in crime, letting out a loud *coo-wee*, a cry she recalled her father had once taught her. By that stage, the Scotsman's fulsome figure had got the better of him. Running out of puff, he bent over, one hand on each knee, cussing under his breath and exposing his bare buttocks to the onlookers, who screamed in horror.

Having realised their plan, the girls met in the laneway next to the local post office. They slid down the stone walls, laughing so hard they could hardly catch their breath.

'Did you see the look on his face!' snorted Betty, holding her stomach.

'He looked like he was havin' a heart attack,' said Lucy Rose, 'his eyes popping out of his head in rage and his balls no doubt bursting out from behind when he bent over!' she hooted.

'Too funny, girls. We make a grand team. I don't know what was more embarrassin' for him, bein' done over for petty crime by a bunch of wee lassies, or showin' his rump to the whole town!' laughed Isla. All the girls fell over each other, rolling about, tears running down their faces and giving high-fives all round.

Before they knew it, the town clock chimed 5 o'clock. 'Jesus, I best be gittin' home. I'll bring the goods to school tomorrow for Part B of the plan,' said Isla.

'Right, but be careful. Don't let your mum see it. She'll have your guts for garters if y' git found out, Isla,' said Lucy Rose.

'I know, I know. Bye for now.' Isla picked herself up off the pavement and scooted back home.

We meet once again, old friend, thought Oliver as he alighted from the train at London station. The trip had become his annual pilgrimage, once each year close to Christmas. This would be his tenth. Each time, on arrival in London, he would post yet another letter to Gerry to remind her that he was close by and still on the hunt for a morsel of truth as to Isla's whereabouts. He would only stay a couple of weeks, first in London and then in Glasgow, before heading back to Melbourne to celebrate Christmas with the family.

For the first four years, Olivia had joined him. Now, however, she did not feel the need to chaperone her brother any longer. She believed Oliver to be more resolute these days, despite the hurt he wore on his sleeve. The absence of Isla in his life had left his heart still gaping, but time had been his friend, enabling him to gather enough courage to get on with life. This didn't mean that he had given up hope altogether, just that he was more prepared to face a probable reality.

The nostalgic air of Christmas time conjured a sense of magic within him, stirring up his hopes and dreams. Those familiar memories of Christmas past, preparing the plate of carrots for Santa's reindeer with Isla, watching her open her Christmas gifts and looking for that hidden threepence in the plum pudding, which was an old family recipe. The joy, the laughter and the warmth of her little arms wrapped around him.

Where there was hope, there was always possibility.

Each year, he stood in the middle of the Christmas markets by the Thames, surrounded by tall candy canes and the coloured Christmas lights of the stalls, their tiny roofs dusted with fresh snow. He would think of happy Christmases with Isla, breathe in the icy air laced with the smell of Christmas spices, burning pine and chestnuts and think of Isla. This enchanting moment refuelled him emotionally. He needed it. Standing there, gazing to the heavens, he was caressed by the movement of air from children skating past him, their joyous cries and laughter adding to the poignancy of the moment. He was there for Isla. Otherwise, he feared forgetting little things about her. This yearly pilgrimage, allowing him to spend precious time with his Isla, reignited the memories that he kept tucked away at other times.

Before taking the train to Glasgow part of Oliver's trip each year involved revisiting the same London haunts he had experienced with Liv. He would dream of news about Isla and if he were lucky, he thought, he might even spot her. But it was this unique moment, standing in the middle of the Christmas market crowd, that was most special to him. Feeling so connected with her reassured him that she was safe, wherever she was.

He often wondered how she would look now she was older, whether she still had a love for music, what school she was attending, what things made her heart sing and importantly, whether she remembered him. In his right pocket, close to his heart, he always carried a well-worn picture of Isla, Larry the dog and himself. The photo had been taken the day before she was taken; it was Isla as he last remembered her. A myriad of thoughts crossed his mind and as he opened his eyes and took in his surroundings again, he tapped his right pocket a few times ritualistically, hoping that his action would travel the cosmos and find a place in Isla's heart.

It was the day after Guy Fawkes Day. Cloaked in secrecy behind the shelter sheds, Isla, Lucy Rose and Betty met before the school bell rang.

'Have y'got the stash?' whispered Betty, looking over her shoulder.

'Sssshhhhh! Jesus, Mary 'n Joseph, you're raising y' voice, Betty!' exclaimed Lucy Rose.

'I am not, y'are! See, the principal'll hear y' from here, Jesus!' said Betty in a loud whisper.

'Listen you two, will you both shut your traps or we'll all get sprung. Now do y' remember our plan or what?' said Isla.

'Yes!' proclaimed the others in unison.

'Good! This'll be fun. But we must be plenty careful. The gym's not in use till Thursday when we have mass there, so let's get it right,' said Isla, trying hard to contain her excitement. 'Let's do it!'

Some 20 minutes later, the school bell rang. All three girls were already seated at their desks, ready for their first class, religion. Once all the other students had piled into class, their grade six teacher, Father Leo, appeared. He was a thin man in his 70s. He had a long face and tight lips, which often displayed morsels of his breakfast cereal. Father Leo did not command much respect from his students and so he carried a trusty cane to threaten or dispense any necessary punishment. The students nicknamed his cane 'McTavish'. Its use often caused raucous laughter from the class, as McTavish would often catapult from Father Leo's arthritic fingers and land in the most unusual places, including harpooning Morag's stomach on one occasion as she entered the classroom.

'Class, class, attention, *attention!*' cried Father Leo in his mixed soprano tone. 'Today, we study the lead-up to the birth of Our Lord, Jesus Christ, as we prepare for Christmas.'

Betty stood up on her chair. 'Is that where Mary was ridin' the donkey, Father Leo? Or is the donkey ridin' her? Eeaww, eeaww!' She jumped down from her seat and the whole class burst into laughter.

'Right, I will not be toleratin' blasphemy here, miss!' said Father Leo.

The whole class let out a long, 'Ooooooooooo!' and contemptuous cheers filled the room.

'Not McTavish, Father Leo, not McTavish!' cried Isla, as she and Betty elbowed each other in the ribs, giggling hysterically.

Father Leo stepped down from the platform in front of the blackboard. In a ninja type movement, he entered the first aisle of desks and in true warrior form, flicked McTavish from side to side, using it as a nunchaku. Both his poor eyesight and his aim failed him. Students fell to the ground in the wake of McTavish's misguided lashings, pretending to be wounded, crying out in pain. In the midst of this kung-fu horror, Lucy Rose crept up behind him and wrote in chalk on the back of his black cloak, '*Suck me!*'

Finally, Father Leo arrived at Betty.

'Not me sir, not me! I promise to be a good girl from now on!' she said, hands in prayer position, looking as angelic as possible.

Father Leo bent over, inches away from Betty's face to ensure that he had the right girl. He slammed McTavish on her desk just as the class belted out another, 'Ooooooooooo!'

'Just git out here, miss. Git to the chapel. Ten Hail Marys and two Our Fathers. I don't be wanting to see y' terrible wee person in my class for the rest of the period. Do y'hear me?' bellowed Father Leo in his high-pitched voice.

'Pardon, sir?' said Betty cheekily.

Father Leo repeated himself, his tone reaching higher operatic notes until his voice eventually cracked.

Betty ran past him to the front of the class and out the door, Father Leo chasing after her, leaving a mob of students feigning death in the wake of his pursuit.

Isla spied Betty running past the class window and waved at her, holding one hand to her mouth and trying to contain her laughter.

Suddenly, Morag appeared at the classroom door.

'*What* is going on here, class? I will not be toleratin' this nonsense. Have some respect, all of you. Do y'hear? *Do... y'hear... me?*'

There was a marked hush in the classroom. No-one dared to look sideways. 'Yes, mam!' they all exclaimed.

'*Do y'hear me!*' said Morag once more.

With gusto, the class repeated that they had.

'Gud! Gud! Now git back to work all of you. Jesus, Mary and Joseph, you're grade six students. Y' supposed to be settin' an example. It's your final year. Wake up to y'selves! Have a gud look at yourselves and for the Lord's sake, grow up, or y' might be answerin' to me next time. And I warn ye, *don't* give me the pleasure!'

Morag exited the room. Not a sound was heard. Isla smiled to herself and thought, 'Now that's my kind of woman! That's *my Morag!*'

The next evening, Oliver alighted from the train at Glasgow. The blast of the Guy Fawkes fireworks was still spilling into the evening air from the previous day's celebrations. The sky was clear and dark blue, pierced by a multitude of twinkling lights, the full moon like a heavenly torch illuminating the world below. There was fresh snow encasing the station platform and a display of fairy lights wrapped around the station's posts. Christmas carollers stood huddled in a group near the exit gate, all wearing red and white scarves and green woollen beanies and holding candles. Oliver stood there listening to *Silent Night,* one of his favourites, placing his luggage at his side.

Whilst he was listening, he turned to look at the train behind him, remembering what it had been like all those years ago when they had tried to recover Isla the first time. He sensed the ethereal presence of Liv and the police behind him. A feeling of loss overcame him. He observed the train's colours, insignia, the shape of its windows, its iron handles. He smelt the puff of engine smoke. His eyes welled with the memories. 'Just like Isla's train,' he muttered softly, 'I was so close back then, yet so far… but I tried. I did all I could. I hope one day Isla knows that. I trust that she will understand that her daddy did not give up on her. I know in my heart I *never* will.' He wiped away a tear then spied himself in the reflection of the train window, gave himself a half smile, tipped his hat, turned back to the choir and picked up his case.

The choir's rendition of *Joy to the World* lifted his spirits. He gave the train one more glance over his shoulder and then headed for the exit. All is not lost after all, he thought.

Chapter 15
This Place
Wednesday 7 November 1961

Jess finished work late. She had a couple of quick nips at the Stromness Hotel before making her way up the hill to home. The arctic gale almost swept her off her feet, freezing her thin bones, the only saving grace the insulation provided by the scotch whisky warming her blood.

Entering the front door, she could smell the simmering fat from the chucked steak and an unpleasant cooked cabbage odour.

'Isla, I'm home. Rough day. Need a shower, be there soon dear.'

'Sure mother, dinner'll be ready in 15. Beef goulash.'

Although young, Isla was a proficient cook. She had shown interest at an early age, which, given her working hours, Jess had encouraged. In fact with her mother's work commitments, Isla had little choice but to grow up quickly.

There was a familiar routine to Isla's Wednesdays after school, as it was not uncommon for Jess to arrive home late on that day due to her work schedule. Isla would start her homework, take out any rubbish for collection the next day and prepare the evening meal. Jess felt a bit guilty stopping off at the pub before heading home, but it was her much needed medicine after a long day at the clinic.

Isla added her final touch of chopped red and green peppers, paprika, tomato puree for the braising steak and a sprinkle of caraway seeds, and then called out, 'Mum, dinner's ready!

They sat at either end of a small dining table. Isla had dressed it with a red checked tablecloth, table napkins, a large candle and a small vase filled with native island greenery.

'Here y'go, I know it's not that exciting but it'll warm us up.'

'Just being clever enough to cook me a meal means so much to Mummy.'

'*Mother,* not *Mummy*, I'm too old for that now!'

Jess looked a little surprised at Isla's abrupt response, which hurt.

'Oh, alright. But no matter what you call me, don't forget, I'll always be your mother.'

Isla did not say a word and focussed instead on her plate. She was getting a bit over chores. Her responsibilities at home affected her free time and in many respects, she felt robbed of her childhood. She was growing up and wanted her mother to validate her more.

'Is anything up, Isla? You look a bit down. Something happen at school today you want to talk about?'

'No, Mother. School is fine.'

'Well, is it piano? Should I have a word to Morag?'

'No, it's not piano. Morag be the best,' sighed Isla, not wanting to talk about her issues.

'Okay, well if you don't want to talk about it, I can't do much, can I? Up to you, love!' Jess said this gently, observing Isla to be out of sorts.

There was a moment's silence. After chewing a morsel of cabbage, she looked over her cutlery and said, 'Yes, Mother, *it is up to me.*'

'What's that supposed to mean, *it's up to me?* I work hard every day to put food on the table, pay the bills, send you to school… what more can I do, Isla? Tell me?' Jess firmly placed her cutlery down.

'I don't know Mother. I guess sometimes, you know, sometimes I miss Dad… my idea of Dad. I miss where I grew up, what I can remember of it. I can't describe it. I feel there's a bit of me missing. You never *ever* talk about him or his family, ever! Why doesn't Aunt Liv ever call? Visit? I don't understand you. There are no pictures of him, his family, nothing…'

'Well I miss him too, Isla,' said Jess, nervously wiping her mouth with her serviette.

'I don't believe you Mother, cause if y'did, y'd talk about him to me. The only person I speak to about him is Morag… she listens.'

Jess raised her eyebrows at the thought of Isla sharing such emotional intimacies with her piano teacher. 'Oh she does, does she? Is that what brought all this on? Perhaps she ought to be your mother then!'

Fighting back tears, Jess gritted her teeth. 'I've had enough of this miss, I may not be mother of the year, but I'm doin' my best, believe me Isla. You're a lucky little girl, luckier than most!'

'Funny you should say that! That's exactly what Dad used to call me!' Isla folded her arms, leaning towards her mother. 'If you really think that, Mother, then you don't know me at all!'

The silence was complete save for the occasional shrill of the polar winds outside. From either end of the table, they looked through each other. For the first time, Jess truly observed that her little girl *was* growing up, she was not so 'little' anymore. She was becoming more self-righteous and opinionated in her attempt to piece together fragments from her past. For a flash, Jess saw Oliver sitting opposite her, that same glint of the eye and aloofness of expression. She didn't like what she was witnessing. Not at all.

Deciding to end the war of words, she stood up, threw down her napkin and with her clenched hands by her sides, said, 'I need some fresh air. We need a break. Please, clean up the dishes, finish your homework and lock the front door, I won't be late.'

She gave Isla no opportunity to reply and marched out of the home, heading for the Stromness Hotel again.

Three hours later, Jess returned home. She placed her coat over the club chair, her handbag at its side. She stoked the fire and added another log. All was quiet in the home except for the shriek of the wind outside. Thanks to Isla, the kitchen was tidy and clean.

Jess crept down the hallway, oil lantern in hand, arriving at Isla's room.

The door was slightly ajar and she saw that Isla was tucked under her blankets, fast asleep. She was tempted to sneak in and kiss her on the forehead, but decided not to in case she woke her. Best to leave the night's bickering to one side and move on.

Whilst gazing at Isla, Jess pondered why it was often so hard for her to be affectionate. Oliver had always managed. He'd made it look easy. *Why can't I?* she thought. *Why do I still find it hard to express myself? Why can't I talk to her about her father's past?* Standing at Isla's door a moment longer, observing her little miracle, she felt the pain of her past choices.

Jess vowed to try and be a better mother, to listen more to Isla. She could never deal with losing her daughter; she would never forgive herself. But at the same time, she had come too far. She had tangled herself in a web of deceit and locked away the truth from her. She must never find out, Jess thought, *never.*

Slowly, she closed the bedroom door and quietly made her way back to the kitchen, bumping against the corridor walls every so often.

She grabbed a half-full bottle of whisky and a tumbler and navigated her way to the club chair in front of the burning fire. Taking a few sips, she placed her glass on the nearby nest of tables and reached down, opening up her handbag. Inside was a small bundle of letters she had picked up from the post office box that day. There were the usual bills and about four letters forwarded from Gerry, with the back of each envelope simply marked, *Sender: O Johnson.*

She raised the envelopes close to her nose, as if sniffing the contents. She didn't open them, she didn't dare. As she peered into the embers, she was tempted for a split second to fuel the fire with them out of frustration. Instead, she went to the bedroom and added them to her collection of saved mail, all marked *Sender: O Johnson*, hidden away in a shoebox on top of her wardrobe.

Jess had never had the courage to open them. She could not face it, knowing they were from Oliver. She was only keeping them for Isla, in case she herself met with an untimely death. *At least if I'm dead, Isla can never judge me*, she thought. She can discover the secret for herself and do as she pleases with the information. She might hate me, but at least I won't be here to suffer the consequences. At least here in Stromness, away from Melbourne, I've been a better functioning mother and given myself a new lease on life, she reassured herself.

In many respects, however, this was a falsehood. Jess had never really recovered from her depression, thus her constant reminders to herself of how well she was doing. The relocation had been a band-aid and that was all. Occasionally visited by this truth, she thought that while none of it was perfect, she was trying to do her best and that was what counted.

Back in the lounge room, she closed the window and soon fell asleep, nestled into the chair and covered with her favourite crochet rug.

Before long, she had the sense of flying high above snow-laden treetops. Although she was only wearing a nightgown, she did not feel the cold. Then she was travelling above a tranquil sea, so still and perfectly reflecting the starry sky that it was hard to discern where the sea ended and the sky began. In a blink, she found herself back in her lounge looking at herself in the club chair, sound asleep. Then the closed window flew open and the clock struck 2.00 a.m. She still did not feel cold but intuitively shut the window again. She saw that the fire was barely burning and used the poker to stoke it, noticing that her body was still sitting on the chair covered by the blanket. She tried picking up the whisky tumbler from the table, but her hands were unable to grasp it. *Strange*, she thought. Then she felt a coolness overcome her and a lightning bolt shot up her spine, making her forehead ache. She sensed a presence in the room. At first it appeared as the foggy outline of a woman. With the dwindling fire giving off a faint glow from the lingering embers, Jess could see a figure not of this world. Rubbing her eyes to focus, she discerned an elderly woman with wide blinking eyes making a whistling sound, swaying and moving her hands from side to side, as if she were dancing to an ethereal operetta. Unexpectedly, the apparition ceased moving. She placed her hands on her hips, extended her neck towards Jess and let out a frightening roar, 'Hello Jessica, remember me? It's your mother, Dorothy!'

The image became clear and Jess could see her mother standing in front of her. Frozen, she was unable to move or speak.

'Ah, yes, it's me alright dear. *Your mother.* I thought it was about time I broke up this little party of yours. Tell me, whatever have you been thinking, dear?

Jess looked at the ghost in disbelief.

'Speak up, missy. Cat got your tongue?'

'No, it's, it's… just that… '

Before Jess could say another word, Dorothy interrupted, 'Just that you didn't expect me, missy?' She laughed.

'No, well… ' said Jess.

'No, well, you just listen to me, young lady. I've been watching you for some time. It's disturbed me, it has. Thought I'd raised you better. I need to go to a place of rest, be with your father, but the boss upstairs says I need to set you straight first, mop up your mess. Again!'

Her mother's harshness made Jess stand up. She peered down at her feet and saw she was a child again. Her weathered hands were small and smooth and as she touched her hair, she noticed she was wearing pig-tails.

'Are you listening to your mother, child?'

Although Jess's appearance had changed, curiously she felt no different emotionally. She was still overflowing with past memories, choices and her constant companion, despair.

Whilst she had never been so bold as to talk back to her mother, now, an unusual courage overcame her and she said, 'What do you mean, "set you straight", "mop up your mess", Mother? I guess there's no need to call you Mumma anymore?'

'Oh, do I sense disrespect from you? Well look at you, look at this place! Long way from home, dear! And neglecting Isla the way you do. Poor little child! Who *is* the child, by the way? From where I'm standing, you don't seem to have grown up at all, missy!'

'The problem, Mother, is you taught me nothing except the fear of you and that bloody wooden spoon.' Jess was now able to pick up the tumbler from the floor and pour herself a half glass of whisky from the nearby bottle. It was just the Dutch courage she needed. All those years ago, she had been unable to speak her mind. Now, robbed of her childhood and plagued by feelings of grief and persecution, she could now at last set the record straight. Taking a gulp of whisky, she wiped her mouth and tossed the glass aside, smashing it on the floor.

'Oh, so you feared me, did you? Well, it was the only way I could control your strident behaviour, otherwise you'd just have disobeyed me, as you always did. I couldn't have your father coming home to that, not the way he was after the war.' She paused, then added, 'Best clean up that mess,' pointing to the broken glass on the floor.

Ignoring her mother's order, Jess continued, 'See? That's the problem, Mother. Frank always came first.'

'*Father* to you!' said Dorothy.

'I'll say what I like... *Mother!*'

'You look a little bit under the weather, young lady. Such a pity to view your decline like this. It's the drink, the demon drink, that's what it is!'

'Ha, you were watching *my decline* when I was a kid, Mother. Or did you miss it? Attention elsewhere? Hmmmm?'

'You're still a child to me, Jessica, always will be!'

'From the day I was born, you failed to feed me emotionally. I was thinning out on that vine a long time before Oliver picked off what was left of me. You made me hate you. You weren't there for me. You might as well have been a ghost then. You didn't know, but I used to creep out of my bed at night and watch you in Father's chair, after he died. Night after night, I visited your sadness, your despair. You tried to hide it, but I saw it eating away at you. You lost your husband and then you checked out until the Angel of Death eventually collected what was left. You left Gerry and me behind. You willed your death. And by the way, good on you Mother for not leaving Gerry and me empty-handed. Oh no! You left us with hands full of *emotional baggage*, stuff that I've been trying to deal with all my life. Look at me, Mumma, look at me! I was just a kid, a kid. You bitch, you Godforsaken selfish bitch! I was just a little girl with a life of dreams ahead of me. You turned me into a nightmare.'

Then she felt herself grow taller and peered down to see that her feet were no longer small, her hands no longer childlike and her hair was pinned back.

'Well bravo, bravo Jessica! I am impressed. I can see that you've picked up a few tips from those Hollywood moving pictures! The courage tempered by a full serving of contempt is breathtaking!'

Jess hardly heard her mother's words, as she was now crying uncontrollably, gasping for air. Hearing her own words spoken aloud had affected her. For the first time in years, she was facing the demons she had been running from all these years. It was as if a valve had been released, the drop in pressure making her giddy.

'Well c'mon, straighten yourself up. I didn't raise my girls to get all emotional like this. Have some respect for yourself, Jessica. What would your father say if he could see you now? Hmm?'

Jess raised her head slightly, glaring at the spirit. 'He'd probably hug me, Mother, that's what parents do, something you *never* did! The problem is that you only had eyes for him. Gerry and I were never good enough. I often wonder why we weren't good enough, why we were treated so poorly, why we had to work so hard so young. Was it me? I know you, Mother, but… I don't *really* know you.'

Jess took another breath, wiped her tears and slowly walked towards her mother.

'You know, I cried the day your granddaughter was born. Not because you weren't there to see Isla born, but because I didn't know what or how to feel after she arrived. I was there in that delivery ward for a short time, alone with this brand-new baby in my arms. Her perfect cherub lips, tiny ears, flawless little fingernails and knowing blue eyes. I looked at her from head to toe. There was no-one to disturb us and in the silence, I thought, Oh, this motherhood stuff, it'll come naturally, that's what God intends. All mothers have doubts, fears about parenthood, about attaching to their child. And as I scanned her tiny body, I waited and waited for *something* to kick in. But it didn't! And you know what, Mother? I felt nothing. Nothing! When Oliver rushed in, he was so happy. I could see how overjoyed he was, how he loved *me* for giving him this very special gift. I watched him as he took Isla from my arms to hold his daughter for the first time. I saw him look into Isla's eyes, I saw him raise her to his face, kiss her and smell her newborn scent. He had this natural biological response to Isla and she to him. I don't know how to explain it, but I saw it. And I felt so jealous. Yes Mother, jealous. Me! I hated myself for feeling that way. In that second, I wanted to be Oliver, I wanted to feel like he felt towards Isla. I wanted Isla to look at me the way she looked at him. But as I said, I just felt nothing. And look at me, Mother. I still feel *nothing! God you must be proud! You taught me so well!'*

'You must feel better getting that off your chest, dear. Not what I came for, but pleased I've given you something to chew over. You never did chew enough, dear. Your father said that too. Always swallowed too soon, never chewed. Chew some more, Jess, you never know, all that *emotional nourishment* you missed out on growing up, well it might only be a mouthful away.'

With that, Dorothy's image vanished before Jess's eyes.

She caught her breath, staring into the failing embers until the room became dark.

Then she opened her eyes, trying to piece together her dream. She looked at the clock: it was 6.00 a.m. Although she was still tired, she felt a cloud lifting off her, leaving a feeling of peace, something she had not felt in a long time. Slowly, this time with contentment, she drifted off again snuggled into her security blanket.

Chapter 16
Good Friends
Thursday 8 November 1961

Isla woke up later than usual. Quickly changing into her school uniform, she washed her face, brushed her teeth and tied her long brown curls into a ponytail. Making her way down the hallway, she heard the clang of dishes and in the kitchen, was surprised to see her mother emptying the contents of a whisky bottle down the sink. Jess peered over her shoulder, giving her daughter a smile.

'What are you staring at, miss? Today is a day for new beginnings. *Today* marks the day when your mother declares no more whisky!'

'What about other stuff?' said Isla.

'What, like wine or beer? That too! Your mother's turned over a new leaf, Isla. I had the strangest dream last night, it was so real. The good thing is that it got me thinking about us, about you. I can't make any firm promises, but your mother's going to try harder from now on. That I promise! I'm doing it for us.'

A weight temporarily lifted from Isla's shoulders. Maybe it wasn't just the dream, maybe her mother had listened to her for a change. Perhaps she's actually noticing me, Isla thought.

For the first time in a long while, Isla sat down to a fully set breakfast table with plates, cutlery, fresh toast and her favourite jams. Jess had cooked Isla her favourite strawberry pancakes and made a mug of delicious hot chocolate.

Whilst Isla was tucking into the morning delights, Jess sat opposite her, sipping on her tea, giving her daughter the widest grin.

'Would you quit staring at me like that, Mother, it's kinda weird!' Isla said.

'I'm allowed to stare as much as I like at my beautiful girl. It seems like it was only a short time ago that we were making our way on that crossing to Stromness. And here we are some six years later and how you've grown. I'm so proud of you, Isla. I don't tell you that much, I know, but I am. And I do love you so much!'

'I know you do Mother and I know how hard it must be for you too without Daddy. I miss him so much, so I can imagine how much you must miss him!'

Jess took a double sip of her tea, not knowing how to reply. 'Oh yes, yes Isla, we both do.'

Isla was able to talk with her mother that morning, something they seldom did. It was a relief to be able to discuss matters troubling her, as more recently, her mother had appeared to show little interest in her.

'And I miss Larry. The memory of him is fading a bit and I'm scared. I want to remember him and I'm scared of losing him forever… just like Dad. Sometimes I just wish I had photos or something to jog my memory. I don't want made-up memories, I want the real thing!'

Jess was stuck for words. She simply nodded, gave Isla a comforting grin, got up from the table to wash her mug and then changed the subject. 'Well, a brand-new day begins. Don't be late to school. Have a grand day and I'll see you tonight. Love you. Best be off. Bye love.' She put on her black winter coat, flung her olive-green scarf about her neck and closed the front door.

Isla's belly was full of pancakes. She sat there sipping the cream off the top of her hot chocolate, quietly staring into the distance. She thought about the time her dad had dipped his fingers into her mug and wiped some chocolate and cream on her nose, and how he'd let Larry lick the remains from his finger. The memory made her feel warm inside. Her lips curled into a smile and she gave a little laugh. *We had so much fun, didn't we*, she thought.

The clock chimed 8.30 a.m. *Oh my God, late again!* she thought. She downed the last bit of her drink, fled the house, ran down the cobbled road to school and jumped puddles along the way.

Waiting at the front gate were Isla's partners in crime, Betty and Lucy Rose.

'Sorry I'm a little late. I know I said 8.30 a.m.,' said Isla, catching her breath.

'We were here on time!' smiled Betty.

'It's pot calling, not kettle, you dummy,' said Lucy Rose.

'Whatever! You know I don't cook much,' said Betty, poking out her tongue at Lucy Rose, 'anyhow, it's all planned, are you ready Isla?'

'Yes, are you in?' said Lucy Rose.

'Yes, of course, comrades. It's ready to go anyway, isn't it? You two just have to do the last bit and that's it! Right?' said Isla.

'Yes, but you're our lookout, Isla. If the coast is not clear, it's your job to signal a red alert. Remember?' said Betty.

'I do,' said Isla, 'do you think I'm stupid or something?'

The girls laughed, 'No comment!'

'You two are impossible! Whatever you do, do *not* get sprung, or we'll be banned from school camp tomorrow.'

The assembly bell clanged at 9.00 a.m., with students scurrying to their classrooms. Following a brief update by the deputy principal, the whole school headed to the gymnasium where their annual end-of-year mass was to take place, presided over by Father Leo.

The gym was not huge. It accommodated about 150 children from preparatory to grade six, together with teachers and other staff. Father Leo was assisted by two altar boys who dutifully fulfilled their sacred functions in creating a solemn atmosphere.

The room was cold and damp. Isla always thought it smelt like rotten apples and sour milk.

Morag sat with the other teachers in the front row. Isla sat in the third row, in a seat closest to the aisle. From there, she was able to see Betty and Lucy Rose, who had secreted themselves behind the long black curtains that provided a backdrop for the makeshift altar.

On each side of the altar table were tall wooden stands, one displaying the hymn numbers and the other, a picture of the nativity scene with Mother Mary holding baby Jesus.

Two golden chalices commanded centre stage on the altar table, one holding the blood of Christ, the other containing holy communion wafers.

So far, Isla thought, Plan B is going off without a hitch. The gymnasium had been locked up all week and the girls' skilfully positioned firecrackers appeared not to have been disturbed. They had taped a circuit of fiery contraband under the altar table and behind the altar stands, and attached a set of Catherine wheels. They'd all joked about their fiery display having the potential to bring about the second coming of Christ.

The morning was windy and gloomy. Snow had ceased falling, but the powdered landscape contrasted with the dark purple-grey thunder clouds. The silence was soon broken by *Spirit of God* sung by the energetic yet tone-deaf school choir, as Father Leo ambled down the middle aisle following the altar boys, one holding a large crucifix, the other a large golden Holy Bible above his tiny head. Where's McTavish? Isla thought, smiling, as he passed her.

Father Leo arrived at the altar and Isla couldn't help but snigger when she saw the altar curtains moving ever so slightly.

Beckoning the altar boy holding the Word of God, Father Leo commenced mass in his broken high-pitched voice, making the sign of the cross. 'In the name of the Father, the Son and the Holy Ghost, I welcome you to this special mass. We are marking the final days of school for the grade six students of Stromness Primary and we bless them in prayers for their future journeys ahead. May the Lord be with you. I now read from the Holy Gospel of John, praise to you Lord Jesus Christ.'

Father Leo asked the altar boy to raise the Bible higher above his head so that he could better read the scriptures with his waning eyesight. Whilst that was happening, the other altar boy knelt at Father Leo's foot holding a set of bells, which he sounded every time Father Leo gave a small kick to his right arm.

Whilst Father Leo struggled through the scriptures, at just the right moment, Isla let out a loud sneeze, signalling to the girls to commence operation Plan B.

Carefully, Betty and Lucy Rose timed the ignition of their matches upon Betty's subdued cough. The curtains were close to the altar so the burning fuse did not have to travel far.

As the petty arsonists were trying not to giggle behind Father Leo, he raised his arms to the heavens and pronounced, 'This is the Word of the Lord!'

As if the heavens had responded with thunderous applause, the percussive explosions rang out, setting off the altar table from its footings, smoke pouring forth. At the same time, spinning fireworks lit up the altar stands in a whistling propellor-like motion. Father Leo jumped ten feet with the sound of the crackers, kicking the bell-ringing altar boy in the head and knocking the other boy flying, the golden Bible becoming a holy catapult. Falling backwards, Father Leo adopted a crucifix position on the floor as one of the altar stands with rotating fireworks landed on him, causing him to let out a high-pitched shrill. Students were screaming, rushing towards the gymnasium doors to escape the hellfire. In the pandemonium, Betty and Lucy Rose slowly emerged from the back drapes to join in the confusion, careful not to be seen. By that stage, Morag and the other teachers were attempting to round up the children, which was akin to herding a mob of cracker-crazed kittens.

In the eye of the holy storm sat Isla, laughing to herself and admiring her handiwork. As Betty and Lucy Rose ran past her, she stood up from her chair, only to be faced by Morag standing over her.

'And where do you think you're going, miss?'

'Um… I'm looking for… I'm heading back to class, ma'am. Quick, we must escape!'

'Are you now? Must we now? Well, we might just have a little chat about this later… if that's alright with you?'

Isla got the sense that Morag had a few clues about the morning's events. 'Yes ma'am, yes!' She swiftly made her escape, collecting Betty and Lucy Rose on the way back to their classroom.

Later that afternoon, Morag entered Isla's classroom. Sister Angela was teaching Latin, with all children holding their heads in their hands, staring at the clock on the wall, waiting for the bell to ring.

'Excuse me, sister, I should like to have a brief word to Isla, Betty and Lucy Rose after the school bell sounds. Would you be good enough to ensure they arrive at my office *promptly*?'

'Of course, of course. No trouble at all. Hmm, less than 10 minutes, it seems. How time flies, I so love teaching Latin,' said Sister Angela, gazing at her watch.

Morag briefly whispered into Sister Angela's ear, gave the three girls a stare and exited the room.

The trio flew into a panic. The fireworks had been the talk of the school that day and although no-one knew the culprits, the teaching staff had a fairly good idea. They could smell three little rats in their midst.

A frenzied series of notes passed between Lucy Rose, Betty and Isla each time Sister Angela turned to chalk the blackboard. Each girl's focus was fixed on the clock's minute hand as it got closer to 3.00 p.m. Isla noticed a bead of sweat drip from her brow. *Ding! Ding! Ding! Ding!*

echoed the bell. The class removed their ink pens from the inkwells, packed up their books and scooted out of the room, ignoring Sister Angela's pleas to complete their homework tasks.

Once the classroom was empty, Sister Angela peered over her glasses at the three remaining students. 'Now you girls. A special visit with Morag. Something you are all looking forward to no doubt. You're lucky the principal is away on leave in London. Could be worse.' Giving them a wry smile, she added, 'Now pack up quickly girls and I'll deliver you as requested. Hurry up and no nonsense please!'

Without delay, the girls were seated outside Morag's office, their knees jumping up and down at varied time intervals, like the wooden hammers hitting the keys on a piano. They gazed at their feet until the large office door creaked open and Morag beckoned, 'Come in girls.'

There were three chairs on the other side of Morag's generous timber desk. Her chair was higher and once seated, she was an even more imposing figure.

'Now little lassies, I'm thinking you all know why you're here?' she said.

'No!' said the girls in unison, staring at their shoes.

'Well, I find that a little hard to believe! You can tell me what you're thinking, or I will DRAG IT OUT OF YOU, it's your choice.' She smiled sweetly at the trio, making them feel even more on edge.

'Was it about mass?' said Lucy Rose.

'Oooo, you're getting a little warmer,' said Morag. 'Who can be cleverer than that?'

'Was it to do with the prayers?' said Betty.

'Not them, but you will be praying this is over by the time I'm done with you!' she bellowed.

'I know!' said Isla. 'It was the firecrackers, wasn't it miss?'

'And what would you three be having to do with firecrackers?' said Morag.

'Well, it was a bit of fun miss, you know, a bit of a muck-up day. We know we shouldn't be doing such things, but the devil Father Leo teaches us about, well he climbed into us all, like possessed us. I had not control of my body and mind, miss. My hands did things I couldn't control no matter how hard I tried. I tried, I did. Even prayed, Hail Mary and all that. How about you two?' said Isla, looking at her accomplices.

The other girls nodded their heads furiously, their knees still bouncing up and down.

'Then, miss, this voice possessed me, directin' the others to do the unimaginable and before long the stage was set to cause an utter chaos. And do you know miss, as soon as that first cracker set fire, I felt that devil leave my body, havin' its laugh, and from what I saw, miss, I was shocked. I was. I could see the others were too. Ain't that right girls?'

Once again the girl nodded their heads in agreement.

'Then like a fiery dragon, one after another those crackers set off and all I could do was hang my head in shame, thinking, what has that devil made me do? That's when I saw Betty and Lucy Rose flee, they was escapin' that devil miss, just like me!'

The story came to an abrupt end and the air was filled with an awkward silence. Morag's leather chair creaked. Her presence filled the room. She slowly leant forward, her nose seemingly inches away from Isla's face, who was seated in the middle of the trio. On closer inspection, she saw Morag's eyes were bloodshot, the bumps on her temples were horn-like and due to the frosty temperature in the room, puffs of smoke appeared to billow from her nostrils.

'Girls, my *dear* sweet little girls. I have NEVER heard such NONSENSE in all my life! The only devil here is mischief, something you three are all good at attracting. You're supposed to be bringin' pride to this wee school. Instead, in trying to resurrect Guy Fawkes himself, you've shamed yourselves and the school. I'm disappointed, especially you Isla, I thought more of you. There's a wee bit of penance to be served here. There's three mops and buckets waiting for you outside the hall, compliments of Sister Angela, and some cloths for the altar table and stands. Off to work now and clean that hall top to bottom. The floors should be fit to eat off once you've finished. And whilst you're mopping and cleaning, I want you to have a good think about your choices. Remember, ol' Morag here has eyes everywhere. Don't forget. Now off you go. NOW!'

The girls jumped out of their chairs but before reaching the door, Morag said, 'Oh girls, I understand once Father Leo has his minor burns attended to, he and McTavish might also be paying you a wee visit in the gym. Give him my regards. Now off with you!'

The girls headed off without hesitation.

As they disappeared, Morag couldn't help herself from smiling. 'Possessed by the devil indeed!' She was strangely proud of how spirited they all were. The thought of Father Leo spread-eagled on the floor made her burst out laughing.

The next morning, Isla joined the 20 other grade six students at the school's front gate, ready to board the big yellow school bus with Morag and Mr Lewis, the history teacher. Isla was so excited to be going on this retreat to mark the end of her primary years. The retreat base was north-east of Stromness in a place called Kirkwall Bay. She had been told all about it by other students and couldn't wait to experience the Ring of Brodgar, the largest Neolithic standing stone circle in Scotland. Mr Lewis had also told the girls in class that this ominous circle was made up of some 21 stones, which stood amongst the heather, rising up from the earth like vertical claws from mystical dragons buried long ago. It seemed like a place of magic and possibility to Isla.

On the last night of the retreat after dinner, awards were presented to the children, marking their efforts for the year and filling them with a sense of achievement and pride. Isla sat on the floor with Betty and

Lucy Rose, wondering if she would receive anything, hoping she would but trying not to be over-confident. Betty won the religious award for best depiction of illustrated donkeys in Biblical times. Lucy Rose won a mathematics award for completing the most complex long division problem ever presented to a Stromness student. The last award for the night was presented to Isla. It was the music award for composition. Morag presented Isla with the gold statuette and Isla gave her a wink, making Morag's heart skip a beat in absolute pride.

After a celebratory dinner, Isla made her way alone out to the open fire, sleeping bag in hand. She wanted some time to herself to soak up the past few days and just be quiet with her thoughts. The fire was still burning brightly, the wood crackling and embers floating up into the night sky like fireflies. The air was crisp and cool. Stars twinkled in the evening sky, little beacons that guided her to inner reflection.

From the kitchen window, Morag observed her seated alone on a log in front of the campfire, with her sleeping blanket wrapped waist high.

Grabbing a bowl of marshmallows and a couple of sticks on her way, she pulled up to sit close to Isla facing the fire.

Without saying a word, Isla glanced at her as she sat beside her, and then stared back into the fire.

'What you doin'?' said Morag.

'Nothin' much,' said Isla.

'Thinkin'?' said Morag.

Isla looked sideways at her old friend and smiled, her eyes returning to the flames.

Morag began, 'You know, when I was a wee little girl, my favourite time on my folks' farm was sittin' in front of the fire. I used to toast marshmallows and wonder about things, you know.' She passed Isla a marshmallow fixed to the end of a stick.

'It's not easy growing up, it's hard Isla. I've never told anyone this, but I'm a little like you. I never had a father growin' up. He died when I was a wee bonnie. Never met him. Saw pictures of him and that was it. So it was just me and my mam. Sort of like you. And though I didn't know my dad, I used to imagine what he must have been like. Big, tough, no nonsense. Perhaps he had a huge laugh, I thought, smoked a pipe and wore one of those peaked tweed caps. He would have loved me, given me big hugs and squeezed me, I convinced m'self. We probably would've even toasted marshmallows together.' She shifted closer, sharing her blanket over Isla's shoulders.

Isla nestled into Morag and looked up at her. 'I miss my dad, Morag. I miss his hugs, I miss him squeezing me too, I miss his laugh.'

'Well, I bet he misses you too, Isla. Why wouldn't he? You are the cleverest little girl I have ever known and the best piano player in the whole of Stromness! He'd be so proud.'

'Sometimes, I find it hard it hard to talk about it. I want to, but I don't want to make Mum cry. I think a lot about him. I wake up at night and feel he's with me. It doesn't scare me. But I wish I could see him just one more time, tell him I love him, show him where I live, what I'm doing. You know, sit with him once more, like this, and just laugh.'

Morag gave Isla a gentle cuddle. Armed with her stick and speared marshmallow, she pointed to the sky, 'Will you look up there missy, at that twinkling ceiling. Sometimes I imagine all my ancestors looking down on me, giving me guidance and reassurance. Urgin' me on, softly prodding me along in the right direction. It gives me strength, the courage to embrace the next day and *squeeze* the life out of it, every last drop. I see that in you lassie. Those ones up there, they fill your soul, they give you spirit. You're a brave one and a smart lassie to boot. And if you look carefully up there, you will see a bright star, and that star may just be your daddy, winkin' his eye at you, tellin' you how much he loves you and what a fine lass you've grown into. He may even send y' a shooting star, y'know, like wavin' at you, if you're lucky. My, he'd be proud as punch, Isla, and don't you ever forget that, will you?' She tweaked Isla's nose.

Isla peered up at her, giving her a warm loving smile.

'I won't,' she said. She was about to say something else but stopped and took a quick breath before catching Morag's eye. 'You know it wasn't the devil that possessed me yesterday, Morag?'

'I know, Isla, there's devil enough in you to let another one in!' laughed Morag, giving her a comforting hug as they both gazed up at the night sky.

Chapter 17
Last Chance Lost

Thursday 9 November 1967

Lucy Rose and Betty sat on the kerb near the school gate, waiting for Isla to arrive. They were exchanging notes from the film *To Sir With Love*, jointly humming Lulu's hit song. Their harmonic pleasures were interrupted by Isla and Jimmy, arriving hand in hand.

'Are you still singing that song?' said Isla.

'I love that film, Sidney Poitier is so smashing, he just oozes *sex* appeal. That smile, those eyes… he's my man!' cooed Lucy Rose.

'He wouldn't give you a second look, with your attitude and all,' said Betty.

'What's that meant to mean? You need a mirror to check in on your own attitude. Your mirror's full of pus, from you squeezing all those pimples livin' on your poxy forehead!' said Lucy Rose.

'Ooooooh harsh, very harsh, nasty even. At least I'm not covered in orange freckles! By the way, ever noticed your hair's on fire, Lucy? Quick, grab a bucket of water someone!' laughed Betty.

'Oh God, stop it you two! Enough with the bitchy comments already. Where's the love? Feel the love girls! Love, peace and happiness, this is the 1960s!' said Isla.

'Yeah girls, feel the love!' said Jimmy.

'I can see you're feeling the love alright, Jimmy McRoberts! And too often from what Isla tells us,' laughed Betty. Jimmy blushed, giving Isla a stare.

Oblivious to his discomfort, Isla said, 'Jimmy's mate, the chemist's son, looks after us and all. Free love without playing Russian roulette, hey Jimmy?'

'Too right love. Don't need a yapping kid to spoil the fun!' said Jimmy.

'You sure about that, Jimmy?' said Betty, holding up her pinky then slowly lowering it.

'Oh, you girls are just too much. Jesus! I'm headed to geography class. Catch you at lunch, Isla.' Jimmy went to head off but Isla pulled him back by his woollen scarf.

'Hey, not before I kiss you, Jimmy McRoberts!' She drew him closer and kissed him on the cheek. 'Now you can go, Jimmy!'

He smiled at her for a moment, turned around and headed up the hill. A short distance away, he called out to her, caught her attention and blew her a kiss before making his way to class.

'Oooooooo!' cheered Betty and Lucy Rose.

'He's a keeper,' said Lucy Rose, 'and hot!'

'He's not too bad,' said Isla, smiling at her comrades, 'but there's so much life in front of us girls, the world's at our feet with many adventures to be had. Gotta get out of this town first! I'm sure there are many more Jimmys in the world!'

'You're such a slut Isla,' smiled Betty.

'Takes one to know one!' Isla winked at her.

'Don't you want to settle down with your man, have a bairn or two, build a home, you know, live happily ever after?' said Lucy Rose.

'Jesus, you readin' too many of those romantic Mills & Boon type books, Lucy Rose,' laughed Betty.

'I think it's way too early for that, Lucy Rose. Been stuck here for too long,' said Isla. 'There's a world out there I want to explore. I want to suck up the air, run free, perform, sing my way around the world. I want to travel to Australia… find my roots and all.'

'Seems to me you're finding enough roots here,' chuckled Betty.

'Betty, you're such a *whore!*' said Lucy Rose.

'As Isla said, takes one to know one, Lucy *loose!*' said Betty.

'Do you two ever give it a rest? Now come on, let's head to class. Miss McAlistair's French Revolution is a bit more bearable than this one here!' laughed Isla.

The girls headed up the hill, with Betty and Lucy Rose playfully pushing each other and trailing behind Isla.

'I feel like the mother hen with you too, Jesus! But I love you both,' said Isla, peering over her left shoulder and giving her friends a grin.

After history class, Isla arrived early for her next scheduled lesson with Morag. Sitting in the music room was always so peaceful and she loved breathing in the serenity. The room had a musty smell about it, probably due to the collection of old books and music scores filling the nearby bookcase. There were occasional photos of a younger Morag with her mother and a young boy Isla assumed was Morag's brother. There were also numerous music trophies and even a gold-plated orchestral baton, awarded to Morag for conductor concert excellence.

Studying the antique bookcase in greater depth, she noticed its fine, intricate, impressive woodwork and classic large paw feet. For a moment, she recalled her father's bookcase, and the familiar scent of the room also jogged her memory. She remembered her father sitting at his piano, pencil clenched between his teeth. She saw him look up from his piano score, flick his hair back and give her his familiar wide smile. Then, Larry was there, jumping about.

Morag's door burst open and the memory dissolved.

'Oh there you are Isla. You beat me for a change! Now, before we start work today with your exam pieces, I need to have a talk with you... a serious one. I've been ponderin' this for some time and given that final exams are only two weeks away, it's now or never.'

Isla was still shaking off her brief dream interlude and trying to focus. Morag's words made her anxious. Was she about to be reprimanded for something?

'Now, as I said, I've been thinkin' lassie, something ol' Morag doesn't have much time for now that I'm school principal. You're one of the best pupils I've had the pleasure of teachin' in a long time. I've never heard a 17-year-old play like you do. You play like the music speaks to you lass, and in so doin' you speak to us, your audience. I float lass, every time I hear ya' play. I cannot describe it, but it's electric. Spine-tinglin' stuff. You have the gift, lassie. You're charmed, or maybe your father is channellin' you, your nimble fingers or both. But listenin' to you play is my bread, butter n' jam, it feeds ol' Morag's soul it does. Anyhow, I'm ramblin' a wee bit, but the point is this: you're too good not to further improve y'self. You deserve a shot at it, the world deserves you give it a shot.'

Morag went to the top drawer of her desk and presented an application form for Cambridge University.

'There it is lass and if you wish, I'll be your sponsor and referee.' She smiled, placing the form into Isla's hands.

'But, Morag, Mum won't agree, she can't afford it, I can't afford it!'

'Just check the addendum to that form lassie, there's a scholarship application. I reckon we can get you there. The audition is in three weeks' time after your final exams. We have worked on that song of yours, *Isla's Song,* year after year and I feel there's enough meat on the bone to impress a panel. It's in a fine state, better than fine. It'd make your dad proud. It'd make me proud, lassie. We can do this. What say you?'

Isla took her time perusing the forms. She got to the last page and a tear dropped onto the page. She reached for her handkerchief and blew her runny nose. She continued to look down at the form, transfixed.

'Well, what say you lass? What say you? We can do it, we *can* do it!'

'You really think so?'

'I do not think so lass, I know so!'

Isla glanced up from the page, her heart full of spirit. 'Alright, let's do it, as long as you're at the audition with me.'

'I wouldn't miss it for the world!' exclaimed Morag. 'Now let's practice, don't you think? Gotta keep up that momentum, lassie!'

That afternoon when Isla arrived home, she was anxious to share the news about her university application with her mother. Jess had had the day off work and was preparing Isla's favourite roast chicken with duck fat spuds and fresh peas.

'So how was your day, Isla? You must be doing lots of work gearing up for those finals, no doubt!'

'Yes, so much to do, but I'm top of it Mum.'

Jess had been making a real effort since that eventful evening when her conscience was preyed upon by visions of the past. After the night, she had kept her personal promise to remain sober and life thereafter travelled along at a reasonably calm pace, apart from its usual ups and downs. As Isla grew, Jess could see more and more of Oliver in her, including his big blue eyes, cheeky grin and the way he used his arms to express his feelings. It was a constant thorn in her side. The guilt of her decision to tell Isla her father had died increasingly haunted her. It even woke her up in the middle of the night. There was no retreat. But every time Isla now called her 'Mum', it reinforced for her that despite all her faults, she must be doing something right.

Besides, she thought, *I raised Isla to blossom into a beautiful, gifted, free-spirited woman.* She has grown into a true force of nature. Just as Jess thought this, she knew she had stolen that opportunity from Oliver, watching their daughter grow into this powerful, headstrong woman, and she knew that she could ill afford to deliberate over her past choices. She well understood her emotional Achilles heel and knew that to venture into that dark place would only cause her to lose her balance on the fine line of her well-travelled tightrope.

'I'm so proud of you, love. I want you to know that,' said Jess.

'Thanks Mum, I can only try. And sometimes it's very trying! By the way, a couple of things, I have something important to discuss at dinner with you...'

Jess interrupted, 'What is it? What is it? News? Good news? I want to hear it!'

'At dinner, Mum. What do you say to me? All good things come to those who wait!'

'Oh, using my epitaphs against me now are we?'

Isla laughed, 'Hardly an epitaph!'

'And the other thing, Jimmy has asked me to the post-exam dance and I want to wear those patent black heels of yours. Can I?'

'Deal, only if you swear you'll tell me that other bit of news at dinner, as you promised.'

'I am a woman of my word, of course. So where are those shoes, Mum? I want to try them on now.'

'On top of my wardrobe miss. But hurry, dinner's nearly ready!'

With the sun setting on another day, the bedroom was lit mainly by the glow of the oil lantern, which Isla carefully placed on her mother's bedside table. Opening the curtain did little to enhance the light.

Standing on tippy-toes, Isla fossicked about the top of the wardrobe until she could feel the outside of a shoebox. She just managed to edge it forward. However in doing so, she caused a nearby box to topple over the edge, its contents of envelopes spilling all over the floor. There must have been at least 50 letters, Isla thought, quickly looking at the bedroom door to check for her mother. She moved the lantern closer to view the envelopes and noticed the date stamps spanned over many years, with the mail appearing to go from Australia to London and from there, get redirected to her mother. Each of the envelopes was distinctively marked *Sender: O Johnson*. That's my father's name, Isla thought, her heart racing and her eyes darting from one envelope to another, confirming their identical markings. *Jesus, what is this? Why hasn't my mother ever disclosed these letters? Some of the date stamps were recent.* The blood drained from Isla's cheeks and she became lightheaded.

'Isla, where are you, love? Did you find the shoes? Dinner's ready! What are you doing?'

Isla quickly packed the envelopes back into the box. She paused for a moment and rather than confront her mother, decided to open one of the letters and discover the truth for herself. Just as she was about to tear an envelope open, Jess appeared at the bedroom door.

'What are you up to miss? I *did not* give you permission to go snooping around my room! Give that box to me!' she said, terrified that Isla had already read one of the letters.

Isla heard her mother, but it didn't register. She was spellbound by the writing on the back of the envelope. *Is this my father's handwriting,* she thought, *could this be him?*

Jess intervened, breaking Isla's entrancement, collecting the letters and grabbing the box from the floor. Isla was left holding a single letter.

'It's none of your business, Isla. I'll get your shoes! Out of here now!'

Isla remained seated on the floor, the glow of the lantern lighting her up from underneath, giving her a ghostly appearance.

'Are these my father's letters?' cried Isla. 'Are these letters from him? Is my father alive? Have you been lying to me all this time?'

Jess's thoughts raced. She had dreaded this day of reckoning, knowing that it might arrive. But she had always hoped that if it did, she would have long since left this earthly plane. In the panic of the moment, her brain went into overload and she spat out, 'It's your aunt, Isla, the letters are from your aunt. Aunt Olivia. *Olivia Johnson.*'

Isla's shoulders slumped, her hopes destroyed in seconds with that one response. For a moment, she had thought her father could be alive. So many thoughts had crossed her mind at once, including the possibility that he was alive, a slim hope, she knew, but something that for a brief moment had lit up her heart. Better a deception and to discover my dad really is alive, she had thought.

'Can I open this letter then, Mum? I'd like to read it.'

'No! I'd prefer not, if you don't mind. I was going to destroy them, all of them. Every time I received a bundle from your Aunt Gerry, it crossed my mind. But I decided to keep them and let you make your own choice when I'm long gone from this world. Now is not the time, Isla. Not now. I've never told you this and it's never been easy for me, but your Aunt Olivia blamed me for your father's death. I spoke to her shortly after his accident. She told me that if I hadn't travelled to England, it never would've happened. He would never have died in that terrible car crash. Her words were so cruel. Unforgiving really. So I cut ties.'

'What *terrible car crash*? You never mentioned a *car crash,* Mother! In fact you've never even told me how my father died. I wanted to ask you, but I never did. I didn't want to cause you pain. I'll never forget that day at Thurso. You told me he was dead. Dead! That's it! I don't remember you telling me anything else. I don't even remember him having a funeral.' Isla was desperately searching her mind for particulars.

'You were so little, love. And I was so devastated. Your father was supposed to meet us at Glasgow and that's where we were when I got the devastating news from your Aunt Gerry. He was driving from London in a heavy snowstorm when the accident happened. His car was found at the bottom of a ridge. He must've lost sight of the roadway. I didn't know what to do, what to say, Isla. There we were, the two of us, no home, no money and for me, no husband. I had to be strong, love. I had to be strong for us. I had no choice. There was no funeral here as your Aunt Olivia shipped your father's body back to Australia as soon as she could. That was another one of our fights. She refused to allow me to bury him in London, as I wanted.

She wouldn't even let me... *us,* pay our last respects. I didn't have one cracker to pay for our fares back to London, where your father was lying alone in some hospital. Told me she would sick lawyers onto me if I refused to let her fly him back to Australia. Well, I couldn't afford legal costs. The house back home hardly had any equity, with your father and I struggling to make ends meet. I was ripped apart in every way. Your Aunt Gerry was struggling for a penny too and couldn't help. As for Olivia? After our last argument, she told me I could rot in hell for all she cared. Seemed she didn't give a damn about you either, love. As you can probably gather, I've never forgiven her. I've never been abused like that in my life. So I decided I had to do the best I could. I did it for you, for us, and it was hard. God's hard, Isla. After that I lost my faith, your mother's ashamed to say it, but that's when I took to the bottle. But I've changed, Isla. You can see that and I did it for you. It's always been about you, love. I love you!'

Jess took a breath, gauging the impact of her story on Isla.

'I know it's a lot to take in, love, but I've been protecting you. Believe me. That's all I've ever done. After the accident, I knew it was just the two of us. I've done the best I could. You were just a tiny child then.'

'But why have you waited now to tell me? And why haven't you told me about these letters and about Aunt Olivia?'

'I wanted you to be old enough to understand. I didn't mean for it to happen like this. I'm sorry. I could never bear to open those letters, not after what your aunt did to us and said to me. Still, I chose to keep them for you, in case you wanted to read them later.'

Isla was still stunned, not knowing what to believe. She needed time to digest the evening's events.

'So, do we still have our house in Australia?'

'No love, your aunt ended up selling it, probably saying your dad died without a will and spinning some story I was untraceable! That woman has a lot to answer for!'

'I see… So… you don't want me to open them now, is that what you're saying, Mother?'

'I would prefer you didn't. It would pain me so if you did. Do you understand, Isla? If I'm true to myself, you know, I'm still hurting and I can well do without pickin' at those emotional scabs. Please believe me Isla, I did it for you love. It was all for you. I put those letters behind me for now, for my own mental health. And I'd ask you to respect your mum's wishes. I'm not saying *never*, I'm just saying now. Do you understand, love?'

Isla was at a crossroads. She harboured some niggling doubts about her mother's story, still hinging her hopes on it all being a lie and that her father was in fact alive, and perhaps even trying to find her. On the other hand, there was a part of her that was drawn into her mother's heartfelt, honest account of past events.

She was also comforted by her mother's recent changes and the fact that she had given up alcohol. She really was trying to do the best she could.

On balance, Isla decided not to rock the boat and show her mother a level of support. *I'll wait*, she thought, *Mum's right, now's not the right time. I can wait, even if it's only for a short time.*

'Here Mum, take this letter. You're right, I can wait.'

Jess's rapid breathing settled and she gently took the letter. Reminiscent of the day she had told Isla of her father's demise, she crouched down and whispered in her ear, 'He'd be so proud of you!'

She hugged Isla in the comforting light of the oil lantern.

Chapter 18

Wild Things Run Fast

After a restless night's sleep, Isla woke up rubbing her eyes and yawning. She spotted her scholarship application on her desk and recalled that she had failed to talk about it with her mother.

Unsettled from the previous night's events, there was still a part of her that regretted handing over that envelope to her mother. *Must push those thoughts away*, she thought, *what's done is done, for now I have to focus on my final exams and scholarship application. My time will come, the right time. Things have a way of working themselves out, I'm sure… at least I hope…* She looked to the ceiling.

Then she jumped out of bed, put on her woollen dressing-gown and fluffy pink slippers and placed the scholarship form in her pocket as a reminder to secure her mother's signature.

Jess was in the kitchen tending to breakfast.

'How did you sleep, love?'

'Alright, not too bad. Tossed and turned a bit. Guess my final exams are playing on my mind,' she said, covering up the real reason for her restless night.

'That's no good, let's get some warm food into your engine to get you through the day. It's a cold miserable day outside, so rug up, love. Winter's on the wing.'

Jess placed a stack of pancakes on the table with Isla's favourite toppings of strawberry jam, maple syrup and cream.

After also placing a mug of hot chocolate in front of her, she said, 'Have you thought about universities? I've had a look at Edinburgh and Glasgow. London's way too far away. There are some really good options

Isla, depending on what you want to do. What have you been considering, love? Arts? Medicine? Teaching?'

'No, not really Mum. None of those. I'm thinking music, you know, composition, performance, voice, probably at some of the colleges or unis near London. *Cambridge*, for example.'

'Cambridge? So far away. It's *too far away,* Isla. And expensive! Why would you want to go there anyway? And music? I know you love piano and you'll always have that gift to be able to play. But for a job? Isla, these are tough times and you need a job that will sustain you. Music is *not* a job. It's a hobby. I couldn't support it, Isla, I won't support such a choice. Look at how your father used to struggle teaching and composing, we could barely survive. That's why I had to work so hard, all those night shifts, whilst he went on doodling songs between students.'

'I wouldn't remember, Mother!'

A tense silence swept over the room.

Jess was concerned that she had gone too far. She looked across the table and noticed Isla's dressing-gown. 'What's that paper in your pocket, Isla?'

Isla stood up, putting down her drink mug and wiping her mouth with a floral serviette. Staring at her mother sheepishly, she said, 'Nothing Mother, just some study notes, keep them close by as a reminder, you know.'

'Have no fear love, you *will do well*. I have every confidence in you. You've worked hard and you'll get the results you need, I just know it! You only need to focus. We'll get you into one of those universities, I know we will.'

'Thanks. I best be off now, running late. See you tonight. Can't eat anymore, but thanks.'

'You've hardly touched your breakfast. Are you alright?'

'Fine. Butterflies and all that, but I'll be okay, I always am, you know me, Mother.'

With that, she disappeared into her room, brushed her hair, cleaned her teeth and changed into her school uniform. She grabbed her school bag but before swinging it over her shoulder, noticed the scholarship application poking its head from the pocket of her dressing-gown perched over the study chair. She seized it, peered down to the bottom of the form at the parent's signature line and signed it *Jessica Johnson*. She folded it, stuck it in her school bag and called out a farewell to her mother.

Two weeks later, the first of five exams commenced. All the students lined up outside the gymnasium ready to be ushered to their desks in anticipation of their English exam. Isla, Betty and Lucy Rose were all jittery, bouncing up and down to keep themselves warm. It was going to be a huge week, one that they had all worked so hard towards, perhaps except for Betty, who had as usual over-indulged down at the pier with the apprentice fishmongers.

'I really need this exam, I need to romp it in,' said Isla.

'Me too,' said Lucy Rose, 'I want to get into one of those posh universities in London.'

'Maybe Cambridge?' said Isla.

'Maybe!'

'Well, I don't know what all the fuss is about, you too. I'm heading to beauty school, going to set up my own shop and all and if you two are lucky, I might even do your hair and nails,' said Betty.

'You are on!' said Isla.

It was 9.00 a.m. and the bell sounded, all students scurrying into the exam hall and taking their seats.

Morag was seated at the front with Mr Lewis and Sister Angela.

'Well, young men and women, the day of reckoning has arrived. We wish you well. You've all worked hard. Pens down at 12.15 noon sharp. You are allowed 15 minutes reading time.' Looking at her watch, Morag signalled, 'Your time starts now!'

The week sped past. It was arduous and all-consuming, however, Isla felt she had done herself proud. Results would not be in for another three weeks. In the interim, Isla had her scholarship interview at Cambridge and Morag had promised to chaperone her. As school had officially ended, she told her mother a white lie that she was joining her friends in Glasgow for the day and staying overnight at Betty's aunt's home. Jess did not mind and felt that it was a fitting reward for all of Isla's hard work.

Isla had also separately reassured Morag that her mother was fine with the overnight arrangements, saying she would've joined them except for her nursing commitments. Morag thought nothing of it and was more focussed on calming Isla and ensuring that she gave the scholarship interview and audition her best shot.

The train trip south was long and it was a relief spotting the Victoria Station sign, heralding their arrival in London. It was only a short walk around the corner to the Sisters of Charity convent, where they were provided with free overnight lodgings. After morning mass at 6.00 a.m. and a solid breakfast of bacon, eggs, toast and black pudding, Isla and Morag travelled by train to Cambridge University.

Although a wintry day, the snow has eased and the sun glistened on the fresh snowfall. The bluestone buildings at Cambridge University were a majestic vista with their iron-barred arched windows partially covered with evergreen creepers. The cobblestone paving and hallway stone arches made Isla feel like a queen. At the rear of the President's Lodge, the Mathematical Bridge connected Queen's College across the Cam River, where students and tourists punted in narrow flat-bottomed boats. The green willows angled their limbs over the banks, providing shade to the water fowl and a foreground that would have appealed to Monet. It was everything that she had imagined and more.

Eventually, they found the exam room and took their seats outside, awaiting Isla's name to be called. The cacophony of musicians tuning their instruments and testing their voices emanated from other hallway doors. Isla thought there was a real feeling of life about it, as if something magnificent would be born from this sheer musical force.

'Johnson, Isla Johnson, come in. Are you her mother, madam?' said the usher.

'No, I'm her supervisor, her teacher. May I?' said Morag.

'Yes, you may. Come in Isla, the panel looks forward to meeting you.'

They entered the room. As usual, Morag's spindly stature overshadowed Isla, who sprang from Morag's silhouette at the last minute to greet her examiners.

'Pleased to meet you Isla, I'm Professor Russell, this is Dr Capaul, Dr Tehan and Professor Clifford. Have a seat, dear. You too, madam,' he said, pointing to Morag. Professor Russell wore a houndstooth jacket, beige shirt and traditional Cambridge tie. He was a well-preserved man in his 50s with blond, greying, wavy hair and emerald-green eyes. His gaze lulled Isla into a sense of security and comfort, despite the nerves in her stomach. His smile reminded her a little of her father's grin, what she could remember of it, the same cheery face that lit up the dullest room.

'We've all read your application,' he said. 'We understand you're awaiting your final exam marks, but assuming all goes well, we will be assessing you today on your interview and your chosen music piece. Do you understand, Isla?'

'Yes sir, I understand,' said Isla.

'So in your own words, Isla, what brings you here?' Dr Capaul asked.

'I love music, that's all,' said Isla. There was an awkward silence and Morag subtly smacked her thigh. The sound resonated, and all the examiners looked up from their papers. Morag ineptly cleared her throat.

'I mean, I just love it, I don't why exactly. It's like I'm standin' in the valley of those Scottish highlands, where wild things run fast… and the music, it just fills me, it fills my heart, my breathing, my soul. I feel the buzz in my fingertips. It's electric. It makes me run and run and soon I'm one of those wild things, but armed with a music that carries me like the wind. It's just me and the music. That's all. We're one. Joined at the hip, you know. And I know whether it be in the Orkneys, London, Australia or wherever, it's the music that matters, because without it, my wildness is lost. My essence is gone. Yeah… that's it,' she said.

Morag nudged her thigh again and gave her an approving grin.

'Thank you, Isla. I think we get the picture. Would you play us your piano piece now? First, please tell us what it is and why you've chosen it?' said Professor Russell.

'That's easy, it's called *Isla's Song*. My dad named it after me. He started it when I was three years old. It was the first piece I ever played, well, I guess not that well when I was so little. There are so many happy memories for me in this piece of music. My dad didn't make it to Scotland with Mum and I years ago, when we came here from Australia. He died on the way in a car crash. But with Morag's help, I continued to work on his song… *our song*, and I hope I've done my dad proud. It's my ode to him. I know he's lookin' down on me when I perform it. He's with me today, I can feel it, he is. And if you listen really carefully, you might just hear him between the notes. That's where the real music lies,' said Isla.

Proudly, she stood up and took her seat at the mini grand piano to the right of the examination table. Morag moved to the entrance door and sat silently cheering on her young protégé.

A moment of silence enveloped the room and then Isla's fingertips began to stroke the ivory keys. A heavenly heartfelt music charged the air. The music transported Isla to a faraway place. She envisioned herself as a young girl with long, curly, wild hair, wearing a free-flowing white linen dress, running through a Scottish valley, each touch of the ivory her fingertips reaching for the heather. She could see herself spinning round and round, growing older with each rotation, her heart brimming with joy, a fulfillment like no other, her laughter awakening every bud to bloom. Then she saw herself as no longer a child but a singer–songwriter in her 20s, staring at the passing clouds, each one painting a different picture, until she spotted a fluffy white one resisting the air current. It stood still above her. The shape was familiar; Isla and her father. A small cloud was connected to the larger by a feathery wisp, shaped like a puppy. Other clouds moved around these two in tune with each note played. The movement was poetry in motion, telling a tale of freedom, desire and achievement, but for Isla, there was a loving tale of contentment about it. Knowing what it meant to be loved.

When the piece ended, Isla gently raised her hands from the keyboard. She glanced once more at the sheet music, as if seeking her father's approval. Then she glanced over at Morag, who was wiping tears from her eyes. Eventually, she stood up and collected her sheet music.

'Thank you, Isla. We appreciate you travelling so far today. We shall be in touch shortly, once your exam marks have been published,' said Professor Russell.

Isla smiled politely, nodded and walked out of the room, Morag behind her. This time, she did not take refuge in any shadow. Once outside, Morag grasped her hand and said, 'You did me proud girl, so proud. I bet you also did your father proud, lassie.'

'I know I did,' said Isla.

'How so, miss?' Morag raised an eyebrow.

'Because he was sitting right next to me on that piano stool, Morag, that's why,' she smiled.

Morag gave her hand a squeeze. 'I think you deserve a hot chocolate as a reward. What say you?'

'You're on, teacher extraordinaire,' said Isla, 'And Morag? I love you!'

Back in Stromness, the transistor radio was turned up to full volume, with Isla accompanying the folksy sound of The Seekers from behind the plastic shower curtain.

'Hey *Georgy girl,* the postman's arrived!' Jess called out. 'Bet it's your marks. They said December first and here we are. Hurry up!'

Isla jumped out of the warm shower, switched off the radio and quickly got dressed. She ran to the letterbox and collected the mail. Amongst the bundle, she fished out a letter addressed to her from Stromness Secondary School. She ripped open the envelope and unfolded the letter, reading her results. Honours in every subject with special commendations for drama and music.

Isla stood in the cold by the letterbox. Light snow was falling, but it only made the moment more magical. *I did it*, she thought, *I bloody did it! I knocked, and now my door to opportunity is opening.* She looked up into the grey sky, snowflakes kissing her cheeks, and yelled, 'I did it! I bloody well did it!' loud enough to unsettle some nearby seagulls resting on chimney stacks.

'Come in, Isla! Come in! Have you lost your senses child?'

She skipped up to the front door, 'Mum, I did it!'

Her mother grabbed the letter and absorbed her daughter's achievement.

'My Lord, Isla! Isla, oh my Lord, these marks are incredible. Congratulations, my darling girl. You have worked so hard and achieved so much. Mum is so proud of you. With results like these the world is at your feet. You can now take your pick of universities, I'm sure, Edinburgh or Glasgow. Either will welcome you with marks like these.'

Isla stopped cavorting about the lounge room, thinking about her audition at Cambridge.

'Yes Mum, I know. Exciting! Have to give it all careful thought. Lots to consider,' she said.

Later that afternoon, Betty and Lucy Rose came around. No-one except

Morag knew about Isla's audition at Cambridge, and Morag thought that Jess had given her permission.

'So I passed,' said Betty. 'That's all I wanted and that's what I got. Mum's teed up my apprenticeship at Shirley's Mane Attraction, the beauty parlour in Inverness, and I start in two weeks. Once I learn a bit, I'll try some fancy new dos on your hair, girls. How'd you two trolls like that? You could both do with wee makeovers. It's no wonder Jimmy dumped you for Charlene, Isla!'

'Oh piss off, Betty, I dumped him. After his mid-thrust condom-breaking episode. He couldn't even get that right. His mate Colin, who used to steal the French letters for us from his father's chemist shop, got him a pack that was too small. And the rest is history. I need a more experienced lover, one who doesn't confuse the size of his pea brain with the size of his wiener. Hopeless! Anyhow, wasn't as if I loved him or anything, he just sorta fulfilled a girl's desires!' said Isla.

'Ooooh, a girl's desires! Aren't we all hoity-toity and so New Age. Free love and all that! Does your mother know about your *girl's desires*?' Lucy Rose said in a smouldering tone.

'Yeah, does Mummy know, Isla? Or do the boys have the only input, so to speak,' laughed Betty, rubbing her hands up and down her thighs suggestively.

'Oh, you two are incorrigible,' said Isla.

'Jesus, what does that even mean?' said Betty.

'She's having a go at our bumpy corrugated thighs, Betty, just because hers are so perfect,' said Lucy Rose.

'Oh my God, you two are hilarious and you know what? I'm going to really miss you and all your craziness! I do love you both,' laughed Isla.

'I'm going to miss you too,' said Betty.

'Me too,' said Lucy Rose. 'Oh and by the way, in case you wanted to know, not bragging, but I got enough marks to get into Cambridge and

I'm doing arts. Greek history and criminology, I think.'

'You just wanna perve at those naked hairy Greek butts,' said Betty, 'I love a man with a hairy butt.'

'Hardly, I'm hoping to squeeze a real one, dear,' said Lucy Rose, lifting her red horn-rimmed spectacles.

All girls let out a burst of laughter.

'What about you, Isla? What are you thinking?' said Lucy Rose, composing herself.

Isla was so tempted to tell her friends about her audition at Cambridge, especially now that Lucy Rose had disclosed her intention to attend the same college. But she fell short of disclosing her dream, afraid of tempting fate.

'I'm thinking I might do a bit of research first on the courses available before I lock in anything. Besides, a girl always needs to broaden her horizons.'

'Look where that got you with Jimmy! Maybe ease back on the broadening stuff, Isla. You don't want another broken condom. Not a good look taking a pram to uni, Whaaa! Whaaaa!' said Betty. She and Lucy Rose laughed and danced around their friend, mocking her.

Isla's impatience grew over the coming days. She had had no word from Cambridge and guessed that she was unsuccessful. She had pinned all her hopes on that audition and didn't know what to do if she didn't get in.

One early morning about a week after her school exam results were released, Isla looked out her bedroom window after hearing the familiar quick step of Morag, who was climbing their front stairs. She was wearing the same black coat she had worn for years. It was adorned with a large silver beetle brooch on its left lapel. She also wore black silk gloves, black stockings and grey velvet motor boots, with a coney fur trim and velveteen uppers. Her now grey hair was kept from blowing in the breeze by a matching beetle clasp. With her nose, known for its ability to sniff out danger, pointed to the heavens, Morag arrived at the front door, giving two sharp knocks on the middle wooden panel.

Jess opened the door to find Morag fishing through her clutch bag.

'Oh, here it is!' she said, waving the envelope at Jess. 'I thought I would deliver it to Isla directly. It was sent to me, as I put the school's address on the form by mistake.'

'I'm sorry?' said Jess. 'What are talking about? Isla has her results already, Morag.'

'No, these are from Cambridge dear, see the wee emblem stamp on the front?' Morag pointed to the school insignia. 'It's her results from the audition.'

'What audition?'

'Oh Jessica, you know, the audition for Cambridge University. The Faculty of Music. You remember dear, you signed the application form.'

'I did no such thing, Morag. I did not sign any application form. When did this happen? How did she sit the exam?' said Jess, distressed.

Morag sized up Jess's anxiety and sensed that Isla had some explaining to do.

'Is Isla in, Jessica?' she said, trying to remain calm.

'Yes, I'll get her, she's in bed.'

'Well, it be 15 past the hour of nine. She mustn't miss any more of this day. Fetch her, please. Tell her Morag comes bearing news from... from Cambridge.'

Whilst Morag waited patiently in the lounge area, Jess prodded Isla out of bed, hurling questions at her in whispered tones about supposed results from Cambridge. By then, Isla had wiped the sleep from her eyes, wrapped herself in her dressing-gown, jumped into her fluffy slippers and scampered down the hallway to greet Morag, who calmly sat there waving the Cambridge envelope back and forth, as if fanning herself.

'Oh my God, it's arrived, it's arrived Morag!'

Jessica joined the party in the loungeroom, '*What's* arrived?'

Isla drew in a quick breath. 'Sit down, Mum, here, sit down,' said Isla, pointing to her mother's favourite club chair. 'I'll grab you some water.'

Then she stood with her back to the fireplace and addressed her audience.

'Now don't go off at me, Mum, please. I just wanted to keep my options open. You always taught me that, remember? You said in life, never nail yourself to one post. You wanted options for me. So when you started talking about unis at Edinburgh and Glasgow, I thought I'd take your advice and check out some other options as well. You know, just in case. Well, it so happens around that time, Morag showed me the scholarship application for Cambridge. For music. Anyhow, I knew you were against me going too far away, but I thought I would give it a go anyway. Y'know, see what happened. So I signed the form for you...'

'You did what!' said Morag and Jess simultaneously.

'And I gave it to Morag to post and I auditioned. Morag took me.'

'You took her!' said Jess, glaring at Morag.

Morag only allowed herself a quick glance at Jess, before turning to Isla. 'So, miss, I became your accomplice, in a fashion?' she said, trying not to smile at Isla's wicked deceit.

'Well no, not like that. Mum... Morag... you know how much I love music. It's a part of me.'

'Oh, I know alright,' Morag said, 'you should've heard her interview, Jessica, now that was something else.' She wiped her mouth with a handkerchief.

'Yes, well, if I had known about the interview, I might have, Morag!' said Jess.

'It's what I want. It's what I want to do. If it's meant to be, it's meant to be. Whatever is in that envelope, that's my future. One way or the other,' said Isla.

Jess slumped forward in the chair, holding her head in her hands for a moment and then clasping them in a prayer position. She didn't know what to say. She was ashamed that Isla had chosen to lie to her and align herself with Morag. She felt belittled that the flaws in their relationship had been exposed to Morag, a woman with whom Isla had now been confiding for a number of years. Jess had come a long way from her nightly benders in front of the fireplace. She had done a lot of soul-searching, yet her journey was far from complete. Now, she knew she could not risk losing her daughter or alienating her by denying her dream to study music. The words of her own mother echoed in her mind.

'Alright, Isla. I'm not happy. I thought I'd raised you better. There was no need to lie to me, to forge my signature, to take Morag on a wild goose chase. Here's the deal. If what's in that envelope says you're accepted into Cambridge, so be it. You'll have my blessings. Might even move closer to you if I have to. *But,* if you're not successful, you'll be going to Glasgow University to study medicine. Is it a deal?'

Morag leant forward from the couch, placing the promising envelope on the coffee table. She sat back again, her hands poised on her nimble knees, awaiting the official outcome whilst reciting Hail Marys to herself.

Isla looked at her mother, and then over to Morag. Slowly, her gaze transferred to that single envelope sitting by itself on the table. She took in a deep breath and said to her mother, 'Deal!'

Picking up the envelope, she slowly tore it open at its end. She slid the letter out, unfolded it and with darting eyes devoured its contents. Without any expression, she slowly looked up over the letter to Morag and her mother.

'Yes, bloody yes! The wild child plays again, I'm off to Cambridge! I'm off to Cambridge!'

Jess stood up, hands fidgeting, not knowing exactly what to say or do, as Isla rushed over to Morag, giving her the biggest heartfelt hug, 'We did it! We did it!'

Morag lifted Isla's petite chin with her spindly forefinger and winked at her. 'That we did, lassie! We sure did!'

Chapter 19

The Wizard of Is

Monday 2 September 1968

Isla stepped off the train at Cambridge Station, hands overladen with luggage. It was the first day of autumn, with the past now making way for further growth and new beginnings. For Isla, it was like a dream arriving there, finally making it after all those years of study.

She dropped her bags and fossicked for the self-drawn map lodged in her coat pocket. *Ah yes, I remember now*, she thought, *the herringbone red brick road to Newnham College.* She picked up her luggage and with that, a sudden warm breeze blew the map from out of her hand.

'Have no fear, damsel, I am to the rescue, with steed awaiting!'

Taken aback, Isla dropped her bags, watching a young man chase her map and try to scoop it from the ground without success, the thermal current whisking it out of his reach. Moments later he returned.

'Well, mademoiselle, I failed on this mission, however, I have a feeling I can still be of some use. I am at your service!'

Isla smiled at his cheeky grin. 'And who may you be, brave knight?'

'Knight, hardly!' he laughed. 'My friends call me the Wizard, because I appear from nowhere and always at the most opportune of moments, my lady.'

'And my dear Wizard, what is your name?'

'My friends call me Wiz for short, though in certain familial settings, I am known as Isaac.'

'I see, Isaac... or Wiz, if I may be so bold. I am indebted to you for your

THE WIZARD OF IS

attempt at rescuing my map, however, now I am but a lost damsel in need of guidance.'

'Again, the Wiz has arrived in a timely fashion. I can guide you and if you're lucky, I can even lead you astray,' he chuckled.

Isla was taken in by his extrovert nature, the way he skilfully deployed his words and how when he smiled, his dimples enhanced his handsome face. His curly black locks bounced off his shoulders, and he was tall and alluring in his pin-stripe trousers, pointed black shoes and maroon braces over a crepe shirt displaying the Trinity College emblem.

'I bet you can, Wiz... Isaac!' said Isla, flirting with her eyes and blushing all at once. 'I am headed with this cargo to Newnham College, but I have no idea how to get there!'

'As I said, the Wiz is at your service. My red MG steed awaits and I think there is just enough room for these bags of yours. Blimey, did you bring the kitchen sink as well?'

Picking up her bags, Isaac led the way to his car, parked just outside the station gates. The roof was down, making it easy for him to deposit her luggage. Whilst arranging the bags, he turned to his waiting passenger. 'By the way, your turn!'

'My turn for what?'

'Your name, it's only fair since I told you mine. A bit of show and tell,' he said, suggestively raising his eyebrows.

'I see. My name, sir, is Isla. That's my name and that's what my friends call me.'

'Well, I shall call you Isla then,' he said, winking at his newfound friend, 'hop in!'

Getting into the sports car, she gazed at him, not believing her luck at meeting him and being driven to college. 'And may I ask, what were you doing at the station anyhow? Obviously not waiting for me!'

'I wish I could say yes, dear damsel, however, my folks had sent me a parcel by rail. It was supposed to arrive but did not. Nevertheless, a much fairer package arrived in its place. How lucky am I! Right spot, right time, you know!'

'You seem to have a lucky air about you, Wiz!'

'Well Isla, it's a two-way street when it comes to luck, dearest damsel!'

Isla inwardly giggled. He was handsome, but the way his eyes popped with expression and his flamboyant hand gestures reminded her of the lanky scarecrow from *The Wizard of Oz*. She pinched herself discreetly, making sure that this was not a dream. *I'm not wearing ruby slippers*, she thought.

When they arrived at Newnham College, Isaac helped her with her luggage to the front gate.

'Men are not allowed past this gate, damsel. If I did so venture, the myth is that I would turn to stone and we couldn't have that, seeing as we've just met. I'm at Trinity College, two minutes up the road. I am sure we will meet again. When the Wiz has a feeling, it usually comes to fruition.' He winked. 'It's orientation week on the main campus, hope to see you there... and good luck, the headmistress is a bit of a witch... so I'm told.' He laughed. 'Ta-ta, fair damsel, until next time. Onward, my steed!'

As instantly as he had arrived, Isaac disappeared down the tree-lined driveway, sounding the horn of his MG in farewell.

Before picking up her luggage, Isla stood at the bronze gates, breathing in their design. The central panels were made up of sinuous acanthus foliage bordered by sunflowers. The gateway arch with two large turrets provided a grand entrance. Behind the gates, she spotted the warm and friendly Queen Anne-style buildings, with crescent gables and multiple windowpanes. The four-storey red brick buildings were reminiscent of a palace, marked by the architectural glory of the Pfeiffer Arch as its entrance.

Clumsily juggling all her bags, she managed to prise open the entrance doors and make it inside the main building. No-one was present. *Must be lunchtime*, she thought. Leaving her belongings at reception, she took the opportunity to explore her new lodgings.

There were so many rooms. She pondered all the amazing women who must have studied here and set the world on fire. There was a long continuous corridor and one of its tributaries was the main hall, suffused with light, topped by a barrel-vaulted ceiling with elaborate white plasterwork featuring the Newnham College monogram in a Tudor strapwork design.

One of the other rooms was the junior common room for undergraduates and a small buttery room, where students met for light meals and drinks. Finally, Isla found the most stunning space she had ever seen, the library. Looking around, she could not believe her eyes, her jaw falling open with amazement. I am such a long way from Stromness now and here is my opportunity to make my dreams come true. *I can do it*, she thought, thanking her blessings.

From the middle of the library's main room, she gazed for a short time upon the barrel-vaulted ceiling. It's so beautiful, she thought, drawn to the combined Wedgewood blue paint and white plaster decorations, the oak structural beams perfectly matching the numerous book stacks.

'Can I help you miss?' asked the librarian.

'No, just looking ma'am. I'm new here.'

'Well, this library is a place for study. It is not intended to be a thoroughfare for gaping mouths. Unless your purpose is to study, best you leave miss. Thank you. And please exit quietly, noise is not tolerated here.'

Isla had almost forgotten what it was like to be at the bottom of the food chain again. Despite the abruptness of the librarian, she could not stop smiling. Nothing was going to spoil this joyous moment for her. Nothing.

Once she had arranged her room keys with the bursar, she settled into her single room and unpacked her personal items, making her room feel a little more like home. She stuck various posters of the Beatles, the Monkees and Frankie Valli and the Four Seasons on her walls. Around her dressing mirror, she placed photographs of Lucy Rose, Betty, Morag and her mother. They filled her soul with happy memories and past adventures. Scanning the pictures, she was saddened that she had none of her father. She tried to remember him, but as time marched on, she had noticed more often that memories of long ago had started to fade. *Sammy, Jimmy, Harry, what was the name of our dog again?* she thought. *Harry... Harry, no, that's not it! Larry! Yes, Larry. Oh my God, Larry, I'm so sorry. How could I forget you, you furry little bundle.* Staring into the mirror, she saw flash by an image of her father. Relieved by the recall, her throat tightened and her eyes welled. If there's one pledge I make to you, Isla Johnson, she said, pointing to her reflection, it's that one day you will get to Australia and make some sense of it all.

Orientation week was starting the next day, so Isla grabbed a quick meal at the buttery before retiring for the night. As she lay in bed, she heard footsteps on the hallway boards outside and the occasional giggles of fellow students. The moon shone into her room through the gable window, bathing it in a dull glow. Snuggling under the covers, she fell instantly asleep and was transported back to Stromness. There she was, standing on a jagged cliff face, its base rocks smashed by turbulent waves. Turning around with her back to the sea, she saw the valleys of Orkney rolling out before her. She was a young girl with a lion heart and a sense of wildness, running down the valley, dancing on air, the wind blowing her in a direction that seemed right to her. She was possessed by a feeling of contentment, a knowing that she had finally arrived.

Woken by the college bell, she sat up in bed, stretched her arms out and thanked the Lord for her sweet dream. My first full day at Cambridge, she thought, giving her arm a small pinch, time to seize the day!

She made an early start exploring the Cambridge grounds, bursting with the colors of autumn. The main college square was full of student life and sprinkled with stalls advertising everything from drama club, varsity press club and rowing memberships. There was also one stall selling tickets to the pre-May ball. She wondered why it was called 'pre-May' but checked out the information and decided it looked like fun and a great way to meet people. The college band, The RhinoBeetles, was playing and the theme was 'Be Hip, Be Cool'. I'm in, Isla thought. Whilst filling in the required form, someone tapped her on the shoulder.

'And look who's here!'

Isla turned around, her mouth agape. 'Oh my God, my God, Jesus, it's you, it's you!'

'You can't get rid of me that easy, *comrade*,' said Lucy Rose.

Isla gave her a huge hug. 'Oh Lucy Rose, it's so nice to see a familiar face.'

'Right on! So good to see you, sister. When did you get here?'

'Just yesterday, a bit of a trek, but the train ride was stunning.'

'Yes, wasn't it. I got here three days ago. From the station, I got a lift to Girton Hall, settled in and here I am! So, are you going to this ball?' Lucy Rose hardly paused for breath. 'They have the main one in May, but this is a bit of a bash for us first years. Could be fun. I'm going. Some guy randomly asked me. Bit impulsive, but I said yes, nothing to lose I guess... Oh my God, Isla, this place is dreamy. I love it. It's so cool. I feel naïve but grown up all at once. Pinch me, pinch me, Isla!' She laughed loudly, sounding the occasional nasal snort.

'Ha, I was just thinking the same. A little bit different from Stromness. Just a wee bit,' laughed Isla. 'I am going to the ball, what the hell, nothing ventured, nothing gained. And besides, I get to meet your new fella.'

'I wouldn't get too excited Isla. We've only pashed once...'

Isla interrupted her, 'You whore, what, already?'

'Well, you know me, I couldn't resist. He's kinda cute, artsy and I love his energy. Not a bad kisser either.'

'You're still a whore, but I'm jealous!'

'Plenty of time to gird those loins, comrade. You might find that prince at the ball!'

'I'm not leaving all those men to you. I'm coming, my friend, so watch out!' Isla winked.

'Oh you are terrible Isla, but I love you.'

'And I love you. It's so good to see you! Next holidays, we must visit Betty in Inverness.'

'Yes, let's. I hear she's perfected the beehive do. Knowing her, she's probably stuffing fake birds in the hair to give it that nesting effect. She always loved a unique touch!'

'Imagine! Oh Jesus, I wouldn't put it past her!'

'Listen, I'm off, have to meet Romeo at the local caf, but I'll catch you Friday night. Wear your sassiest dress. We'll teach these local lads how we Stromness girls can party!'

Lucy Rose blew Isla a kiss and skipped off across the college lawn.

That afternoon there was a concert recital at the faculty of music. Isla decided to have a look and check out the local musical talent and competition. She had already put her name down to join the band. The concert hall was staged with a performance area surrounded by tiered red velvet seating, enveloped by a room of dark oak panelling to ensure maximum resonance.

Isla took a seat at the back looking down on the stage. Not long after, she was joined by the Wiz.

'Oh damsel, fancy seeing you here!'

'You're not stalking me, are you Isaac?'

'Wiz.'

'Pardon, oh yes, Wiz.'

'Not I am not. You see, in our brief interlude, I had no chance to mention I'm studying first year arts and music. I play violin. Saw this on the bulletin and decided to come along. And you being here, well that's a bonus!'

'Mr Smooth, as always, *Wiz!*'

'Charming, as always, *Isla*. How about a cup of bean at the local after this, if I may be so bold, damsel?'

Isla gave him a sideways glance, her eyes having been fixed on the stage. 'Alright, but be a good boy. After all, we are Cambridge students.'

'I agree with the Cambridge bit, as for the rest, you might have to excuse me.' He boldly but lightly took hold of Isla's hand.

'You are the cheeky one. Patience is a virtue. Now the concert's starting, zip those lips and listen.' She removed her hand gently from his clasp.

After the recital, they ventured to the Cambridge Cuppa, just around the corner from King's College.

'I've got a better idea, as the Wiz often does. Let's head instead to the University Arms. I feel like something a little stronger than a cup of tea.'

Soon after they arrived, Isla shuffled into a booth, her hands fidgeting. *Well I'm here*, she thought, *might as well make the best of it.* Besides, she was determined to show this London boy what Scottish girls were made of. 'I'll have a double Johnny Walker on the rocks thanks.'

'Oh… okay,' said Isaac, peering into his wallet, making sure that he had not spent all of his parents' allowance.

Moments later, they clinked glasses, stout meeting whisky, Isla's eyes meeting his. They shared their stories in between laughs and a few more shouts of spirit and ale. Even though she liked Isaac, there was something about him that niggled at her. She couldn't put her finger on it, save that he seemed too good to be true, so her intuition was on high alert. He came from wealthy London stock, and his father was a successful commercial lawyer who had also graced the venerable halls of Cambridge. At Eton, Isaac had been a vice-captain and captained the rowing quad. Why me? Isla thought. This guy could have his pick of girls. She wondered if it had truly been fate that had led to their meeting, or if Isaac had somehow planned it.

'Okay, damsel, last drinks on me. The Depth Charge! Are you up for it?'

'Is this another one of your conjurings, Wiz?'

'Far from it! You Scots reckon you can hold your liquor, we'll see!'

Moments later, Isaac returned to the table with two pints of ale accompanied by shot glasses filled with Drambuie.

'Now, the aim is to drop the shot glasses into the ale and scull. First to finish wins. On the count of three. Ready, down the hatch, one, two, three!' said Isaac.

They grabbed their glasses, dropped in the ominous charge and sculled. Isla raced home like a true champion, flipped her pint glass over, raised her arms in the air and cheered loudly, 'Scots one, Brits zero! Woo hoo! Winner, winner, chicken dinner!' grinding her fists together in a victory gesture. 'Winners are grinners! So much for the Wiz! The Wizard of Oz... no, no, the Wizard of Isaac... no... the Wizard of Is.' She could hardly contain her laughter.

'Oh now, don't get too cocky, damsel. We have four years ahead of us and many more drinking competitions ahead.' He pointed at Isla with a big grin. 'Time to go methinks, I have a huge day tomorrow!'

'Oh you do Wiz, Wiz, Wizzie,' said Isla, her tongue engaging way before her brain had time to kick in. She flopped back on the seat, her arms splayed at her sides. 'Hey Wizzie, turn off that button that's making this room spin, will ya!'

'Oooh, and who's the little Scots girl who can't hold her liquor, hey?'

'I'm Australian, *actshooley*, and I don't mind sayin' I've got a bit of larrikin in me, so no room for your wizzer, Wizzie. Oops!' she said, letting out a loud burp. 'Oh sorry Mr Wiz, not very ladylike of me.' She burped again. 'I can usually hold me manners in… if you know what I mean?'

'I'm beginning to get the drift, Isla! Well, tick-tock, I better get you out of here, you half-breed or whatever you are.' He laughed.

Isla could barely stand up. Isaac slung her arm over his shoulder, assisting her out of the hotel. The fresh night air hit her senses with a harsh slap. 'Where am I?'

'Cambridge, damsel. Let's walk you home.'

As they approached Newnham College, Isla found a park bench to sit and catch her breath. She straightened her attire, pulling down her woollen cardigan sleeves, brushing down her front and pulling her hair back from where it was wildly draping all over her pale face. Isaac moved in closer to her on the seat, making a fake yawn action to wrap his left arm conveniently around her. Slowly, he moved in on her lips and kissed her briefly but passionately. She gently pushed him away, his image a little blurry, but her heart pounded against his, her body finally giving in to her desires. He was manly, slightly muscular and was looking at her with comforting eyes. She wanted him. Slowly, she pulled his coat lapels closer to her, forcing his face to hers. She kissed him back, the tips of their tongues touching and making Isla let out a small sigh. Then their mouths were locked with intensity and passion.

Suddenly, Isla suffered an unfamiliar peristalsis approaching her throat at a rapid rate, causing her to abruptly turn her head and vomit all over the iron arm of the bench.

'Oh my Lord,' she said, thrusting forward to gush another stream of semi-digested whisky. 'Oh my God, how embarrassing!'

'Well, I do declare that's Brits one, Scots nil, damsel!' said Isaac, jumping out of the way, laughing. 'Are you okay? Let me at least walk you back to Newnham.'

'No,' said Isla, 'it's just there, I can see the light. I'll be fine, please, enough shame for one night.'

'Well, if you're sure… the Wiz will make his exit. Until next time, damsel!' He bowed.

By the time she had finished her last purge, Isaac had disappeared, armed with a pocketful of her dignity.

Chapter 20

Judgement of the Moon and Stars

The following morning at 8.30 there was a loud banging at Isla's dormitory door. 'Are you in there, Isla? Isla? You awake? Hello!'

Awoken by the racket, Isla shoved the pillow over her head and yelled, 'Go away! I'm dying a slow death!'

'Come on, let me in, people are staring!'

'Jesus, can't anyone just die!'

She crawled out of bed, put on her dressing-gown and well-worn fluffy slippers, rubbed the sleep from her eyes and opened the door.

'Oh my Lord, it's you, Lucy Rose! What the hell are you doing here at this ungodly hour? Even Jesus was given three days before his resurrection!'

'It isn't Easter and besides, there's a sale on in town. We girls need some shopping therapy before Friday's ball. Oh, and there's a try-out for the choral at Selwyn College.' She broke into an arpeggio.

Their conversation was interrupted by three nearby dorm doors opening, mops of hair poking out and voices shouting, 'Will you shut the fuck up!'

'*Ladies*! Get stuffed! What would you hags know anyway? You are looking at a virtuoso!' Lucy Rose continued her scales, one hand on chest, the other extended to the right.

Isla grabbed her scarf and pulled her into the room with such force that the two of them ended up on her bed with Lucy Rose on top of her.

'Bit awkward! Now get off me!' screamed Isla. 'You weigh a ton!'

'With pleasure! And what is it with your breath, it smells like spew!'

Isla had a flashback to the night before and cringed with embarrassment. 'Oh nothing, let's just say I had a big night that ended badly.'

'Ooooooh, tell me more!'

'That's plenty for now, comrade. Let me wake up first. Might need some pineapple juice for the vocals if you want me to audition with you.'

'But first, to buy party dresses!' said Lucy Rose.

Both mothers had provided their girls with preliminary funds meant for life's vicissitudes, but this was a day for reckless spending. Every girl needs a party dress, Isla thought.

After a cuppa at the local eatery, they explored the college boutiques.

'Everything's so expensive!' said Isla.

'I know,' said Lucy Rose, 'I saw this fancy-pants dress shop around the corner from here that hires out ball gowns and party frocks. Let's have a peek.'

The girls entered Cinderella's, grinning from ear to ear like two kids let loose in a lolly shop. Trying on one gown after another, Isla finally settled on a floor-skimming dress in luxurious black velvet with flutter sleeves and a V-neckline. It's open back had a slender tie, making a dramatic finishing touch and hugging her slim figure.

Lucy Rose chose a cobalt-blue satin Loretta swing dress with a fulsome tulle petticoat. 'My mother's pearls will be the perfect finishing touch,' she smiled.

After seeking the proprietor's advice on shoes, both girls exited the store wearing a retail therapy glow and armed with two large shopping bags each.

After a spot of lunch, their next stop was the chorale audition at Selwyn College. They filled out the audition forms and waited with at least a hundred other potentials, sitting on the pew, fidgeting, waiting nervously for their numbers to be called.

'I don't see why I should have to wait so long with this riff-raff, Isla. I mean, once they hear my voice, they will be convinced there are such things as fallen angels,' said Lucy Rose, her hands resting over her heart.

'Personally, I would have thought your sound was more like someone squeezing a cat to death!' said Isla.

'Bit harsh, but I suppose you don't know talent when you hear it, love!'

Just then, Lucy Rose was called in.

'Number 52 please.'

'Wish me luck!'

'You'll have better luck if you give the panel earplugs,' said Isla, laughing loudly.

Lucy Rose entered the doorway but not before using her middle finger to give Isla the bird from behind her back.

Moments later, she returned. Isla could see that she was less than happy with her performance.

'They said I need more training, that my pitch was less than perfect and that I have a habit of gripping my larynx on the high notes, which results in screaming instead of singing. Well, I told them all that they must be blind and deaf. Fancy not seeing talent when it's right in front of them. Jesus, some people don't know anything about talent. Dumb stuck-up bitches. Anyhow, you're in next. If I didn't make it through, God help you!' Lucy Rose grimaced.

'Number 53, please come through,' signalled the audition monitor.

'Here I go!'

'Don't forget to give them my best.' Lucy Rose gave Isla a big cheesy grin.

'Back at you!' said Isla, poking out her tongue.

Lucy Rose held up both thumbs and pulled a face.

Isla was taken down a hallway and into a music room with a raised timber ceiling, which gave the space a sense of openness. When the three women on the panel introduced themselves, the echoes of their voices pinged about in Isla's head, impressing upon her the room's resonance.

'Now Isla, we are singing a cappella today. What song would you like to perform?' one of the judges asked.

'*Downtown* by Petula Clarke,' said Isla.

'Very well, when you're ready dear.'

Isla breathed in just enough air to support her voice. As she commenced the song, she hit every note with precision and delivered a pitch-perfect performance. Her openness of sound vibrated through the room, piquing the interest of each judge on the panel, causing them all to raise their heads from their note-taking and peer over their half-rim glasses.

As she concluded the song, the judges formed a brief huddle, whispering to each other. The middle judge broke the pack and said, 'Very nice dear, next time a classical tune might be more appropriate.'

As she went to leave the room, Isla thought that Lucy Rose was right for a change.

'Oh, and by the way Isla, are you free to start Thursday 6.00 p.m. at the chapel? Sharp. Music will be provided on the night and we will be short-listing you as a lead choral solo member. Thank you for coming, dear.'

Isla thanked them and headed to tell Lucy Rose the good news.

'How did you go Isla? I bet the cows gave you the once-over like me?'

'Well, sort of, but then they offered me a spot and all,' said Isla, trying to curtail her excitement.

'Oh well, some you win, some you lose. They obviously don't know a good thing when they hear it. I think I'll take up drums instead. I've always had good rhythm, well at least that's what the fellas tell me.' Lucy Rose laughed.

'You are a *nasty* one, Lucy Rose, a totally *nasty* young woman. Your mother would wash your mouth out with soap if she heard you.' Isla smiled.

'She'd have to catch me first,' snorted Lucy Rose, poking Isla in the side.

It was Friday night and Isla had finished her first week of lecture introductions and tutorials. *The workload was going to be arduous*, she thought, but she counted her blessings at being able to study at such a prestigious institution. She would ensure that she scored at every goalpost.

The formal ball was being held in the main hall at King's College. She was to meet Lucy Rose at the venue, rather than travelling together, mainly because her comrade had a mysterious male chaperone whom Isla was dying to meet.

Arriving in her gown, reminiscent of Audrey Hepburn's in *Breakfast at Tiffany's*, Isla took a moment before entering the main hall to scale the steps to the Gothic chapel. She was mesmerised by its pointed arches, elaborate tracery and stained-glass windows. The chapel also piqued her interest because it was the home of the famous King's Choir, one of her competitors in the college choral circuit. She wrapped her arms about herself in the chill of the evening air. The sky was clear, mapped with twinkling stars. She noticed one slightly yellow star. It was impressive, solid and surrounded in an audience-like fashion by other smaller interstellar bodies. Fleetingly, she recalled her scholarship performance and then her audition for the choir and smiled about all the cosmic possibilities that lay ahead.

She entered the ballroom with the confidence of a movie star on the red carpet. All eyes were fixed upon this new college girl, who was full of presence and individuality and a certain air of unpredictability. She promenaded down the middle aisle to the bar.

'Pimm's and lemonade please.'

'And how old may you be, miss?' said the bartender.

'Twenty-one of course, sir. I'm not one for fibbing and I have a reputation to think of!' Isla prayed no-one had heard her.

Sipping her drink through her straw, she explored the room, feeling comfortable in her own space for the time being. *After all, it was not often a girl had the so-called privilege of being present in a male-dominated college,* she thought. Transfixed in the moment, Isla hardly felt Lucy Rose tap her on the shoulder.

'Finally! Where have you been? I've been looking for you everywhere.'

'I've been here and having a lovely look about. I'll mingle later. You look ravishing, by the way Lucy. Oh my God, if only Morag could see us now.' Isla grinned.

'And you look stunning too Isla. I wish I had your figure. That dress is incredible. You look like a Hollywood star. And your hair, oh my Lord. You are sex on a stick! You should wear your hair up more often.'

'Ha! I don't know about that. Any talent about?'

'For sure, but I'm here with Romeo. You know Isla, there's something about him. He's a good kisser and all. Wants to move to second base all the time. I tell him no. I'm just not certain about him. One minute he's all over me like a rash, next minute he goes MIA. Peculiar. We'll see.'

'Where is he? I'm a great judge of character, you know me. Besides, we sisters need to stick together!'

Lucy Rose scoured the room over Isla's shoulder, checking for her man. 'There, there he is! Over there. Oh look, he's seen me, he's coming over.'

As Isla turned around, she got an eyeful of the encroaching Romeo and violently coughed, spraying Pimm's and lemonade all over him whilst Lucy Rose was trying to introduce them.

'This is Isaac,' said Lucy Rose.

'Oh, I'm so terribly sorry *Isaac*! Look, I've ruined your jacket.'

'Fancy seeing you here!' said Isaac, using his handkerchief to wipe down his tuxedo jacket.

'Yes, *fancy!*'

'Oh, you two know each other?' said Lucy Rose.

'Yes, you could say that!' said Isla.

'Oh, yes... yes, we met earlier this week. You know, one of those intro stalls about clubs to join, college excursions, *etcetera, etcetera*,' said Isaac, fumbling for words.

'Oh!' said Lucy Rose. 'It must have been memorable, although you never mentioned anything to me. Come to think of it, neither did you Isla.' She smiled, intrigued.

'Well, you meet so many girls first week here at college and... '

Isla interrupted him, 'I bet you do!'

Making his escape, Isaac said, 'If you ladies would excuse me, I might tidy myself up in the bathroom.'

'Oh, *I don't mind.* Besides, I'm sure you can handle yourself just fine. I bet you're a *wizard* at multi-tasking,' said Isla.

'Yes, well... well, later,' said Isaac, lightly kissing Lucy Rose on the cheek and then scampering off to the men's room.

'So what's the story there, *comrade*? I didn't come down in the last shower, you know,' said Lucy Rose.

'Well,' said Isla, taking a sip of her cocktail, 'I'm glad you asked, *comrade!* I met Isaac at Cambridge station the day of my arrival. Told me he was there collecting a parcel from his folks in London.'

'That's where I met him too! Oh Jesus, and that's exactly what he told me his reason for being there was!'

'So, into his so-called steed I jumped, delivering me to Newnham,' Isla continued. 'We had one date, he snogged me, I was so pissed I vomited straight after round one. He left me on a park bench in a pool of yuck and I haven't heard a word from him since. Calls himself *the Wizard*. I call him the *wanker!*'

'I knew it! I knew it! I could feel there was something not quite right with that fellow! What is it we say? Never try to outsmart a Stromness lassie, you might end up with more than you bargained for!' Lucy Rose knocked back her glass of bubbles.

'I have a plan, for *mister wet behind the ears*. Let's see how much of a wizard he really is! But I need your help. Are you in?' said Isla.

'Am I in?' said Lucy Rose. ' Does a Scotsman wear *naething* under his kilt?'

The two girls grabbed a fresh glass of champagne from the passing tray, clinking flutes to seal the deal. They hatched a cunning plan, marking judgement day for the Wiz.

Isla made herself scarce for the rest of the evening, milling about with fellow music undergraduates. Meanwhile, Lucy Rose was busy plying Isaac with champagne, charming him and appeasing his overfed ego.

As the hours drifted towards midnight, Lucy Rose led Isaac to a private nook at the rear of the hall, close to the River Cam. Under the stars, Isaac moved in on her. Holding and then kissing her hands, he professed his love for her, slurring his words, dribbling between sentences.

'That's beautiful, Isaac, or is it Wiz?' said Lucy Rose, removing her hands from his and cupping his face in her hands. 'But, you see, it's like this… ' Isaac tried to move closer to kiss her. 'No, no, no, it's like this, I don't have the same feelings. I've tried, but you just don't do it for me. And I have tried, believe me.'

'But I wuve you, my chicky doo dah,' said Isaac, 'my pinky winky, snuggly wuggly.' He rubbed his nose against hers.

'Your what? I'm not your *chicky doo dah, pinky winky or snuggler…* I'm not your chicky. You don't do it for me. You're too proper… you know, stuck-up. You deserve someone stuck-up like you. Anyhow, this little chicky is *chooking* off. Stick your pinky-winky where it fits!'

'Oooh, don't be like that. I wuve you, I do. Really. There is no other woman like you.'

He leant in to kiss her, licking his lips, and within seconds of their lips meeting, he turned his head and spewed vomit all over his dinner suit pants and patent black leather shoes.

'Oh, what a mess, Isaac. But I guess you'll be alright to find your way home, hey Wiz!' Lucy Rose pointed at him, gave him a wink and turned her back on him to head up to the rear entrance door of the college.

As planned, Isla appeared from nowhere, as striking as ever, her figure etching a sexy outline on the night's palette.

'Oh, feeling a little blue, Wiz? Oh well, Aunty Isla has come to your rescue. Never say I don't look after you.'

'I don't feel good, Isla. I feel like shit. Too many bubbles. Everything is spinning like crazy!' Isaac bent over, holding his head.

'Never mind. It will all be fine. Let's get you home. You do look like shit!'

'How, how? I can't even walk. Leave me here, I'll be fine.'

'Oh no, only a selfish, non-caring and self-centred person would do such a thing, Wiz. I'll take care of you, don't you worry my friend.'

Looking up at Isla and barely able to focus, Isaac said, 'You know, you know, I never meant to hurt you. You know that I have feelings for you, I do, believe me. Lucy Rose… well she, she threw herself at me. I was all about you… only you,' he said, turning to vomit again.

'There, there,' Isla said, patting his back, 'come with me. I'll punt you home to Trinity. Give you time for your tum-tum to settle. And think of how romantic it will be. No judgement from me, just the moon and the stars. No judgement whatsoever.'

A short distance from the nook, Isla commanded a long boat for the journey home. She assisted Isaac over to a nearby seat on the bank, hitched up her gown, took off her stilettos and climbed onto the boat.

'Come on, get in, you'll be fine, Wiz. You can do it!'

After two failed attempts, Isaac managed to gain focus, settle his balance and steer his right foot onto the boat. Isla quickly clasped onto his hand, pulling him into the boat. In doing so, Isaac fell over, making the boat rock and Isla nearly to lose her footing. As all this was happening, Lucy Rose reappeared from a distance to watch their plan unfold.

'Jesus, you nearly gave me another baptism,' cried Isla, regaining her balance. 'Now lie there and don't move, or I'll hit you with this pole.'

'Ooohhhh, I don't feel good, Isla. Why are the stars moving around in circles and why's the moon rotating like that?' Isaac turned his head and spewed again.

'There, there, it will be alright, Wiz. Don't worry now. Isla will take good care of you. Close your eyes and have nice dreams about all the lovely girls you've met at the station over the last week. Be like counting sheep I guess, you'll be asleep in no time.'

Isaac's face was covered with chucky bits of vomit. His eyes soon rolled back into his head and his body was splayed across the hull of the small boat.

As planned, Lucy Rose and Isla met on the Mathematical Bridge at the rear of King's College the next morning at 9.00 a.m. They were greeted by a growing crowd, all cheering, hooting and laughing, pointing to a boat tied below. The girls shuffled to a prime viewing position at the front and looked down. They saw the flat-bottomed boat with a punting pole as its mast and a handkerchief tied at the top. The small boat was secured by a mooring rope, giving the vessel enough length to allow it to navigate the Cam's midstream current. In the centre of the boat, Isaac was struggling to free himself from the ropes attaching each of his hands to the oar riggers. He was screaming abuse at Lucy Rose and Isla, which was hard to hear due to the cheers and celebratory mood of the crowd. His pants and underwear were pulled down around his ankles, exposing his manhood, and his shirt and jacket were stained with the remnants of his over-indulgence the night before. The boat was positioned perfectly for all on the bridge to get a first-class view of the Wiz's wizzer.

'I wonder who would do such a terrible thing!' said Lucy Rose, raising her hand to her mouth to hide her grin.

'I have no idea,' said Isla, 'but whoever it was, you wouldn't want to cross her… or them. Savage, absolutely savage, comrade! Have a good look, Lucy Rose. Thanks to a wee bit of Scottish intervention, he's now the Wizard of Was!'

The girls bid him a cheeky farewell, locked arms and headed to the local for a well-deserved, celebratory hot chocolate.

Chapter 21
This Flight Tonight
February 1972

Isla gazed out of the plane window and waited for the other passengers to board. The rain droplets on its surface appeared as pearls, preventing her clear view of the tarmac. It was late and she let her mind wander, reflecting happily on her years at Cambridge.

Majoring in music composition and performance, she had passed her degree with honours. Apart from her studies, much of her final academic year had been taken up with exams, practical workshops and concerts. When she wasn't studying, she was earning pocket money playing solo gigs at the local pub, where she would try out her original music on the patrons.

Lucy Rose had completed her degree the year before and headed to London to work for a well-known book publisher. Isla missed her terribly. However, it gave her more time to focus on her curriculum and less on extracurricular activities, such as boys and beer.

She thought with great fondness of her end-of-year showcase performance where she had performed in front of industry professionals. Morag and Jess had attended that evening, although they were not seated together. Morag had never really taken to Jess. Isla often thought perhaps it was due to Morag being over-protective and a little partisan given Isla's disclosures to her over the years.

Isla had explained to her about the hidden box of envelopes and Morag was always direct with her, expressing her concerns that she believed her mother was withholding information. Never accepting why she had been given such limited information about her paternal family and the details around her father's death, Isla understood Morag had her back. 'It just doesn't add up lassie!' These words haunted Isla occasionally.

There was a part of her that just wanted to retreat from her history, fearing the unknown and its potential repercussions. Although she loved Morag, she was afraid of losing her mother and so there was a need to trust her. Isla was well aware her maternal relationship hung on a tight thread, but her mother was the only family she had. She could never understand why her paternal family had deserted her, although a part of her often wondered about the letters in the shoebox from Aunt Olivia. For the time being, any betrayal of her mother's trust outweighed her curiosity, despite Morag's probing.

Outside of her studies, Isla had many fond memories of her time spent at university. Her intimate short-lived romantic liaisons with Kevin, the engineering student, who had no impulse control when it came to sex, red wine and strawberry pancakes with cream – in that order. Her intense sexual encounters with Oscar, whose passion for rugby union matched his voracious sexual appetite off-field. He tackled her in bed as if he were on the playing field, their sexual antics lasting for hours, leaving Isla with the feeling of having played back-to-back matches. She could hardly walk the next day and during their encounters, regularly wished that she had worn a whistle to call for time out.

She also smiled remembering her romantic days with her favourite, Freddie: their dates punting along the Cam, enjoying picnics in the daisy fields and spending untamed summer nights making love amongst the secluded foliage spanning the riverbanks. Freddie's delicate and sensual touch was a memory indelibly imprinted on her mind. The thought of his naked body pressed against hers and the musky smell of his scent still sent a charge of electricity through her.

One of her most exciting days was receiving the formal letter from an eminent London performance agent, who wanted to sign her up after her showcase performance. She recalled Morag's cries of excitement over the phone when her star pupil called her with the good news. She dropped the phone and Isla could hear her screaming and imagined her jumping up and down with glee. Whilst there were none of Morag's excited antics from Jess, Isla could tell her mother was pleased and her congratulations were heartfelt.

Remembering reading her agent's letter, Isla placed both her hands on her heart. She glanced at the night-time sky outside the plane window and thought of her father, knowing that he would be looking upon her and beaming with pride. His wide grin and sparkling eyes flashed in front of her momentarily and she was immediately possessed by a comforting warmth, reassuring her that he was close by.

Her thoughts were abruptly interrupted by the cabin crew's announcement, 'Please ensure your seat belt is fitted and your seat is in the upright position. Your flight to Paris will arrive at approximately 9.30 p.m. Now sit back and relax. We trust you enjoy your flight with British Airways.'

I can't believe I'm going to Paris, she thought. *I cannot wait to see a city I've heard so much about. The City of Romance. Imagine me, auditioning in front of all those record label executives! Who would have thought.* She smiled.

A world of potential lay at her feet.

The flight arrived in Paris on time and Isla collected her luggage and hailed a taxi to transport her to the Marais area, where her agent had arranged accommodation for her.

The drive from the airport was magical. *Oh my God, I'm here, I'm actually here!* she thought, as they passed the Eiffel Tower, Notre Dame and the River Seine. She pinched herself just to make sure. Despite the cold outside, she wound down the window and stuck her head out into the chilled night air, filling her lungs, feeling a certain *je ne sais quoi*, making her ride into the centre of Paris even more exhilarating.

The taxi stopped at a small street just off the rue des Petit Champs.

'Le voici, mademoiselle. Numéro trente-six pour vous. Neuf francs s'il vous plaît.'

'Certainement monsieur. Merci beaucoup. Bonne nuit,' said Isla proudly, knowing that her French classes at Cambridge had paid off after all. I feel like a local, she chuckled to herself. *I am a real mademoiselle now*, she thought, collecting her bags and entering the tiled foyer of her apartment building.

Although her agent, Johnny Black, had arranged this apartment for her, he would not disclose the owner's name for fear that she would become starstruck before her audition the following evening.

Exhausted from the journey and the day's excitement, Isla slowly climbed the carpeted staircase. At level three, she located her apartment number and dropped her baggage to retrieve the keys. Inside, the apartment was modestly lit by a couple of stylish French lamps. There was a crystal vase on the kitchen counter filled with freshly cut flowers and a small cane basket overflowing with chocolates, coffee, biscuits, fresh bread and milk. Johnny's business card was attached. 'Bienvenue!'

Despite her weariness, Isla managed a smile, which lit up her face. Through the doorway, she could see the bedroom and a very inviting bed, its covers turned back, primed for its exhausted occupant. Forgetting to turn off the lights, she climbed into bed and immersed herself in the scent of fresh linen and lavender. Within seconds, her eyes closed and she drifted off to sleep.

The following morning, she stirred when the sun streamed in through the tall iron-framed windows. On her bedside table, the alarm clock indicated 9.00 a.m. and she decided she had better get up and enjoy the day. Her audition was scheduled for 7.30 that evening at the Moulin

Rouge. She only intended to stay in Paris for four days and so she wanted to make the best of it. There was so much to see and do.

After a quick shower, she made herself a pot of coffee and some toast with strawberry jam. It was peaceful sitting at the small dining table and gave her an opportunity to take in the beauty of the apartment.

It was a generous size, with old brown herringbone parquetry flooring warmly contrasting with the white walls and floor-to-ceiling oak panels. The dwelling was bright and positive, the large double windows graced by black wrought-iron balconies letting in plenty of light. There were intricate Louis XIV mouldings and marble mantels with gilded French mirrors in the lounge area and bedroom, framing built-in iron fireplaces. In the centre of each of these rooms was a large ceiling medallion from which hung crystal chandeliers.

The apartment was styled with softly patterned fabrics in muted colours, *objets d'art*, cabriole sofas, Louis chairs, French candles and freshly cut flowers. It was just as she had imagined Paris would be, and more.

Finishing her second cup of coffee, she peered out the window, gazing at the rooftops of Paris that seemed to shine with their patina of zinc. 'Wow, I am actually here, and not too shabby for a highlander!' she laughed.

Exiting the apartment building, she navigated the narrow cobblestone streets of the Marais. A little peckish still, she popped into a nearby patisserie to purchase a *pain a raison*, a pastry shaped like a snail and filled with French custard and raisins.

After leaving the shop, Isla noticed a tall skinny man with a long black beard wearing a black fedora. She followed him down the street and watched him enter Sacha Finkelstein's Jewish bakery. The shop was packed and people were lining up outside. She managed to get a glimpse in the front window and spied the freshly baked Jewish goods such as challah, cinnamon chocolate babka and mazurka pastries. *Gosh, if I lived in this city, I would put on five pounds a day*, she thought, wondering how the locals remained so thin.

Around the corner, she came across Izrael Épicerie du Monde, displaying shelves crammed with spices and jars of oil from around the world, beans from Costa Rica and caviar from Iceland. Enough food for one morning, she smiled to herself. I'll start salivating if I see any more food.

She was almost skipping down the streets and found herself constantly stopping to admire grand mansions and peer at carvings and statues. She was surrounded by so much history that until now, she had only read about. Now, she was actually living it.

During her time at Cambridge, apart from her music, she had developed a love of literature and had read a number of novels by Victor Hugo, one of her favourite authors, including *The Hunchback of Notre Dame*. Her favourite, however, was *Les Misérables*. Whilst ambling down the Parisian streets, her mind lost its way in his storytelling. Curiously, she ended up at the Place Des Vosges, an area whose former residents not only included the mistresses of French kings, but Victor Hugo himself.

She sat on the grass in the public square area, her stockinged legs extending from her purple suede mini-skirt, her feet with the brown ankle boots crossed over. Her light-brown velvet jacket and mauve woollen scarf protected her from the cool sun-kissed day, and her long, wild, curly locks bounced in the occasional breeze.

She rubbed her hands together, taking in all her surroundings including the once-aristocratic mansions now converted into trendy bars, restaurants and galleries. They captured the style of the local Parisians with their chic, expensive and sophisticated fashion sense, and a piece of prose from her beloved author Victor Hugo came to mind. 'As the purse is emptied, the heart is filled.' She smiled to herself, now truly understanding what he meant.

At 4.30 pm, she returned to her apartment for a quick rest and to freshen up for the evening's audition. She was immensely grateful to her agent for lining up such a rare opportunity. Executives of record labels from London, Germany, Paris and Spain were going to be present and she knew that this moment in the spotlight could propel her career in the music industry.

After some vocal warm-up exercises and guitar playing, she headed to the Metro bound for the Moulin Rouge. The train arrived later than expected, but she had allowed plenty of time to prepare herself and settle her nerves.

From the Metro exit, she spotted that Paris icon in the distance, the Moulin Rouge. Painted in candy colours and topped with a windmill, it was exactly how all the photos depicted it. Butterflies invaded her stomach. *I can't believe I'll soon be standing on the stage where Edith Piaf and Josephine Baker once sang!* she thought. *Where are those Hail Marys when I need them, Morag?*

With guitar case slung over her shoulder, wild curly locks protruding from her woollen beret, she announced her appearance to the front of house maître. 'Bonsoir monsieur, je m'appelle Isla Johnson. Je suis ici pour l'audition.'

The maître checked his records and nodded, leading her through the main performance area and backstage to the green room. The décor of the main performance area was elaborate, with mirrored walls and sparking chandeliers. The stage was ample, framed by a proscenium arch and with red velvet curtains and lavish gold rope ties. Tables and chairs were sprinkled about in cabaret style for the audience, each table adorned with a small posy of flowers, a modest French lamp and an ashtray.

In the green room, Isla noticed six other people, all busily tuning their instruments and humming vocal scales. The maître quickly ushered her inside and said, 'Stay here please, miss. You will be called soon.'

Isla nodded, trying to hide her quivering hands. She leant her guitar against the wall and sat on a nearby chair, staring into one of the dressing-room mirrors. *Okay, I was excited, now I'm shitting myself,* she thought. *C'mon Isla, pull yourself together. This is what you've been waiting for. You can do this. This is what you've worked for. Dad, if you can hear me, now would be a really good time!* Taking in a lungful of air, she was halfway through a Hail Mary when she heard, 'Miss Isla Johnson, to the stage please.'

Before retrieving her instrument, she looked into the mirror again and said aloud, 'Alright girl, you have this!' and left the room amidst the quiet chuckles of her fellow performers.

She stepped cautiously onto the stage and positioned a stool centre downstage. There was one single beam of light spotlighting her from above.

'Good evening. Isla Johnson?' said one of the judges.

'Yes sir, good evening,' said Isla.

'We will address you in English, if you are fine with that Isla?'

'Yes, that will be fine, thank you.'

'I know it is a little difficult to see us from the stage, however, I can tell you that we have representatives from RCA, Warner Music, EMI and Universal here. We also have two executive producers from Germany and Paris and a manager all the way from Australia, who previously worked with Pye and Phillips.'

Isla interrupted. It was hard to hear the shadowy figure. 'Did you say Australia, sir?'

'Yes I did. Why?'

'Oh, you may not pick it from my accent, but I was born there a long time ago!'

'Looking at your CV, an impressive CV too I might add, you're only 22 years old. So in my years, that is not too long ago,' he said, letting out a laugh. 'Perhaps you have brought the sun with you today to make you shine. Now, please take your time. We only run these auditions twice each year and we all want you to do your best. That's why we called you here in the first place. So relax. When you are ready, Isla.'

Isla took a long, deep breath, held it and let it out slowly. She closed her eyes and pictured her mother, her father and finally, Morag. In her mind's eye, she recalled her recurring dream of a girl running through the Scottish highlands, carefree, easy, grinning with excitement standing on that cliff precipice, heart content, soul overflowing with emotion. She was ready. She opened her eyes, her fingers drawn to the guitar chords, and commenced strumming, her voice eventually partnering the music to *Isla's Song*. Morag and she had finessed the song some time ago, and thanks to her Cambridge tutelage, it was now truly complete and ready for an audience. It was her song, its roots vested in her father's inspiration. It was a song that captured her feelings of love, hope and importantly, a coming together of souls.

As she sounded the last note, there was complete stillness in the room, a disturbing silence that at first pained her, undermining her expectations and ego.

She unhinged her guitar strap and jumped down from the stool, walking off stage left. Before she reached the wings, however, she heard thunderous applause from the darkened tables below. She could discern people standing up, shouting her praises. The maître signalled at her to get back on stage. At first, she didn't register his cue, but then realised what was happening. She gathered herself, her heart rapidly beating, and slowly returned to the spotlit area, not wanting to appear over-confident but then suddenly finding herself taking an unconscious and spontaneous bow.

She gave a broad smile. Coming up from her second bow, she glanced to the heavens and thought, We did it Dad! We did it!

Chapter 22

In France They Kiss on Main Street

Making a quick exit out the stage door and navigating the cobblestoned laneway, Isla heard someone calling her. 'Wait! Isla Johnson, is that you? Wait!'

She turned around, trying to make out the figure calling her name. Before, she knew it, he was upon her, saying, 'Sam, here, Sam Fraser. Nice to meet you.'

He extended his hand and she reached out to shake it.

'Pleased to meet you, Mr Fraser.'

'Oh no, too formal, call me Sam,' he smiled, releasing her hand when he realised he had clasped it a little longer than was comfortable.

Trying to appear assured, Isla said, 'Do you often go chasing young women down Parisian alleyways, Mr Fraser... I mean Sam?'

'Only if they're worth chasing!' He smiled cheekily.

'Oh, I see! And what possible worth could I have to you?'

'Well, that's what I'd like to chat to you about! One Aussie to another,' he said.

At first taken aback by the comment, she realised he must be the Australian who had been sitting with the other music producers at the Moulin Rouge.

'Yes, I like to know certain things, especially those things that matter. How about we indulge in a café latte together and I'll explain it all to you? I know a little place around the corner, La Mère Catherine. Sort of an eat and run place, so I won't hold you up, I promise!' Sam crossed his heart.

Isla seized the opportunity to look at her apparent admirer properly under a streetlamp. He had shoulder-length curly brown hair, high cheekbones, perfectly shaped eyebrows and oval chestnut-coloured eyes. He had a wide grin, emphasising a cleft chin, and an angular jaw, giving him a sense of both strength and reliance. He was slender, toned and tall. His presence exuded a warmth that made her feel at home. She finished by observing his lips, which were fulsome and very kissable.

'Is anything wrong, Isla?' said Sam, interrupting her assessment.

'Oh no… no,' said Isla, shaking herself off, 'I was just… I'm happy to join you for 20 minutes,' she said, checking her watch, 'but if I am to join you, I'll need a whisky on the rocks after that audition… make it a double!'

'Okay, you're on. Forget the coffee. My shout. Let's do it! I'll match you!' said Sam.

They turned the corner and Sam headed into a brasserie, which had previously served as the church presbytery of Saint-Pierre de Montmartre. Here goes nothing, he thought. Poking his head out from the main door, he signalled to Isla, 'This way, quick. Last table inside by the window. It's perfect!'

Despite having her guitar slung over her shoulder, Isla still managed to navigate the narrow entrance. By the time she entered the main foyer area, she could see Sam seated at the window table, past a row of tables and chairs, waving his arms about, 'Here! Here Isla!'

I might be slow, but I'm not deaf, she thought.

Releasing her guitar strap and placing her beret and coat on a nearby wall hook, she finally sat down at the table. It felt good taking the weight off her feet, and she briefly took in her surrounds. The interior had dark timber walls, exposed wooden beams and terracotta tiles. It was furnished with large crocks, and framed oil paintings of Montmartre landmarks. Red-and-white checked tablecloths adorned the tables.

Candles dripping on their wine bottle holders burnt brightly on each table, setting a romantic mood for its patrons.

'How do you like it, Isla?' said Sam, like some tour guide.

Before she could respond, a waitress approached them. She was wearing a short white cotton skirt, black blouse and red apron, and was ready for action with pad and pen in hand.

'Bonsoir, que voulez-vous?'

'We would like two double shots of whisky on the rocks, s'il vous plaît, mademoiselle... Oh, aussi des frites, merci beaucoup.'

The waitress jotted down the request, tore the entry from her pad and placed it in a small wooden holder on the table. 'Merci. À bientôt.'

Isla was mildly impressed with this Aussie lad and his easy command of the local language.

Tumblers arrived filled with the Scots' honey elixir.

'Cheers!' said Sam, raising his glass to Isla's.

'Cheers! Now tell me why I'm here.' Isla gazed into Sam's eyes, searching for the truth.

'Oh yes, why you're here. Well, that's easy, I'm now your manager. There's much to discuss.'

Isla spat out her mouthful of whisky, 'You're what? There's what to discuss?'

'Much! Well, I came to your rescue actually. You should be grateful. After you finished your audition, which was not bad, mind you, Max from RCA and Jeremy from Warner got into a bit of a shouting match over who would sign you up. I had to bust them up. A bit of a scuffle really. Pity you rushed off. You would've loved it. Anyhow, where was I? Oh yes, the scuffle. I decided to kill two birds, so to speak, with one stone.'

The waitress delivered the hot chips midway through Sam's pitch. He sculled his whisky, demanding another two.

'Twenty minutes... remember?' grinned Isla.

'I'm getting there, hold your horses.' Sam raced on, 'Now, birds and stones, that's it. Anyhow, I knew they were gunning to contract you. And why wouldn't they with your talent? So, calling on my days at Universal Studios, I decided to play a cunning little game and tell them I was your manager. They probably know your agent, but I gathered they wouldn't know about any manager, so my caper was safe. I gave them my card and told them you would sign up for the best price. Said for them to call me by the end of the week with their best offers. No muckin' about… I said their *fair dinkum best offer,* Isla. Pure gold! I'm proud of m'self. You're a lucky girl, you are. Imagine how much money I just made you, not to mention a solid record deal with one of the best recording companies in the world. Your agent will love me… oh, and a guaranteed launching pad to make you the success you deserve to be. Your music is going to be the next thing! I can feel it! The world's gonna be at your feet, I know it!' Sam performed a drum roll on the table, before clinking whisky glasses with her again.

Isla was silent for a moment, wondering who the hell was seated opposite her, trying to comprehend what Sam had done. She did not know whether to burst out laughing or run for her life.

'I'm sorry, I'm sorry! Let's just peddle back a wee time. You did what? You told them what? You're my what? Oh my Lord!' She slumped back in her chair. 'Now I've heard everything. You don't even know me, Sam Grazer!'

'Fraser,' said Sam.

'What?'

'Fraser, not Grazer, as in short for trail blazer.'

'If you say so!' she said, knocking back her second whisky. Just then the waitress passed by their table and Isla asked, 'Excusez-moi, puis-je en avoir deux autres, s'il vous plaît? And some more chips.'

The waitress smiled at her, 'Pourquoi pas, mademoiselle!' In a flash, a further two whiskies landed on the table.

'Look, I'm sorry Sam. You seem like a nice fellow and all, but this is way too fast for me. I don't even know you, and you don't know me!'

'Look Isla, this is how it is in the recording business,' Sam said, turning serious. 'When you hear top-class talent, you pounce on it. This is the dawning of the Age of Aquarius and all that, babe. At the audition, I sat there, shut my eyes and listened to you. It was like listening to an angel. I was floating on air. And that song. It was syrup on toast, dripping with emotional longing and all that. It was stunning, Isla. Truly! If you have two of the biggest chiefs in music studios arguing over you, you've got it. The wow factor. Your music speaks to the soul. And so I thought to myself, I'm hopping on this bus. I want a ticket to ride. I've got the experience. I've got the know-how. I talk the talk. I could make you a star. I know of your agent, he'll love me. So what do y'say? C'mon Isla, what do you have to lose?'

Isla looked into his dreamy eyes. There was a spirit about him that she had not encountered in any other man she'd known. He didn't seem to be a con man. There was something genuine about him that was hard to put her finger on. He seemed trustworthy and as she pondered these thoughts, it dawned on her that she was being impulsive. What the hell are you doing, Isla Johnson! She set out the pros and cons in her mind. What to do, what to do, she contemplated. What would Morag do? Where are you when I need you, Morag?

'Okay, time's up! Do I have a new client or not?' said Sam. 'I have two in Australia, one in London and two in Germany. You would be my first Scottish artist, well, one with Aussie roots. C'mon Isla. Jump! No regrets! I promise I won't let you down.'

'Sam, I have to tell you, I don't know what I'm doing… I'm not usually like this… well, a bit, but yes… okay! Let's give it a go. I'll call my agent in London. There's something about you, don't ask me what… but let's give it a go. A trial period of 12 months, and I want that record deal signed up by week's end. It'll impress my agent. Best price, as you said. Understand. Comprenez-vous?

'We're friends now, Isla. *Comprends-tu?* N'est-ce pas?'

'Yes, it seems so, but you're my manager first. Okay... Am I really saying this?'

'Yes, you are! No regrets, babe. I'll pitch you for gigs, get you the best coin possible. Your agent will love me!'

With that, Sam raised his hand, attracting the waitress's attention.

'Let me guess, encore deux?' the waitress said, smiling.

'I think a bottle of your finest French champagne is in order, please!'

The room was already slightly spinning for Isla. It was a night of swift decisions, wild choices and celebrations.

The champagne bucket arrived, chilling a bottle of Belle Epoque. With a pop of the cork and a slow pour, their bubble-filled glasses were soon clinking.

Just at that moment, an accordion player passed their open window, marking their special moment. This is perfect, Isla thought, as she saw the clock across the road, realising that the 20 minutes with Sam had turned into a lazy two hours.

'L'addition s'il vous plaît!' said Sam. Without much haste, the bill arrived. 'There will be many more celebrations like this one, Isla!'

Isla smiled, his words singing to her soul.

They exited the brasserie into the outside chill and the crisp night air went straight to her head. *It was that last glass of champagne*, she thought.

'I have a great idea. I want to show you something, Isla, if you're up for a small trek. Follow me!'

Making their way down rue Lepic, they ascended Montmartre hill, reaching the staired balcony area in front of the cathedral, a symbol of conservative order in years gone by. In front of them was a spectacular birds-eye view of Paris, including la Tour Eiffel in the distance. The flicker of streetlights paved the way to the distant horizon as they sat on the marble steps, king and queen of their realms.

'Isn't it wonderful?' enthused Sam, arms outspread. 'Just imagine that one day, each and every one of those lights represents a fan of your music and these steps are your stage. Your music will light up the world, I just know it, and it's a privilege to be able to flick the switch on for you, Isla Johnson.'

Although Isla was listening to him, she remained mesmerised by the illuminated scene below them.

Sam cut through the silence. 'I think we need another name for you though, you know a *stage name*. Hmmm let me think... I know! The name of your first pet and the street you first lived in.'

'Okay. My dog was called Larry and my street, well, that's a little harder, I don't think my mother ever told me. I remember it was near my school and that's it,' said Isla.

'Well, that won't do. Here's an idea! You could use my street, Glover Street, so that makes it *Larry Glover*. Yes, I can see that working for you, *Ladies and gentlemen, at great expense to the management, let me introduce you, all the way from the Orkney Islands via Australia, to Miss Larry Glover...* drum roll!'

Sam took a few steps down from Isla. 'Alright, we may need to brainstorm this. Stand up with your back to the cathedral. Now point with your left hand, as if you were holding a sword out to your fans. You know, Isla, give me a bit of Joan of Arc. Now don't move, look commanding, no smile!'

Isla took Sam's directions seriously, marking her spot on the stairs imperiously. To Sam, with the backdrop of the holy cathedral, she looked like an angel and it gave him an idea.

'That's it! That's it. Take two... *Ladies and gentlemen, at great expense to the management, let me introduce you, all the way from the Orkney Islands via Australia, to Joni Saint Claire!* Round of applause, if you please!'

Below Isla, like a humble servant, Sam clapped and wolf-whistled. A lamp on the cathedral wall perfectly spotlighted her, and Sam looked at her longingly. He was lightheaded and his heart was ready to leap from his chest. He could not take his eyes off her and continued to shower her with applause.

Like some royal princess, Isla descended the well-worn marble stairs to join him. As she faked a royal sceptre, donning Sam, Sir Lionheart, he got down on one knee. 'Arise, mere mortal, for this day you will stand beside me as my lionheart, brave, ferociously loyal and protective of your queen. Arise, arise!'

Sam stood up, exploding with laughter. 'You're not my bloody queen, you're Joni Saint Claire! And what a night this is!' said Sam, moving closer to her on the step.

'And what a night it is, Sir Lionheart!'

There was not a soul to witness the crowning ceremony, which was only occasionally interrupted by the distant sound of traffic. They looked into each other's eyes searchingly, wondering how they had arrived at this spot. Sam drew Isla even closer, holding her tightly to his body, feeling hers pressed against him. Gently, Isla cupped his face and brought their lips together, satiating their longing with a passionate kiss. They each understood that their deal had been sealed in more ways than one.

I've never felt like this before, perhaps it's the bubbles, Isla thought.

As they broke for air, Sam whispered, 'Wow, you really are something... special. It's late, you've missed the last carriage back to the Marais, so how about slumming it at my pad in the 18th arrondissement? It's cosy, nothing flash. Not a palace, but I love it. What do you say, *Joni Saint Claire*?'

'I say yes, besides I'm absolutely bloody freezing my tits off here!'

'Language, my dear, hardly fit for a music queen,' Sam teased.

Hand in hand, they departed for Sam's nearby apartment. By the time they reached the bedroom, they had fully disrobed, catching each other's lips between falling garments, leaving a trail of clothes behind them.

The rays of an early sunrise filtered through the tall windows, illuminating their naked bodies nestled together on top of the bed linen. Isla wrapped her legs loosely around Sam's lean muscular torso, and Sam again ignited Isla's pleasure by gently kissing her mouth and neck. Overcome with passion, Isla released her legs, allowing Sam to explore her sweet-scented body. He softly cupped her breasts, lightly flicking her aroused nipples with his tongue, leaving her writhing. Although he had been with plenty of other women, Sam was full of wonder and excitement. This was like a sensual awakening for him. It felt so good, so special. He gently kissed his way to her vulva. Using one finger, he rubbed her sweet spot, making her twitch with ecstasy. His other hand softly circled her nipple, gently squeezing it. Isla's back arched, her pleasure zones ignited. Another of Sam's fingers stroked her pubic hair, deliberately fingering her opening intermittently, making her body arch. Isla tried to slow her breathing, knowing Sam would take her to the brink. Each time Sam's finger eased inside her, he took all the light in the room with it, and she had to catch her breath again. In response, she pushed her hips forward as his finger performed tiny, tight, urgent circles on her hooded pleasure spot. Slowly, Sam removed his fingers, licking the juices and sharing them with Isla, delicately rubbing his fingers over her lips and then passionately kissing her.

'I want you inside me now, please Sam, I want you.'

He gently slid inside her, and she raised her pelvis in ecstasy. Her breathless moans filled them both with passionate waves of rapture. As the rhythm increased, Sam gently prodded Isla's sweet spot once more, softly pressing and rubbing it, provoking an increased flow of juice and her exhilaration. Isla kissed the nape of Sam's neck, licking his sweat, consuming his spicy odour.

'I'm going to come, Sam.'

'Me too, babe. God, you are so beautiful!'

Sam raised himself above her, biting his bottom lip, entwining his fingers with hers, and they came together, Isla's head flung backwards as she groaned with delight, her fingernails almost piercing the flesh between his neck and shoulders. Then they lay in each other's arms, soaked in sweat and wetness, their breathing ragged.

'Oh! Wow! That was incredible,' sighed Isla.

'You're incredible,' said Sam, lightly brushing her hair from her forehead and snuggling up to her, 'so incredible.'

They closed their eyes and nestled together as one.

After 3.00 p.m., Isla was awoken by a mangy black cat meowing outside Sam's window. She rolled over to discover her lover's absence, though his musky scent was a pleasant reminder of the previous night. She looked around the apartment. It was an open space, quaint and bohemian. From the bedroom, she could see a small kitchenette and a lounge–dining area with colourful curtains and pastel footstools, a small table with oval-backed chairs, multi-coloured ceramic vases filled with market flowers and original portraits seemingly acquired from the nearby Place du Tertre.

'Bonjour!' said Sam, entering the bedroom with a tray of coffee, croissants and strawberry jam. 'How did my mademoiselle sleep?'

'I had the best sleep ever, better than I can ever remember!' said Isla, sitting up in bed and rubbing sleep from her eyes.

'I did too, didn't even hear you snore,' said Sam, grinning.

'I don't snore!'

'You're so cute when you get annoyed.'

'Ha! Wait till you see me get angry!'

'Seriously, I had the best night, Isla. You are magical and not *just* a pretty face it seems.'

'Don't forget the singing bit!'

'Oh yes, you can sing too… and compose. Never heard a singing orgasm before. God, did I get lucky!'

'Ha! Yes, you did get lucky Mr Fraser, and don't you forget it!'

'At least you got my name right this time, Joni!'

'Oh yes, Joni Saint Claire, I remember now, the name you chose for me. I love it Sam, I really do. It has a ring about it. And just to think you christened me outside the basilica. It's blessed, and I'm blessed to have met you.'

'At last some praise, keep it coming,' said Sam, beckoning with his hands.

'That's enough, don't want to stroke your ego too much!'

'Stroke anything you want, dear Joni,' smiled Sam, pouncing on her and nearly toppling the breakfast tray.

'You are the most wicked boy I have ever met, Sam Fraser, but I like you!' She kissed him deeply, cradling his face with her small hands.

'And I like you, mademoiselle, and I look forward to many adventures ahead. Speaking of which, given I had your details from the audition, I contacted your agent and told him the good news. He's stoked of course that I'm managing you... well, I sold it to him, but he's even more excited that we have such great interest from two highly endorsed record labels. Lots to do, songs to write, perform... Oh, and the stellar news for the morning! I have you a gig, or rather your agent got you one, playing at the Shaftesbury Theatre Westend on Monday through to Saturday. We have to curtail your trip by a day and head back to London. I know the Shaftesbury is usually a musical theatre venue, in fact *Hair* is on at the moment, but given the music genre and their current audience, we thought it worth a shot. Bit of a one-off, but I reckon it could pay dividends. You know, a new era of music, the dawning of the Age of Joni Saint Claire. What do you think?'

Isla peered over her coffee cup, 'I think it's bloody fantastic!'

'Thought you might. Now finish up your morning coffee and those croissants, there's much to do. Oh, and we're going shopping. You need a new style, you're too Cambridge at the moment, you know, private school like, trying too hard. Paris has some great options. Not too dear.'

'What do you mean *too Cambridge*? I like my style!'

'Gotta own your new title, Isla,' said Sam, lightly flicking her nose, 'you know, stake a claim. If we can't find some gear here in Paris, my mate Freddy in downtown Soho is just the man to help you discover your inner Joni Saint Claire. Before long, you'll be starting a new fashion trend. I know it!'

Looking out the French windows, Isla noticed her furry visitor had disappeared. *Black cats are bad luck*, she thought, *so I'm glad it's gone.* Sam left the room and minutes later, Isla could hear the sound of the shower from just outside the bedroom. The steam rolled into the bedroom, like a Scottish mist. Finishing up her coffee, she carefully listened for movement, then jumped out of bed, quietly stomping her feet up and down on the spot, punching the air with her hands. Then she leapt back into bed as if nothing had happened. Am I a lucky girl or what! If only Lucy Rose and Betty could see me now, how they would joke knowing their close mate finally got to kiss a man in Paris. And what a man!

Thanks for sending me this angel, Dad. I count my blessings. Sam's pitchy singing from the shower made her grin even more. *Yes*, she thought, Joni Saint Claire has arrived.

Chapter 23
The Circle Game

23 December 1977

'Hey, come see, hurry Isla! You're on the front page of *The Times*. "Saint Joni Blessed Amongst Brits – Sweeps the Awards." Oh my Lord! Look at you, what a knockout. And *I'm* not lookin' too bad either,' said Sam, staring closely at his picture in front of the media wall.

Isla rushed in from the bathroom, towel wrapped around her, her long curls still dripping wet. 'Hand it over mister, I want a look-see!' she said, snatching the tabloid from him.

'Oh wow, let me read. "Joni Saint Claire, talented Scottish musician, swept the inaugural BRIT Awards last night, winning Best New Artist, Best Single of the Year for *Isla's Song,* Album of the Year for *Isla's Song,* British Female Solo Artist Award, blah blah folk singer's meteoric rise for folk singer blah blah blah"… '

'Hang on, hang on! Keep reading, c'mon,' said Sam.

'If I must: "British Producer of the Year, RCA Records … blah blah… Ms Saint Claire was seen arm in arm with her manager, Mr Sam Fraser, who has taken this folk singing sensation to heavenly heights."' Isla shoved the paper back at Sam.

'There! See? See? Who's the boss… who's the boss man!' Sam teased, gently prodding her with the newspaper and circling her.

'Okay, I give up! Come here, a hug will have to do, lover boy!'

Sam picked her up, swinging her about. 'I am so proud of you babe, proud of us both. Together, we're an unbeatable team!'

Held in Sam's arms, Isla kissed him gently. 'I can't believe it, Sam.

The ceremony last night, all the glitz, the press, the hype. But you know, inside, there is still that little Aussie girl who sings from her heart and loves to write. It's the simple pleasures… and you're one of those!'

'Good to know! And by the way, a little less with the simple bit!' Sam laughed. 'You are one special gal and I'm glad I chased you down that alleyway all those years ago.'

Isla laughed, 'And I'm glad I didn't run, you freak!' She kissed him again. 'Oh shit, I forgot to tell you, Mum wants us to join her at Aunt Gerry's this year for Christmas lunch. I'm so sorry, it totally skipped my mind, with the awards night and all. Are you able to come with me? Please? I know we had planned our own private lunch.'

'Well, I guess,' he smiled, 'whatever the plans, I just want to be with you, so if it's at Aunt Gerry's and you're there, then so am I!'

'Great, it's 12 noon. She's just moved. I think to Fulham, close to the Thames. I'll need to check the address. No presents necessary, all sorted. Oh, except the one you have for me,' she said, pinching Sam's cheeks.

'You're a naughty one! Don't go all rockstar on me!'

'I know, but I have a reputation to live up to now and naturally, I have learnt from the best!'

She looked at the kitchen clock. 'Fuck, I'm late… again! I have that album signing at RCA. Max will hit the roof if I'm late. Best fly, babe. See you at the theatre, we can discuss the tour plans. Have a great morning. Love you!'

And with that, she was gone. Sam couldn't resist picking up the newspaper to read the article again, punching the air with his fist. Lookin' the goods, my man, lookin' da goods! he thought.

Olivia and Richard arrived in London after a long-haul flight via

Singapore. Both were grumpy, their hunger pains getting the better of them. They took a cab and Olivia gave the driver their address at Hotel Ritz, Westminster.

'Let's go to that little pub near Harrods for a bite to eat, darling. Not been there for years. I'm famished. I could eat a horse. How about you?' said Olivia.

'Two horses,' said Richard.

'Wonderful, we'll drop off our luggage, freshen up a tad and then head out for a meal. Perfect!'

In the cab on the way to Harrods in Knightsbridge, Olivia noticed a long queue outside a well-known record store. She glanced at the posters with the face of Joni Saint Claire littering the shopfront windows, heralding the next Scottish sensation.

'Must be a record signing for that young artist. I read an article about her on the plane. Quite the rising star, that one. Joni something ... damn, her name was on those posters. Anyhow, quite the talent. They're saying she's the next big thing! Bigger than The Beatles. Imagine that, Richard?'

'Yes, imagine,' said Richard, more interested in the roadworks on the side of the carriageway.

'Oh come on love, pick yourself up, get excited, we've not been to London for years! In fact, I haven't been since I was here last time with Oliver. I'll not forget that either. You know, Richard, it's like I've shut all that away in a dark closet and I'm too upset to open its doors and revisit it all. It stabs me in the heart every time I think what that witch did to Ollie and more so, to little Isla. Depriving the poor child of a father. Us of a niece. What sort of mother does that, Richard? Seriously! A putrid soul!'

'I'm afraid a soul to pity, Liv. She couldn't have been thinking straight, surely. It's not normal,' Richard said, facing Olivia and gently patting her knee. 'It's just not normal.'

'Hmmm... anyhow, let's not think about it, I only get upset, not only for Ollie but for that poor child.'

The cab pulled up outside the Elephant and Wheelbarrow pub. The roadside kerbs were filled with snow, the street trees decorated with fairy lights. Two large ornamental candy canes stood on either side of the main entrance, reminding them that this was indeed the festive season.

They sat at a small table, drinking stout and eating bangers and mash. It was still early and for a Friday night not overly busy. There was a hush between the couple. Olivia reminisced about Isla, wondering how she had grown up, where she was living, whether she remembered her brief time in Australia. And then she tuned into the music playing on the radio in the background above the white noise of the patrons. *There's something about that tune*, she thought, *where have I heard it? I know it. Where?*

She became increasingly perplexed. When the song finished, the radio announcer said, 'Don't forget your last chance to book for this spectacular show, the award-winning Joni Saint Claire in concert. Season ending Christmas Eve at the Theatre Royal, Drury Lane before she starts her world tour. Special Christmas Eve performance. Good seats remaining. Call the theatre, book now. Spoil yourself and your loved ones this Christmas.'

Olivia dropped her knife and fork. 'Did you hear that Richard? It's that girl. Joni-what's-her-face. Can we go to her show? Last one tomorrow night. Let's treat ourselves.'

Before Richard could answer, Olivia jumped up from the table, headed to the bar, requested a phone and telephone index from the publican and called the theatre for tickets. She returned moments later looking pleased with herself. 'Good job I'm a woman of action! Tickets booked. 7.00 p.m. show.'

'What show? What tickets?' said Richard.

'You know, that girl on the posters I told you about. The ones I saw, the one on the wireless just now. Joni Saint Claire. There's something about her music I connect with. Anyhow, it will be good for us. I haven't been to a concert in such a long time, love. Humour me, pet.'

'Don't I always, *dearest*?' said Richard, wondering what the hell she was talking about.

'Now do you ever hear me complain, darling?'

Richard gave her a half smile before finishing the sausage on his plate.

'I thought so, *dearest*,' she said, giving him a sly wink.

———

The sound of the telephone abruptly awoke Isla. She placed the pillow over her head, craving some uninterrupted sleep after a huge show the night before. The ringing ceased, only to start up again.

'Can you get that Sam?' yelled Isla. 'Who rings at this ungodly hour?'

'What, what? I can't hear you, I'm in the shower!'

'Oh, Jesus and Mary, don't worry!'

'What?'

'I said *don't worry!*' Isla leant across to the other side of the bed and picked up the phone, 'Hello! Who is it?'

'Is that any way to speak to your mother?'

'Oh, it's *you*, Mother! I'm so sorry. Late night,' she said, sitting up in bed. At that moment, Sam entered the bedroom, dressed only in a towel, wondering what all the commotion was about. 'Who is it?'

Isla covered the phone, 'It's my mother!' She rolled her eyes.

'Hello. Are you there dear? Hello, hello?' said Jess.

'I'm still here, sorry. What's new?' said Isla, squinting when Sam opened the bedroom curtains, the sun partially blinding her. 'Shut them, for God's sake!'

'I beg your pardon, are you telling me to shut up, miss? I'm still your mother and will not be spoken to like that!' Jess was unimpressed.

'No Mum, I was talking to Sam.'

'Well, he won't be sticking around too long if you speak to him like that, dear. I thought I'd raised you better than that!'

'No Mum, I wasn't, I mean I didn't… oh look, I'm sorry, I'm only just waking up, let's start again. What can I do for you, Mother?'

'Well, hello to you too. I *can* call you to just say hello, you know. I *am* your mother. Just because you're all famous now, doesn't mean I'm not good enough to talk to. It's hard enough to get through to you as it is! Anyhow, I didn't call to reprimand you, I called to tell you that as it turns out, I will be at your show tonight as promised, but Aunt Gerry can't come. I called Morag. Thought she might come along. I know you'd love to see her. You know, she still runs around town telling everyone about you and how proud she is and all. You'd think she was your mother and not me. She came to London yesterday, staying with some cousin. So it's all worked out well, she's coming. I'm at Gerry's at the moment. She has all the kids here for Christmas lunch tomorrow. Bodies sleeping everywhere. You haven't forgotten, have you? And you're bringing Sam, I gather? Aunt Gerry wants to know. You know what's she's like! Oh, and thanks for getting back to me as usual.'

Exasperated, Isla was struggling to get in a word. She thought, *she still thinks I'm that wee girl she can boss about.* 'Yes, I've got all that Mum. Sam *is* coming tomorrow, so sorry, meant to confirm.' Isla was looking at Sam's half-naked body in the sunlight streaming through the window. *God, tomorrow he won't know what hit him*, she thought.

'I'll bring Morag to the stage door after the show. No doubt she would love to see you, Isla. Now, I'll get off the phone. You seem a little grumpy. You obviously need more sleep, especially if you're performing tonight. I can hear it in your voice. Mothers know best. See you tonight. Bye love.'

Before Isla could bid her mother farewell, the line went dead.

'Why does she always do that to me, trying to control me, even from a distance. *Oh my God.* It absolutely shits me. I am so over her sometimes, Sam. At least it will be great to see Morag!'

'Oh come on, give her a break Isla. She's your mum. She cares for you. I think you forget sometimes what she's been through, raising you without a husband, in a faraway place, having to provide for you, being responsible for you.'

'Oh, so now you're taking her side. I can't believe this, after all I've told you!' said Isla, frustrated by Sam's partisan approach.

'I'm not. I'm not. You know I love you. It's just... I feel sorry for her now and then. From what you've told me, she doesn't get it. She seems to mean well, babe, that's all I'm saying. It's just her social and emotional cues, they're a little misplaced sometimes.' Sam sat down next to Isla on the bed and wrapped his arm around her.

'I know Sam. I get where you're coming from. But don't think you know *the whole story*. Maybe one day,' she said, taking hold of his chin and softly kissing him on the lips. 'I do love you. Now get off this bed, close the curtains and let me get some more shut-eye before I rip your towel off and ravage that sexy body of yours!'

'Hmm, might skip the curtains and ravage you right back,' exclaimed Sam, returning her kiss.

'Enough, tiger, back into that cage,' laughed Isla.

Sam jumped off the bed and closed the heavy velvet drapes. Despite the window coverings, Isla could still make out his shadowy figure at the end of the bed.

'You know I love you, Sam. Right? You're my rock and never forget that.' Isla rolled over and retreated under the blankets. Sam digested the remark for a second, blew her a silent kiss and exited the room with a bounce in his step.

It was 7.00 p.m. and after sharing a customary Pimms and lemonade at a local pub, Olivia and Richard headed to the theatre and arrived in time for the curtain opening.

'God, how much did you pay for these seats? Front row centre!' said Richard.

'Don't trouble that little mind of yours, darling. You know me, I always get what I want! Besides, it's Christmas and I thought I'd treat you. It's all about creating memories, darling.' Olivia tapped Richard on the knee.

'Hmm, *you're* treating *me*. I see, and would that be with my money?'

'Well darling, you know better, what's mine is mine and what's yours is ours! Now sit back and enjoy. I'm looking forward to hearing this girl and seeing what all the fuss is about.'

Just then, the curtains opened to reveal a vivacious young girl sporting a bottle-green plaid mini-skirt, beige woollen stockings, knee-high brown leather boots and a cream blouse, her vibrant locks grazing the collar. A piece of red and green tinsel formed a belt wrapped around her tiny waist.

'Good evening everyone. I'm Joni Saint Claire and Merry Christmas to you all. Thank you so much for spending your Christmas Eve with me. I plan to make this a little different tonight and perform my favourite Christmas carols for you, but with a touch of my style. I hope you enjoy them. Christmas brings back many memories for me. One of those memories is sitting on my dad's lap, singing some of these carols. They are cherished memories that I hold close to my heart. I hope tonight, in the tradition of Christmas, we get to make some more wonderful memories together. Bless you all.'

After two hours of solid performance, the concert ended with a standing ovation. Olivia stood front and centre, clapping and simultaneously struggling to pull Richard up from his seat to join her.

'Richard, follow me, I'm going to find the stage door and get that girl's autograph. A star is born, Richard! A star is born!'

Seated with Morag towards the back of the stalls, Jess was annoyed, as her vision had been impaired by a column for the entire show. As soon as Isla concluded her performance, Morag jumped from her seat, letting out a wolf-whistle and wiping her eyes to address the flood of joyous tears.

'Isn't she wonderful, Jessica! That's your daughter. Oh my! Bless her, she's done me proud, that wee lass.' Her clapping accelerated with exuberant force. 'To the stage door, I want to hug my little prodigy and congratulate her. Oh Lord, I'm so proud of her, Jess.'

'Good, I'll show you the way, Morag. And by the way, I am very proud of my daughter too and she knows I am.'

'I know you are, Jessica. What mother wouldn't be!'

Morag and Jess stood outside the stage door at the end of the alley, rubbing their hands to warm up. The door frame was decorated with Christmas lights, their colours reflecting brightly onto the snow beneath them.

Olivia turned the corner to the alley and spied the stage door, its bright lights a beacon in the wintry landscape. Getting closer, she saw two women standing outside of it. More fans no doubt.

Arriving, Olivia directed herself to them. 'Excuse me, ladies, is this the stage door?'

Jess turned around and saw Olivia, her jaw dropping as if she were a ghost from Christmas past. Spontaneously, her stomach flipped and blood rushed to her head, making her giddy.

'Jessica, are you alright? You look like you've seen an apparition!' said Morag.

For the first time in a long time, Olivia was speechless, unsure of what she was seeing, unsure how to react, her emotions brimming. Her eyes darted about Jess. *She's aged somewhat*, she thought, *but it's her, the one and only Jessica Johnson!* So many questions came to her mind. Where is my niece? for starters. Olivia clenched her fists, tightened her arms and locked her knees.

From the end of the alley, Richard called out, 'It's bloody freezing out here, Olivia! Are you done yet?' His words were muffled to Olivia's ears and she just stood there mutely, fiercely staring at Jessica.

Jess, on the other hand, turned towards Richard's voice, even though she could barely make him out. *I'm trapped*, she thought, and her legs were about to collapse beneath her.

Then the stage door burst open and Isla and Sam appeared.

'Mum, Morag!' said Isla, giving them each a hug. 'So great to see you both! How special. Oh Morag, at last I get to introduce you to Sam in person. Told you about him in the letters I sent you.'

'Oh my, it's so good to see you. Give me a warm hug. Bit chilly *out here* at the moment, I can tell you that!' Morag said. 'And yes, Sam. Much more handsome in person than what can be conveyed in the written word!'

'Pleased to meet you, Morag, I've heard so much about you. Good evening to you too, Jessica,' smiled Sam.

The scene played out right in front of Olivia's eyes and she realised she was eye to eye with her niece, Isla. Not Joni Saint Claire, but Isla, Oliver's daughter. *And the spitting image of him too*, she thought.

With a twist of emotion, a lump formed in her throat and her eyes welled with tears. She so wanted to hug her, to hold her, to tell her how she and Oliver had looked for her and how her father had never given up. Fortuitously, her practical nature stepped up to the occasion. Smiling inwardly, she took but a moment to cook up a much better plan. Rather than creating a scene, Olivia felt sure that her plan would not only protect Isla from the adverse fall-out of this moment, but serve up to Jessica a welcome dessertspoon of retribution.

'Joni, I'm so sorry, I don't mean to break up a family reunion. *Family* means the world to me, so I understand. Besides, your mother will no doubt want to *whisk* you away for some celebratory eggnog. I just came to say how wonderful you were. A standout!'

'Oh, thank you. You are too kind,' said Isla.

'No, not at all. Could I trouble you for an autograph, dear?' Olivia caught Jess's troubled gaze.

'Not at all, who do I make it out to?'

'Just Olivia will be fine.'

'I love that name. I once knew someone named Olivia.'

'Oh really? Not that common in Australia.'

'Are you from Australia?' Sam asked.

'Yes,' said Olivia.

'Me too, and Isla, I mean Joni, well that's her stage name. Mum's the word. We don't advertise her heritage all that much, as she really grew up in Scotland,' said Sam.

'Oh really, well that's a long way from Australia for your parents to travel,' said Olivia.

'No, well, it was Mum who brought me here. Dad died on the way over,' said Isla.

Olivia's tongue seemed fixed to the roof of her mouth. It took all her energy to refrain from slapping Jessica across the face at that very moment. Instead, she took in a deep and silent breath, trying to smile through her pain and grief. 'Oh, that must have been terrible for you and your poor mother.'

She gave Jess the evil eye, a powerful glare that did not escape Morag's attention.

'Well, Isla's going on a world tour after Christmas,' Sam continued. 'If you're back in Australia by then, here's my number, call me. I can arrange two VIP tickets, being a fellow Aussie! You'll see we're at the Hilton in Richmond. Please keep it confidential.' Sam passed Olivia his card.

'Oh, of course, that would be wonderful. My husband Richard and I will definitely be back by then and we shall attend with bells on, the ones we saved from Christmas, of course,' she quipped to dull her pain.

Turning to Richard at the end of the alley, Olivia called, 'Coming, dear! That's my husband down there, he'll be a frozen moment by now. Anyhow, lovely to meet you Joni, or I hope I can call you Isla, Mum's the word!' She placed her index finger over her lips. 'Thank you for the offer, Sam. It's been such a pleasure meeting you all. As promised, Isla, we certainly did make a memory tonight! I so look forward to seeing you all very soon. Have a wonderful Christmas.' Olivia shot a final arrow at Jess before pivoting on her heel, 'It's such a wonderful time to spend as family. I'm sure your mother would agree. Ta ta!'

'Are you alright, Mum? You look like you've seen a ghost!' said Isla.

'Said the same thing to her, I did, Isla. Ah yes, must be that wee bit of Charles Dickens that continues to lurk around these alleys. Best be home before midnight!' said Morag.

'Oh, you and your ghosts, Morag. I miss your stories, you know. Let's find a warm drink somewhere close. I'm ravenous,' said Isla.

'Yes, please! With marshmallows,' said Sam.

The stage door slammed shut and they all walked arm in arm up the laneway, all except Jess who was left there standing. She sensed that this was the beginning of the end. There was nothing she could do but wait, and maybe pray. *God deserted me so long ago*, she thought, *I wonder if he can still hear me. If ever I need a miracle, it's now*, she pondered, knowing that a wolf was coming to her door and this time there was nowhere to hide.

Chapter 24
The River

'Merry Christmas, babe,' said Sam, kissing Isla on the back of the neck and spooning her under the warm blankets.

'You too, beautiful man. Look, it's snowing!' said Isla, peering out the bedroom window. 'I love snow at Christmas, it reminds me of Stromness. There's something magical about it. It's like this heavenly dusting of snowflakes filling the cracks in a year gone by. Erasing any mistakes, laying a fresh carpet for us and paving the way for a new year, full of hope and dreams.'

She got out of bed and stood at the window. 'Look at it Sam, look at this stunning vista. So finely dusted, glistening in the morning sun. When I was a little girl, I used to think the snow on all the rooftops was God's icing, like on cupcakes.'

'We are the poet this morning! Romantic even! What was in your hot chocolate last night? Perhaps give up your songwriting and take up prose,' smiled Sam, joining her at the window, holding her tightly from behind and kissing her neck again.

Isla backed into Sam's body, feeling him against her. 'What did I ever do without you?'

'Oh, I don't know, I often ponder that thought,' chuckled Sam.

'Oh God, I wish we could spend all day here together in bed. You and me. Aunt Gerry's is going to be absolute torture. I know it! Bring your earplugs, the whole tribe is coming.' She sighed.

'And who is the *whole tribe?*' Sam raised an eyebrow.

'You really want to know? Well, here goes. There's Mum of course, Aunt Gerry and Uncle Bob, Billy, who works as a customer services officer at London Airport mainly so he can watch planes take off and land, Gertrude and her three kids Oak, Clay and Phoenix, all to different fathers. Talk about confusion on Father's Day. Then there's Phillip, who's gay, but no-one is supposed to know that, though the nail polish gives it away kinda. And finally, Margaret, who's married to Russell, with four kids: Gerry, named after her mother, Barbara, named after Russell's mother, Shirley and Chip. God knows why those names. So the day should be an absolute delight! God help us!'

'And do you keep in contact with this family of rabbits?'

'You have to be joking,' laughed Isla, screwing up her nose. 'I usually send Aunt Gerry birthday and Christmas cards and that's it. I know Mum keeps in contact a little more. Occasionally, Aunt Gerry has forwarded mail, cards and all that in the past, you know. We're not really all that close. Don't know why I've not seen Aunt Gerry and her fam more over the years. She and Mum seemed close. Bit funny when you think about it. Guess Mum and I were too far away, who knows? But Mum insisted this year that we all spend Christmas together. I think she misses me and all that. Anyhow, it's only a day and with you there, it will be just tolerable.'

'So what time and where?'

'Twelve noon. Fulham. Government housing area.'

'Nice, commission flats by the Thames. Stunning. Hope we all fit in!' laughed Sam.

'It's actually a commission *home* I'm told and it does have river views. Sort of upmarket in a way,' Isla smiled and faced Sam.

'Oh, river views, something for us to aspire to one day!'

Isla lost herself in his dreamy green eyes, wondering what it might be like spending her life with this man.

'You are a beautiful man, Sam Fraser... seriously. I love you. There, I said it. I'm sorry if I don't say it enough, Sam. You know me. I guess it's... '

Sam interrupted her before she could say another word. Lovingly, he cupped her delicate pixie-like face with his right hand, gazing into her eyes, tenderly kissing her lips. 'And I love you, Isla Johnson. I have the moment you walked on stage at the Moulin Rouge. I just knew it. I'm beginning to know more and more about you, wee lassie. That's our adventure, getting to know more about each other. And I so cherish the thought!'

Isla kissed him back, their tongues meeting in heated passion, each gasping for breath. They fell back on the bed together. Isla's hand wandered to take control of Sam's now swollen phallus, rubbing it around her moistening entrance. He glided his fingers over her nipples, gently flicking them to increase her pleasure. Softly, Isla guided Sam inside her and he thrust smoothly in and out, his hand massaging her swollen clitoris in circular motions. They kissed each other passionately and as they neared orgasm, Sam thrust faster and harder. Wrapped in each other and drenched in each other's love juices, they cried out simultaneously in shared pleasure.

Then they collapsed into each other's arms, their rapid heartbeats gradually returning to normal. After a while longer, Isla rolled on top of him. 'I've never felt this way about anyone, Sam. I'd hate to ever lose you. You won't leave me, will you?'

'What brought this on, babe? Of course not! You're stuck with me… that is, until you decide to sack me and kick me out,' said Sam, stroking her curly locks.

'Good. It scares me, that's all. I don't know why. Don't think I'm some mad possessive type. For some reason, Sam, it just frightens me.' Isla nestled her head into Sam's chest, a little embarrassed at having exposed her true feelings. *Oh God, I hope he doesn't think I'm some weirdo*, she thought. *Shit, I shouldn't have said that.* Too late now, she pondered, digging herself further into Sam.

Sam wondered where Isla was coming from, never having gleaned any sense of insecurity from her. As they lay there, the grandfather clock chimed 10. 'Well, we best get up, shower and head to a world of chaos,' said Isla.

'Merry Christmas, babe!' said Sam.

'The roll in the hay was my present, not even gift-wrapped,' Isla quipped.

'Very funny! No, let's do presents after, it might be the best way to end this day, it seems.'

Isla got out of bed, put on Sam's dressing-gown and bent over the bed, tweaking his nose. 'That it might be,' she laughed.

After she left the room, Sam rolled over, put the pillow over his head, let out a scream of triumph, then sat up in bed fist-punching the air.

At Gerry's door, Jess knocked at first and then pounded her fist on the door to be heard over the commotion within. Midstream her assault on the door, Margaret opened it, nearly copping Jess's fist in her face.

'Oh Lord, I've been out here bangin' away. Thank God you heard me, it's freezing out here. River's even frozen over in part.' She rushed inside to warm herself.

Making her way down the narrow hallway, she could hear a percussion of screams emanating from its tributaries. Finally, she arrived at the not-so-grand lounge–kitchen area where trestle tables had been set up in a 'U' shape in readiness for Christmas lunch. A fresh pine tree awkwardly balanced in a stand stood in the corner of the room, brightly adorned with a mix of baubles and painted cardboard children's decorations. Coloured lights were wrapped around it, flashing on and off, with a tinsel star standing proudly on top to mark the occasion. Bundles of presents tied with a variety of ribbons were splayed across the floor at the base of the tree.

'There you are!' said Gerry, entering in a fluffy pink dressing-gown, wearing furry slippers with rabbit heads, a lit fag protruding from her lips.

'Sis, great to see you. It's been too long!' said Jess, hugging Gerry.

'Yes, way too long. Must confess love, you haven't been the best in communicating with me,' said Gerry offhandedly. 'Been wondering if you were still alive!'

'Oh well you know, time flies and I've been so busy. Isla consumed my time and all.' Jess walked over to the Christmas tree, her back to Gerry.

Yes love, but she's been off your hands for a time since uni, hasn't she. I just thought… well, I've missed you that's all. You are okay Jess, aren't you? The black dog's not back, is it?' Gerry was being careful not to unravel her.

'No, I'm fine. It's just work, sis. I've decided to move closer to London, so there'll be no excuse in the future.'

'Oh, wonderful news.' Gerry approached her. 'Come 'ere, give your older sister a hug!'

The two embraced and were soon interrupted by a mob of children invading the room, yelling, 'Santa's come, Santa's come! Where's my present? I want my present! Can we open them now? Can we? Can we? Please Nana, please!'

Gerry turned around to the infant pack and roared, 'Now listen you lot, get up to the bathroom, brush your pegs and your hair, get dressed and once everyone's here, it's then we'll be opening your gifts, only then! You hear me? And only if you're good!'

A bunch of doughy eyes looked up at Gerry and they all nodded before scampering from the room.

'There, I still got it, sis! They be feared of me for the time being. As proven with their parents, the listenin' turns to deafness at about age 13.'

'Morning Jess, Merry Christmas!' smiled Bob, his rotund body parting the wave of kids like Moses.

'Merry Christmas, Bob,' said Jess.

'It's like a bloody daycare centre, this place. Least you know you're alive,' said Bob, hands on hips, having a loud chuckle to himself.

'Will you get those other buggers out of bed, Bob. They've all had a sleep-in, there's a lot to do before Isla's here and I need some help!' said Gerry.

'Isla's bringing Sam, her boyfriend… and manager too, Gerry,' said Jess.

'Good. It's been so long since I've seen her. Seen 'em both in the papers though. Quite the looker that man of hers.'

'Yeah, well I don't get to see her much these days either, part of the reason I'm moving south. I miss her.'

All of a sudden, the smash of glass was heard coming from the front room. 'What the fuck!' Gerry stormed into the hallway. 'Will all you fuckin' lazy arses get yourselves out of bed and act like parents for a change? Jesus, Mary… I'm not your bloody slave! D' ye hear me!' Gerry drew on her cigarette and brushed the fallen ash from her dressing-gown. 'GET UP, or I'll be wringing your bloody necks!'

Bob gave Jess an awkward smile. 'I'll get you a cuppa, love. Looks like you need one. God knows I do!'

Jess turned to look at the tree. Hanging there was a framed photo of Jess and Gerry as kids with their mother. Jess remembered well when the photo was taken, being the first Christmas after her father's death. A sadness possessed Jess's face in the photo. Their mother had been drunk most of that day and Jess was sent to bed early for some mild misdemeanour, crying herself to sleep. *Merry Christmas, little Jess*, she thought. *God bless us all this day.* She reached forward, glanced about and turned the frame to face the tree.

Some two hours later, Isla and Sam arrived at the front door bearing gifts. Struggling with the bundle of presents, Sam managed to knock on the door. Shortly after, the door opened.

'Hi, I'm Billy. You must be Isla and… '

'Sam, Billy, pleased to meet you.'

'Come through… oh, and Merry Christmas to you both.'

'Merry Christmas to you too,' said Isla and Sam in unison.

After hanging up their winter coats on the wall pegs, they arrived at the end of the hall and entered the kitchen area to absolute pandemonium. Bob was on the couch drinking stout, Gertrude was chasing Oak and Clay about the trestle tables, Phoenix was finger-painting, with most of the paint decorating her dress, and Margaret's children were playing a game of pin the tail on the donkey, with Phillip attempting to control the game, spinning the children about and directing them towards a donkey picture on the wall, which looked more like a lopsided llama.

'Where is the bloody potato peeler, Mum?' Margaret asked.

'Third drawer over there, Margy. Use your bleedin' eyes!' said Gerry, wiping her hands on her apron. 'Oh my Lord, shh everyone, we have guests!' She had just seen Isla and Sam at the entrance to the room.

Clapping her hands together and then wolf-whistling, she eventually made the room come to a standstill.

'Now everyone, this is Isla and her friend, Sam. Please behave yourselves today. We're wanting to make a good impression on our guests. Welcome Isla and Sam, to our mad but humble abode. You are our very special guests today and I want you both to make yourselves at home.' She smiled, giving them both a warm hug.

Jess went up to Isla and affectionately kissed her on the cheek. 'Merry Christmas, love, I've missed you. You need to make a bit more of an effort. Nice to see you again, Sam. You know, I've told her I'll be dead one day and she'll regret not visiting me more.'

'Good to see you again, Mrs Johnson,' said Sam, extending his hand to her.

'I told you before Sam, call me Jess. No formalities necessary. I see you're keeping my girl well.'

'Oh Mum,' said Isla, embarrassed by the comment, 'I keep *myself* thanks. This is the era of the independent woman and as for me, I'm free, wild and mostly in control, aren't I Sam?' Isla elbowed him in the ribs.

'No comment,' said Sam, smiling.

After introductions all round, Gerry handed Isla and Sam a glass of passionfruit spumante. 'Enjoy loves, I bought this special at the grocers. He told me it was a good drop and very festive. Worth lashing out a bit at Christmas, especially for my niece. Bought a dozen, so we won't run dry today! There'll be no-one wanting for a drink this day. Not in my house, hey Bob!'

'No love, never in this house,' muttered Bob under his breath, hidden behind *The Times*.

Gerry popped the cork, filled the wine glasses and encouraged everyone to clink their glasses. 'Here's to a wonderful day and most of all to family! Cheers!'

Gerry sculled her glass, topped it up and clapped her hands to command everyone's attention again.

'Alright Billy, now put down that bloody plane. You're in charge of cutting the beans. Gertrude, after you've changed Oak's nappy... I'm gathering that's the shitty smell wafting about... wash your hands and start peeling the spuds with Clay and Phoenix. Hand over the peeler to her, Margy.'

Gerry spotted Phoenix's pout. 'And yes you too, miss! You eat at our table, you contribute! You hear me?'

Phoenix glared at Gerry, stomping her left foot and sticking out her tongue.

'Phillip, you can help Russell salt the pork and chicken... oh, and stuff it with some lemons?'

'Stuff what? And how do you stuff it, Mum?' said Phillip.

'Oh Jesus, the chicken, Phillip, and you should know what needs stuffin', God knows I'm guessing you stuff enough things up your arse.' Gerry laughed.

'There you go again, trying to out me in public. I'm sick of it, *Gerry*. I've told you I'm no poofter, okay!' said Phillip, putting on Gerry's rose-printed apron.

'Yeah, leave the boy alone Mum. If he likes it *that way*... no harm done, hey boy! He's not harmin' anyone,' said Bob, attempting to rescue his son from further embarrassment.

'What *way*? Fucking hell, I've told you, I'm not gay!' said Phillip, spinning around to face the kitchen window, placing both hands on his hips. 'You're all so annoying, I hate you!'

'Now where was I?' said Gerry. 'Oh yes, Margaret. Wait! I need a drink!'

Gerry poured herself another glass of spumante. 'Share it around, Jess, share it around.'

'Gerry, you need to pace yourself. You're just like Mum. She could never handle the demon drink and let's face it, neither can you!' said Jess.

'Oh lighten up, love. It's Christmas.' Turning to Isla, she said, 'She always gets like this, doesn't she Isla? Or is it Joni? Joni, Joni Joni!' she chanted, dancing around with a half-bottle of spumante in her hand, nearly clocking Bob in the head. 'Now, back to Margaret. Round up those rug rats of yours, Hewie, Dewie, Louie and Minnie.'

'Mother, it's Gerry, Barbara, Shirley and Chip!' blurted Margaret.

'Oh, that's right, love, *Chip* off the old block. That be you, Russ,' laughed Gerry.

'Jesus, *Gerry*, you can be such a *biatch* sometimes,' said Phillip, tossing back his long black locks.

'So cheeky, Phil,' said Gerry, pinching his cheek. 'But he's soooooooo cute when he gets a little upset with his mummy!'

Gerry swivelled about to Margaret. 'Whatever those little darlings are called, I want you to get them to set the table for me. Can you do that. Margaret? Do I have to keep asking you? I don't want to keep asking you!'

'You've just asked me, Mother! I get it, okay, okay!' said Margaret, trying to round up Shirley and Chip, who were running around Bob's chair in circles.

'I know, I know, but I usually do ask you more than once and I'm just tryin' to save my breath!' Gerry stooped over the island bench, slightly breathless, holding a half-full glass in one hand and a cigarette in the other. 'Now Jess, you're the waitress, fill up the glasses, mine too dear.'

As the kitchen cuckoo clock chimed three, everyone was finally seated, wearing coloured paper bonbon hats, blowing party whistles and speaking over one another. The air was thick with laughter, screams of joy, cries and chatter.

Sam and Isla were seated to Gerry's left in the middle of the U-shaped table, with Jess to the right of the couple. Gerry clapped her hands, stood up, nearly losing her footing, and using a spoon, hit the side of her champagne glass to gain everyone's attention. She took another sip of spumante, which seemed to make her speech fuzzy. It was difficult to know if the sentence was ever going to end.

After Gerry thanked everyone for coming and contributing to the day, she gracelessly resumed her seat with the assistance of Jess, who knew all too well her sister's issues with the devil drink. It was a family trait after all.

'Please Gerry, no more now, you've had enough!' said Jess, stroking her sister's hand.

'I'll let you know when I've bleedin' well had enough, little sis. Besides, Christ is born, it's been 12 months since his last birth. Wish I could say the same about the rabbits in this household!'

By then, Sam was wriggling his buttocks from side to side on the wooden chair, taking small sips of sweet sherry to ease his nerves. I knew it would be bad, he thought, but I had no idea I'd be stuck eating Christmas lunch in a nuthouse.

'I told you!' whispered Isla, squeezing his knee.

'You owe me big time, babe… and I know just how you might repay me!' smirked Sam.

Interrupting their hushed conversation, Jess turned to Sam and asked, 'So tell me, what plans do you have for my daughter next year? I hear a tour is in the offing.'

'What the hell?' Sam was momentarily distracted by Clay and Chip on all fours crawling under the trestle tables, screaming like Apaches. 'Ah, yes. That's the plan, Jess.'

'Get back on your chairs, you little buggers!' cried Gerry. 'Jesus, can't you control your kids, Gertie and Margy? And Billy, put down that bleedin' plane and stop teasing Oak with it, will ya? You'd think you were 10 years old. Sit down and eat your meal!'

'Yes Mum, but I wasn't teasin', I wasn't,' said Billy, his eyes filling up.

'You are such a baby sissy, Billy. How old are you? Go on, cry, why don't you!' sneered Phillip.

'Pot callin' the kettle black, Phil, you're the biggest sissy here. I've seen the make-up hidden in your drawers,' said Margaret.

'Oh Mum, she's been goin' through my drawers again. Anyhow, it's not mine… it's, it's Barbara's. I was going to give it to her all wrapped up nice and that,' said Phillip.

'Pity you had to stop to put on some lippy before you wrapped it up,' said Gertie.

'Oh fuck off, you're all shits. I hate you!' said Phillip.

'Now, now, CHILDREN, behave. Bob, can you please do *something*?' said Gerry.

'Listen to your mother,' said Bob, 'we have guests, you know!'

'Oh! Well said, Bob! That's my Bob. He's a penny-pincher for words, my old man. His words count for so much, you know Jess.' Gerry took another swig of bubbles.

Jess turned back to Sam.

'I'm sorry, Sam, you said plan?'

'Yes, that right, we're going to Australia. Isla and I decided it would be a great opportunity, riding off the success of her new album. Besides, she tells me she has family there!'

'Ooooooh, Australia, will you fancy that Bob. We'd love to go to *Australia* one day too, wouldn't we Bob?' said Gerry.

Bob looked at her, grumbled something and then stuffed his face with some lemon chicken.

Jess's heart sank. 'Really? Australia? Not much to see there from memory.'

For a moment, she was transported back to the stage door, facing Olivia.

'Besides, Isla's family would no doubt all be departed by now. Not heard from anyone since we left all those years ago.' Jess wiped her mouth nervously with a Christmas serviette.

'Oh really, Mother? It's strange, isn't it, that after all these years, no-one from Dad's family ever wrote to us. I often wondered about that. Kind of weird. Perhaps they had no time for me? Though I do recall that box of envelopes on your wardrobe shelf from Aunty Liv, so you told me.'

'Olivia. Yes, I remember her,' said Gerry. 'Thought its shit didn't stink, that one. A doctor or something. Did you get mail from her, Jess love?' She winked broadly at Jess, not having heard Isla's previous comment.

'Yes, ages ago,' said Jess, attempting to change the subject. 'Anyhow, I wouldn't be bothered going to Australia. You should try and hit the US market, like The Beatles did. Much more interesting places to discover. Broader audience. More money, I bet. I'd give Australia a wide berth if I were you two,' she said, shifting uncomfortably in her seat.

'You know, now we're all adults and that, I can tell you, I can,' said

Gerry, swinging her champagne glass in her hand, taking the occasional gulp, 'I never once received a letter from the bitch Olivia, but your father, Isla, yes, your father, well he sent me letter after letter after letter. A veritable post office, I was. Wasn't I, Bob? Naturally, I sent them all to your mother. Didn't I, Jess? Well, none of my business really. Besides, your mother and me lost a bit of contact really when you trekked up to the Orkneys. That's right sis, isn't it?'

Jess nearly choked on her pork, unable to cough up a chunk stuck in her throat.

'Quick, get her a glass of water Gertie, she's choking,' said Gerry. Bob quickly stood to lend a hand.

'I'm alright, stop hitting my back, Bob. I'll be fine,' said Jess.

Isla interrupted. 'I'm sorry, what did you say Aunty? That Dad was sending you letters regularly and you were forwarding them to my mother? Is that what you said?'

The realisation of what she was saying made Isla's voice brittle and her eyes welled up.

'Yes, love. I assumed your mother would've shared the letters with you. And for a few years back then, he'd come and visit me. Not that I let him in. Sent the boys in blue around to visit us now and then, didn't he Bob? Askin' us some questions and all. But, you know, despite all that, I always liked your dad, but not our business, was it Bob? Was it Bob?' Gerry elbowed Bob in the ribs, realising she had let the cat out of the bag. 'I'll tell you what love, there's still a few here I haven't forwarded, let me get them for you.'

Jess was speechless, not knowing what to say or which way to turn. Gerry stumbled to the bureau near the Christmas tree, got down on all fours and fetched out a shoebox full of envelopes from the bottom drawer. She passed them over to Isla. 'There you go love. Merry Christmas from your favourite aunt!'

Gerry stumbled to her chair, holding onto it for grim life, feeling the impulse to projectile vomit.

An unspeakable rage was bubbling inside Isla. She carefully lifted the lid on the shoebox. Inside, there were numerous envelopes, spanning the years, all clearly marked with Australian stamps. On the back of each envelope were written the words, *O Johnson*.

Oh my God, Isla thought, the letters in Stromness were not from my aunt, but from my father. Fuck, he's alive!

Isla stared at her mother, wanting to remove her limbs one by one. A voiceless scream possessed her.

'He's alive, Mother? My father's alive!'

'Of course he's alive, pet. He's been writing to you. Didn't your mother share his letters… ' Gerry stopped and before she could do any further damage, Jess piped up.

'I can explain, Isla. Please, before jumping to conclusions, let me explain love!'

Isla abruptly stood up at the table. An eerie hush possessed the room and she leant into Jess so they were only inches apart. 'My father's alive. You lied to that little girl and let her grow up without a dad. You are a despicable human being and I NEVER want to see you again. You understand Jessica? NEVER! I'm done. From this day, I have no mother! I need to get out of here, Sam.'

'Oh love, don't be like that. There's plum pudding and brandy custard. I dropped some sixpences in the pudding as well,' said Gerry, trying to make the peace.

'My mother might like them, Aunty. A penny for her thoughts!'

Isla made a brisk escape out the front door.

'Thanks, everyone. It's been, well… an enlightening day really,' said Sam, who went to follow Isla and then returned to collect the box of envelopes. 'Bye all! Nice to meet you. We really must do it again sometime.'

Making it to the street, Sam did not see where Isla had gone. He put on his woollen coat and wrapped his grey woollen scarf about his neck. A warm Aussie Christmas wouldn't go astray, he thought.

He passed a dead-end street, which led to a pathway running adjacent to the Thames River. There was an old wooden bench, surrounded by snow, looking out onto the frozen waters and its grey surrounds. Seated there was Isla, her arms wrapped around her stockinged legs, her eyes fixed on the river.

Sam sat beside her, gently placing his arm around her. Neither of them said anything for some time, Isla staring at the frozen river. Unexpectedly, she spoke.

'I'm numb, Sam. I'm really numb. I can't feel anything. Nothing. And I'm so scared. Why can't I feel anything, Sam? I want to feel something. But I sit here and stare at the frozen river, wishing for a pair of skates to skate away on.'

'Don't try and think, babe. Too hard to process now. Let's be quiet. Let's just sit here. Listen to the distant sounds of Christmas. Catch our breath. All that matters is that we're here together. Just you and me. For the moment, that's all that matters, that's all we have. Let's just *be*, babe.'

The wintry breeze swirled about them. Then Sam lifted her chin with his finger, drawing his lips close to hers and softly kissing her. 'I love you, Isla!'

'I know, and me too, but what happens now, Sam?'

'What happens now is that we sit here, as one. We don't just skate away. I'm not leaving your side, do you hear me? The world might have changed forever this day, Isla, left your heart with a gaping hole, but it doesn't mean we can't build a bridge together.'

He gave her shoulder a squeeze. He kissed her forehead. And although a million thoughts were flittering around her mind, Sam's words comforted her and she knew that things were going to work out.

Chapter 25
Come to the Sunshine

The next morning, Isla and Sam were woken by the constant ringing of the telephone. It stopped for a time, then rang again. Sam checked the time and it was only 8.30 a.m.

'God, who could be ringing this early. Should I pick it up?' he said.

'Do so at your own peril,' said Isla, rolling over and putting her head under the sheets.

Then it stopped. Sam quickly lifted the receiver and placed it on its side to avoid further incoming calls. There, I'm a genius he thought, snuggling into Isla.

'Fifteen more minutes babe, then we need to head to the airport. Let's not be late for a change! Destiny... the land of milk and honey, cobber!'

Isla said nothing, thoughts about her father preoccupying her. Gradually, however, she was gaining a bit more clarity, and vague yet happy childhood memories floated in and out of her consciousness.

On the other end of the unanswered phone was Jess, a broken woman, who had not slept all night. As she dialled for the sixth time, all she could hear was an engaged signal. She realised any hope of a connection was futile. She retired to Gerry's lounge room and sat in their mother's old wingback chair. It's scent was familiar and Jess slowly drifted off, plagued by her nightmares.

'Are you in there Jess? Oh, there you are,' said Gerry. 'I'm just heading to the corner shop to grab some milk. Won't be long. Might pick up some miracle cure for a sore head too. Jesus, that spumante packed a punch. Listen love, I know we need to talk after yesterday's fiasco. I remember bits 'n pieces. The bits that do come to mind make me feel sick to my guts.

We *really* do need to talk it out Jess… like old times. Is that okay?'

Jess stared into the fireplace without saying a word. Her thoughts were spinning wildly and although she heard Gerry and was listening to her carefully, she remained silent, her gaze fixed, her body motionless.

'Alright love, I know you might be a wee bit angry still. As I said sis, let's chat, I'll be back soon.' Gerry headed for the front door. Before closing it, she called out, 'I do love ya sis!'

That morning, London traffic was worse than usual, making Isla and Sam late at the airport. Their flight, however, was on time. Bolting from their cab into the airport, they arrived in the nick of time.

'I knew it, I knew it,' said Sam, huffing and puffing, 'we're always late!'

'Don't look at me, babe, you're my manager. You need to lift your game, obviously!' Isla smiled.

'Very funny!' said Sam, poking out his tongue. 'Where's your passport?'

'You have it!' said Isla. 'Don't look at me!'

'Oh my God, oh my God, it should be in this pouch!' said Sam.

'Passports and tickets, sir, please,' said the airline officer at the boarding desk.

'Hold your horses… shit, where are they? Fuck, they're not in here! My coat pocket… no, fuck!' Sam ran his hands through his hair in panic.

'Sir, there is no need to use such profanities,' said the officer, giving Sam a very stern look.

'Yes, babe, no need to use such profanities. I'm shocked. I'm so sorry sir. I will give my staff a sound talking-to,' said Isla, waving the tickets and passports in his face and quietly chuckling.

'Oh my Lord! Thank God! Where were they?' said Sam.

'In my pouch, not yours, Skippy!' laughed Isla.

'Very funny miss!' said Sam. Before he could say anything further, Isla placed her index finger on his dry lips, 'Now, where were we? Oh yes, hand the nice man the tickets and passports, Sam, there's a good boy!' As the officer checked the travel documents, Isla gave him a cheeky stare, saying, 'It's no wonder we're always late for our flights. Very hard to get good staff these days!'

'Indeed, madam, indeed,' he said, stamping the tickets whilst Sam smacked his forehead with his hand.

Around the same time at Gerry's home, Jess's trance-like state was interrupted by a loud knocking at the door. 'I'll get it!' she called, easing herself up. 'I'm coming, *I'm coming,* Jesus, hold on!'

Opening the front door, Jess was confronted by two austere police officers in full uniform, wearing their traditional bobby helmets. 'Good day, who are you ma'am?' asked the older one.

'Jessica Johnson, officers. How may I help you?'

'Is this the residence of Mrs Gerry McIntosh, ma'am?'

'Yes, why? What's she done now?'

'Is there a Mr McIntosh? Is she married or does she have a partner?'

'Yes, but why… what's wrong, you're scaring me!' Jess turned around and yelled out to Bob. Moments later, he stumbled down the stairs.

'What is it? Can't a man get some shut-eye? Still feel pissed from yesterday! What is it, Jess?'

'Are you Mr McIntosh, sir?'

'Aye, that's me. Who wants to know?' said Bob, puffing out his chest in his stained white singlet top, which only partly covered his protruding gut.

'Good morning, Mr McIntosh. I'm very sorry to awaken you, however, I'm afraid I'm obliged to deliver you some very distressing news.'

Jess immediately grabbed Bob by the shoulder.

'I'm sorry to say sir, your wife's been involved in a terrible car accident. A tragic accident. She's been killed by a hit and run driver, crossing over Lyon Street. Been shopping, it seems. We are sorry, Mr McIntosh. Please accept our deepest condolences. Here is a card with the relevant contact numbers and they will be able to assist you at the hospital, where she's been transported. Again, we are so very sorry, sir.'

Jess closed the door slowly. It appeared the Bob had not heard one word after 'she's been killed', collapsing into Jess's arms, clinging to her and sobbing uncontrollably. Jess stood there, supporting her brother-in-law, wanting desperately for some emotion to trigger inside of her. She so wanted to feel something, but the revelations from yesterday continued to overcome any feelings. They were lost somewhere; she was lost somewhere. She desperately wanted to rediscover herself, to feel complete, but her true feelings continued to escape her. She stood there lifeless and detached. All she could do for now was hold Bob tightly, comfort him with her embrace and gaze at the picture of Gerry and Bob hanging crookedly on the wall.

The trans-continental flight was long and arduous and when they finally touched down and Isla's feet stood firmly on Australian ground, a weird sensation overcame her. *I do feel I've been here before*, she thought, *it feels familiar, how strange. And just to think, this is where it all began. My past is about to catch me up.*

'What are you doing standing there, babe? You look like a stunned rabbit. Let's grab our cases, catch a cab and head to the Hilton. I think a lie-down and a bit of shut-eye will do us both good. Be nice to be horizontal. We only have a day or two to rest before the real work starts.

What do you think, madam?'

'Oh, madam says great idea. Let's do it. I'm exhausted, Sam. Sorry if I'm a bit, you know, vague, lots going on in my head, you know… '

Sam looked at her lovingly. 'I know, babe, I know. I can't even imagine. Hey, just for the record, I think you're doing an amazing job… coping. You're a special gal!' Kissing her softly on the head, Sam overloaded himself with their luggage. They processed through customs, hailed a cab and headed for the Hilton Hotel and some necessary shut-eye.

Their accommodation stood opposite the Melbourne Cricket Ground, adjacent to the Treasury Gardens, very central and close to public transport. The train station was just across the road. All this information and more they gleaned from a happy, loquacious cab driver who not only shared his personal life story with his weary passengers, but all the local tourist information and upcoming events.

'Did you know, Melbourne is the cultural capital of Australia? Some sheila named Joni Saint Claire is opening a show here next week at Her Majesty's Theatre. Love her stuff. Jesus, mate, is she hot. Have you checked her out? Love to give her one!' he said, smiling at Sam in the rear-vision mirror.

'Yeah, me too mate,' said Sam, elbowing Isla, 'she is pretty hot. But boy, I hear she has a temper!'

'Well, I heard she is beautiful inside and out,' said Isla.

'Well, don't mind me saying, I'd like to turn her inside out!' laughed the driver, raising his eyebrows in the mirror.

He gave Isla another look, 'Hey miss, has anyone ever told you that you look a bit like Joni? She's just a bit thinner than you, bit more gaunt, that's all!'

The taxi pulled up at the Hilton. Isla fossicked through her handbag and pulled out a $20 bill. 'There, that should cover it, tip included.'

Concierge collected their bags. As they alighted from the cab, Isla turned about and stuck her head in the window. 'Oh, one more thing, driver, she's not *that thin*! Ciao for now!'

Soon after, they were in their suite where they kicked off their shoes and lay spread-eagled on the king-size bed. There was a knock at the door. 'Coming,' said Sam, muttering, 'what now?' to himself.

A bellboy handed him a telegram addressed to Ms Isla Johnson. Sam quickly turned the message over to discover that it was from Jess.

'Who was that?' said Isla with her eyes closed.

'Telegram, for you. It's from your mother!'

'Oh my God, how did she track us down here?' said Isla, sitting up to tear open the telegram.

'I think I blabbed it to that woman at the stage door that night, when your mother was present. Remember? Oh shit, that reminds me, I mustn't forget those tickets I promised to leave her.'

He looked at Isla, whose face appeared to be drained of blood as she stared at the piece of paper in her hands.

'What's wrong, babe? You look like you've seen a ghost!'

'Gerry's dead, Sam. Killed in a car accident on 26 December. My God. I never got to say goodbye. Christmas was so fucking awful. So many questions… shit! I so wanted to speak to her, Sam. Out of anyone in my family, she might have given me some real truths. It all makes sense now, why my mother kept her at a distance for so long. Anyhow, I'm just too tired to get into this now. Sorry Sam. Let's get some sleep. I need sleep right now.'

'Okay, let's sleep and we'll talk later. You have a lot goin' on, babe. Be kind to yourself. Things will reveal themselves bit by bit and I'm here with you every step. For now your show must be our focus. Lots to do over the next few days with rehearsals, album signings, television and radio appearances. The Melbourne memory lane tour will have to wait a few days. I need you to be Joni Saint Claire for now. Can you do that for me?'

She smiled at him. 'You know, I'm so lucky to have you, Sam. I couldn't do all this alone! And, yes, I can do it, for us!'

Without saying a word, Sam gave her his cheeky grin and jumped into bed with her, spooning her lovingly. Isla closed her eyes and whispered her aunt a *God bless*, recalling faded images of a small child meeting her aunt for the first time at London Airport all those years ago. Her wide smile full of teeth, her bright blue eyeshadow, her wet kiss and smell of cheap floral perfume mixed with tobacco. Most of all she remembered the physical warmth she exuded. *Aunt Gerry knew my father was alive all those years*, she thought, *all the lies… so many lies. To what end? Why? Stop it! I must shift my thinking away from Mother, at least for now. Bless you Aunt Gerry, all is forgiven.*

Isla's thoughts slowed and soon she was asleep nestled in Sam's arms, feeling safe, secure and exactly where she belonged.

The interior of Bob's house resembled his scattered thoughts. He sat in his favourite armchair most of the time, whisky in one hand, cigarette in the other, alternately sipping and smoking. Jess was worn out by the comings and goings in the house, the well-wishers and the post-funeral food parcels left at the front door. She had never quite realised her sister's popularity. She grieved all those years in Stromness when she had rarely visited Gerry. They had been close growing up. Gerry had always protected her. However, after arriving in Scotland, Jess hadn't been able to face her with all the deceit that she was harbouring. She could never bear to tell Gerry the lies around Oliver's supposed death. She knew that Gerry was not that accepting of her choice to remove Isla from Oliver in the first place, so she would not have approved of her lying to the child about her father being dead. I shut the cupboard door on that one, thought Jess, easier to manage the façade alone without sharing my burden. Why did you have to let the cat out of the bag on me, sis? I suppose it wasn't your fault really. What did Mum used to say? 'Man proposes, God disposes.' Well, He's really dumped me in the shit this time! Perhaps I deserve it after all.

Gerry's passing left a real hole in the house. It was too quiet. The stillness was interrupted every so often by the chimes of the grandfather clock and the flapping of shirts and nappies on the backyard clothesline. They were sounds that reminded Jess that her mother's spirit was close by.

'I'm making a cuppa, Bob, would you like one love?' Jess asked him.

'That would be nice Jess. Real nice.'

Soon enough, the kettle was whistling on the stove and Jess carried a tray over to Bob with a fresh pot of tea, floral china cups and saucers and a plate laden with Bob's favourite chocolate cream biscuits.

'Milk, Bob?'

'Oh no thanks. Black will be fine.'

Jess poured him a cup. He extinguished his cigarette in the nearby ashtray and as she handed over the teacup, he topped it up with some whisky from his flask.

Sitting down opposite him after pouring herself a cup, Jess waited a moment before saying, 'Now Bob, I know you're dealing with a lot. I can't imagine really. I know you miss her, we all do. She lit up everyone's heart and soul.'

'Why did you wait all those years to visit, Jess? Gerry would often ask me. She thought she had done something wrong. You never wrote to her. You rarely called her. You would've only seen her once or twice since movin' north. Where did you go, Jess? I mean, I know where you were, but where did you go, what were you thinkin' lass? You hurt her, you did.' Bob downed his cuppa and helped himself to a second, adding another little tipple of whisky.

Jess started to well up.

'I don't know what I was thinking, Bob. I really don't. I had troubles of my own. After leaving Melbourne, I needed to sort myself out. It took time, longer than I ever imagined. I was fit for nothing, except working to make ends meet and looking after Isla. Sometimes I gazed at those wild seas in Stromness, waves thrashing about in the strong gales. They would look at me, Bob, all angry like. No matter how hard I looked back at them, they'd become fiercer, until I could look no more. And you know, as time went by, I realised it wasn't the waves staring at me all angry like, it was me holding up a mirror to myself. And I didn't like what I saw.'

'Well, it happens to us all, Jess. We make choices, some good, some bad, but either way, we have to make the best of what we choose. Often there's no turnin' back, is there? Takes courage to do so.'

Jess carefully picked up her teacup, not taking her eyes off Bob. She felt the warmth of the tea on her lips and it grounded her in the moment, a moment that she wished she had been able to spend with Gerry instead.

'No, there was no turnin' back Bob. Perhaps I wasn't brave enough. I made some bad choices, I did. And I sensed Gerry knew I did. They were choices born out of my fog. I wouldn't listen to anyone and I wish I had. I really do, Bob. But I was scared and I feel I let her down. I feel I've let so many people down.'

Jess placed her cup down, holding her face between her hands in shame. 'I fear I really messed up big time… and now it's too late!'

Bob took a quick sip of whisky from his flask and then gently patted Jess on the knee. 'There, there love. Remember that old Bible story about casting stones? We all make shite decisions, but it's ownin' up to them. Seekin' forgiveness is a humblin' journey and sometimes that's all we have left. I'll pray for you lass. I will.'

He sat back in his chair as Jess composed herself. 'I think I'll be okay here now, lass. I'll really miss that old bugger, but I have the kids about me and I'll never be visited by loneliness. I know if Gerry was here, she'd be givin' you a good talking-to and have you catch the first plane to Australia to tell your girl what you just told me. I reckon she's got a tough skin that girl of yours, bit like her aunty, but inside, I sense she knows how to forgive too. You've got nothin' to lose and everythin' to gain. So what about it? Hey?'

What Bob said made a great deal of sense to Jess. *I do have nothing to lose*, she thought. She straightened her dress and collar. Looking at Bob, she leant forward and grabbed both his hands lovingly in hers. 'Nothin' to lose, Bob, as you say. I just hope a spoonful of atonement is met with a measure of forgiveness. It's not going to be easy.'

'Give it time, go easy on yourself and be brave, love. You have my blessin',' Bob looked up to the ceiling, made the sign of the cross and added, 'and Gerry's!'

Pulling himself out of his chair, he walked over to the kitchen cabinet, removed a Mexican cookbook from the shelving and retrieved an envelope from inside.

'You know, one of the kids got this cookbook for her at a Mother's Day stall one year. Think it was sixpence. Billy complained they charged him too much. Anyhow, none of us liked Mexican much, so Gerry hid her stash in it, thinking I didn't know. I caught her a few years back sticking a few pound notes in an envelope and slipping it into the book. I asked her what she was doin' and she told me that each year she would put away some money for your birthday, in the hope that one day she would see you face to face and light up your day with a cash surprise. Suppose with the chaos at Christmas, she forgot to give it t'ya. So here it is, love. Only wish Gerry could see y'face. Put it towards the airfare back to Australia. Now off you git out of here. No time to lose!'

He took hold of Jess's arms and added, 'She did love ya, you know. She always did. Just never got to say it that often to ya, ya know.'

He gave Jess the envelope. As she opened it, she spied a wad of bills, held it close to her heart and hugged Bob, this time, with tears spilling down her cheeks. 'I loved her so much, Bob.'

Chapter 26

If

5 January 1978

Olivia and Richard had missed Christmas in Melbourne and Richard had surprised her with a short stay at Lake Como before the trek home. It had been a rough few days for Olivia not being able to tell Oliver the news but now, finally, they were home. It was far too delicate a concern to telephone him, and she wanted his reunion with Isla to be just right. *Who knows what he'd do*, she thought. *You can't trust men to act rationally.*

She was prepared to take any flak for not disclosing the news sooner, confident that her plan was solid. Despite her clear thinking, she was beside herself with excitement. She had gone over and over in her head that fateful meeting at the stage door and was thrilled that she would soon be able to share the wonderful news with her brother.

'Will you drive faster, Richard! You're driving like an old codger!'

'I'm going as fast as I can, *dear!* If you hadn't asked me to go to the Hilton and pick up those tickets first, we might have beaten this morning's peak-hour traffic!'

'Well move it, I have a plan and it can't wait any longer!'

'I know *dear,* I know. Always the plan!'

Outside Oliver's home, Olivia exclaimed, 'Finally!' and hastily exited the car without waiting for Richard to open her door. Her high heels appeared to grow wings as she practically ran to Oliver's front door.

'Ollie, Ollie! Love! It's me, Olivia. Open up, wakey, wakey, rise and shine!'

Oliver stumbled out of bed, put on his dressing-gown, rubbed the sleep from his eyes and opened the door. 'Olivia, Richard, what are you doing here so early? When did you arrive home?'

Olivia bowled past him without answering and headed to the kitchen. 'Cup of tea anyone? You two sit in the lounge. Your sister will be in shortly with the news of the hour. Special news, Ollie, headlines, just for you, darling brother.'

Soon after, she entered the lounge where Richard and Oliver were seated on the Chesterfield couch, which had seen better days. She pulled up a maroon velvet chair after placing the teacups and pot on the small wooden coffee table.

'Now, I have something very important to tell you, Ollie darling and… ' Oliver was about to speak, 'and I don't want you interrupting me!'

'This is enormously upsetting but joyous all at once. I'm so excited to tell you Ollie, aren't I, Richard?'

'Oh for God's sake Liv, just spit it out, tell me!' roared Oliver.

'Oh well, if you're going to be like that… '

'TELL ME!' said Oliver.

'I'VE FOUND ISLA! I SAW HER! There, I said it!' Olivia exhaled deeply and fanned herself.

'What? Isla? You saw her? Where? How do know it was her?' said Oliver.

For the next half-hour, the three of them discussed how Olivia had come upon Isla. She described every detail of Isla to her father, her wild stunning features, her quirky mannerisms, her handsome manager, Sam, and her international accomplishments as a singer/songwriter.

Oliver was brimming with excitement, leaning forward to take in Olivia's every word, crying tears of joy. He sought comfort in a velvet cushion, every so often burying his face in its softness.

For her part, Olivia was centre stage, acting out her meeting with Jess, the shocked look on her face, the timely opening of the stage door and Jess's discomfort as she stood there knowing her long-held secret was out.

'It was all so dramatic, darling, I couldn't have written a better script myself! Now, the cherry on the pie is this, dear Ollie. When I met her Sam, he kindly offered me two VIP tickets to Isla's opening concert. Her stage name is Joni Saint Claire, mind you. Mum's the word. The tickets are for this evening. Front row. I'm not going, neither is Richard. I want you to soak it up, alone, there with your daughter. She doesn't know you're coming. She probably doesn't even remember that Sam offered me the tickets. We picked them up before heading here. Isla didn't know it was me at the stage door. I didn't let on. Thought I'd let that witch of a mother stew in her own juices for a while. That Jess must be so violently ill now knowing what I know that you now know... if you know what I mean, darling. Anyhow, these are yours!' She waved the tickets in front of him. 'How you arrange to catch up with her, well that's where my plan ends. It's over to you now, my darling brother.'

She beckoned Oliver to stand, kissed him on the cheek and held him tightly, whispering into his ear, 'I love you little brother. You never deserved what she did to you, you never deserved to miss your li'l one so much. Don't let her get away this time, love.'

Oliver was overcome by the news. Am I dreaming? he thought.

'Off we go, Richard, I need a Pimms! Is it too early? Perhaps! Maybe a glass of bubbles might be better. Let's leave Ollie in peace. No doubt he has lots to think about. Oh, I'll leave the tickets on the hall stand. Enjoy, darling brother. I want to hear all about it.' She blew him a kiss and left, with Richard tagging behind.

That evening, Her Majesty's Theatre was overflowing with Joni Saint Claire's fans. Her biggest fan, however, was seated in the middle of Row A. The years had been kind to him, a few more wrinkles but not overly, his hair as thick as ever, highlighted with flashes of steely grey, his eyes retaining their cheeky sparkle. Oliver was dressed in a traditional tuxedo with white stone cufflinks, black bow tie and jet-black patent shoes. His curly hair was slicked back and he wore round tortoiseshell-frame glasses. A white silk handkerchief emerged from his jacket pocket as a finishing touch.

He had not had much time to gather his thoughts, consumed by so many emotions during the day. It had all happened so quickly. Any minute he would wake up to find that this was not really happening. He had waited so long for this moment. He sat there nervously, beads of sweat lining his brow, his hands unconsciously wringing the program. A sudden hush consumed the crowd when the opening music heralded the start of the show. The long red-velvet stage curtains gradually peeled back to reveal its star, Isla.

Twenty-two years since Oliver had laid eyes on her and there she stood right in front of him. She is so beautiful, he thought, watching her commanding presence onstage. She was wearing a fitted emerald-green evening gown, a white feather boa and several brightly coloured rings. Applause welcomed in this new goddess of music and she stood there, raising her arms in thanks, smiling from ear to ear at her adoring audience, her eyes sparkling under the spotlight beam.

The continuing ovation became muffled to Oliver's ear and he could no longer see this rising star called *Joni*. Instead, he saw a wild little girl boldly grinning back at him, wanting to share his piano stool to play him another tune. His memories flashed back to where it had all begun. He recalled bolting up those stairs at St Vincent's Hospital to hear the news of Isla's arrival, the smell of her newborn head and how he had lovingly nursed her in his arms for the first time. Isla's first steps and her colourful birthday parties, Aunt Liv taking on the role as games coordinator. Life had been grand. How had it dismantled so quickly? Where did those precious years go? I have missed out on so much!

His thoughts drifted further and he recalled those Saturdays spent at Dom's Deli sharing a milkshake with Isla, laughing and talking in the front window surrounded by red geraniums. And their sing-alongs motoring along in his prized Chevy.

He had a little chuckle to himself remembering Larry the labrador and the dog's loyal attachment to Isla. In particular, his protective growls offered to any passers-by who couldn't resist the temptation of bending down to greet her. I miss that dog, he thought.

His thoughts flashed back to the days spent at the piano with Isla, writing her song, teaching her scales and their songs together. Special moments that had created a unique bond between father and daughter, he thought. God, I have so missed her. All these years, I have had this gaping hole in my heart wondering where she was, what she was doing, whether she even gave me a passing thought.

What did I do that was so wrong? he thought. Why did Jessica do this to me? I was a great father, we made ends meet, I loved her and supported her. I loved Isla. She might as well have thrown me in jail to rot. Jess planned this, he thought. It must have taken some effort, with a little help from her sister. How could Gerry do this to me? I always got along with her. Thought we knew each other. Wonder how Jess would've felt if I'd done this to her? Difference is, he thought, I would never have been so cruel and callous. How could another human being treat the father of their child in such a way? I mean, it wasn't as if I were violent to her or Isla. I was Jess's loving partner.

All those years ago on his last trip to Glasgow, at the station, Oliver remembered how he had been determined to try to put all this behind him. How he was prepared to move on with his life, as best he could, despite an ever-present canyon of despair. I did my best, got on with my life, in my own way. But now, here I am, sitting in a theatre, watching my daughter perform, a young woman I don't even really know. That very thought terrifies me. I want to meet her, I want her to meet me. But what if she rejects me? What if I never get to speak to her properly? I want her to know my side of the story. Is that selfish? Does she need to be burdened with it? Perhaps she wants to know?

Oliver looked to the ornate ceiling above, praying for guidance.

He was so uncertain as to how to approach her, what to say, what to do. It was like walking on a rickety wooden bridge traversing two cliff faces without a safety net. But he was determined to cross over, reunite with Isla and rediscover lost time, at any cost. He did not know exactly how it would play out, but whatever form it took, destiny had brought him and his daughter here and he was determined to play it out and accept the consequences.

Looking at Isla now and still finding it difficult to believe he was there, Oliver became more orientated. Momentarily, he captured her eye. She didn't look at him with recognition, but it was a look nonetheless, with a warm inviting smile. I'll take that, he thought, it's more than enough for now.

My girl's home, finally, my *li'l one* is home.

Chapter 27
Conversation

8 June 1955

'Daddy, let me play. Can I show you something please, Daddy!' cried Isla, pulling on her father's dressing-gown.

Oliver removed the pencil from his mouth, took off his reading glasses and peered down at his little girl. 'Come here, li'l one. What are you doing up so early?'

He picked her up and sat her on the piano stool next to him.

'Daddy, I've been practising my song we wrote!'

'Have you, li'l one? Show me.'

Isla delicately spread her fingers before placing them decisively on the keys. Oliver had written the music in an age-appropriate format for Isla. With her eyes focussed and wearing a determined look, she played two verses and the chorus of *Isla's Song*.

Upon completion, she lifted her hands elegantly and beamed at her father, smiling proudly.

'Oh my goodness, li'l one, you *have* been practising. That was perfect, just perfect.' Oliver cuddled her, kissing the top of her head.

'Let's write some more, Daddy!'

'Okay, let's do a bit more before brekky. What do think about this?'

He had been thinking about the tune and how to make it flow effortlessly, and Isla's playing had given him just the right inspiration.

'Something like this… ' said Oliver.

---

5 January 1978

Slowly coming back to earth, Oliver refocussed, orientating himself back in the theatre, listening to Isla finish playing the last bars of the music to *their song.*

Isla took a deep breath. Silence enveloped the stage and her spellbound audience. She appeared to wipe her eyes, warding off the emotion welling inside her. Gracefully, she rose from her piano stool and walked downstage.

'It is fitting that I concluded this concert with a song dear to my heart named *Isla's Song*, written by my father when I was just a wee lass. I hoped you enjoyed it, as I do each time I get to play it. It connects me with a past which lights up my soul. Thank you all for joining me here tonight. It was so special to perform in my homeland for the first time and so wonderful to have you as my audience. Thank you.'

Taking her final bow, she stepped graciously backwards to resounding applause and the grand curtains folded in front of her.

Her performance had ended, but Oliver knew the real show was about to begin.

He was still standing, clapping explosively and wiping away tears, as the curtains hid his li'l one. He wanted to turn to the house and exclaim, *That's my girl!*

He found it difficult to move from his position, shuffling about on his feet and not knowing what to do next. The lead-up to the event, discovering the whereabouts of his daughter, sitting in the audience watching her perform, had been all so overwhelming. His limbs were heavy and he felt numb. He resumed his seat.

'Excuse me, sir?' said a woman patron trying to manoeuvre past him. 'Excuse me, would you mind letting me past!'

Oliver just sat there, speechless, paralysed, hearing nothing.

'What is wrong with you? Louis, can you believe this man? Does he expect me to jump over him? Are you listening to me, you ignoramus!' she exclaimed.

'Don't worry Beatrice, let's go the other way! Let's not cause a scene dear,' said her husband, grabbing his wife by the hand and gently pulling her in the opposite direction.

As he pulled the woman away, Oliver turned his head, suddenly picturing Jess drawing a young Isla away from him. She was resisting her grasp, screaming for help.

He jumped to his feet, yelling, 'Leave her alone, she's mine! She's *my* daughter!'

There was a sudden hush. The husband let go of his wife in shock and she stumbled towards Oliver.

'You, sir, are a freak! Get some help!' said the woman, as her Louis again grabbed hold of her hand. 'C'mon dearest. That's enough. Leave him be.' They scurried from the now empty row of seats, leaving Oliver standing there alone.

Isla, I have to see her, he thought, coming back to the present. He took his handkerchief and wiped his face clean of sweat and tears. He then combed his hair, straightened his spectacles and filled his lungs. There, pull yourself together, you've waited for this day for so long, don't fuck it up old man.

Scoping the theatre, he saw it was almost empty. He checked left and right, then headed to the stage stairs on the prompt side, taking them two at a time. The stage manager had vacated her post and forgotten her opening night gift, a dozen red roses. Perfect, he thought, a present and a cover-up all at once.

He hurried down the narrow corridor backstage, brushing past theatre staff, technicians and other performers, not knowing where he would find Isla. He stopped a passing male crew member wearing headphones and said, 'I have these roses to deliver to Miss Joni Saint Claire, I'm one of her publicists, which way is her dressing-room?'

'Oh, Joni, around that first corner on your left and her dressing-room is the second on the right. You'll see it. Her name's on the door, mate.'

Oliver thanked him. Soon, he was standing in front of a door facing a bright star with the name *Joni Saint Claire* emblazoned on it. He took a deep breath and knocked three times.

'Come in,' called a female voice.

As he entered, he saw Isla sitting in front of her make-up mirror in a white dressing-gown, removing her stage paint. 'What is it, sir? Can I help you?'

Oliver extended the bunch of roses. 'These… these are for you. Admiring fan. Thought I would deliver them.'

Isla had not yet turned around. She was still facing her mirror and Oliver was only able to see her reflection.

'Just leave them on the chair,' she said, pointing to a nearby chaise without paying her guest much attention.

Nevertheless, as Oliver walked over to place the roses down, her eyes followed her visitor in the mirror with some curiosity.

'By the way, wonderful performance tonight, ma'am.'

Isla didn't answer, pivoting on her chair to face him. There was silence as she scanned him. She couldn't make sense of it but thought there was something familiar about him.

'Who are you? Have we met before? What are you doing here?'

'I told you. Just delivering the flowers, ma'am.'

'I don't know you, do I? I can't put my finger on it. Do I know you?'

Words failed him. He was back again in that theatre seat, his limbs heavy and his speech pressured.

'Are you alright sir? You look like you've seen a ghost! Here, sit down, I'll get you a glass of water.' Isla disappeared into the bathroom to fetch him a refreshment. 'Here, drink this up, it will make you feel better.'

Oliver quickly quenched his thirst, adjusting himself on the chaise.

Isla moved her chair closer to him. 'Do you feel alright? Your pallor scared me. Thought you were about to pass out. And how would that look, a stranger collapsing in Joni Saint Claire's dressing-room?' She smiled.

'Thank you Isla, I'm feeling much better,' said Oliver, looking down at his now empty glass.

'I'm sorry! What did you call me?'

'Isla, I called you Isla,' said Oliver, now peering into her blue eyes.

Isla did not say a word. She searched her visitor's face, taking in his curly brown-grey locks, his jawline, the creases framing his lips and his familiar green eyes. Uncomfortable, she clasped her hands tightly, leaning into this unknown and curious visitor.

'I'm sorry, sir, but really, who are you?'

His tears fell slowly. Looking squarely at her, finding it difficult to speak, he said, 'Li'l one, I'm your father!'

Isla immediately stood up, holding her hands over her mouth, backing away and colliding with an adjacent costume rack. 'What's your name?'

'Oliver, Oliver Johnson. Your mother is Jessica Baker. We lived in Camberwell. You were taken from me by your mother in November 1955… to London then to Scotland and God knows where. And I've been with you in spirit since the day I lost you.'

He stood up and walked towards her, overcome with waves of emotions at every pace. Not knowing what to do, he instinctively and slowly held out his arms to his daughter, longing to hold her.

Isla stood motionless, not knowing what to do with her arms. She often complimented herself on being in control, even when she was out of control. It was something Morag had taught her growing up, about taking control of situations and being a strong, educated and capable woman. Now, however, that rug of learning was wrenched from under her. She was adrift at sea, no Morag, no lifebuoy, all alone. Her initial instinct was to rush forward and lovingly embrace her father, hold him tightly, after having lost him so many years before. However, she harboured a belly-full of anger buried deep inside her, a discontent that she had never fully explored. As she stood there, she thought, *This should be the best day of my life, what is happening to me? What the fuck is happening to me!* Impulsively, she walked towards Oliver and hugged him loosely, her chin resting on his shoulder. The smell of his aftershave was familiar and unconsciously, her embrace tightened. Oliver returned her embrace, whispering into her ear, 'My li'l one, I *never* thought I would see you again!'

Suddenly, the dressing-room door was flung open. It was Sam.

'What the hell! What's going on here?' he shouted.

Isla pulled away. 'I'm sorry! I can't do this Oliver. I just can't do this. I'm sorry. I don't know what's wrong with me. I don't... I can't... I can't. Please leave. Please *just go!*'

'But Isla, I'm so sorry. I didn't mean to... What's... ' said Oliver.

'*Go!*' she shouted.

'Oliver... *your father*?' said Sam. 'I thought... '

'Just *shut up* Sam. For once, *just shut the fuck up!*' said Isla.

Stunned, Oliver retreated. Not knowing how to react, he wrote his address and telephone number on a piece of paper and gave it to Sam. 'If she changes her mind, she'll find me there. Please, take it son.'

Just as he was leaving, Jess crossed his path and bowled into the dressing-room.

'Ah ... you told me to shut up,' Sam said to Isla, 'but I was coming to tell you that your mother flew to Melbourne to surprise you. So... surprise! Best I go and give this little family reunion some privacy.'

'You're not going anywhere, bozo,' said Isla, pulling Sam to her side.

'Jessica!' said Oliver.

Jessica, ashamed to acknowledge him, continued looking at Isla.

Oliver gave Jessica another look, shook his head and tugged her arm to gain her attention. He took a moment. 'You know, I don't hate you Jess, I feel sorry for you.' He turned back to Isla, gave her a last glance and left the room, closing the door behind him.

'What the hell are you doing here, *Mother!* I told you I never wanted to see you again!'

'I thought I would surprise you, Isla. I want to speak with you. Christmas Day was such a debacle. I need to tell you things. Explain myself. Since Aunty Gerry passed, things have become clearer to me and I want you to know about them. It's important to me!'

'Oh, so *now* you want to speak with me. You *need* to tell me things. Well, good on you, Mother! It's always been what *you want*, what *you need*. Things might be clearer for you, but you have fucked my head rightly. My father, *my father,* comes into my dressing-room after 22 years to hug his only daughter, a daughter you took from his arms. You never asked him for permission, you just took me like some piece of property. Worse still, Mother, you never asked me. "Oh Isla, do you want to travel to the other side of the world, away from your father, his family, your friends and spend the rest of your life thinking your fucking father is dead?" You fucking selfish bitch. You've never prioritised anyone's interests except your own. And because of you, when faced with my father tonight, I stood there like some fucking stone statue feeling zip! I'm so fucking angry. I'm angry at you, I'm angry at me and I'm even angry at him, come to think of it, for not trying harder to find me. What the fuck! How messed up is that! So be proud, Mother. Congratulations. Go tell your friends you're the mother of Joni Saint Claire, be very proud. To the world, having reared me, you're a great success. But you know, as far as Isla Johnson is concerned, you failed as a parent! You failed dismally. As a person and a mother, you failed in even proportions, because your only thought was about yourself. No-one else. Just you! Now get out of my sight.'

'Are you finished, missy?' Jess said, speaking down to her in childlike fashion. 'Well Isla, I'm sorry, I am, but you need to understand, I did it for you, for us. You were my priority, always have been!' She approached Isla with outstretched arms.

'I call it bullshit, Mother. Don't you touch me, don't you ever touch me again. You have only thought about yourself, what *you* need, no-one else. Well, Mother, perhaps I need to take a leaf out of your book and start thinking about me. Sam, *get her out of my sight! I never want to see you again!*' She rushed to the bathroom, slamming the door, and stood over the basin, white-knuckling it, sobbing inconsolably, finally collapsing to the floor in a foetal position.

'I'm sorry Jessica, but I think you had best leave,' said Sam.

Jess looked bewildered, lifeless even. 'Yes, well, it seems that way. Here's my number. Would you please contact me to let me know how she is, Sam? I know it puts you in a difficult position, but please, just do this for me? I'm her mother.' Jess wrote her details on the back of a theatre napkin.

'Sam, I know she hates me. Perhaps she's got reason to. But I'm not a bad person. Truly, I'm not. I did what I thought was best, what I thought would give me the best possibility to be a good mother to her. That's all. I'm far from perfect. We *all* make mistakes. Perhaps some more than others. But you have to believe me Sam, I'm not the bad person she thinks I am.' She wiped away her tears. '*Please* be in touch… I'm sorry. Tell her I'm sorry.'

Jess left quietly and Sam put her napkin in his trouser pocket. The room was left empty, quiet and soulless. He moved the roses on the chaise to sit down and gazed at Oliver's note, which he was still holding. Placing his hands in a prayer position, he raised them to his forehead and thought, what now?

'About time!' said Olivia, barging through Oliver's front door. 'I've been knocking and knocking. Let me put the kettle on, I want to hear all about it.'

'Come in, please, don't mind me!' said Oliver, following his sister to the kitchen.

'Now, c'mon, spill the beans! I want to hear from go to whoa,' said Olivia, busily arranging the teapot, cups and saucers, 'isn't she just wonderful, Ollie? Oh my God, that voice!'

Oliver held onto the kitchen sink, letting out a sigh. 'Well sis, it was wonderful, she was wonderful, more than wonderful, my heart leapt out of my chest, so many memories, so many thoughts flashed by. I was totally, utterly overwhelmed. I think I stayed in that state from the time you told me the news about Isla. But sitting in the theatre, watching her, hearing her, it was all too much. I was cherishing every moment but at the same time grieving the times lost to us as father and daughter.'

He took his tea to the kitchen table and Olivia sat beside him. She held his hands, which were quivering. He wiped a tear away and continued, 'Anyhow, after the concert, I made it backstage. I didn't think about it much, I just made it my mission to find Isla and I did. As I opened her dressing-room door, she was sitting in front of the make-up mirror. She didn't turn at first, but I could see her spy me in the reflection. All I wanted to do was run up and hug her and, you know, blurt out, "I'm your Dad!" and all that. I waited for the right moment and when it eventually happened, it was nothing like I'd imagined.'

'Oh dear!' said Olivia. 'But how could you possibly have imagined what it would be like?'

'I told her I was her father. We hugged, or rather, I hugged her. Liv, it was awkward ... for both of us. I can't put my finger on it. And then, well, she became so upset she asked me to leave. I felt it was way too much for her. It didn't feel natural or... or anything. I can't explain it.

I left my details with her friend, who came in at the end. Didn't know what else to do.'

'Sam?' said Olivia. 'That's her friend's name. He's a lovely man, the one who gave me the tickets.'

'Yes, yes, that's his name. To make matters worse, Jess of all people showed up! It appeared she was uninvited judging by the icy welcome. And you know the funny thing was, when I saw her, I wasn't shocked, a little surprised maybe, but I felt nothing, except an overwhelming pity for her. I guess after all these years, sis, I've been able to deal with my anger, my initial hatred for her, for what she did to me… *to our child.* But I've moved on. I must've moved on to respond to Jess in such a way. Despite trying to forget, to bury memories that ripped my heart apart, I now realise that I have this chance to revisit the past, and who knows, to be a father to Isla once more, however that looks… with what time I have left. I want so much for us to reunite. I do. Do you think it's asking too much, Liv? Do you think I'm being selfish loading her up with my needs? I don't want her to suffer. The way she looked at me and her lack of affection, I could tell Liv… I could sense her suffering. This sadness came over her and consumed her like a dark cloud. I don't want to cause her trouble and I don't want to push her over the edge at the height of her career. God help me, Liv.'

He took a long breath and held his head. So many considerations. For a short time, both of them sat in the kitchen without saying a word. It didn't feel awkward. Olivia knew her brother just needed time to gather his thoughts and settle.

Ten minutes passed by on the kitchen clock before Olivia was ready to offer her brother some well-intended sibling advice.

'Ollie, darling, you have never wanted her to suffer. I've watched you and I know you better than anyone. This reunion was a lot to take in for both of you. Who knows what that witch has told her over the years.

So *patience,* dear brother, is your friend. Incidentally, I bought your daughter's LP today and played it. Did you know on Track 5 Side A there's a song called *Isla's Song*? Guess she played it for you last night too!'

She reached out to her brother, wiping a fallen tear from his chin.

'She's *never* forgotten you Ollie, and I have no doubt curiosity will eventually corner this little cat. Just a little more time, a pinch of patience and a nicely drawn pot of tea for you and Isla to sit down and have your long-awaited conversation. I have a gut feeling, little brother, that that *wee lassie* did not hop on that plane without good reason. It wasn't just for her tour. She came all this way to find you, dear. Now… chin up, drink your tea. Your marvellous sister is taking you to buy a new suit and if you're lucky, jam scones and cream at the Block Arcade.'

'What would I do without you, Liv?'

'Oh, I don't know, sleep in longer?' laughed Liv, blowing him a sentimental kiss, which he caught mid-air, smiling and placing his hand over his heart.

Chapter 28
A Melody in Your Name

10 January 1978

Sam and Isla had finished their meeting with a journalist from *The Australian Women's Weekly* magazine. Despite some probing questions, Isla had been careful to keep her past private. Trying to adopt a more adult approach to matters, she had no intention of embarrassing her parents. Sam was always there to provide his sage advice, but she thought that a little secrecy went a long way in maintaining an element of mystery, befitting for a well-known performer. *It kept her audience intrigued and her fans wanting more*, she thought.

After the reporter left, they sat alone in the large lounge area of the Windsor Hotel. The once-jewel in Melbourne's crown was now a little outdated, with tired furnishings, unpolished brass chandeliers and threadbare carpets doing little to highlight its once stand-out Victorian features.

'One more scone before we leave, babe?' said Sam, covering the remainder with strawberry jam and lashings of fresh full cream.

'Better watch yourself, Sam, your belt will be gaining another notch!'

'You'll love me no matter what size I am,' Sam grinned, scoffing down the last scone.

'Not if I have to fit you into a lounge chair using a shoehorn!' Isla smirked.

'One cheeky smile deserves another.' Sam wiped cream from his mouth with a serviette. 'Have a look at this.' He passed her a scribbled note.

'What's this?'

'It's your father's details. I think you should give him a call. The show's settled in and you owe it to yourself.'

Isla sat still, not saying a word, just staring at the note.

'C'mon. You remember Christmas Day at the river. This is unfinished business. You need to do this for you, babe. I know it must be bloody scary, like throwing yourself into some void, but you don't want to live the rest of your life filled with regret. I truly believe that the part of you that you thought lost at that crossing to Stromness all those years ago deserves a reunion with that brave, scared little girl. You need to be able to make sense of things, Isla. It can only help you moving forward. I saw it in Oliver's eyes too. He's also trying to make sense of it and he needs to find that lost part of himself. Please babe, I have a good feeling about it, you won't regret it. What's the worst that could happen, hey?'

Isla sat there for a moment longer. She neatly folded the notepaper and placed it in her jacket pocket.

'You're right Sam. All my life I've felt a tiny part of me missing. I've tried to over-compensate at times, been brave, forthright… even arrogant at times. And since meeting Oliver again… I've had time to think, to let things settle, find their level. I've always been adventurous, but this time the stakes are much higher. It's weird, I feel some awkward attachment to him. It scared me at first, but I'm okay now Sam. I am. I agree I need to heal my painful memories, to give me some clarity. I know he's the one holding the key to my questions. Moving forward, I need to get this tormented monkey off my back!'

'Music to my ears. You know I'd support any decision you made. I couldn't be prouder of you, babe. Really! You're an incredible woman, even if you are getting a bit pudgy in your old age.' Sam laughed.

'Pot, kettle, mister! And by the way, I couldn't do it without you, even if you are a pain in the arse sometimes.' She smiled at Sam.

'I'll take that and raise you one!' said Sam, leaning forward and gently touching her nose with his forefinger.

Back at Camberwell, a short, sinewy woman with long, grey-blonde hair knocked on Oliver's front door. There was no answer. She turned about and headed to the front gate, only to be confronted by Oliver, holding a loaf of bread and a bottle of milk.

'Jessica, is that you? Well, this is a surprise! Again! I'm astounded that you would even show your face about here. I'm guessing that no doubt you want something. One of your flaws, I'm afraid. Call me judgemental. So what do you want? Spill it out because this is the last time you'll cross my path!'

Jess looked about and observed a passer-by. 'Can we go into the house at least, please Oliver?'

Oliver did not really want her in his home. There were too many memories, some of which he feared might resurface and make him grieve even more. He stood looking at Jess for a moment, checking in on himself, and was surprised by his apparent lack of feelings towards her. She meant nothing to him emotionally, or that was what he kept reminding himself. Even so, despite his theories as to why Jess had abducted their child, he had never heard an explanation from her own lips. It was a piece of the jigsaw that he had wracked his brains over for years and now with her standing in front of him, his curiosity grew.

'Alright, Jessica. But not for long. You checked out of my life long ago.'

As Jess entered her former home, an eeriness overcame her, the atmosphere pricking her conscience. Past memories threatened to prise open distressing doors closed long ago. They were painful, even confusing, due to her failure to confront them all those years ago when instead, she had assigned them to her psychological archives.

Her senses were bombarded by the dusty smell of the drawing room, the chesterfield, the sight of the old bookshelf with music sheets strewn over it and joint treasures from another life, the clicking of the metronome that Oliver had often forgotten to stop before running his errands. Her eyes also landed on a picture of Isla on a shelf just behind the piano. She was five years old and cuddling her puppy, Larry. Even at that age, Isla's smile showed her essence, her wildness and her joy of life. Jess wondered what it would have been like for Isla if she had never removed her. How would she herself have coped remaining here? Had her decision to relocate been the most prudent one? She shook her head as if to erase such thoughts. *Don't go there*, she thought, *don't double-guess yourself. Live with it, Jessica, live with it. They were your choices.*

'Would you like a glass of water, Jessica?'

'No, I'm fine thank you.' Jess took a seat on the velvet club chair.

Oliver dragged out the piano stool and sat opposite her. 'Alright, Jessica, let's cut to the chase, why here, why now?'

Jessica was taken aback by Oliver's abruptness. She had expected him to be cold towards her, rejecting, but she did not recall him ever being so sharp and cool all at once, almost businesslike. He was foreign and icy towards her, even dismissive. *I wonder if he agreed to let me come in because he also wants something from me*, she thought. *It must be that. Maybe if I offer him something, he might help me. I've got nothing to lose.*

'Before we get into that, my first priority was to come here and talk to you. I know I don't deserve your time, but I owe it to you. Honestly, Oliver, I don't know where to begin. I don't. I have done so much soul-searching, I've turned myself inside out. I made choices, some impulsive, some planned and some reprehensible in hindsight. But I made them nonetheless and I've hurt people like you in doing so. I'm not here to plead my case, but I need to explain myself. I'm not asking for forgiveness.'

'Just as well, Jessica. You'd be short-changed on that count, so don't bother.' Oliver folded his arms.

'We had such a wonderful life before Isla was born, Oliver. I loved you so much. You were everything I dreamt in a man. I had nothing to gauge a relationship against, given my parents, but I just knew you were the one. I was safe with you and loved. Then Isla was born. I wanted to be the best mother. I wanted to be everything my mother wasn't. I had no doubts about you. You were a born father. The best dad ever. But me, it scared me, Oliver, it filled me with fear. I never wanted to be my mother, but she haunted me at every turn. Still does! I started to question my actions. Was I caring for Isla as I should? Was I holding her the right way? Was she attaching to me the way she should? If she fell over, was it my fault? If she cried during the night, was it because I didn't feed her enough, hold her enough? I looked at the two of you together, and your love seemed so effortless, so compelling. What was it, I would often think, what did you give our child that I didn't? I watched her look at you with total adoration, from the day she was born. Those eyes never looked at me in the same way. They still don't. It broke my heart in pieces and eroded my rational thinking. Bit by bit I could feel my body consumed by this blackness, this grey cloud. It was like falling into a hole, Oliver, and I couldn't pull myself out. I tried, I tried so hard, but nothing I did made any difference.'

She took a spell and Oliver could see her becoming emotional. He felt transported back in time. Although Jessica had never expressed herself to him in such a fashion, her past actions were now starting to make better sense to him.

'I'm sorry, Oliver,' she said, wiping dry her eyes, 'I just wanted to be the best parent to Isla, and I wasn't. Remember her first day of school? I couldn't even make it to that on time! I was a shit mother, a failure. It got to a stage where I wasn't sleeping, I was hardly eating and I was being admonished at work for stupid mistakes. I couldn't breathe, Oliver. I thought I could fix myself, but it got worse. It was then Gerry offered me a short stay in London, as you know. But I thought I needed more than that. I blamed you. I know on reflection it seems crazy, but I thought maybe it was you making me feel that way. Maybe he's poison to me, I thought, that's why I'm feeling this way. Maybe my cure, my hope, is to get away from it all. Escape. And with our child. Maybe I could start over again with Isla. Erase my past mistakes and do things better this time. My plan gave me hope, Oliver, and that's all I had. I'd thought about knocking myself off many times. Some nights coming home after work on the tram, I thought about stopping off at that bridge crossing the Yarra River in Richmond, taking off my heels and just jumping. I knew Isla would be okay with you, and that you and she would be better off without me. I did, I truly believed that Ollie. And it tore me up, it ripped my soul apart. I didn't want to die, I wanted to live, but this voice kept urging me and it really scared me. Eventually, I got to the point where I couldn't cope any more. So I did it, I took the easy option and took Isla away from you. I stole her and effectively killed you instead of me. After all these years… and what for? I hurt you, Oliver. I hurt you in the worst possible way. It is unforgiveable, I know. I'm surprised you even let me in.' She looked up. 'I'll have that water now if I may?'

Oliver gazed at her for a moment before registering her request. 'Sure, I'll get you one.' He went to the kitchen and fetched two glasses of water, catching his breath at the sink. You did seriously maim me for a time, Jess, he thought, but you never quite killed me.

Returning to the room, he put the glass near Jess on the coffee table.

'Thank you. I know there's lots to say and now may not be the right time. It's a lot to take in,' she said.

'Yes, well, I get the drift Jessica, more than you might believe. You see, over the years, I've had time to think. A lot of time.'

'Isla is an incredible woman, Oliver. We did that. You did that. She has your spirit, your love of life, your musical talents, your looks and cheekiness. She is a caring person and we should be so proud.'

'But I don't fucking know her, Jessica! Are you stupid? All these years, no word, no sign. Year after year, I travelled back to London and Scotland looking for some clue. Your sister was no help. She'd slam the door in my face. Letter after letter I wrote you and Isla and not even a postcard in return. You ripped out my heart, Jessica, and then crucified me. I have no feelings for you whatsoever. You disappoint me. You disgust me. I forgive you, I want you to know that, but I will never forget what you did to me and my relationship with our daughter. You single-handedly destroyed that. Why? Because you didn't have the decency to confide in me, to trust me to help you. I tried Jessica, God knows, but you didn't let me in. You shut me out, took our daughter and from what you're saying, blamed me for your issues.'

'I didn't mean to, I didn't mean to Oliver, I'm sorry, I am. I know you don't believe me and I can't do anything about that. I'm not making excuses, all I can offer is an explanation, one that falls short of acceptance, I get it. But I made choices that prevented me from turning back. All I could do was move forward and pray for God's forgiveness, as He was the only one I knew who would offer me such undeserved comfort.'

Jess took a sip of water before leaning forward on her chair to bridge some distance between them. She took in some air. 'I know I don't deserve it and you probably don't care, but I need a favour from you, Oliver.'

Oliver abruptly stood up so that he was almost leaning over Jess. 'Oh here we go, I was waiting for this! The heartfelt explanation, the throwing yourself on the floor at my mercy and then the favour. The Jess of old reveals her true colours again! Well, look around sweetheart, there aren't any more children to steal and you've robbed me of being a dad.'

Oliver's reaction made Jess recoil in her chair. A vision of her drunken father, strap in hand, flashed through her mind. He immediately noticed her reaction and headed over to the piano to put some distance between them, leaning against it.

The room descended into stillness again. Waiting for the right moment, Oliver looked across at her. When he could see that she had gathered herself, he said softly, 'I don't understand it, Jessica. I tried. I gave you everything I had. I would've been a great dad to our child and you stole that from me, and robbed our child of a father. You have to live with that, Jessica. Not me. I have to live with the loss of what might have been. As I said, I *have* forgiven you. But I will never forget what you did, explanation or not.'

Jessica knew he was right. She had thought about it long and hard over the years. She had to live with her choices.

'Oliver, I just ask you to hear me out and then I'll be gone. You will never have to see me again. Isla walked out on me in London the day before Gerry's death. There was an incident at Christmas lunch at Gerry's. One thing led to another, there was a family argument and Isla told me she wanted nothing further to do with me.'

'What was the incident?' said Oliver.

Jess conveniently omitted telling Oliver the whole truth, failing to disclose she had told Isla her father had died. Readjusting her position in the chair, she thought it best to soften the blow.

'The incident… well, look, I don't need to go into details, but Gerry had had a few, you know what she was like, and anyhow, she retrieved some of those letters you had left under her door and gave them to Isla. The incident was over you. Understandably, when Isla found out you had been sending letters, she hit the roof and that was it. Sam chased after her and the next time I saw her was in the dressing-room with you.'

'I see, I see. So why did you follow her to Australia? Scared she was going to come looking for me?'

'No, not at all. I knew that was on the cards. I didn't want to lose her. I don't want to lose her. I love her, Oliver. I'm her mother. She's my daughter. All those years, what we've been through… and I don't want to lose her now. Please Oliver, talk some sense into her. Help me mend the bridge. Explain to her what I did for her, why I did it.' Jessica was now standing, desperately holding out her hands to Oliver.

Oliver stood upright from the piano. A sudden strength overcame him, his fists clenched at his sides, his jaw locked with intent, his piercing stare now fixed with contempt.

"'She's my daughter… all those years what *we've* been through… I don't want to lose her now… " Jesus Jessica, black hole or not, you have learnt nothing! I didn't write this song for you to play, Jessica, you chose your own tune. You're the one who danced to this melody, not me. You are still the cold, selfish, heartless person I came to know. Over the years, it's the way I reconciled your cruel actions and you know, hearing you now, I think I got it pretty right. Perhaps you are your mother after all. From what you told me about Christmas, it seems Isla has made her choice, just like you made yours so many years ago. Try living with it, Jessica. I did! After all, you gave me no choice. Now, get out of my house before I throw you out!'

Oliver's face was bright red and the veins were protruding from his neck, his eyes glaring. Jessica did not recognise this man. Her shoulders drooped and she bowed her head, feeling reduced in size. Her visit had been for nothing. She collected her coat and hurried to the door. Oliver slammed it behind her.

As he did, his legs crumpled beneath him, and he slid down the door frame using it as a brace. He sobbed loudly, gasping for breath, realising he had been conning himself over all these years. He did feel something after all; the pains of nostalgia. Wiping away a stream of blood pouring from his nose and trying to contain the tremors in his hands, he sat against the door, wondering if he would ever hold his li'l one again.

Chapter 29
Not to Blame

Isla knew it rude to call without warning, but she needed to feel some control about the situation. There were so many times in her past where she felt she had had no say, where she had simply done as she was told. This time she was determined to call the shots.

From their hotel, she bid Sam farewell and caught a tram to Camberwell. Staring out of the windows to the streetscape, her mind was invaded by hazy memories of a past long gone.

Everything seemed much busier than her childhood recollections. She reflected on the times she had shared a milkshake with her father, choosing her favourite ice-cream at the local milk bar and running freely with Larry in the park. Instead of smiling, she became emotional, shedding a quiet tear. It was all a reminder of things past and how her life might have been if she had not been relocated. Although she had much to be grateful for, she was filled with angst. Her mother had denied her the opportunity of a relationship with her father. She wondered what had possessed her. *How could she have done that to me?* she thought. *If she loved me, why would she do it? And what about my father? If he loved me, where the hell was he?* Her fists tightened. That wee child who had roamed freely about the hills of Stromness, twirling about, arms spread, welcoming the cool air with abandon, had grown up. She was now a well-known artist, in love with a man who genuinely stood by her side and unquestioningly had her back. Isla had the world at her feet and yet there were important pieces missing. As the tram approached her stop, she hoped that Oliver had some answers for her. She deserved to know.

Upon alighting the tram, her memories were again triggered and she was visited by a sense of familiarity. The day was warm and a slight breeze swept across her cheeks. She walked past Camberwell Primary School and thought how much smaller the main building looked to how she remembered it. She recalled the concerned look on the principal's face when she handed her mother her purse as she was being hurried into a taxi on that fateful day. What was her name? Mrs Heads, Headswill, Heading? She remembered Oliver attending her school recital and how she played the bare bones of *Isla's Song* for her school. Her heart lit up as she remembered how proudly her father had gazed upon his little princess and how thrilled she had been to complete the song without missing one note. How I clung onto that song over the years. It was like a piece of driftwood in the middle of a vast ocean for me, the one thing connecting me to my father. Despite appearances, I was such a wee lost girl at times, adrift and confused. If it had not been for Morag rescuing me and setting me straight, I could have easily been swallowed up by the swell. Thank God for Morag.

Isla opened the wooden gate in the picket fence. In front of her she imagined a much younger version of herself. So innocent, her light-brown curly locks tied in a red-checked ribbon, wearing a frilly blue dress paired with white patent leather buckled shoes. Her cheeky grin, her questioning emerald-green eyes looking to grown-up Isla for answers. *What I would tell you if I knew then what I know now*, she thought.

She was just about to knock when the door unexpectedly opened and there she stood, face to face with her father.

'I heard the gate open and saw you from the drawing room. I had to rub my eyes, to be honest. Thought I was imagining things, but I'm so glad I wasn't. Come in, Isla.'

He was a little thinner than she recalled from their first brief meeting at the theatre, although his signature smile continued to light up his face.

'I'm sorry I didn't call. Hope you don't mind me turning up like this.'

'Not at all, not at all, now come in, I'll put the kettle on.'

Oliver directed her to a chair in the drawing room. 'I'll just be a tick, how do you like your tea? You do have tea, don't you?'

'Yes, that would be lovely. Just with a dash of milk please, no sugar.'

'Great, won't be long!'

For a short time, Isla was left to her own devices in the drawing room. Memories floated in and out. There on one of the dusty bookshelves was a framed picture of her and Larry. She picked up the frame and smiled as she remembered Larry being particularly mischievous that day, chewing up one of her sandals. She recalled her mother reprimanding Larry. Afterwards, Isla had given her pup a big hug to make up for his punishment. Her father had captured that moment on film.

'Anything to eat, Isla?' shouted Oliver from the kitchen.

'A biscuit might be nice,' she said, replacing the picture on the shelf.

She faced her father's old Steinway. How grand it still is, she smiled. Slowly, she glided her fingers along its dusty frame and then opened the keyboard cover. One by one, she tinkered with individual notes, before pulling out the familiar piano stool and sitting down.

Gently, she placed her fingers on the keys. Momentarily, she was distracted by an image at the corner of her eyes. It was that little girl again, the one at the front door she had conjured. Barely able to reach the keyboard, she stood there grinning, leaning against the piano, anticipating Isla's next move. It was such a long time ago, but she remembered climbing onto the piano stool and playing music for her dad.

She started playing *Isla's Song*. As always, she performed it without the need for sheet music. It had always been her lifeline to her father and she had never let go of it despite the passing years. This song had connected her to her past. In part informed by Morag's wise teachings, the song always filled her with hope, joy, love and a longing for reconnection. To let go of it would have been like catapulting a part of herself to the cosmos. She knew she could never do that, fearing the irreversible consequences. By hanging on, she was saving herself, giving herself a sense of hope that one day, she might find peace of mind. *Today is that day*, she thought, and she continued playing like never before. Note after note, the music filled her soul, brightened her spirit and rejuvenated loving memories from a time long past.

Oliver entered the room, tray in hand bearing a pot of tea, teacups and a plate of teddy bear biscuits and Anzac cookies. He placed it on the coffee table and approached Isla. She didn't look at him, the music possessing her in these familiar surroundings.

Slowly, he sat down to her left, proudly watching her play an old familiar tune. Her image transformed before his eyes and he imagined another time. There was his little girl once more with her signature grin, wearing her blue dress, hair tied in a red ribbon, her feet in white patent shoes unable to reach the foot pedals.

Isla's trance was broken by her father's presence. She lifted her left hand from the bass clef, allowing her father to take over and improvise, whilst she played the treble part. This was the lifeline connecting her to her father. They were reunited in music.

When they finished playing, the Steinway continued to reverberate for a time. They both sat there in silence, allowing the vibrations to resonate through them. Then, still looking down at the keys and without raising her head, Isla whispered, 'Dad, why didn't you find me, *why didn't you*?'

Oliver was momentarily lost for words. 'Hmmm,' he said, nodding and standing, 'let's have that cuppa.'

He pulled up a chair and poured the tea, handing her a cup. After pouring his own cup, he cleared his throat, praying his words would be well received.

'I searched for you for many years, Isla. Your Aunt Liv travelled with me for several years, but later it was just me. Year after year I searched, but nothing. And then, when I couldn't find you, all I could do was hope and pray that one day we might be reunited. It seems now that day has finally arrived.'

He took a sip of tea before continuing. 'The day your mother took you, your aunt and I headed to London straight away. We started our search at the main rail station. It was a frantic time. All we wanted was to find you and bring you home. On that day, by chance, I spied you and your mum in a carriage bound for Scotland. Despite our pursuit, we narrowly missed you and all I could do was place the matter in the hands of the police and God. We did end up tracking down your Aunty Gerry, as I knew she would know your mother's whereabouts. Even put the cops onto her. Gerry had always been kind to me and we got on well. However, when we turned up on her doorstep, I don't know Isla… she wasn't straight up with me. Something wasn't right. I could feel it. Anyhow, despite my endeavours to find you in London and Scotland over nearly 10 years, you remained hidden from me. I even sent you letters addressed to Gerry at least two or three times each year. I never heard back. But I always had you here, love,' he said, placing his hands over his heart, 'I always did! You were my world. Your disappearance killed me inside.'

Oliver put down his cup and retrieved a handkerchief from his pocket and wiped his eyes and nose. 'Oh Isla… ' He looked longingly at his daughter, desperately wanting to embrace her but holding back for the right time, if it arose.

'Do you remember that concert on my last day of school, Dad? How I performed our song, *Isla's Song*? You were sitting in the audience, giving me your signature wink. I looked up at the end. You were so proud of me. I was so happy. One of my treasured memories. I became so scared of losing memories like that, Dad. I was afraid that I would forget you. But it was our song, *Isla's Song,* that saved me. When I was unpacking my school bag in Stromness, I found your sheet music. The song had travelled with me, like a faithful companion. But it was much more than that, it was my lifeline to you and our memories together.'

Isla stopped for a moment, taking a deep breath and trying to gather her composure.

'The one thing Jessica did was ensure that I had a piano. Suppose she did something right. I had this piano teacher, Morag. Fierce lady but she turned out to be my guardian angel. Smart as paint too and we worked on *Isla's Song* together. She got me, Dad, and I loved her. I miss her.'

'Has she passed?' asked Oliver.

'No. No doubt she's still putting the fear of God into her students. But she had a heart of gold beneath that tough exterior and she was blessed with a powerful intuition. She had Mother's number and I felt protected by her. Anyhow, with her help I got into Cambridge on a scholarship, I graduated and the rest is history.'

'So how did you find out about me, Isla?'

'Christmas lunch at Aunty Gerry's. Actually, things weren't adding up a little before that, but Mother had gone through a tough time. I decided not to rock the boat, you know, give her the benefit of the doubt. Apart from Morag, she was all I had.'

'So what happened on Christmas Day. Was there *an incident*?' said Oliver, recalling his conversation with Jessica.

'You could say that. I went with Sam, that guy you met at the theatre the other night, well we're actually going out. Alcohol somewhat lowered inhibitions at Gerry's that day. One thing led to another between Gerry and my mother and next minute, Gerry was showering me with letters from you that she had forgotten to forward to Mother. I thought initially they were from Aunt Olivia, as I'd found some hidden in Mother's room at one time and that's what she told me, but I never opened them. Decided to trust her. *Silly me.* Anyhow, at Christmas, it all came out about you, Dad, the lies about your death, everything.'

Oliver flinched, but said nothing.

'Y'see, I thought you were dead, Dad… all those years. My mother told me you had been killed. I'll never forget it. It was on the pier when we were waiting to catch the ferry to Stromness. It was a wild day, the hurling wind and the oceans angry as all hell and she told me you were dead. But you couldn't be dead, I kept telling myself. How could you be? And how could you do this to me? Me, a little girl, afraid, feeling alone, abandoned. I was holding my mother's hand anxiously, wondering if the sea was going to eat me up as I climbed on that boat. I was so numb Dad, I felt nothing but fear. I knew then that you weren't coming to join us, ever, that I had lost you forever.

'And when it came out at Christmas… well, there I was again, that wee lass sitting on that bloody windy pier at Stromness, alone, afraid, trembling. I ran out, Sam in tow, and spent the rest of the afternoon curled up against him, dealing with so many mixed emotions, anger being at the top of the list. I mean, how could she have done that to a child? What was she thinking? Why did I deserve that? What the fuck was she doing, Dad?'

Oliver took another drink from his teacup, being careful what to say, not wanting to overstep the mark and risk offending Isla in any way. At the same time, he too was trying to contain his rage at Jessica's actions. She had lied to him on her recent visit, not disclosing full details of *the incident*. So she killed me off, he thought, that's how she tried to bury me in Isla's thoughts! Isla's right, what the fuck *was* she doing? How could she, depressed or not, visit her problems on a child, deprive Isla of a dad and me of a daughter. I get it now, he pondered. After all these years, the pieces landed for him. She didn't use her depression as a shield, she used it as a sword against me to justify her actions and blame me instead of taking responsibility for herself. And how easy, he thought, killing me off to a five-year-old child who wouldn't ask too many questions, and then tucking her away in a godforsaken place at the other end of the earth. There's no climbing out of this hole for her, Oliver thought.

'Listen Isla, it took me a long time to deal with your abduction. So many sleepless nights, I tossed and turned and I was no better for it the next morning. Or the one after that. There were never any answers, just more questions. My efforts to find you mounted up as one failure after another and it ate away at me. Each time I looked in the mirror, bits of me started to disappear. I began failing to recognise myself. If it wasn't for your Aunt Olivia and Uncle Richard, I don't know where I would be. One day, I guess I just woke up to myself. Reality smacked me across the back of my head. Sadly, I determined that it was unlikely I'd ever find you and I left it in God's hands, hoping he would one day bring you to me. I never lost hope, Isla. Never! Hope was what kept me going. And after a long time, I lost my bitterness for your mother. It was the hardest thing ever losing my contempt for her and her actions, harder than wanting you back, because it was the contempt that kept driving me, giving me hope that the wrong had to be righted. But in the end, it was something else. Much more powerful than contempt or hate. It was forgiveness. I chose to forgive her. I took control. It was my choice, not hers. Taking that control was the most empowering thing I have ever done. It wasn't easy. Don't get me wrong, Isla, I'll never forget what she did to me, to you, but I forgave her. And when I did that, it gave me my life back and fuelled my hope for a reunion with you one day. And here you are! My prayers have been answered.'

Oliver was fumbling with his hands, wringing them, trying to prevent the inevitable flood of tears.

'Your mother can justify her actions till the cows come home, Isla, but at the end of the day they are her reasons and she has to live with them, not me. I've done nothing wrong. I was a good husband and I wanted to be the best father. She took that from me and she took you from me. That realisation must… it has to… burn at her core, for it seems that after all this time, she is the loser. She still isn't taking any responsibility for her actions and the emotional and physical carnage she caused.'

Isla sat there consuming his carefully chosen words, pinching herself from time to time that she was *actually* with her father, sitting in a room where she felt she was finally home.

'Well, I don't get what she did, Dad. I don't. I need more time to process. I'm sorry, but I can't be as forgiving as you. I'm trying, I am. But… I just can't.'

'Give it time, Isla. Patience is your friend. Just let your thoughts settle first, try not to judge or blame. In good time, the answers will bubble to the surface. I can't say when, but they will, li'l one.'

Changing tack, he said, 'Remember these Teddy Bear biscuits? Sometimes I would butter them for you and you would squeeze them together and lick the butter from the sides. You were such a cheeky li'l devil.' He smiled.

'I do remember and some would say I still am!' laughed Isla, wiping away a tear.

'There is so much to think about. I'm so blessed God paved a way home for you. To be here with me… God, Isla. I've so missed you. I have never stopped loving my li'l one. Never!'

Oliver's dam of emotion finally burst. Holding his head in his hands, he sobbed uncontrollably. Isla immediately stood up and placed her arms around her father from behind, crying with him, both of them in a whirlpool of emotion.

They freely and unashamedly let their feelings out, allowing their pent-up feelings of grief to run their course. After a long silence, Oliver stood up, turned to Isla and held her by the elbows. Softly, he wiped her eyes with his handkerchief.

'No-one is to blame, li'l one. Blame gets you nowhere. We invented it to alleviate responsibility. Bit like judgement. An old Franciscan monk once told me, "You can sit back and judge your parents for all their failings, and you might learn from them, but then you get to grow up and make up a whole set of your own." Remember that! If there's anything this old man has learnt over the years it's that it makes a lot of sense to kick blame and judgement to the boundary line. It won't help you win the match.'

'Dad, you always knew the right moment to say just the right thing. I do remember that!'

'Well, this old man hasn't quite lost his marbles yet.'

Isla saw his nose was bleeding. 'Dad, your nose, what's wrong? It's bleeding!'

'Oh, nothing to worry about. It's okay.'

'You need to get that checked. Could be blood pressure or anything at your age.'

'Don't you worry yourself. Doc's checked it all. Now, if you like and your schedule permits, how about coming with Sam to your grandparent's shack down at Rosebud? Despite their passing, Olivia and I still use it. Kept it in the family. We still have a small boatshed on the beach too. I'll invite Liv and Richard. A family reunion of sorts. What do you say? No pressure!'

'Dad, I wouldn't miss it for the world. How about this Sunday? Noon?'

Oliver grabbed a pencil off the piano and wrote down the address on a scrap of paper. 'There you are, the address. We'll have a barbie at the boatshed. No need to bring anything except yourselves.'

'Great. Can't wait Dad! Is the boatshed painted blue and yellow stripes?' she asked, smiling at her father.

'Yes, it is! Gosh, you were only five when we were last there!'

'Well, you see, I haven't lost my marbles either! Must run in the family.' She laughed and then tightly embraced her father again. 'I'm home Dad, at last… I'm home.'

Chapter 30
Nothing Can Be Done
Four Weeks Later

Oliver sat patiently waiting for Olivia at the coffee shop in Brunswick Street, just around the corner from her private consulting rooms. It was early morning and the cup of bean was just what he needed to recharge his mind. With his knee bouncing up and down, he nervously flicked the pages of *The Age* newspaper, failing to absorb any of the news.

From a short distance away, he heard Olivia's approaching cries, 'Here, darling, here, I'm *so sorry*. Caught up… I know… again! Hope you've not been here long.'

As a waiter passed, Olivia caught his eye. 'Short espresso please Vincenzo, extra hot, grazie! Now, brother of mine, what's the urgency?'

Oliver folded up the newspaper and placed it to the side, then took a sip of his now lukewarm coffee. 'I need your advice sis and as always, I know I can count on you!'

'Yes, of course you can pet.' Olivia tapped his right hand. 'But before you spill the beans, I just want to say how it warms my heart to see you with Isla. I've not had a chance to tell you, but she's grown into such a beautiful woman. She has your heart and soul, Ollie. Nature beats nurture every time. 'Oh, and I loved getting to know her Sam too. It was a little awkward at first, given our first meeting at the stage door, but he's such a stellar fellow. If I was any younger …'

Oliver interrupted, 'Now, now Liv, settle down.'

'I won't! I never will. You know that. On the outside, the drapes might be drooping somewhat these days, but there's always the fun factory. I'm still a girl of 27 at heart!'

'That I know!' Oliver laughed loudly.

'There you are *signora*, nice and hot, just like the lady,' smiled Vincenzo, serving Olivia her coffee.

'Told you Ollie, *nice and hot,* I'll take that! Now enough of me, what's on your mind?'

'I don't know how to say this Liv, but my leukemia is back and my specialist told me last week that I best attend to my affairs. He can't say how long I've got. There's nothing more they can do! It's such a shit thing to happen but there you go, and I don't know what to do.' He grabbed Olivia's hands, taking a quick sharp breath, his lips quivering.

'Oh my dear Ollie. I'm so, so sorry. Is this the specialist you've been seeing for some time, Dr Oswald?'

'Dr Owens. He ran some tests last week. I've been so tired, been having nose bleeds and I've noticed my skin is becoming speckled with pink dots, like before. He only delivered the bad news a couple of days ago and in my inimitable style, I've been stewing over what to do.'

'Oh darling, you should have called me. Fuck this cancer! Gutless bastard it is. I'd like to get it in a room and clobber it. Are you sure the doctors can't do anything for it? They did before.'

'Nothing! And the worst is, I don't know how to break it to Isla. Things have been going so well, Liv. I am loving our time together. It's been so special and now, I feel like I'm losing her again.'

'Well you need to be frank with her, Ollie. You need to sit down with her and spell it out. It's not your fault. She'll understand. She has to!' said Olivia, trying to be firm but strong for Oliver.

'I don't want to lose her again! She's been through so much, Liv, and this might be the final straw for her. Her last concert is only four days away and I don't want to ruin it for her.'

'You won't darling. Fuck the concert! She needs to know. You are her father. She's a strong girl. She has our family genes after all! Come here and give me a hug. We both need it!'

They sat there tightly embracing each other, not wanting to let go, their grip broken only by the passing Vincenzo who said, 'I told you signora, *nice and hot!'*

Olivia turned to him with a wink. 'He's *my brother!*' All three burst into laughter, a welcome release of tension for brother and sister.

Oliver arranged to meet Isla the following day at Frog Hollow Reserve in Camberwell. It was a picturesque parkland that Oliver had often frequented in his youth playing cricket.

When Isla was little, he would often take her to the park to play on the swings and in later times, they would visit with Larry.

He was hoping that the area would conjure happy memories for Isla. She was between shows that day, so he knew her time would be limited. The timing was not optimal, but he needed to let her know, for both their sakes.

Seated on a park bench, he had not been waiting long before Isla pulled up in a taxi. She was wearing brown sandals, a green checked dress, her curly locks restrained by a dark green headband. Although she was not wearing any make-up, her skin glowed in the sunlight, her eyes were clear and her lips ruby red. Spotting her father from the short distance, she ran to him, giving him a welcome hug, and then joined him on the park bench.

'Dad, how are you?' she said, smiling. 'You know, don't laugh, but I *love* calling you that. Sounds funny, but after so many years only *thinking* that word, it's so nice to be able to say it out loud and proud.'

'After so many years, I love hearing it,' said Oliver, taking her hand with a grin on his face.

'Now, what is it? I told you I haven't got long unfortunately. Got to get back to make-up and hair by 5.00 p.m. Not that I don't want to see you. I want to spend every moment I can with you. It's such a wild ride, retracing my roots, spending time with you and the fam. The best ride ever in fact. My dreams have truly been answered, Dad!' Isla rested her head on her father's shoulder.

'I feel exactly the same way, li'l one. More than you know. And I'm so proud of you, all you've achieved, the talented and wonderful woman you've grown into. You're incredible and you warm my heart each day. But I must tell you something that's been on my mind.'

Isla raised her head, giving her father a worried look. 'You look a bit tired, Dad. Is everything okay?'

'Well, no, li'l one. I'm sorry. I haven't told you my whole story. Didn't want to worry you.'

'What do you mean?' Isla reached for his hands.

'Three years ago, I was diagnosed with leukaemia after a raft of tests. It was followed up with chemo treatment, which nearly killed me due to my immune system shutting down. After some time, I eventually got through it all and luckily, went into remission. My oncologist was surprised at the time. It was a gift from God. Time passed and I didn't give it much thought until lately. I've been feeling very tired, not myself. I thought it was due to all the excitement with you in my life again after so long, but then the nose bleeds started up again. So I went back to my specialist… more tests and yes, the cancer's back. This time with a vengeance, it seems. I don't know how long I have, li'l one. I wish I did, but it's in God's hands now.'

He looked into Isla's eyes and could tell his heartfelt well-intended message had wounded her terribly.

She sat there, not saying a word, her eyes flitting side to side, her breathing becoming increasingly shallow, as if she were gasping for air. Memories flooded her, flashed before her, transporting her back to that day at Camberwell Primary School when her world was turned upside down. The concerned look on the principal's face through the rear window of the taxi as it sped off; those churning butterflies in her stomach when she boarded an aeroplane for the first time; bursts of a cold breeze chilling her body on that pier in Stromness; being lied to by her mother about her father's death. She experienced again her extreme anger with her mother. Unexpectedly, her mother's drunken states and volatile moods confronted her and again, there she was alone, standing on that cliff face gazing into the starry skies pleading for her father's ear. Finally, her mind revisited those black memories from Christmas Day at Gerry's, where lies and deceptions had unveiled themselves. Isla was numb, remembering sitting on that bench seat with Sam, looking at the Thames, desperate to just skate away, to escape. A heavy voice from that day invaded her thinking. Run! Run, Isla! Run!

Now, here she was again, lost and alone in the world.

Overwhelmed and overcome by a sense of abandonment, she released her father's hand and stood up, moving away from him.

'I don't understand. You said you told me everything… you said. You told me, no more secrets. You said that I could count on you. But you lied, Dad, you lied. I found you again, you found me, but what for? As quickly as you came back into my life, you're leaving me again. I can't deal with it. I can't lose you again. I just can't! Fuck you! Fuck you for making me love you again. Fuck you for losing me again. You're no better than that witch of a mother of mine.'

Oliver could see the contempt in her eyes, and he pleaded, 'Li'l one, please… '

Before he could complete his sentence, she abruptly interrupted, 'Don't call me *li'l one*! Don't call me *your daughter*. Not now, not ever. Leave me alone. I've tried to be strong, Dad, but I just can't take it anymore… I can't!' She turned her back on her father and ran as fast as her legs could carry her.

As Oliver watched his daughter disappear, droplets of blood began spattering down onto his trousers. He was feeling dizzy, the park and his vision of Isla running off into the distance blurred. There was a taste of blood in his mouth, a struggle to breathe and then, darkness fell upon him.

A passing elderly couple approached his unconscious form and called an ambulance. Soon after, Olivia and Richard arrived at St Vincent's Hospital upon hearing the news that Oliver had been transported there for urgent medical attention.

That evening at the theatre, Isla took her final bow for Wednesday night's performance. *Three shows to go*, she thought. Hurriedly, she headed to her dressing-room. She had not yet had time to process fully the events of the day. Given the show, she had no choice but to compartmentalise matters, something she had learnt to do from an early age.

'Good show Joni, really edgy tonight! Gritty heart-wrenching stuff. Loved it!' said the stage manager when Isla brushed passed him.

If only he knew why, Isla thought.

She was met outside her dressing-room by Sam, 'Babe, good show, *different*, but still good!'

'You have no idea! I've had a bitch of a day, Sam. Turns out my family gets the gold medal for hanging onto secrets. Can you believe Sam, my dad has terminal cancer! Good of him to tell me! Terminal cancer!'

She burst through the door and plonked herself down on the couch. Sam took a moment to process the news by getting a glass of water. He pinched the bridge of his nose and said, 'Wow… cancer! Jesus.'

'What the fuck have I done to deserve this, Sam? What have I done? I'm surrounded by so-called victims, but it's me, I'm the fucking victim. I didn't ask for any of this!'

'Isla, I need…'

Isla interrupted him. 'I mean, first I get kidnapped, then I'm told he's dead. I have my suspicions but still, I choose to trust her and her family. Then I get told, oh by the way, just a little translation issue there, he's not dead really, he's alive and in Australia, but forgive me because I wasn't thinking straight at the time. Then I travel here, for some work, granted, but mainly to meet my father. I finally reconnect, at first not sure, because forgive me, I'm a little confused. Then I let him into my world, I trust him, I get to know my father and then, what the fuck, he tells me, "Oh by the way, sorry love, it's been nice reconnecting, but I'm dying and on my way." You know, *bye, bye,* greener pastures, God and all that! What the fuck! Does anyone give a damn about me? Sam, do you? Do you have any secrets I should know?'

'Pause there for a minute, babe.'

'No, I won't fucking pause there. I'm so angry Sam. I could explode! Really! Who do my parents think I am? I didn't ask to be brought into this godforsaken world. It was their choice. Inside of me lives a wee girl who feels an immense pain from my past and no-one seems to give a damn. I'm not some dog they can pick up and cuddle when they want, I'm their daughter! I grew up wondering what my father would be like. I looked into those stars each night, I made wishes, Sam, I imagined what it would be like to be held by him, I didn't give up my memories of him. And now, I have fallen in love with my dad all over again. I feel like I've become that little girl again and I need him more than ever. But he's going to leave me, Sam. I can't do it, I'm not being left again. I can't do it anymore, Sam.' Wiping her tears, she sat alone sobbing on the lounge.

Slowly and gently, Sam approached her. He eased his way onto the couch and lovingly placed his arm about her, holding her, protecting her from the outside world. Isla put her head on his broad shoulder.

After a while, he said, 'Isla, babe, you know I will always have your back.' She looked up and before she could speak, he gently placed his finger on her lips. 'Please listen before you say anything.'

Isla stared into his trusting eyes and nodded.

'I want you to stand in your dad's shoes, just for a minute. When you were five, you were taken from him. He had no say in that. Can you imagine how he felt? His heart would've been ripped apart and to add salt to the wound, year after year he returned to London and Scotland to find you, without success. He wrote to you time and time again with no response. Time passed, and you were both drawn to the stars in the night sky, both gazing upwards, wondering about each other, praying for each other, holding onto your memories, fearing losing any sense of each other. When you look at it, Isla, in spite of the tyranny of distance, you and your dad have always been together in spirit. The only thing that kept you apart were lies told by a woman haunted by her own issues. And now you have been reunited. That intense feeling that your heart guarded all these years has been fortified, enriched by an attachment that was there from the year dot. Don't cut the umbilical cord now, Isla. He loves you. You love him. Perhaps there's more to this cancer thing, perhaps he was waiting for the right moment. It can't have been easy for him either. Don't give up on him, babe. You need each other now more than ever. Life is full of regrets, don't let this be one of yours.'

He bent down and kissed her cheek, wiping away her tears. The quiet was broken by the telephone ringing.

'Hello? Sam speaking. Oh, okay nurse, can I take a message for her? Alright then, I'll put her on. She's here with me. Babe, they want to speak to you.'

'Hello, who is it?'

Isla listened intently without saying a word. After a short time, she passed the phone back to Sam.

'What's wrong babe? What's it about? Everything okay?'

'It's Dad. He collapsed in the park where we met today and was transported to St Vincent's Hospital. Aunt Liv gave them my contact details. They said I should come in.'

'Okay then. What are you thinking?'

'I'm thinking you're right. Don't get a big head. But you are! I'm so exhausted Sam, been mulling this over all night and you're right. No regrets, I say. Can you please drive me?'

'Of course. For the record, you always make the best choices and that's one of the reasons why I love you.'

Chapter 31

The Priest

Summer, 1954

'Daddy, hurry up, help me build a sandcastle!' said Isla, bucket and shovel in hand.

'Okay, okay, li'l one. Let me get these chairs out of the boatshed first. Mummy wants me to set up the umbrella.'

'Okay, but hurry Daddy, I want to build it and then swim. Can we collect shells after that?'

'So much to do, Isla. You sure are the busy one, miss!' Oliver winked at her.

'She doesn't get that from her father, does she?' said Jess, putting on her tortoiseshell sunglasses and a broad sunhat.

Oliver was going to bite back but thought the better of it, biting his tongue instead.

After setting Jessica up with the umbrella, he joined Isla at the shore.

'You know Isla, when Daddy was your age, my dad and mum used to bring Aunty Liv and I down here all the time. And my dad would build castles with me.'

Isla smiled, filling her bucket with sand and patting down after each scoop.

'Put yours here Daddy, next to mine. We'll build the biggest castle ever and then the mermaids will visit and sing to us. I want to be a mermaid, Daddy!'

'Why, li'l one? You'd have no legs!' he laughed.

'Yes I would Daddy. When you get out of the water, your tail grows into legs and then you sing, that's what my teacher reads to us. You know that book, *The Little Mermaid*?'

'Oh yes, I remember,' grinned Oliver, 'but if you were a mermaid, I would never see you as you would live in the sea, li'l one.'

'Oh yes, but I would visit you. I would visit you every day and sing to you. You would hear me, even if I wasn't here. And if I ever got lost, all you'd have to do is listen and find me. Mermaids are so pretty, Daddy.'

'Well li'l one, I love you just the way you are! I'm sure you're going to grow up to be much prettier than any mermaid. And I promise wherever you are, I will hear you, no matter what!'

'Pinky promise, Daddy?'

'Pinky promise, sweetheart,' said Oliver, linking little fingers with her .

Isla jumped out of Sam's car and burst through the entrance doors to the hospital reception.

'Oliver Johnson please, where is he? she abruptly asked the hospital receptionist.

'Hold on miss,' she said, flicking through the patient register, 'oh yes, there he is, level four, room six.'

Sam joined her, puffing, 'I know, I heard, level four, room six. Let's go!'

When they arrived at the ward, Olivia and Richard were outside Oliver's room, pacing. Liv looked up when she saw Isla and Sam running down the corridor towards them.

'Oh darling, I'm so glad you got the message. I had no idea how to contact you. I'm sorry. Gave the charge nurse your details at the theatre. I didn't know what to do.' Olivia hugged her.

'It's fine Aunt, really. I needed to know and I need to be here.' Isla gave Sam a look. 'Can I see him?'

'Yes, of course. We've been with him all afternoon. He's just come out of emergency. Had some internal bleeds, but all under control. He's a bit weak, but conscious now. We've just come out for a spell. Don't normally smoke, but God knows I needed something! Nicotine and fresh air, call me a naturopath, darling!'

'I'll wait here, Isla, unless you want me?' said Sam.

'No. I'll be fine. Besides, I need to talk to him if that's okay?'

'Good… oh yes,' said Sam.

Isla crept into the room and pulled up a chair to be close to her father's bed. Gently, she placed her hands on his and looked into his eyes. 'Hi, Dad! See what happens when I leave you alone?' She was trying to hold back her tears.

'Yeah, it only gets me into trouble!' smiled Oliver.

They looked at each other, wanting to speak, but awkwardly not knowing where to begin. With one deep breath, Isla tapped his hands reassuringly. 'Dad, I'm sorry. I had no right. I'm ashamed I spoke to you like that, I don't know what came over me. I was possessed or something. I just, I just get so, so… ' She placed her head on Oliver's covered legs, quietly sobbing, whilst Oliver softly stroked her hair.

'It's okay, li'l one. It will be alright. I understand. It's a lot to process. I know how much I've missed you over the years, I can't imagine what it's been like for you. And here I am, lumbering this on you as well. Believe me, I didn't want to. I didn't have the heart to tell you earlier. I just didn't have it in me to risk losing you again. I couldn't… '

Isla raised her head, 'Dad, it's not your fault. I know. I didn't handle it very well. I should've been there with you in the park when you collapsed. Some daughter I am! I'm sorry. But I'm glad you're here, being looked after. I'm okay, Dad. Yes, it's been tough. I grew up thinking you were dead… then you're alive… and when I finally find you, you say you're going to die on me again. My mind just went into a spin. But I came to my senses, nudged by Sam a wee bit, and I realised it wasn't all about me anymore, it was about us. And by running off, I forgot about you and your feelings. Don't get me wrong, I hated what you told me at the park, but I get it. I do! So you're stuck with me like glue, for better or worse. Let's make the best of it, hey, and fuck the cancer!'

Oliver smiled at her. 'Is that the sort of language they teach you at Cambridge? Funny, I recall the same turn of phrase being used at Melbourne Uni.' Their laughter filled the room, making it feel a lot less clinical.

'Two of a kind, Dad!'

'Peas in a pod, daughter of mine!'

Isla bent over the bed and gave her father a heartfelt lingering hug, never wanting to let go of him.

'I have three shows left, Dad, and I want you there for the big finale. You, Aunt Liv and Uncle Richard. Do you think you'll be okay by then to come? No stress, I totally get it!'

'I wouldn't miss it for the world, li'l one. Nothing will hold me back!'

They embraced again before being interrupted by the night nurse. 'Now dear, time to give your father some much needed rest. He's had a big day! Tell the other visitors outside it's time to head off. Visiting hours resume at 9.00 a.m. tomorrow.'

Isla kissed Oliver and said goodbye, turning at the doorway to wave at him before closing the door behind her.

Soon after she left, a Franciscan monk from Box Hill, Father Angelo, arrived. He was part-time theologian and part-time priest for those wanting God's ear. He was a tall man whose belly beneath his long brown robes disclosed a liking for food and perhaps a good red wine or two. His grey locks curled at the ends, touching his broad shoulders, and his bushy eyebrows and sunken cheeks gave way to a fulsome grey beard in need of a good tidy-up. Angelo found Oliver staring out the window of his room, mesmerised by a stationary tram in Victoria Street.

'A penny for your thoughts, Mr Johnson!' Angelo said in a thick Irish accent.

'Oh, I'm sorry Father, I didn't see you there, I was lost in a moment.'

'And what moment might that be, sir?'

'Just a moment, that's all!'

'Oh yes, life is made up of so many. Before long we've collected a lifetime of them. Some we'd choose to forget, some taunt us I'm sure and others, well, we don't want to let go of them!'

'Ah yes, I get your drift Father.' Oliver smiled at his welcome visitor. 'So many moments.'

They spoke for some time. Oliver told him the whole story, summarised but compelling nonetheless. He told him about rediscovering his daughter, his bond with her and his fears surrounding the terminal illness. Angelo sat there, content to listen, interjecting with a kind word every so often, reassuring Oliver and putting his mind at rest as best he could.

'You know sometimes I wonder, Father, why me? What did I do to deserve to cop all this? Or Isla for that matter? If it wasn't bad enough that I had her taken away from me early on, I feel it's happening all over again with this blasted cancer. It's not fair. I know that's a selfish thing to say, others being worse off than me and all, but it still seems bloody unjust. What's the Big One thinking?'

'Yeah, it is unjust. But as my nanna said, Face the sun, but turn your back on the storm.'

'Your nanna's a wise woman. Took me a while to realise that Father, but I did when I gave up looking for Isla all those years ago. It's just this cancer thing, prodding at old wounds, causing me further pain. It hurts. By Jesus, it hurts… I don't know how to deal with it. I haven't got time to deal with it, more's the point. I just want her to be okay, Father.'

'From what you've told me, she's a pillar of strength that one. She'll be okay, and her bloke seems like a good stick too. And listen, God's waitin' for us all at those pearly gates. No-one knows for whom that bell tolls, my son. So live like there's no tomorrow, grab that girl of yours, don't let go and smile broadly into that sun of Nanna's. God bless you Oliver. I'll be prayin' for you.'

Oliver's cheeks filled with colour, his eyes brightened and his mouth curled upwards. 'Thank you Father, best medicine I've had for ages. Bless you!'

The next day, Sam arrived at Oliver's hospital bed before Isla. She was at a photo shoot and interview for the *Sun* newspaper as publicity for her final show.

'I'm a little early Oliver, Isla's at a shoot, thought she'd be here by now.' Sam vaguely scanned the room.

'Come in, I've been up with the birds and the trams. Miss my own bed to be honest. Glad you're here. Anyhow,' he said, sitting himself up in bed, 'good time to have a quiet word with you, if it's okay?'

'Sure, no probs. Shoot!'

Sam pulled up a chair closer to the bed.

'A couple of things. First, the bloods came back this morning and they're not too flash. I was hoping to be out of here tomorrow, Friday, you know. Doesn't look good though. But I don't want Isla knowing. I'll do my best to get to her final show on Saturday, but she mustn't know. I don't want her worrying. I'll be fine.'

Sam nodded, thinking how another secret might not go down too well with her.

'Now, secondly, I have to talk to you about something that might seem a bit uncomfortable, given you hardly know me and all, but Isla loves you, I can tell, and that's enough for me. It's just that when I pass on, I need to know she'll be alright. I have a will. Did it a couple of weeks ago, after I got the news. I've left all my property to Isla, including the home in Camberwell. All you have to do is give my lawyers a call. Their business card is in the drawer there, Freeman & Co.'

Sam opened the drawer of the bedside table, recovered the card and immediately placed it in his jacket pocket.

'You can trust me, Oliver. I'll take care of things... But I kinda need a favour from you as well? I sorta came a little early this morning... well, intentionally.'

Oliver looked bewildered, wondering how on earth he could assist Sam.

'Sure, if I can I will, son.' He adjusted himself in bed.

'Well, I'm a proper kind of guy, that's all... '

'Yes?'

'And, well, I need to do things properly.'

'Ah, yes?'

'Well, you see, I've never done this kinda thing before.' Sam was choking on his words.

'Oh hell boy, just spit it out will you, time's a little scarce these days,' he grinned.

'Shit, well, I love your daughter Oliver and I want to ask for her hand in marriage, that's it! Damn, I said it!'

'Why didn't you say so? Of course, I would be so proud to have you as part of the family. I am thrilled. Music to my ears and no doubt to the rest of the Johnson clan. It's like that sun just hit my face again!'

'You know, my nanna used to say that!'

'I stole it from a priest!' Oliver chuckled.

'Please don't tell her yet, I want to surprise her after her final show on Saturday. I'm picking up the ring this morning.'

'Mum's the word, son!' said Oliver, smiling with delight, picturing Isla in a wedding gown.

'Great, well, all sorted then. Phew, I was imagining the worst!' He smiled. 'I betta fly.'

'Aren't you meeting Isla here?'

'Oh yeah, um, tell her I'll catch her at the theatre. Lots to do! Thank you, thanks so much, Oliver. I'm gonna be the best husband to your daughter. Promise!'

'I have a good feeling you will, son!'

Sam grabbed Oliver's hand and shook it vigorously.

'Oh, and don't forget, Mum's the word!'

'Mum's the word,' said Oliver, copying Sam's intonation, giving him a cheeky wave and watching him scurry from the room.

The morning hours were consumed by the usual medications being dispensed, observations and a visit by Oliver's team of specialists. In between times, his thoughts were drawn to his daughter's wedding, knowing that he might not live long enough to attend. He pictured himself walking down the aisle in a formal black tuxedo and bow tie, lapel adorned with a single white rose and gypsophila, arm in arm with Isla. He guessed the wedding would be at the Holy Spirit Chapel at Newman, where he had boarded all those years ago whilst at university. Olivia would be wearing some standout eye-popping dress, hair up and with a stylish hat pinned to her head. As they slowly approached the altar to the tune of *Pachelbel Canon in D Major*, he imagined the sun shining through the chapel's grand lead-light windows, making for a truly magical moment. How proud I look, he thought. And what a beautiful bride she is… my daughter. A warm feeling swept over him, but not for long.

'Knock, knock! How's that father of mine travelling today?' said Isla, bursting into the room.

'He is well,' said Oliver, gathering his thoughts,' probably being discharged tomorrow and all the better for seeing you. How did the shoot go? Still can't believe I have a famous daughter. So proud too!'

'You need to get your strength back to be ready for Saturday night's show, so I popped into that little bakery around the corner and got you two of your favourites, a strawberry iced vanilla slice and a chocolate éclair! I got an extra vanilla slice for Sam.'

'You know how to hit the spot, li'l one. Brings back memories of Dom's Deli. Do you remember?'

'How could I forget those milkshakes, Dad! My belly still craves them.'

Their discussion was interrupted by the tea trolley. With cup in hand and savouring every sweet morsel of the cakes she had brought, they sat there soaking up their time together, talking, laughing, reminiscing. Am I really here? thought Isla. What a wonderful moment.

'Oh, by the way, Sam popped in this morning, nearly forgot to tell you,' said Oliver.

'I thought he was going to meet me here, thus the vanilla slice. Oh well, more for you. Did he say anything?'

Oliver smiled broadly on the inside. 'No, nothing really, just wanted to see how I was. He was in a bit of a hurry with work things. Good lad he is!'

'God, he's hard to pin down sometimes. I'd be lost without him though Dad. Don't tell him that, by the way. Pinky promise?'

'Pinky promise, li'l one!'

'Good to see you're getting a bit of colour back. You worried me yesterday. Now, Sam has four front row tickets for closing night. They're for you, Aunt Liv, Uncle Richard and Sam. There'll be some VIP do after if it's not too late for you. No stress if you're too beat. I've arranged two weeks off after the show closes. Hoping we can spend some quality time together. Maybe even go for a wee break, you know, drive along the Great

Ocean Road, take in the sea air and find some places to stay along the way? What say you, ol' man?'

'I say enough of the ol' man, for a start!' laughed Oliver. 'But, yes, that would be wonderful. I would love it!'

'Great! Sorted! Now, I just have to sort out that mother of mine. God, she keeps calling me at the theatre, the hotel, I don't know what to do! I've had her, Dad. I let her know how I feel and she needs to respect my wishes. To be honest, thought she would have headed back to London, but I suppose with Aunt Gerry gone, she has no-one.'

'I see, well that's your business, li'l one. I've made my peace long ago and your mother knows how I feel. Don't want to trouble you with that. It's between us... but she knows.'

'I'm still processing, Dad. I told her I never want to see her again, but never is a long time. I don't know how I feel, to be honest. In one sense, I hate her, but after talking to you, I feel pity for her. I wax, I wane. All those years, she was my focus. Now it's our time and my focus is on you. She can wait till I'm ready... if I'm ready.'

She drank her last drop of tea, wiped her mouth with the hospital napkin and pecked her father on the cheek. 'If you need a lift home tomorrow, let me know. Bye for now and enjoy the other vanilla slice. Sam's tough luck!'

And like a mini tornado she was gone. It was times like these that Oliver had to pinch himself, hardly believing that he was reunited with his daughter. Although visits tired him, he savoured every moment, discovering more about Isla's past, her achievements, her escapades, the things she held dear to her heart; the things that made her soul sing. I'm a lucky man, he thought, his eyes becoming heavy before he drifted off peacefully.

The next day, Oliver's oncologist, Mr Seal, was performing his Friday morning rounds. Stopping by Oliver's bed with the charge nurse, he dutifully checked Oliver's hospital records clipped to the bed end. The nurse gave him the latest blood results.

'Well, Mr Johnson, how are you this morning? Nurse tells me that apart from visitors, you slept for most of the day yesterday and then into the night. Bit tired, are we?'

'Must be, I suppose, yes. The visitors do drain me a bit but I love seeing them. They brighten up my day.'

'Yes, I understand, but you mustn't overdo it,' he said sternly. 'Now I've checked your vitals, they seem okay, your blood pressure is a bit low, we'll up your medication on that. Your white blood cell count is getting worse, I'm afraid. Naturally, that accounts for your fatigue and energy levels. I am concerned about your immunity and risk of infections, Mr Johnson. You need to take care, do you hear me?'

Oliver nodded, the doctor's words beginning to fade into a blur.

'Do you hear me?' the specialist repeated loudly.

Oliver shook himself out his confused state and nodded. 'Yes, I get it. So am I right to be discharged this morning, Doc?'

'Hello? I'm sorry, have you been listening to me, or am I simply wasting my time? Am I wasting my time, Sister Butler?'

'No Doctor, I mean Mr Seal,' said the nurse, trying to hide behind her clipboard.

'Mr Johnson, if you don't want to risk your life, risk infection and bring on a hastened arrival at God's waiting room, I suggest you remain here until we can at least generate some more hope for you on the white blood cell front. I can't even guarantee that at present. I've told you, Mr Johnson, if you were at a train station, the next stop would be the terminus. So please listen, and do as I say. Do you hear me now, Mr Johnson?'

'Loud and clear, *Mister* Seal. Oh and Doc, next time, don't forget to bring your manners in here with you. Your attitude is crying out for a renovation!'

Mr Seal took a small step backwards, glaring at Oliver and not knowing what to say, whilst Sister Butler slowly lowered her clipboard and let out a small titter.

'What are you laughing at, Sister Butler?'

'Oh nothing Doctor, I mean *Mister Seal*,' said the nurse, winking at Oliver from behind her boss.

Chapter 32

Blow the Candles Out

It was Friday, 6.00 p.m., and as arranged, Liv arrived at Oliver's room with tuxedo in hand, Richard following behind.

'Are you sure you won't get into trouble, darling? I mean why couldn't you wait for tomorrow night, love? You might be feeling a bit stronger.'

'Time is of the essence, sis. Tomorrow night is too far away. Please, just support me on this. Richard, tell her to support me!'

'Oliver, you are impossible!' said Richard. 'Quick, hop up, I'll help you get into this penguin suit. God, it needs a good dry-clean. How many mothballs do you have in that wardrobe of yours?'

Olivia stood guard down the corridor at the nurses' station. Once they were out doing their observation rounds and the coast was clear, she gave Richard the signal, waving about her red silk scarf. Oliver got into a wheelchair and Richard transported the chariot to the lift. Oliver was wrapped in a grey hospital blanket, wearing Richard's thick, black-framed glasses and Olivia's blond hair piece.

'You look like our mother, darling!' exclaimed Olivia.

'Shut up sis, say no more!' Oliver smiled.

Once the lift doors opened, Richard rapidly shoved Oliver inside whilst Olivia hastily pressed the ground floor button. The doors closed just in the nick of time, narrowly preventing a nurse from entering. 'Ta ta!' waved Olivia. 'So sorry, pet!'

Before long the trio were on their way to Her Majesty's Theatre.

'Are you okay, Ollie?' Olivia asked.

'I'll be fine, Liv. Don't worry about me. I want to do this. I need to do it. Now, do you know what you're doing? Have you spoken to Sam?'

'Yes, yes, it's all under control. Got it!'

'Good, I know I can count on you. Does my hair look alright?'

'I think I preferred you as a blond, darling!' said Olivia, squeezing his chin.

At the theatre, Richard pulled up outside the stage door where Sam was waiting.

'Are you really sure this is a good idea, Oliver?' said Sam.

'Don't bother, darling, he's on a mission!' said Olivia, helping her brother from the vehicle.

'I'll be fine. Just get me to the wings at the right time and I'll do the rest, Sam. This means the world to me, you know. Let's do it!'

Richard left to park his car, whilst Olivia and Sam assisted Oliver down the hallway into a vacant dressing-room.

'There, you'll be safe here, well away from Isla. I'll come and get you. Won't be for a little while but I've left you some water and other goodies. You'll need the energy,' said Sam.

'Any gin, darling?' said Olivia.

'As they say in the classics, Aunt, later!' smiled Sam, making a hurried exit.

'Aunt my foot! Did you hear what he called me? My God! Are the wrinkles really showing up, Ollie? Am I getting that old haggard look about me? Note to self, apply more Oil of Ulay.'

'Sis, they're not wrinkles, just the dried-up beds of happy times. Now, please fetch me a glass of water.'

Oliver's inbuilt metronome was anxiously ticking away in his head, sweat was beaded across his brow and his heartbeat was rapid. Lightheaded, he reached for a piece of chocolate, savouring its sweetness.

There was a knock on the door and Sam entered. 'It's time Oliver. Let's do this!'

Down one corridor and then another. Finally, after climbing a set of stairs, Olivia, Sam and Oliver arrived at the prompt side wings of the stage. Oliver leant against the stage wall to catch his breath, then brushed down his suit, fixed his hair again and stood there anxiously, awaiting his cue. A trickle of blood emerged from his nose, which he quickly wiped away.

Olivia grabbed his hand and held it tightly. 'Love, this is your dream and I'm so proud of you, little brother. After all you've been through. I love you so, so much Ollie!'

Applause from the audience died down as Isla introduced her final song.

'Ladies and gentlemen, as my final song for the night, I want to play you something very special. It's not really a song, more like a lifeline to my father, with whom after many years, I've recently reunited. You might have read about it in the papers. It's true, it really happened and it's so magical. This is a song we shared a lifetime ago, a song that has stayed with me always. My dad wrote it for me and named it *Isla's Song* and now I'm blessed to share it with you.'

Sam gave Oliver a gentle push from behind and he walked onstage to join his daughter. As soon as Isla saw him, although she was in shock, she ran up to him, hugging him, holding him in the spotlight, a place so deserving of the presence of them both. Momentarily, they stood there filled with joy, their eyes fixed lovingly on each other, whilst the audience gave a standing ovation.

'Dad, what are you doing?' cried Isla.

'I'm here to play our duet, of course! Are you up for it?' Oliver guided his daughter to the grand piano.

Elegantly, they took their seat at the piano and after the audience had hushed, they commenced playing, accompanied by Isla's rich vocals. Crotchets and quavers bounced from the keyboards, with father and daughter playing as one, reunited, each feeling the other's emotions drive their soulful tune. Olivia looked on from the wings, tears streaming down her face, squeezing the life out of Sam, who was gasping for air.

The song transported them on a journey to their shared past, from the drawing room at Camberwell, to Isla's school, to parties and playdates and birthday celebrations and Larry the labrador.

Before *Isla's Song* drew to its close, Isla was transported to a sheer cliff face in Scotland, her locks blown about by tormented winds, ocean waves crashing below her feet. She stood there peering out to sea, in search of her father. Waiting. She was steadfast and resolute in her desire to find him, never giving up hope. Before long, she spied this man making his way to shore, rowing with passion and a steely determination. Getting closer, Isla could see it was her father. Relief overcame her. At that very moment, the seas grew less angry, the winds subdued. Isla floated back to the present and noticed her father's fingers finally lift from the keys in unison with hers. She was whole. Her journey was complete.

Hugging each other, they stood and bowed to a rapturous, jubilant audience who were on their feet, clapping and cheering.

With the curtain closing, Oliver felt giddy. The room was spinning and sweat was running from his brow. In his dazed stated, he noticed blood pouring from his nose, staining his white shirt. Then his legs gave way and he collapsed.

Isla was pulled down with him, still holding onto his hand. She screamed for help, gently caressed his face and knelt beside him. 'Dad, please don't give up, stay with me, don't leave me, please!' Her tears mixed with his blood as Sam rushed to her side.

'Please Sam, do something, please, I can't lose him, please help him!' she cried.

Richard and Olivia hurried to his side as well. Oliver was barely conscious.

'Hold on Dad, hold on, I'm with you. I'm here, I'm not leaving you,

I never will Dad,' said Isla, as the ambulance officers arrived with a stretcher.

Olivia, Sam and Richard stood outside the ambulance whilst Isla climbed inside to be with her father.

As the ambulance officer went to close the rear doors of the van, Isla looked up and saw her mother in the middle of the street, staring at her. A single street lamp dimly lit Jessica, who wore an empty expression. Her legs barely supported her. Her hair was untidy. There was a grey hollowness about her gaze. Wind swept about her, stirring her hair and clothing, but she did not move.

Like the girl on the cliff, she was still, but there was no-one waiting for this girl.

Chapter 33
Shine

The final show. Not exactly the way Isla had envisaged it but at the same time, much more than she had ever expected. The curtain was about to close on one chapter of her life, paving the way for the next.

She stood in the wings with Sam by her side holding her hand. They could hear the audience shuffling into Her Majesty's Theatre, like some distorted noise. Despite the distraction, Isla's eyes were fixed on the stage, designed especially for tonight's show.

The lighting was soft. A violet spotlight enveloped the black grand piano placed centre stage. It was a warm, comforting light, filling Isla's heart with joy, a befitting symbol honouring her father. Memories floated by: learning to play piano with her father; performing duets together; penning tunes together – well, she smiled, her father mostly, with her happily assisting. Most of all, she remembered their laughter and the sense of security of having her father nearby.

Her eyes moved to the rear wall upstage. It was painted gold, with gold stars of various shapes and sizes. A projection with an occasional shooting star split across the interstellar collage. The image transported her back to Stromness, where she used to stare up at the sky, fearing losing the memory of her father. The way she spoke to the heavens, hoping he would hear her, and how she held close those feelings of connection to him. As long as I have the stars, she would think, I have a map to my father's heart and a lifeline to him.

From the wings, she could see that the red velvet curtains were drawn, hiding an array of fairy lights suspended from a beam within the proscenium arch. Their luminous splendour provided a magical foreground. The strings of lights on each side framed the stage. The setting was exactly the way Isla had pictured it in her dreams over the years. *It's my place of refuge*, she thought. *This is exactly how I remember it. It's beautiful, perfect in every way.*

She gave Sam's hand a little squeeze, feeling her engagement ring rubbing against his finger. It made her face light up.

'I love you Sam,' she said, turning to her fiancé.

'Back at you babe. I'm so proud of you. Harry the puppy and I both. Nothing like getting engaged with a baby canine in tow. Imagine the rumours.' Sam giggled quietly and gently kissed her on the forehead. 'Chookas babe, see you on the other side.'

House music filled the auditorium as the curtains opened, revealing the redesigned staging. Isla stayed in the wings, watching Sam take his seat front row, leaving an empty seat next to Olivia and Richard. Oliver's seat.

The lights dimmed and as the music concluded, there was a brief overture of Isla's well-known songs. Then she stepped out from the wings to greet her fans. She hesitated at first, looked to the heavens and said to herself, *Yes, I'm ready, Dad, I am.* Unexpectedly, she felt the warmth of a hand holding hers. She looked down and knew she was not alone.

Head held high, she walked to centre downstage to her grand piano. Standing beside it, she was framed by fairy lights and shooting stars.

'Ladies and gentlemen, I welcome you with all my heart to my final performance in Melbourne, for this run anyhow. I am pleased to let you all know that this wonderful city is about to become my full-time home. Yes, I've decided to move here... '

The audience responded with adoring cheers and applause.

'Thank you. As you know, I was born here and I'm so excited. Tonight is a very special performance for me. I promise I'll try to keep the tears at bay. It's not only my final performance but it's a night of farewells.'

She looked down to Richard, Sam and Olivia, seeing her aunt already
fossicking through her handbag for tissues. Then she looked at the
vacant seat next to Sam. She stared at it for a little while with reverence,
then tilted her head back to keep any tears from escaping and took a
deep breath.

'I really look forward to sharing this performance with you. Melbourne
has been so kind to me, in so many ways, and I have prepared something
very special for you tonight. I'd like to sing for you a cappella, *Fear a'
Bhata*, translated from old Scot's Gaelic as *The Boatman*. It's a song from
the late 18th century that captures the emotions of a young girl courting
a handsome fisherman and the feelings she experiences during their
courtship. As many would know, although born in Melbourne, I grew
up in Scotland, on Stromness, an island in the north surrounded by wild
seas and sheer cliffs. It's one of those songs that always sang to my heart
and soul, and it's travelled with me over the years into adulthood. You
will be able to follow the English translation to the lyrics above me. I hope
you like it.'

After the applause died down and the audience stilled, Isla shut her
eyes. The warmth of the spotlight caressed her cheeks. And there she was
again, transported to a cliff at the northernmost tip of Stromness. The
warmth from the lights moderated and she felt instead a breeze blowing
against her tiny frame and the spray from the surf wetting her face; tasted
the moist salt air filling her lungs and heard the waves crashing discord.
Inhaling deeply, she fell into her body and opened her eyes to see the
audience sitting on the edge of their seats, spellbound. Quietly humming
a first note to herself, she began to sing.

O Boatman, no-one else
I often look from the highest hill
That I might see my boatman
Will you come tonight, or will you come tomorrow

Oh sorry will I be if you do not come at all

My heart is broken, bruised

Often tears are running down from my eyes

Will you come tonight, or will I wait up for you

Or close the door with a sad sigh?

My darling promised me a gown of silk

That and a fine tartan

A golden ring in which I'd see a likeness

But I fear that he shall forget

I gave you love and cannot deny

It's not love that lasts a year or a season

But a love that began when I was a child

And that will not wither until death do take me

My friends say often

That I must forget your image

But their counsel is as unfathomable to me

As is the returning tide

O Boatman, no-one else.

Isla concluded the song and there was a suppressed hush that paid a respectful homage to her journey. Within moments, however, the quiet was interrupted by a chain of applause, erupting into a standing ovation. She looked down and saw Richard hugging Olivia, whose face was glistening with tears. Sam was also wiping his eyes, blowing air kisses to his future bride.

She stood there with arms outstretched, bowing, soaking up the moment, revelling in the applause for herself and her dad. Then she walked to the piano. The audience resumed their seats, anticipating her signature song.

Gracefully, Isla stepped into the violet cone of light, at ease and comforted, another star shooting across the stage as she took her seat.

She smiled, recalling Morag once telling her on school camp how a shooting star was her father waving at her. Carefully, she placed her fingers lightly on the ivory keys for the last time this night. With composure, she looked to the heavens, winked and positioned herself ready to play their favourite song.

Reunited forever, she thought, raising her hand to her lips, blowing her father one final kiss.

Author's Thoughts

Isla's Song commenced its journey some years ago in Dublin, when I attended a presentation by world expert on International Child Abduction, Dr Marilyn Freeman, at the World Congress Conference on the Rights of Children. Her compelling paper resonated with me.

Aligned with my leanings, Dr Freeman appeared to have an avid interest in the jurisprudence governing international abduction and relocation cases, but she also had a focus on how we might improve situations for children who are victims of unilateral relocations and their ongoing psychological ramifications.

The first kernel of pen to paper emerged as a draft screenplay, in which I collaborated with Phillip Claassen. Despite receiving some very positive feedback, I was dissatisfied with the characters' lack of complexities and their story arcs: I couldn't totally relate to the characters; I couldn't visualise them adequately; I sat uncomfortably with them in their world, like some distant passenger.

There were many hours spent riding my bicycle along the undulating hills of Phillip Island, piecing bits of the story together, making it less opaque and more real. Coincidently, as my vision became more apparent, a brief to appear landed on my desk in Chambers in early 2021. The facts aligned with my story and filled my creativity with further tributaries that added to the story's rich tapestry. This case transformed the previous movie script into a more heartfelt story, as I could now see every character grow in strides, each telling their side of the story. For the first time, I truly started to engage with them and understand their relationships, their struggles, their desires. And I was able to accomplish all this without judgement.

There is at least one thing that I have learnt as a Family Law Barrister of over three decades; you must never judge your client. You must listen to them carefully, take their instructions and advise them accordingly, including matters such as the risks of litigation and cost consequences. But, you must never judge them, for to do so to me would be a breach of my privilege, being a confidential voyeur into their private world.

In writing this book, however, an insurmountable hurdle presented itself in terms of setting this story in current time. Since 1980, the Hague Convention on the Civil Aspects of International Child Abduction is the main international agreement that covers international parental child abduction, through which a parent can seek to have their children returned to their home country. It was drafted to ensure the prompt return of children who have been abducted from their country of habitual residence, or wrongfully retained in a contracting state not being their country of habitual residence. The Convention also deals with issues of international child access. It became effective on 1 December 1983. In 2022, there were 103 parties to this convention.

It is worthy to note even when a country is a signatory to the Hague Convention (and has an agreement with Australia), this does not necessarily mean it will effectively enforce its treaty obligations.

The Australian Central Authority in the Attorney-General's Department is responsible for administering the 1980 Hague Convention on the Civil Aspects of International Child Abduction. The convention is a multilateral treaty in force between Australia and a number of other countries. It provides a lawful procedure for seeking the return of abducted children to their home country, and assistance to parents for access arrangements for children overseas.

Not long after the 1980 Hague Convention, the United Nations Convention on the Rights of the Child was signed on 20 November 1989, effective as of 2 September 1990, after being ratified by the required number of nations. As of 31 December 2022, 196 countries are a party to this Convention, including every member of the United Nations except for the United States. It is an international human rights treaty, which sets out the civil, political, economic, social, health and cultural rights of children.

Fortunately, over time, the voice of a child has become a central focus to legislation and social services worldwide. However, there is still much we can do, due to our courts and governments often falling short of invoking the best outcomes for children, hamstrung by court costs, delays, inexperienced judicial officers being appointed and government policy.

Given certain resources and interventions now available to parents and children in cases of international abduction, it seemed more appropriate to place my story at a time where parents were basically left to fend for themselves in such situations.

Reflecting on the issue of abduction, it is hard to imagine how a parent would emotionally and psychologically process the loss of a child. Unlike today, in years past, the loss was often terminal. It is one thing to consider a parent's grief in such circumstances. However, I always feel in such cases that it is the children who are the major victims, scarred with ongoing psychological damage well into their adulthood.

Dr Marilyn Freeman has stated in her research, 'Abduction and its effects linger for many years after the ending of the abduction.'

Children remain at risk of emotional and psychological difficulties as they enter late adolescence and young adulthood.

Such 'at risk' behaviours might manifest in alcohol/drug abuse; problems trusting people; lack of impulse control; feelings of insecurity in intimate relationships; abandonment issues; difficulties in settling down in any one place. It does not follow that all such child victims suffer from the same problems. However, they are at risk; in my experience, the abducting parent usually has little or no regard for the emotional backlash of their poorly constructed psychological dam wall. What we often see is a latent and predictable deluge of emotional grief and pain for the child.

Writing this book was like sitting on a couch with a bowl of popcorn nearby, watching the story and its characters unfold before my eyes. I wanted to get across that pain felt by each one of them; the difficulties behind their choices; the repercussions of choices made. As stated, the aim was never to judge any of them but to provide a point of view, an explanation for their actions, forming a basis for an understanding at least.

In my experience, it is usually the child who sits mid-field in the battle between the parents. And despite the child's unconditional love for his or her parents, time and time again, I see parents abuse that love and instead, choose to continue to fling hand grenades at each other. Their lack of insight is measured only by their lack of priorities.

In the case of international abduction, prior to the Hague Convention, the world stage offered the child very poor shelter. Often the child felt he or she was abandoned, left alone in a windy desolate wasteland trying to make sense of the abducting parent's actions and explanations and the left-behind parent's apparent failure to seek him or her out. A perfect storm for emotional fall-out.

About the Author

Darren has been a Family Law Barrister for over 30 years. He worked as an Associate in the County Court prior to signing the Bar Roll in 1990. He is an accredited Mediator and Arbitrator and a Mentor for Juris Doctorate Law Students at Melbourne University.

Darren was also a Steering Committee Member on the Family Violence Taskforce reporting to the Royal Commission on Family Violence.

He is a Director of Pacifica Congress and a member of the Victorian Bar, the Medico-Legal Society, the American Bar Association and the Association of Family and Conciliation Courts. Darren is a committee member for the Victorian Bar Ethics Committee, the ADR Committee and the Health & Wellbeing Committee.

Darren is also a professional actor, author and producer. He has appeared in many television shows and theatrical productions. In 2018, he co-founded TO BE LOVED NETWORK LIMITED, a registered charity that provides resources to children navigating family violence and parental separation. He has written a children's book, *Tommy & Tiger Terry* and his film, *Tommy*, is a compelling resource that has won many awards. It was nominated in the best film category in 27 festivals, including BAFTA and ACADEMY qualifying events. In 2023, it will be embedded into the Court's High Conflict Model across the USA, for the education of parents and ultimately, the advancement of children's best interests. Darren has also co-founded a Family Law podcast, with Caroline Counsel, *Done & Dusted*. In 2022, Darren was awarded Barrister of the Year at the Australian Law Awards.